QUEERING HIM

QUEERING HIM

KATHERINE WELA BOGEN

CAT'S ELBOW BOOKS

Published by Cat's Elbow Books

catselbowbooks.com

Copy edited by Alison Kerr Miller
Cover Artwork by Nicola Callahan
Interior design by Zoe Norvell

Library of Congress Control Number: 2025907890
ISBN: 979-8-9986873-0-3 (print)
ISBN: 979-8-9986873-1-0 (ebook)

First Edition

To all bi people everywhere:
You are precious and holy and sacred and safe here.
Thank you for defying the limiting conventions of love,
expression, intimacy, and sex. Your bravery expands the world.

To all the slutty girls:
It is not your responsibility to carry other people's shame for them.
Your sexuality is not grotesque. Your pleasure is not problematic.
Those things are gifts. Enjoy them.

CURTAIN

Avra had fucked it. She knew from the dried snot beneath her nose and the crusty sleep sand grinding into her alligator eyes and the quiet and the cold. Probably she had fucked it badly enough that Kieran wouldn't ever look her in the face again, and her belly twisted around *Serves you right* and *goddamn coward* and *Jesus, my head* and *I hate you so much* and *Please, god, please don't ever leave me* and *Do what you want, I guess* and the big one, the ground beef of it all: *Prove the thesis. Prove me right. No exceptions to the rule, not even you.* She woke to rumpled sheets and her phone case hard against her wrist and a gaping black hole of worry and self-loathing and abandonment trauma on the bed to her left, crawling toward her like her own sick, masochistic shadow. The room smelled like stale beer and not sex, which was strange. She wasn't sore. Her pelvis was unaffected, her skin absent bruising, which was terrible. Her teeth were fuzz-filmed like a muffin left to die. Her head was pounding—pounding—an evil cerebral percussionist playing a musical gray-matter joke. Maybe she'd never care about music again. Maybe she'd spend the next year buried in the bowels of a breakup album, some sad indie girl crooning sympathetically about crying at the grocery store in her headphones, which she rummaged beneath the pillows for but couldn't find.

This was Karly's guest room, Avra thought. The Pepto-Bismol pink of the comforter reminded her how badly she wanted to puke, and she almost did, for dramatic effect and symmetry with the empty feeling in her chest cavity: her stupid, useless chest cavity. She ached in part because of the hangover, which was rolling over her like a train on a murder spree, swerving off the tracks toward birds and rabbits, trying to kill anything precious. The other half of the ache came from that anticipation of karmic vengeance, the knowledge buried beneath her lungs that the universe would serve her worms henceforth, and she would eat them, and maybe that would kill her, or regret would kill her, and if those things combined didn't manage her death then maybe Kieran would. The proper end to their absurd effort, an obsession doomed from the moment it first sank those schadenfreuden claws. He had the right, if anyone at all, Avra thought. If he ever came back, that is. If he ever even spoke to her again.

CHAPTER 1

OCTOBER 2008

They met in sophomore English. Well, no, that's not quite true. They met as children, tiny two-foot-somethings. This was before she converted to Judaism and chopped her hair and changed her name and burst from a stifling closet. She made a spectacle of herself in front of the upstanding, decidedly heterosexual church-goers of Ridgefield, Connecticut—population eight thousand, ninety-seven percent white, a place where Manhattanites go "to autumn," the citizenry of which has voted Republican in every damn election since ten thousand years ago, et cetera.

His mother was her CCD teacher. Or maybe her sister's. Peripheral childhood memories blur, palm-smeared and sticky across a canvas. Finger an inch or so off the pulse point. For any of you unfamiliar, CCD stands for the Confraternity of Christian Doctrine, a "religious education program" (a bona fide brainwash-ing technique) that the Catholic Church designed *for kids.* Even as a six-year-old, she knew something was wrong. But she went every week, per her own mother's instruction. Seemed hypocritical, given that her mother was usually shepherding the girls to CCD so she could begin drinking earlier and with more privacy. While her mom drank, sniffed, and occasionally smashed things, Avra studied recitation, worship, and how to kneel.

In the tumult of learning and unlearning goodness and god-liness, realizing she liked girls (not good or godly at all, then), yawning through the predictability of small-town homophobia, and ignoring the persistent sense of being unloved by her mother, Avra just didn't realize he was there. When she felt dramatic—and she frequently felt dramatic—Avra thought about it as "the before." For most of "the before," her name was Katherine. She had to write a paper on the meaning of "Katherine" during middle school and encountered a description that crawled her skin: *pure, innocent, and virginal.* It was difficult to believe that the universe spat her out only to hand her such egregiously limiting epithets. But she must have been, once. Before her mom hightailed it south, chasing coke all the way to Florida. (She caught it—how fortunate for her. Less so for her little left-behind daughters.) Before her dad fell into a tumbling panic over raising them all by himself or reclaimed his Polish Jew traditions or learned to say the word "tampon" without wincing. Before they stopped going to church—no more CCD, no more Dead White Jesus—and started going to synagogue. Before she decided her name meant fuck-all and changed it to Avra.

The name Avra was an angst-fueled reformation of the self, the feminine iteration of Avraham, or Abraham. Abraham, as in the Very Old Testament. As in, leader of the Jewish people, great Patriarch, in a cozy little covenant with God. She imagined herself the usurper of some holy throne. Avra, the will-be-Matriarch. Avra, the people's warrior. Avra, ruler over man. Avra, inevitable in her triumph. Avra, whose Ashkenazi kin shall inherit whatever earth they have managed to wrest, evermore brutally, from Palestine (she learned that in an Arab-Israeli conflict course at a liberal arts college in Massachusetts, when she was around twenty). At a tightrope-walking sixteen, Avra understood what so many still refuse to acknowledge—that women are meant to be liberators. Queer women? Liberators who have better sex (she learned that from the internet).

And he was Kieran. By sophomore year, Kieran was precisely what you'd expect from a boy thus named. Dark-haired, dark-eyed, cruelly handsome. Taller than he had any right to be. Sixteen and desperately frightened and angry and eager to push his ample luck. Charmless, but adored. Blunt, for the sake of "honesty." No therapist would call him callously unemotional, but they wouldn't immediately protest. Any worth their salt would say something about "the Man Box," maybe, or "socialization via the father." He was an athlete (the clichéd American tradition). The Abercrombie-clad automatons of Ridgefield High School—Avra steeped the epithets in bitterness—accepted him gladly. He wasn't their leader, but he was never their subject.

Avra shopped at those dimly lit, cologne-soaked goth clothing stores, past which wholesome suburban parents hurried their curious children while navigating doomed, economically sagging malls. Avra's spiked 'do barely reached one inch past five feet. She was soft and uncoordinated, faked periods during gym, sang first soprano in the choir, and auditioned for every school musical. She was what the next generation might describe as "cringe." In fairness to her, she leaned in, ignoring the steady stream of mockery, stockpiling her grit. In third grade, as the students selected their school band instruments, Jon McEwan declared, "Girls don't play trombone." Avra—never to be instructed—made her choice. She stayed in Concert Band for eight years, playing badly, out of spite.

So, in some moment buried within the wreath-clad graveyard of youthful memories, they met as small children, before Avra's mother ran toward the rush of something powdered, before Kieran's father knew enough to ask the question, before Avra came out, before Kieran was kind. Before any of it mattered. They met again—and it counted, this time, the way that a kick to the stomach might count, or a broken molar—their sophomore year, in English class.

Broadly, Avra was good at prioritizing. As soon as the bell rang, she was focused, engaged, and brilliant. Avra knew that she was brilliant; she could be the first to answer the question, and often was. Avra knew that she could intimidate her classmates; she could trade analyses with the teachers, and often did. She was not popular, or cool, or pretty, or liked—or likable, really, she knew that, too—but she was fucking smart. Smart was safe. Nobody could hate you all that much for being too smart. But the thing is, Avra was also gay—loudly gay, shamelessly gay. And people could certainly hate you for that.

As soon as the class bell rang, Avra assumed her practiced role of devoted student. But before the bell? Before the bell was always (well, as of this year), always Isabella. Avra glanced up to greet the arrival of her desk neighbor and was smitten. Warm-cinnamon-gusts-of-air smitten. Smiling-before-she-realized-it smitten. "I've been staring moon-eyed at you for three full months and I sometimes doodle our initials and wrap them in an inky heart" smitten. You know, the gross kind.

Isabella was a transfer student from some art school in the Carolinas. Avra learned of her—their graduating class had seventy-two kids in it, *everyone* learned of her—on the very first day of term, but she never expected Isabella to become her friend. Isabella was a dancer. Feminine, lithe, gorgeous, Bambi-eyed, lightly freckled, and femme. Her hair had salon highlights, her mouth a cupid's bow. She was even *dimpled*, for chrissakes. This girl could have been Ridgefield royalty—could have ruled with the iron fist of Regina George, could have decked herself in Hollister finery and made even the manliest of manly boys buckle their manly-boy knees to swear fealty. She didn't. Isabella kept somewhat to herself, gracious but never performative, thoughtful, generous. She did her best to get to know Avra. Every day, she dropped her bag clumsily (the only clumsy thing she ever did) on the desk beside Avra's, grinned, and shared some benign gossip. She bumped their knees, and asked about Avra's "day so far," and did the gay-girl look-too-long and maybe. Maybe. Avra still didn't know, but let her stomach curl pleasantly at Isabella's nudge, at the lingering scent of peppermint lotion on her hands.

In her desire to enjoy the deliciously deliberative is-she-isn't-she, Avra tried her hardest not to be distracted by Kieran, who was miming using an invisible penis as a sword—held with both hands between his long legs—and swashbuckling with his friend Will, who swung back, laughing. Last week, the teacher had revealed that many of Shakespeare's sword lines were Elizabethan-era dick jokes. The clarification had caused an uproar. Avra thought idly that Kieran and Will's antics looked vaguely masturbatory. She could say as much, and they would be embarrassed. But then the bell rang, and invisible penises were sheathed, and Isabella turned to face the front of the room, and—reluctantly, for Isabella was still smiling—Avra did too.

Kieran didn't often speak up in class, but when he did, he was contrary. Somewhere along the trajectory from "sweet benign child" to "popular churchgoing athlete," he had learned to advocate for the devil. Throughout their Shakespeare term, he irritated Avra with his shallow reading of *Romeo and Juliet*, *Hamlet*, even *A Midsummer Night's Dream* (a critique of obedience to patriarchy that Avra admired). Today was *The Taming of the Shrew*. Avra hated Petruchio—the gaslighting, the manipulation, the reward, the punishment.

Kieran, prompted by the overzealous Mr. Bennard for an interpretation, said only "Funny wedding stunt, I guess," and Avra bristled, as she always did when people behaved in a manner so utterly pedestrian.

When she scoffed, the noise wasn't loud, but it didn't have to be.

"What?" Kieran was annoyed, confrontational. Avra was ready.

"Genuinely can't believe I'm wasting a class on Shakespeare listening to your lack of insight." Avra didn't necessarily *enjoy* being mean, but Kieran gave off such a "no one has ever been mean to me" vibe that she almost felt she owed him the growth experience. Mr. Bennard—the English teacher, who wore thick woolen socks with his decades-old Birkenstocks and used the phrase "y'all" with all the irony of a man who had never left New England—shifted nervously from foot to foot. Avra usually gave incisive commentary. Avra usually raised her hand. Avra was a smart girl, in theory. Avra did not know what she was getting into.

The rest of the class did, it seemed. The usual ambient sounds of stirring bodies and scratching pencils and flipping pages had paused. Her classmates were silently observing. This was Avra's first moment of concern, the *uh-oh* that arrives slightly too late to be protective.

He was noticing her.

Kieran Monahan was noticing her, his eyes narrowed and trained on her face, an embarrassed flush on his Apollonian cheekbones. Avra had expected a retort, expected something cutting and vile and flavored with misogyny. It didn't come. He simply stared, eyes boring, until Avra began to itch under the gaze. For a smart girl (in theory), piecing this puzzle took longer than it should have. Kieran was popular, influential, and brutish. He could be vindictive. It was one of the few things Avra sensed they'd have in common. Avra, meanwhile, was the one queer girl at the hetero hop, Jewish in a town of Christians, captious, disliked, leader of the misfit crew only when the misfits hadn't found a slightly more popular crew with which to shelter, and—quite suddenly—*vulnerable*. The resultant frisson of fear was enough to palpitate her heart. Kieran was still looking at her, calculating, head slightly tilted. Mr. Bennard coughed to break the tension. When it didn't work, he clapped his hands, smiled tentatively, and made a desperate I-smell-bullying-risk-but-am-too-anxious-to-do-anything-about-it pivot.

"Who else has thoughts?"

But Kieran's voice—toneless now, more menacing for it—had returned. "No," he said, drawing out the word so that the N lasted a bit too long. "No, I want her to say what she means."

"I mean that Shakespeare was a genius, and you chronically fail to do him justice. Petruchio isn't just some goofy guy. He sucks—he *sucks*. He's controlling and cruel and unpredictable. Like, the wedding is awful. Just another one of his ridiculous stunts to prove that Katharina has no agency."

Kieran looked chagrined, like he genuinely had missed all of this, which spurred Avra's annoyance. She barreled on. "I mean, he doesn't let her sleep. He doesn't let her *eat*. Heaps of sexist, patriarchal viciousness and all you've got for us is *funny wedding stunt*? Honestly, we're here to do a close reading." Avra had a talent for making sweeping statements, invoking the collective: *We* share this goal. *We* do this work. Valiant, given that few of her peers would have intentionally included her within a collective of any kind.

"Why do you have to overanalyze everything? Books don't all have some secret hidden meaning." His tone was turning caustic, defensive, which was a relief—and since when had he noticed her analyses? Avra had never considered what he thought of her comments. She wondered now, but not for long. Time to duck and parry.

"First, this isn't a book. It's a play." Kieran's fist closed atop his

desk as she spoke. "Second, analysis is one of the great joys of experiencing literature, and if you had more than a half-dozen brain
cells to shake together, you'd already know that"—she paused for
a second before plunging on—"and I'd be spared this tedious conversation." Him, with the lack of brain cells? *Him?* Her brain was
not connected to her mouth. She was reacting, lashing. Caught in
a corner. Or, maybe she wasn't. Maybe she was advancing. Seeing a
weak spot and choosing to press. Both. Both, probably.

"Are you calling me stupid?"

"If the dunce cap fits." Ableist, but she didn't know it in 2008.

"Man, you really are a fucking bitch, aren't you?" Ah, the misogyny. There it was.

"Enough," interrupted Mr. Bennard. Avra had forgotten him,
in all her fight-or-flight (all her weave-and-dodge). He looked
furious. She rarely made teachers even mildly peeved, never mind
furious. She suspected that calling a classmate stupid may have
crossed a line. Perhaps also the "bitch" comment. Maybe the "fucking." They were, the two of them, in trouble. Another thing they
had in common, then.

"Ms. Bergmann, Mr. Monahan, I am up to *here.*" Mr. Bennard
raised his hand to his head, actually quite high off the ground,
maybe six foot two, and Avra noted the formal invocation, the
weaponization of their surnames. (She had accepted this half of
her labeling with gritty acquiescence. Bergmann: Yiddish-flavored
German. It meant "mountain man." She had mulled it over during
the Katherine-to-Avra transition before deciding, yes, she would
keep that part. *Mountain Man.* Strong. Isolated. Resilient. A lot
Jew-y and a little Butch. She didn't know what Monahan meant.
She'd have to google it.)

"Both of you, join me outside the classroom, please."
Mr. Bennard's voice was clipped, carefully controlled, his

I-am-very-laid-back Hawaiian shirt offering little comfort. The class muttered and *ooh*ed as he turned and marched from the room. Avra rose to follow. Kieran, swinging a sullen kick at the leg of his desk on the way, tramped out as well. Isabella reached for Avra's wrist as she went, gave it a conciliatory squeeze, and Avra grimaced down at her, as if to say, "I probably deserve this." She did.

Outside the classroom, Mr. Bennard lectured in the classic tradition of concerned high school English teachers. Avra tried to listen, caught words like "respect" and "compassion," but Kieran had his arms crossed and was staring at the ceiling, and damn it, if he wasn't going to pay attention, neither was she. Instead, she watched him. The pinched expression on his (admittedly gorgeous, in an irritating sort of way) face. The hard set of his shoulders above crossed arms. The way his feet were planted slightly wider than his hips. Not bored, then. On guard. Distant, maybe. Enduring. He had clearly been lectured often, and at length. She could tell from the long-suffering glaze over his eyes, the knotted cords of his forearms. Avra remembered meeting his father—a pompous man, loud, a banker—at their middle school graduation and disliking him even more than his already obnoxious son. Kieran's father had arrived late, sat apart from his wife, and let his phone ring during the ceremony. Avra had even watched him wink at the older sister of one of her classmates before he left. Typical midlife man, attempting roguish charm but landing directly on creep-factor. She experienced a brief stab of pity for Kieran before tuning back in to Mr. Bennard, who was wrapping his oratory up with a nice, "and I expect you each to apologize to the other—a genuine, heartfelt apology, *ifyouplease*—before returning to our class."

Mr. Bennard turned and left, then. And isn't it just like an optimist to leave a mouse all alone with a cat? The sound of the door swinging closed echoed briefly through the corridor, and Avra was suddenly very aware of the empty hallway, the tinny hum of the fluorescents, and Kieran's eyes were still trained on the ceiling, his arms still held protectively over his chest, his feet still firmly planted. She wondered how long it usually took him to come back from dissociation after a sermon. Her empathy was short-lived, however. Avra was anxious to rejoin her peers. She *hated* to miss a lesson, hated to fall behind, hated to lose out on any opportunity to prove her brilliance. She spoke first.

"So, I really shouldn't have—"

But Kieran cut her off. "No."

"What I think we have to do is really—"

"No." He became monosyllabic when his guard was up. Avra filed that away for future use. If she ever needed this boy quiet, all she had to be was cutting.

"Will you just let me—"

"Stop."

"But he *just said* we—"

"Don't apologize. It's crap." His eyes were off the ceiling now, directed at Avra's (impatient, endeavoring-toward-contrite) face, and he was taking slow steps toward her. She unconsciously crossed her arms, matching his posture. At her movement, Kieran swept his gaze down Avra's body, head to toe, before training it somewhere near her right shoulder and saying, low and inappropriately frustrated, "Never apologize if you don't mean it." She blinked at him, unsure why this would matter. (People provided insincere apologies all the time, she was certain of that. Her mother had made her certain.) Kieran took another step forward. There wasn't anywhere for Avra to go. Another step. Another.

He was in her space. Avra could see the fine hairs of his not-quite-visible mustache, a bit of dryer fuzz on his shirt collar (a polo, of course). She kept her eyes on his neck, on the blue vein to the right of his Adam's apple. They were taking too long. Mr. Bennard would come out. Or some student would walk down the hall. Somebody would check. One last step forward, and Avra's back was against the lockers. She could feel a combination lock just beneath her shoulder blade, the hard steel edge pressing coolly through the fabric of her shirt. Her breath was shallow. There was less than a foot between them, and Kieran was so tall. Avra had never really noticed how tall he was. He spoke again, his voice laced with a threat so casual it could have been mistaken for earnestness. "You should be nicer to me." There was an edge, a little sliver of pleading. A joke, absent humor. "I could really fuck up your life, you know." A promise.

It was what Avra needed to hear.

He was too close. He was breathing down at her, the warm gust against her nose. She could smell something cafeteria-sweet— a Capri Sun, maybe, or Gatorade. Setting her jaw, Avra forced herself to lift her eyes to his face, raised her chin, pulled her shoulders back, and sneered. She knew how to play defiant, having spent ample time on a stage. She had stood in front of audiences of peers who didn't really like her all that much and tap-danced, in a Snoopy costume, on purpose. Stood—determinedly unbothered—in front of her high and manic mother as she laughed and screamed, smashed lamps, broke windows, begged for cash. Stood in front of the Straights of Ridgefield High and heard every slur from *lezzie* to *muff muncher* to *dyke*. Avra knew how to jut her hip, roll her eyes, clench her fists, and bury the fear where it couldn't surface. *Save it till later, baby. Never let them see you cry.* By sixteen, Avra had earned the attitude of someone who understood that sticks and stones had serious competition.

Kieran raised an unconvinced eyebrow at her bluff. He had experience, too, with condescension, humiliation; he knew how to play haughty, how to stare down some frightened thing—she supposed this skill had been gifted from his father, a man with a startling penchant for shouting at student athletes during intramural games. Avra grated against Kieran's pride, and she realized now what her peers already knew, what had rendered them classroom-quiet only minutes ago: Kieran's threats were not empty.

He put a hand on the locker beside her head, palm flat against the painted metal, and his too-close, sharp-boned face was carved into disdain. She could read the urge to hurt her in the edge of his mouth, the skin of his wrist, and was morbid in her curiosity.

"Fine," Avra said, breaking the silence, knowing some this-might-end-in-horror game was about to begin, knowing just as well that she could lose. "Fine," she said again, placing both of her small hands against Kieran's broad chest and pushing him firmly away. He was warm. She wished she hadn't noticed.

He didn't stumble. His eyes flashed briefly, but he backed up two whole paces. "I'm not sorry," Avra continued. "I won't say it. I wouldn't mean it. You wouldn't either. And it's not as if you've told me anything I don't already know—I *am* a fucking bitch."

She turned abruptly and walked into the classroom without a rearward look. Kieran remained in the hallway for a long moment. Avra imagined him taking a deep breath to gather himself, imagined a blank universe of Kieran's habits. She felt more than saw him follow her through the open classroom door, several paces behind. Throughout the remainder of class, when she caught the displeasure on his face, Avra allowed herself a moment of dangerous debate: What had bothered him more? Her cruelty, or the way she could show her back? Her snapping, or her leaving?

In the subsequent weeks, Avra found her mind irritatingly preoccupied with their proximity. She had some difficulty sleeping (his hand against the locker). She struggled to focus (his eyes scanning her body). She rewound and examined the scene (his breath against her face). She looked for Kieran in every hallway, around every corner. Prophetic, premonitory—he was always there.

CHAPTER 2

SEPTEMBER 2009

Avra was overworked, overwhelmed, and running late. She balanced her PSAT prep book, an annotated copy of *The Bell Jar*, two notebooks, a double-shot latte she was probably too young to drink, and her choir binder—sheet music organized chronologically in order of performance, not alphabetically by song title, she wasn't an animal—all quite precariously as she scurried toward her locker. Missing the bus would mean a mile-and-a-half walk uphill to the library, where her dad picked her up after he finished work. In her rush, she didn't notice Kieran (and she always noticed Kieran), didn't brace for the inevitable, intentional, targeted impact.

Kieran, for his part, rounded the corner, saw Avra coming, stepped decisively into her path, and swatted her collection out of her arms. Avra, clumsily grasping, just managed to rescue the latte, which slopped hot liquid over her wrist. The rest plummeted.

"You," she spat coldly, her eyes watering as tumbling tomes landed painfully on her foot, which would certainly bruise, "are a stereotype."

"Okay," he replied, unbothered, watching her stoop to collect her fallen cargo. Avra did her best not to spill any more of the drink. "And your shit is all over the floor." Mark Carlesson—authoritarian, boorish, vile—guffawed loudly. *Absolute gorillas.*

Avra took a moment to compose herself from her place on the ground, refusing to look up at the twin pillars of self-satisfaction. She knew they wouldn't do anything *worse.* Their mission had been accomplished. But still. Her foot.

She addressed Kieran—Mark was a non-entity, they both knew—with a *Buffy* quote she was certain he wouldn't catch (a subtle, nerdy comfort in a moment of familiar shame). "Why are you always around when I'm miserable?"

"You're always fucking miserable," came the bored reply.

It was truer than the cinematic response: something about the heroine being alone. Kieran would happily do this in front of others. Did, in fact, every few days. What is violence without a jeering audience? Mostly, he walked into her, forced her to drop things, loosened the straps on her backpack, flat-tired her shoes. That is, when he wasn't slamming lockers next to her head, or knocking her lattes off the lunch table, or grabbing her notes during class and snapping pens open onto them. She rather thought that tactic was as much a punishment as a crime, as he inevitably ended up covered in ink, and his clothing cost more than her notebooks.

She smiled humorlessly, finally looking up from the ground and coming face-to-knee with Kieran, who was always too fucking close to her. "Gee, can't imagine why." Avra—belongings held protectively to her chest now—stood quickly, turned her back on Kieran (she hoped he hated that, hated when she was the one to leave), and hurried to her locker, twice as late for the bus, twice as bruised as before.

Avra had learned, over a year of escalating intrusions, to watch for Kieran. She watched for his backpack in the classroom, to pick

a distant seat. She watched for his head—bobbing above the rest—
in the hallways, to plan an escape route. She watched for his gaze
in the cafeteria, to brace for an insult. Somewhere along the way,
watching *for* Kieran had simplified to watching him. Noting his
mood (risk reduction, nothing more). Noting his company (iden-
tifying possible accomplices, enemies). Noting his triggers to avoid
them, or to press on them when she wanted (his triggers like feeling stupid, or unimportant, or underestimated). Avra enjoyed the
pressing, when she could get away with it—it felt significant to
demonstrate her resistance, in small ways, and frequently. So, she
would press in the presence of teachers. In a crowded room, when
her arms were empty and there was at least three feet of distance
between them. In the company of, well, not so much *friends* as
potential allies, should an interaction sour beyond Avra's anticipation. She ignored the needling urge to discover what he might do
to her then, too.

As Kieran orbited, Avra observed. In the cafeteria, he would
tilt his head back to laugh, dark eyes glimmering, and Avra would
stare at his open throat. Around his friends, his guard came down,
and he could be playful. Almost funny. He wasn't always *like this*.
Certainly, to Avra, Kieran was always, always *like this*, but there
were moments—absent her company, witnessed from a safe distance—when he could be nearly human. Avra recognized the
softening relief of a mask allowed to fall. In those moments, she
noted internal whispers of compassion, an odiously mushrooming
interest. A year had passed, now, of Avra trying to catch the times
(few and far between) when he wasn't behaving like such a penis.

Like Tuesday afternoon, at lunch, when he had rested his head
against Will's shoulder—an ill-fitting, *intimate* gesture—and Will
had let him. Only for a moment. Kieran had seemed to thaw, to shift
like a leaf catching sunlight. There was something habitual between

them that Avra knew to her bones. She knew it from Isabella, kissing her sweetly at her locker. Isabella, tucking a lock of hair behind her ear before heading off to her class. Isabella, hugging her gently each morning as she got off the bus, careful fingers on Avra's waist, just beneath the hem of her shirt, touching her skin.

Avra could smell queerness a mile away. She wondered for a long time whether all rainbow teens could do that—sniff the air and find each other, tugged beneath the belly by some bizarre gravitational pull. Seeing Kieran and Will was a splinter under her fingernail, a tilting off of her axis, a learning and an unlearning. Avra *knew* that subconscious seeking of comfort, that subtle blend of fear and shame and desire (concealment, ironically, leaves a trace). Knew it like a lullaby sung to soothe the Baby Gays: *You will find each other, and spring will come. Something will break open. Keep looking, keep looking.* Knew the hurt and the want, the could-be-platonic PDA. For a brief flash, she felt such benevolence for him, saw him so clearly, that her own empathy wrapped a ruthless fist around her heart and squeezed.

But the other boys had noticed too.

"Wake up and decide to be a faggot today?"

Avra felt the snapping of a single horsehair, sensed the plummet of Damocles' sword. She froze, sat straighter, her own meal forgotten. She tuned out Isabella, who was discussing an upcoming calculus test with mounting anxiety. Tuned out Isabella, which she almost never did. Tuned out Isabella because she had to watch Kieran.

Kieran's mask slipped back on like a stone dropping to the floor of a pond after wasting its skipping momentum. He performed nonchalance in the immediate but cinematically lazy push off of Will's shoulder; the well-practiced, not-at-all pained separation of comforting body from comforting body. He turned his face to the other boys with a set, threatening expression, jaguar smile not meeting his eyes. "Call me faggot again." The table went quiet before the topic turned, but someone pulled Will into a headlock, someone clapped Kieran on the back, and the sword was tugged out, just halfway. The group was savagely approving, Kieran's threat successfully registering as certified proof of Heterosexual Masculinity.

Avra saw through it. She saw everything. It moved something in her, the shock of affinity with *this* boy. When she tuned back in to Isabella, her face was warm, her palms flat and trembling on the lunch table's particleboard surface. Isabella didn't notice. Kieran would have, Avra knew.

She was still thinking about it nearly two weeks later.

Motivated by the halfway point between rage and grief, the tender balance of sympathy and self-centeredness, Avra had approached her social studies teacher Friday of that week and asked for faculty sponsorship to start a Gay-Straight Alliance. This was not a new idea. She and Isabella had discussed it with fellow eccentrics, Teo and Deirdre. Since Avra had come out, other students had begun anxiously emerging from their own closets. Not directly, necessarily, but via veiled statements made in class or the halls: "How do you know that character is straight?" "Think I could take a girl to prom?" "Ms. Thompson is kind of hot." "So is Mr. Park."

Avra wished that her sudden determination to start a GSA was fueled by a desire for community safety, or some beneficent hope for building queer solidarity. However, if she was honest with herself—and Avra did strive to be honest with herself—she doubted whether she ever would have sought faculty sponsorship if not for the lunch table incident. There was something unexpected *happening* to her—some nonsensical protective instinct, one quarter self-preservation, three quarters pity. Some vicious, demanding urge to keep Kieran from being hurt. It was possessive, and ghoulish, and sick. Other people had no right—only Avra. Other people had no reason—only Avra. Later, she might consider it Stockholm Syndrome (the pressing need to justify his cruelty toward her by fabricating a connection). At the time, if she had examined it closely enough, she may have identified a desire for power. Perhaps she wanted Kieran in her debt—wanted to prove that she had influence too. She could protect him. She could open doors for him. He should stop being so goddamn mean to her.

This is how, three weeks later—mid-October, just before her seventeenth birthday—Avra could be found handing out flyers announcing the first Ridgefield High School Gay-Straight Alliance meeting to the students gathered in the courtyard, just after lunch. She had chosen this time strategically—late enough in the day that people were awake, and close enough to mealtime to mitigate homophobia fueled by hanger, perhaps catching her peers in pleasant enough moods that they wouldn't tell her to fuck directly off.

Matt Tetrault, an upper-echelon basketball boy with prom king potential, and Darren Collins, a clowny sophomore made more popular by his success on the baseball field, were playing hacky sack halfheartedly by the stone seats. The ball made that predictably crackly *whushp* every time it landed on the concrete. They ignored Avra when she passed and she returned the favor, not bothering to offer them a flyer. She had a mission.

When she approached Will—next to Kieran again, a careful foot of bench between them, no contact today—Avra cleared her throat before speaking. "First Gay-Straight Alliance meeting, next Friday after school. Bring friends. If your parents are homophobes, don't tell them. If you don't want to come, kindly dispose of this flyer." Blunt, to the point, no shake in her voice. Avra was good at this. Her performance today: *queer, unafraid high school girl talking to jocks like they could not touch her.*

Will didn't make eye contact. Avra read into this about a dozen bruised and wretched things. Her chest hurt.

Kieran was always going to be the wildcard here. "Fucking dyke." It wasn't loud. It didn't have to be.

Will froze next to him, shuffled his leg another three inches away—an act of terrified semi-solidarity noticed by both Avra and Kieran, whose face betrayed a shiver adjacent to regret. The hacky sack landed several feet away with a *whushp* and Avra did not look at it.

But the slur hung suspended—bladed, fractal consonants, a poltergeist of self-loathing warping Kieran's tongue into weaponry. Avra felt the smooth paper of the flyer she was holding under her thumb. She counted to four in her head while sucking a deep, soothing breath into her belly, where she held it for a slightly longer count of five, just like her therapist instructed. The air was chill against her wrists, the neck of her shirt suddenly too tight. She breathed out for a count of six and noted the stone patterning of the knee-level bench, the red sheen of Will's tousled hair, the pink of her own sweatshirt sleeve, the deadened yellow of mid-fall grass.

Typically so quick to return a jab, Avra had no rebuttal. She *was* a fucking dyke, proud and (usually) shameless. She dated the femme, Bambi-eyed dancer. She kissed her girlfriend in the hallways, held her soft hand between classes. She argued for gender-bent casting in theater productions, chose queer poets for readings in English, quoted LGBTQ+ activists during social studies. She wore buttons with upside-down pink triangles and a sweater that said "I'm gayer than I look." She fantasized about girls, about goddesses, about the tender flesh of women's thighs. Watched lesbian porn. Liked to feel Isabella's fingers under her shirt, against her skin.

The compassion fulcrum pivoted, and Avra tried to follow. Kieran was performing what he knew, and it wasn't an excuse, but perhaps it was a reason. The sympathy was subconscious and insistent, and Avra knew Kieran's fear like a siren song, and she should not have been on the sacrificial altar.

Back still to Matt and Darren, Avra flitted her eyes automatically toward Will, then to Kieran while she wrinkled her nose in an *Oh, really?* instinct she couldn't quite suppress.

Kieran—who had caught the glance toward Will—adopted a headlight-deer expression of tunneled panic. Avra watched the understanding zoom toward him in the split second after that glance.

He knew that she knew. Knew she had recognized him, somehow. He was a cornered stray about it. The veins in his neck banded furiously, his hand flexed involuntarily on his thigh, and the moment elongated—one solitary flyer held between them, Avra's thumb obscuring the lettering, no boy reaching to take it. Eventually, Kieran broke the gaze. Avra almost dropped her extended hand, almost admitted defeat, but then, to collective surprise, Karly Edwin—beautiful, magnanimous, beloved, a cheerleader—stepped lightly around Darren and Matt and reached for the paper. She must have been watching the hacky sack game. She must have wondered whatever made it stop.

"Thanks!" Karly said brightly, smiling in a proactive bystander way, only marginally easing the nuclear tension the rest of their classmates had hungrily noticed. Avra and Kieran in close vicinity was a frequent showdown setting, and here Avra was, looking at Kieran's face, and here he was, shifting—prepped to pounce—under her insolent scrutiny. She wondered if he'd ever hit her. For a long moment, she pictured it—Kieran, rising to his feet, striking her face in front of their scandalized peers, leaving streaked red fingerprints across her freckled cheek. Something reckless in her hoped he would, wanted to know what it might take, wanted to give him a reason. Some twisted intrigue suggested it would feel different, somehow, from her mother's hand.

Will cleared his throat, Matt said, "Nobody wants your fucking flyers," Karly shot him a quelling look, and the benches buzzed
eagerly with the hum of anticipated antipathy. Avra—instinctively
seeking an ally—glanced over at Karly, who shrugged, flashed
a cautioning smile, and blinked twice: *You might want to get out
of here.* Avra took the cue. She tried to ignore the gleeful collective suspense as she walked back inside, swinging the flyer from
a performatively loose hand, denying her classmates the barbarous
satisfaction of observing her sadness, her fear.

People enjoyed Avra and Kieran's mutual dislike. They'd
witnessed this against-the-ropes sparring, this noxious mutual
obsession, over one climbing, clawing high school year. A harsh
and guttural year, filled with swift retorts and close-to-the-bone
"jokes"—the worst of Avra's viciousness pretending to be funny. As
the show unfolded, people were simply too entertained to intervene. Near the end of their sophomore year, almost six months after
the English class altercation, Matt had murmured during one of
their numerous disputes that it was like being at a dogfight, and
Avra understood at once. Something about the violence of the
thing was tragic, sure, but as one lost a muzzle, the other a man-
gled paw between snapping teeth, their classmates stood transfixed.
They watched between their (whole, undamaged) fingers. Whistled.
Only ever half closed their eyes.

CHAPTER 3

DECEMBER 2009

In the months following the "dyke" comment, Avra turned seventeen, time accelerated around another up-tempo semester, and Kieran adjusted his animosity from something like a nine to a six. Maybe a seven. We'll call it a six-point-five. Avra and Kieran still noted one another. They walked to class several paces apart, him always following behind, his bayonet gaze trained on Avra so intently that the back of her neck prickled in recognition. She'd linger near his locker with her arm slung confidently around Isabella, twirling the dancer's hair between her fingers and grinning, sneaking glances of Kieran and Will's platonic performance over her girlfriend's soft shoulder. Sometimes, Kieran caught her eye from behind Isabella's head. Sometimes, he held her gaze for long, serpentine moments. Their classroom barbs had been downgraded to eye rolls and huffs of disagreeable air. She wasn't being shoved or walked into. Her notebooks were ink-free. Her lattes evaded the floor. She should have felt relieved.

She felt like crawling out of her skin.

Avra still demanded attention—showing off in class, handing

out flyers for the fourth, fifth, and sixth GSA meetings (either the district parents had succumbed to the changing times, or her peers had indeed disposed of the evidence), auditioning for the supporting role in the school musical—but she learned some social graces as her chronic hypervigilance waned. She learned whom to compliment, and how generously. She learned that a well-timed smile after a peer's contribution in class made her seem less the insufferable know-it-all. She learned that fluttering her eyelashes at belligerent jocks was enough to both shut them up *and* garner the once-over, and she slowly learned that her body was ... Well, it was a good body to have. She was not thin, but her shape approximated an hourglass and gave the supple suggestion of Venus or Aphrodite—at least, that's what she told herself when her inner critic said "fat," which, at the time, Avra understood to mean "undesirable." This was before she learned about fatphobia. Growing into her body—her fuckability—more or less excused the transgression of her queerness. She still kissed Isabella in the hallways, only now the boys paused to gawp rather than hurling invectives. All this skill-building had garnered Avra invitations to a few mid-popular birthday parties, reciprocated compliments, moments of camaraderie, and even laughter at her less caustic jokes. If Kieran was the charmed prince, Avra was the rebel queen, each endeavoring to win the favor of the court.

Winter break was several days away and the anticipation palpable. A very pretty senior girl asked a sophomore boy to her family's holiday party, and the students were happily scandalized until her best friend impatiently corrected the wayward rumors: "Christ, he's her *cousin!*" Classmates loudly announced to teachers that they'd need to take the last two days off before the break, because their families were going on their annual holiday vacations (to Florida, Hawaii, Aruba, "the slopes," "the cabin." Rich kids, am I right?).

Members of the cheerleading squad taped mistletoe to their boyfriends' lockers, and the hallways dripped merrily with the threat of mononucleosis—the "kissing disease." Finals were behind them, and jubilation shimmered.

The last day before break, so few students bothered to show up that the senior lounge was opened to underclassmen, and afternoon classes were canceled in favor of study periods. Avra sat on a hard, armless blue couch in the lounge, imagining the rest of her high school career laid out before her like a script. Three more semesters and she would be free from this exhaustingly liminal space, where she was not liked but not disliked, not invisible but hardly noticed, not popular but not detested, queer but without community. The boredom of the thing was enough to shudder her spine. She was just considering pulling out a journal and drafting yet another version of her five-year plan ("escape plans," she lovingly called them) when the weight on the couch cushion beside her dipped, suggesting close company. Then the body flopped down in front of her to sit on the ground, shoulder nearly touching her shin.

To Avra's right was a familiar backpack—black with a red strap, Nike swoop emblazoned on the top. She had watched for this backpack. She knew its owner.

"Hey," Kieran said, not even turning to look at her. He was facing the opposite wall. Avra hesitated, giving him time to elaborate. He did not.

Kieran's friends were wealthy and popular and had no doubt either wheedled parents into calling them out sick, or been swept away on glamorous trips, or they'd simply decided—as the children of the influential sometimes could—not to show up. It was a wonder he was here at all, but perhaps his father's job didn't quite cover vacation costs for Kieran, his older brother, and his four sisters. Or, maybe his father was using the excuse of "vacation deadlines" to dedicate time to an affair. Avra always thought he'd be the type to have affairs, to abandon his family over the holidays, to whisk some pretty young thing off to ski the Alps under cover of "business." The kind of good Christian man who judged others while living proudly in a glass house. She wondered if Kieran's dad ever used words like "faggot." Regardless, Kieran was quite alone.

"Hey." Greeting returned, the two sat in silence. Avra did a quick vicinity scan. One boy sitting on the adjacent couch, nose buried in Dickinson (charming, Avra thought). Two girls by the water fountain, in eager conversation. A group of friends at the other set of couches, facing toward the courtyard windows and watching something on a small, square screen. They laughed loudly. The Dickinson boy didn't even glance up. Nobody was looking, nobody paying them any mind. And even if the fountain girls *were* to glance over, Kieran was on the floor, just in front of Avra. They'd barely glimpse the top of his head.

Avra felt a brush of warmth at the front of her right shin and started. Kieran was slanting toward her, his back pressed in a tentative line against the front of Avra's legs. He did not rest his full weight against her, but leaned forward slightly, as if to ask "Is this okay?" An absurd non-question. The interrogation of consent through subtlety of body language. After a moment of Avra decidedly not moving away, not shoving him off, not asking what the fuck he thought he was doing, Kieran relaxed a bit more, and the pressure against Avra's legs grew heavier. It was overly intimate. It was a system shock. They had not built up to this. And yet here he was, lingering, almost *affectionate*. It was such a 180, she may have snapped from the whiplash if it hadn't felt so earnestly correct, so very much in tune with *finally*.

Avra—touch-starved now that Isabella was away on break, that was as good an excuse as any—let herself enjoy the pressure. It felt like the comfort of a weighted blanket after a panic attack, like an admittance of kinship, like a brief allayment of chronic violence. She wondered skeptically whether Kieran sought anything specific, what he meant by this display, what he needed from her. He still had not looked back. Craving clarity, Avra cleared her throat. Her voice low, she asked, "All right?"

When, once more, he didn't reply, she changed tack. "Looking forward to the holiday?"

The question was left to dawdle, similarly unanswered. Kieran moved as if to look over his shoulder, but stopped with his head at a forty-five-degree angle, like he couldn't quite force himself to finish the turn. Avra could see the tilted profile of a tall, tousled boy who was very, very pretty, and somehow small despite the lank. She imagined that holidays in Kieran's household would include an enthusiastic celebration of the birth of Jesus Christ. A household that would certainly be familiar with Kings, Judges, Leviticus, Romans, and Corinthians. A household that would feel landmine-loaded to Kieran, who had once put his head on Will's shoulder, who had once called Avra a dyke, who had once seen her eyes move toward Will and back. Avra, who had clocked him, by some witchcraft trick or miracle. Avra, who had never said a thing about it to him or to anyone else. Avra wondered idly where Will would be for the holidays. She wondered less idly whether her silence had soothed Kieran's animosity.

Kieran tilted forward again and moved to rise. The pressure on her legs was gone. Avra expected him to grab his backpack and make a quick exit. They didn't ask each other personal questions. They didn't *talk*. They were not friends. Kieran reached back for his bag, but rather than swinging it up over his shoulder, he dragged it across the couch. Rising slowly—unwilling to draw attention—he settled next to Avra, twelve inches between their bodies. Much less space than was appropriate for adolescent enmity. Avra half wished there were more people around. If this was meant to be an apology for the dyke thing, he was squandering the chance to do it right (i.e., publicly demonstrating a tremulous alliance). People could not be cruel to her if Kieran extended the protection of his company. Briefly, Avra imagined the proximity to power. Such a possibility felt baby-new, calf-clumsy. Besides, Avra knew that Kieran would reserve his right to be *most* cruel, in perpetuity—it was part of their pact.

They sat still and baffled on the couch. Kieran's hand was pressed flat against the fabric to his left, close to Avra's thigh, but not touching. His palm was facedown, too far extended from his body to be comfortable. He was reaching. She thought it odd— nobody really sat like that. An invitation, then. Avra could be smart in practice as well as in theory.

She surveyed the vicinity. Certain no one was looking, Avra let her right hand fall to the couch beside her, turned her head slightly to watch Kieran from behind a sheer curtain of wavy brown hair, and brushed her pinky against his.

The effect was immediate. His finger twitched, as if it had anticipated the contact, but did not pull away. Kieran shifted nois- ily, cleared his throat, and sat up straight, still not looking at her. He had all the subtlety of a trumpet. Avra's heart began to beat more quickly; her vision narrowed to Kieran's profile. The downcast eyes, absurd jawline, dark sideburns, red mouth. The spine pulled taut like a bow. She almost smiled. He was responsive like this, nervously risk-taking, allowing himself to be some version of vul- nerable. Avra thought soberly that she liked him much better this way. Imagined him on strings like a marionette, her fingers dancing, and Kieran dancing.

And then, the pinky beside hers moved. Rather than pulling

away, it snaked cautiously over Avra's, the slow drag across her skin sending glittering sparks up her wrist, over her palm. The shock of contact radiated outward from the place where Kieran's finger barely caressed her own. Her mouth felt suddenly too wet. Her lips tingled; a flush moved hungrily up her neck and cheeks. Something was twisting in her gut, some satisfied, fervent, crawling thing. Something saying, "Yes, of course, absolutely." Their pinkies were linked on the couch between them, invisible to the few potential onlookers, and sending waves of confused heat through Avra's belly. She tugged gently, almost like a childhood promise. The pinky crossing her own tugged back, two gentle pulls. Somewhere, bones were breaking, birds were crashing into windows, pawed animals were howling. Somewhere, the gates of hell were threatening to open. To pull them all toward torture and carnality.

Here on the couch, Kieran finally (finally) met Avra's eyes. His face was stone, revealing nothing. Then, a small twitch at the corner of his mouth, an almost-quirk of his eyebrow. It wasn't a smile, but it wasn't his typical scowl, either. Avra's eyes softened into amusement, and her lips tightened into what would have been a grin had she not been so valiantly fighting to keep her features composed. Then, like a cat realizing it had wandered into the wrong house, Kieran schooled his expression back to blankness, removed his pinky from Avra's (she mourned, momentarily), and rose from the couch. He slung his backpack across his shoulder, turned toward the main office and the school's front entrance, and walked slowly away. Avra watched him go, his tall, graceful body shrinking as the hallway framed his silhouette. He did not turn to look.

CHAPTER 4

JANUARY 2010

Upon the return from winter holiday, students tried their best to maintain a sense of cheer. Each carried around a tiny, internal reserve of happiness, stored up from full days out in piled snow, fuller nights of sleep, home-cooked meals, gifts, and the promise of a fresh term. Avra, for her part, carried a budding sense of sexual chaos the likes of which she had not experienced since discovering an illustrated copy of the *Kama Sutra* at her aunt's house when she was eleven and staring at bare breasts for an entire afternoon. She had spent the last several weeks repeatedly rotating her last interaction with Kieran like a doorknob in her head, and was considerably less rested than her monosexual peers. The memory had been worried smooth by Avra's rumination. He hadn't meant anything by it. It was some fluke, a violation of the universe's logic. No cause for alarm.

Alarming or not, things were changing. Kieran no longer stalked her through the halls, and Avra's shoulders dropped from their usual place up around her ears as she rushed from class to class. She missed the constant company, his warm proximity. Avra was always so *bored*. She resented herself, somewhat, for the way she craved his attention, the little fixes she sought throughout each day. He still watched her, still caught her eye over Isabella's shoulder, still rolled his eyes when she spoke up in class, but there was something else. Some wicked, unspoken thing. His gaze would linger, considering, on Isabella's hand, touching Avra's waist beneath her shirt. When Avra made a particularly sagittal joke, he would smirk appreciatively. Once, when she snapped at Matt for knocking over her trombone case in the hall ("Matthew Tetrault, for a so-called paragon of athleticism, you are *genuinely* a fucking oaf"), she thought she'd heard Kieran laugh—a brief, stifled snort.

The changes were subtle, yet Avra was not the only one who noticed. Their peers stopped pausing to assess risk each time Avra and Kieran were in proximity. Fewer boys antagonized Avra in their quest for Kieran's approval of, or participation in, some casual hallway harm. Once, at lunch, Avra even saw Will grin at her from across the cafeteria. She was certain it had been a mistake—a trick of the light, some confusion-induced hallucination—but then he nodded at her in class, later that very same day, and she recognized the grin for what it was: decency.

By February, the boys' varsity basketball team had qualified for the state finals, with Kieran as their shooting guard. Avra strove not to care about their success, not to feel some tiny burst of hometown pride when she heard the morning announcements hail the daring courtside maneuvers of the Ridgefield High School Cowboys, but to no avail. She *cared*. How *embarrassing*. The cheerleaders' "Save a Horse, Ride a Cowboy" routine should have enraged her—no queer rabble-rouser raised in the intimidating shadows of second-wave feminist aunties would *ever*—and yet she sometimes hummed it to herself on her walk between classes, or smiled encouragingly at the upperclassmen girls practicing their pyramid for laughs in the hallway. With this slate of athletic successes (the gladiators, the concubines), archaic traditions trundled back to Ridgefield High.

On game days, while students waited for the buses, the cheerleaders and other willing women gave back massages to members of the team in the senior lounge. It was a tradition dating back to the 1720s, probably. Avra watched with disgusted fascination as Karly, head cheerleader now, cooed in Matt's ear that she just *knew* he'd have a great game, and ground the heel of her hand into the meat of his shoulders while he tried (with limited success) to appear unaffected. Several minutes later, Matt was Silly Putty. Avra noted that Karly's hands were moving down his arms, massaging his biceps, which he flexed instinctively. It was appalling. It was grotesque. It was almost precious. Avra knew a mating ritual when she saw one. She had experienced enough crushes, read enough pornographic fanfiction, seen enough Hollywood movies, spent enough gasping evenings with Isabella, to recognize extended foreplay. Matt (bless him) was resting his chin on his chest, his eyes closed, a cat-got-the-cream expression on his usually churlish face. Avra was too busy watching them to notice that she herself was being observed.

"You!" A masculine voice punctured her inspection.

Avra didn't quite go rigor mortis, but she did balk slightly, anticipating some accusation of perversion for which she hadn't summoned a defense.

"Yes?"

"Make yourself useful, why don't you? Kieran doesn't have anyone." It was Garrett, a senior boy with more social sway in his big toe than Avra could fit in her entire body. His tone was mocking, and a ripple of laughter moved through the gathered crowd—basketball players and cheerleaders and eager onlookers, all of whom knew the acrimonious history between Avra and Kieran. Matt didn't even lift his chin. Avra understood. Hypnotizing, the touch of a woman.

"Do it, you won't!" came a sweet, piping voice from behind her. Tati, sophomore, new to the squad this year—a "flyer," they called her, because she got tossed into the air at games. At least, from what Avra had heard. She had never attended one, usually opting instead to dazzle at this or that rehearsal, finish homework at the dining room table, marathon Pokémon on her Game Boy, or tear through all the smutty sapphic literature she could find at the local public library (heartbreakingly, not much). Avra turned to look at Tati, who grinned cheekily. "Come on, Avra—let bygones be gone, or whatever." Upon glancing around, Avra was surprised by the pleased anticipation on the faces of her classmates.

Finally, Kieran made his obstinate contribution. "Leave it. She's not going to do it." It was low, a bit gruff, and performatively dismissive. He seemed to their group of observers to be letting Avra off the hook, but she knew better. This wasn't designed to absolve her—this was designed to provoke her. It was a dare, and Avra was wavering. She didn't know how to back down from a challenge, and found, quite fervently, that she didn't want to. She wanted to touch him. To see if she could make his head droop like Matt's, make his brow relax, feel his traps shifting under the skilled pressure of her hands (learning to give back massages is a queer femme slumber party rite of passage). At the memory of his pinky brushing across the back of her hand, Avra bit down a threatening shiver.

"Like hell," Avra shot back at Kieran (challenge accepted) and her peers crowed happily.

"Get in there, girl."

"Push over, you guys."

"Give her some room!"

If Avra had been prone to making messianic jokes, she might have referenced the parting of a sea, sarcastically called herself Moses, but this was not the audience. Instead, she stepped lightly over crossed feet and backpacks and used shoulders as handholds to move through the crowd before settling herself on the couch next to Kieran. The same couch. It felt almost ritualistic. There was humiliation to this, but also satisfaction. A sudden, crystalline knowing of one's place in a grander order. Avra raised her hands, took a small, steadying breath, and laid them on Kieran's shoulders.

Applause broke out.

"Jesus, enough!" Kieran was snappish and rigid beneath her touch. He may have provided the challenge, but he was not enjoying the role of "spectacle."

Karly intervened, as much to her own benefit as Kieran's. "For real, you pervs. No reason to stare while I'm over here getting Matt to make *faces*." Matt shook off her hands and wiped a button of drool from the corner of his mouth.

"Are not."

"Am fucking too, I had you *purring*." Karly could be funny, and generous, and a bit mean. Avra liked her, thought semi-regularly of that diplomatic GSA flyer intervention, of Karly's ability to sense quicksand and step lively. She was one of the first to come around to Avra once she had stopped being so insufferable. She had even urged Avra to come to a game, not for the guys, but "so you can watch me cheer!" Avra suspected that Karly was kind of gay, from the way she could flirt, effortlessly, no matter the gender of the stammering recipient. Her spotlight-stealing intercession effectively shifted group focus. As sets of eyes diverted from Avra and Kieran, Avra felt him relax slightly underneath her hands.

Avra arranged her face into an expression of apathy before shifting her thumb to the soft place between Kieran's neck and shoulder and pressing down in long, slow strokes. Her fingers met and pulled apart. Pressed, and separated. She moved the kneading touches thoughtfully down either side of his spine, careful to work the skin beneath his shoulder blades, over each of his ribs. If she had a better knowledge of anatomy, she'd have paid equal attention to all muscle groups. As it was, she tried to cover as much ground as possible. She gripped his shoulders between small palms and dragged her hands languidly over his biceps, stopping at the crook in his elbow. She let her forefingers brush swiftly against the sensitive skin below the hem of his T-shirt sleeve before starting once more at his hairline. It was meditative, almost. Like what she imagined it might be to throw pottery—taking strength from the forearms, guiding the fingers to press just *there*, softening the palms.

Kieran, for his part, melted. Avra sensed the creation of a core memory—the texture of his skin under her hands, how he eventually relaxed enough to press back into her thumbs, how he *gave*. It struck her that touch was another form of communication. Her hands and Kieran's skin whispering back and forth, sharing some or another profound secret. Avra thought briefly of Douglas Adams, and *The Hitchhiker's Guide to the Galaxy*, and the answer to the Ultimate Question of Life, the Universe, and Everything—42. As she skimmed a wanton thread of contact once more over the skin at the intersection of Kieran's neck and shoulder (it was warming, and how satisfying, how delightful), Avra decided that *touch* was certainly a better answer than 42. And then she was grinning at the absurdity of someone with her degree of nerd credibility touching Kieran at all. Kieran, who had probably never watched *Star Wars*, or *Lord of the Rings*, or *Battlestar Galactica*, or any of it. Impossible. Ridiculous.

Kieran had three freckles behind his right ear. The hair at the bottom of his neck was the softest. Short, downy strands tickled her knuckles as she worked. Avra forced back the wild urge to card her fingers through them and tug. She thought his head might drop back. Thought he'd willingly bend to her if she learned to pull just right. She pressed her thumbs behind Kieran's ears, smoothed them down either side of his neck, and felt his intake of breath rather than heard it. His blood moved under her fingertips. When she dragged her thumbs back up the way they'd come, ending at the notch behind his jaw, below his earlobe, Kieran let out a faint contented noise, and Avra's stomach tied itself into furious, jubilant knots.

She thought she was gay, before him. And truly, she should have hated him for the years of torment. There were things she disliked—that he could still scare her if he wanted to. That she always knew where he was in a room (across the cafeteria, third from the right in class, corner of the longest blue couch in the lounge, in the center of the pack during gym). She disliked the girlish urge to preen when he watched her, the way he distracted her from Isabella, the way she'd started wearing mascara to school. She should have hated that his skin was pink beneath her hands, and that she'd always know how little pressure it took to summon that capillary glow. She should have hated the desire to scrape her teeth across the shell of his ear, lick his pulse point to feel it leap under the heat of her tongue, run the flat of her palm down his chest, trail a fingertip over his hip bone and test whether he was ticklish.

She was taking liberties now. Brushing softly against the hairs at the nape of his neck, over and over while he shifted between her fingertips like a charmed snake. She kept the contact as light as possible, and watched goosebumps erupt across his skin. Kieran was pressing back into her hands, turning his head to reach her touch, and Avra was drunk, the power intoxicating. She scraped over his scalp with her nails, unhurried, lazy, and knew his eyes were closed. She wanted to hold him in this trance, to stay in it herself. The back of his neck was starting to bead sweat, perhaps from the mortification of being so erotically mauled, perhaps from the effort of cutting off the noises he might otherwise make. Avra reflected briefly on their history of loathing, and a bubble of humor popped in her throat. She breathed out a small laugh and very nearly pressed her forehead to the back of his skull but resisted the preposterous call toward tenderness. Kieran, usually so sensitive to any perceived slight, heard the laugh and did not freeze or pause. He simply continued turning his head, tilting back toward her hands (the windmills), toward Avra (the imagined, retired enemy).

"You're doing me next time." It was Garrett again, expression too keen. He was watching Avra's hands at the nape of Kieran's neck and crossing his (too large, certainly) arms. At this, Kieran did freeze, caught in an uncommon moment of surrender. Inwardly, Avra swore at Garrett. *Genuinely? Fuck you.* Suddenly, like an old film rerun, Kieran was off the couch, Nike-swooped backpack hurled over his shoulder. He walked quickly toward the empty bus lot, did not say thank you, did not turn around, and Avra loathed their mutual cut-and-run aptitude. She knew she was blushing furiously. The degradation, the pulse she could not ignore between her thighs, the damp of Kieran's sweat still cooling on her fingertips, and the rage at rapture, interrupted.

Not entirely gay, then. Not quite gay.

Avra surveyed the group defensively, prepared for further comments, but none came. Garrett was still eyeing her consideringly. Tati's eyebrows were hidden by her bangs. Karly was shooting Avra a wide-eyed look of . . . consolation? Avra didn't have the space to interrogate that gaze—or to consider what others had seen—before her eyes alighted upon someone else: Isabella, standing sentry by the water fountain and staring at Avra over the back of the couch, a stricken expression on her otherwise lovely, fawnish face.

CHAPTER 5

JUNE 2010

Karly Edwin was throwing an end-of-year party, and Avra was invited. Karly had been sympathetic when Isabella dumped Avra sometime in March ("Oh, babe, I'm so *sorry!* Her loss, future ladies' gain, right?"). She was affectionate and charming and bore Avra's queer identity as a badge of honor—how *progressive*, a *lesbian* friend! At her locker, Karly fiddled with the rings on Avra's hand, said she *wished* she were gay because Matt was *exhausting*, and the girls around them tittered in alarm. In burgeoning high school bestie tradition, Karly texted Avra pictures every few days: her outfits of choice, the cover art from a sapphic film, even once an astounding picture from that one afternoon in senior lounge—Avra behind Kieran on the couch, hands on his neck. Kieran's eyes were closed, his face slack and satisfied (Avra saved it, opened it every quarter hour, zoomed, stared, stored it in a dedicated album on her home computer). In the weeks following the Isabella breakup, Karly invited Avra to sit with her at lunch, as Isabella shored up support from Teo and Deirdre. "We'll show her," Karly would say, protective and performative, slinging a slim arm around Avra's hunched shoulders.

When Avra did see Teo and Deirdre, she felt like a politician whose plans had been revealed to the opposition. Once, Deirdre brought Kieran up in conversation, her eyes trained so obviously on Avra's face that Avra had the savage urge to reach out and poke them. Hard. Avra maintained a stony neutrality. She could feel their judgment (not entirely gay, then, not quite gay), their confusion (but we thought you liked girls?) as she walked the halls in cropped sweaters and floral skirts that Karly swore looked, "absolutely amazing on you, babe—lesbo librarian chic!" Avra didn't bother correcting the slur. It was bizarre to be the queer kid adopted by the head cheerleader, but Avra supposed every misfit had their token moment in the sun.

Undoubtedly, Avra had become prettier during junior year. She had a different confidence in her soft, curved body now that it was no longer the target of so many jokes. She'd started Accutane over winter break, and her skin glowed after six months of chapped, peeling lips and white-hot headaches. She grew out her hair, letting the wavy brown burst from the root, and chopped off the dead bleached ends. Over the course of Karly's attentive instruction—"You're such an autumn—wear deep greens, they'll bring out the hazel in your eyes"; "Apply blush on the top of the cheekbone, not the whole cheek!"; "Girl, you'd look great in a wedge"—Avra had learned to make her queerness palatable, even alluring. The bullying stopped entirely. Girls were quick to choose seats next to her in class. At sleepover parties, Avra was the stuffed animal in a game of tug-of-war—whose bed would she share? Like, *hypothetically*, which of the girls would she most want to kiss? Why? When did she *know?* *How* did she know? The girls liked lesbian porn too. Did that make them, like, *gay* or something? What little social capital Avra had was quickly monetized.

Avra felt some guilt, but not enough to shed her new "queer

femme" aesthetic (heavy emphasis on the "femme"). She supposed
the breakup with Isabella had made her more pitiable—the pretty,
dumped, sad, *human* gay—and thus less of a target. Guys noticed
her now, Garrett foremost among them. He complimented her
clothes, offered to carry her things between classes, even begged
her to come to his games. When she confronted him—"You know
I'm still gay, right?"—Garrett had laughed and retorted, "Given any
back rubs lately?" Avra flushed deeply and handed over her books in
horrified silence. She had been compelled by the shimmering allure
of popularity to become consumable. The fuckable gay. The tame-
able gay. The curable, reformable gay. And Garrett liked a challenge.

Avra was halfway certain that her invitation to Karly's party
was—unofficially—as "the entertainment," in that she'd entertain
half a dozen questions about what it was like to hook up with girls
before she became too drunk to answer. That was the plan, anyway.
Avra, who remembered hiding liquor bottles from her mother when
she was barely five years old, had never tried alcohol before. She was
terrified, and aching for something new, and reckless in her social
ascendancy, and besides, she was seventeen now, which must have
been the legal drinking age *somewhere*.

So, the weekend after finals, Avra dressed up in a high-waisted
black miniskirt, black tights, black platform boots, a black crop top,
black eyeliner, and red lipstick before her dad—mortified at her
outfit, unsure how to intervene—dropped her off at Karly's house.
He hesitated in the driveway, the car silently idling, before turning
to Avra.

"You know, if you feel unsafe . . ."

Avra finished the thought: "I can call, and you'll pick me up."

He continued, haltingly: "I haven't seen you . . . dress . . . like
this . . . before."

"They're Karly's clothes. I haven't dressed like this before." Avra could see her concerned, egalitarian father struggling with how best to ask his anti-dress-code, subvert-the-dominant-paradigm, smash-the-patriarchy rebel daughter *why* she had chosen this outfit without implying that she *shouldn't* have chosen this outfit. Before he could form the words, Avra pushed open the door to his Prius. Thumping music flooded the car. Inside the house, someone was blasting Pitbull. Avra and her father shared a well-timed grimace.

"Is your phone charged?"

"I'll see you tomorrow, Dad." The dismissal was clear. They exchanged quick *love you*s. The gravel crunched under his tires as he drove away.

Karly found Avra immediately. She was waiting in the foyer, as if anticipating Avra's arrival. "You came!" She grabbed Avra's hand—conspicuous, intentional—and tugged her toward the finished basement. Avra had been here for a sleepover just last month. Urged on by the other girls, she had done a dramatic reading of her favorite queer fanfiction, rated NC-17. It was enormously fun. Finally, Avra's contributions, her geekdom, and her advanced knowledge of human sexuality were valued.

The basement space wasn't small, but perhaps felt more so because of the press of bodies. There was a living room with a pull-out futon and a coffee table, one bedroom, a tiny square kitchenette around the corner, and a full bath. A pair of French doors opened onto a broad back patio facing the lawn, which sloped downward over an acre and a half before meeting the edge of thick, slasher-esque woods. Avra could see coolers set outside and soon learned that they were full of Sam Adams, Mike's Hard Lemonade, Smirnoff Ice, and Jell-O shots ("Tati made them!"). Inside, a mirror-paned bar cart displayed every liquor Avra could have imagined, and several she didn't know existed. She recognized Jack Daniel's and had a brief, vivid memory of pouring the sloppy brown liquor down the sink while her mother slept. A beer-pong table was set up by the stairs, the couch pushed back to facilitate a carpeted dance floor.

Karly looked iconic in a short denim skirt and skintight navy tank, pulled down just low enough that the lace from her Victoria's Secret bra peeked alluringly over the top. Once Avra was set up comfortably in a dimly lit corner, prepared to people-watch, Karly curled into her space, a mischievous grin on her very pretty face.

"Plan to do another reading tonight?" Karly prompted. Avra laughed self-consciously, and Karly's grin stretched charismatically. "Could you *imagine* the boys? They would die."

"I'll brush up on my mourner's kaddish."

"What?" Karly's face was blank.

"It's a Jew thing—a prayer we say over the dead." *I was being witty*, Avra thought.

"Oh, right, I always forget about that." *Wrong audience.* "Pretty please take shots with me tonight?" Karly laid her head on Avra's shoulder and gazed up with puppy eyes. Avra shook her head as if to say, *You are impossible.*

"Only if you show me how."

Karly winked in agreement and pushed off from Avra's side. "I'm gonna go find Matt—he gets needy if I leave him alone for like ten fucking minutes, I swear. You—go, mingle. Grace is here and I know she was excited to see you . . . MATT!" Karly shouted in the vague direction of the crowd and moved to seek out her not-quite boyfriend. Avra looked around for Grace, a flautist in her year who sat next to her in social studies. She wondered momentarily if Karly was already drunk. She wondered also what the fuck she was doing there.

"Want one?" Garrett appeared at her side, holding a Mike's and looking both eager and lecherous. He didn't wait for her response before pressing it into her hands with an up-down glance and a "Nice skirt." Avra didn't answer but took the bottle. It was open. "Will and I are playing pong next. Root for me?" Certain that being seen at Karly Edwin's party, cheering Garrett on by the pong table while drinking a Mike's, would solidify her place in the no-lon-ger-a-freak echelons of Ridgefield High, Avra agreed with a pasted smile. She took a swig from the bottle Garrett had procured— probably, she shouldn't have. She knew better than to sip from an open beverage, but thought *Fuck it.* The drink was sugar-sweet and hit the back of her throat in an "alcohol is poison and your body instinctively knows it" sort of way. Avra tried to ignore the pulse of her anxiety, in time with the music (Black Eyed Peas now—who was in charge of this playlist?). She took another drink.

An hour later, Avra had finished two Mike's, Grace had joined her over at the pong table ("I'm terrible at this game." "Girl, same." "Do a Jell-O shot with me?" "Yes please."), Karly had deposited another open bottle into her hand, and Kieran had arrived. Avra could read his mild intoxication in the liquid movement of his body, the red flush on his neck, the way he hugged Will for about two seconds longer than was strictly hetero when he joined them at the pong table. She hoped that he hadn't driven himself. A voice at the back of her head complained that he should be more fucking responsible. She pushed it away. No Kieran tonight. That way led to confusion and sweaty palms and entirely-too-detailed fantasies and general badness. Her treacherous stomach swooped when he caught her eye over the table. Kieran immediately pushed back his hair, stood up a bit straighter. (*Self-conscious*, Avra interpreted. *Nervous.*) When Avra raised her bottle in nonchalant greeting, Kieran inclined his head, turned to mutter something to Will, and made his way toward the lawn to rummage in the coolers. Avra forced her eyes forward.

Someone dimmed the lights. A game of Truth or Dare started

up on the couches. Tati was dancing with a Solo Cup in her hand. Avra thought shrewdly that this was the high school party of Hollywood. What a glorious, meticulous act—everyone knew their role. Boys shotgunned beers in the yard and came back inside laughing and leaning on each other (the rare physical contact they were allowed) and cursing jubilantly and smelling like sour hops. Girls wound their waists and bared their midriffs and picked "dare" when they were brave and "truth" when they were defiant and weaponized every piece of their wiles, reaching for the scintillating illusion of power. Grace was watching Will from under her eyelashes and saying things like, "Nice" and "Killin' it!" every time he sank a ball (he and Garrett had beaten three other doubles and taken smoke breaks besides). Avra was buzzed (perhaps significantly), but not *drunk*. She overenunciated to mask her tipsiness, hit consonants hard when people asked her a question, point-blank refused to slur. It was probably noticeable.

When Will and Garrett triumphantly defeated their fourth set of challengers in a row, they left to join the game of Truth or Dare, spurred by Grace's subtle but strategic cajoling. Avra, pleasantly intoxicated, moved to follow, but Karly interceded.

"Babe, first of all, Lily brought punch. It's lethal, and you *absolutely must* try it. Second of all, she told me she hooked up with Darren but he was super bad at going down on her, and I think you should give him some pointers." Avra's brain took a few seconds to catch up, but when it did, her laugh came out as a snort.

"What? Why me?" She had slept with all of one person, ever. Karly looked at her like she was being stupid on purpose.

"Because you fuck girls! And I'm betting you're good at it. Or, at least better than Darren. I mean, Isabella stayed with you for what, like a year and a half? You must have been doing something right." Karly was pink-cheeked and grinning, her words a bit too loud and close together. Avra knew she was bold even before booze, so let the assumptions slide noisily by. Karly could get away with pretty much anything. "Okay, don't move—I'll go get Darren."

Avra widened her eyes. "Please, please do not." Giving guys at a high school party cunnilingus pointers sounded . . . well, honestly, it sounded like a very good time, but—in Avra's experience, which consisted pretty much entirely of reading through instructive erotica with curious friends—sober and private sex education was typically more effective than drunk, public ridicule. Besides, the room was starting to turn, and she couldn't trust that she'd explain the full anatomy of the clitoris right, and she might giggle at the word "labia" or confuse the class with her differentiation of "vagina" versus "vulva" or lose the thread as she emphasized the importance of *consistency* and *pattern* and, also, Karly was already gone. Avra stood alone by the bar cart, deliberating an exit strategy. The game of Truth or Dare on the couch had hit a rhythm. Avra felt no urge to join. She was barely noticeable and wished to stay that way.

She glanced down at the cart and the Jack Daniel's label swam lazily in front of her eyes. Damn. What was a good Jack Daniel's mixer? Mom kept Diet Pepsi in the fridge. Always diet, so she could stay thin, but Avra was pretty sure the cocaine helped with that. *Don't think about your addict-alcoholic mother at a popular-kid party during your first experience with booze, you maudlin little shit.* Avra pressed her thumb and forefinger together, grounding. *Do not fuck this up for yourself.* Intimidated by the liquor selection, Avra swayed backwards, as if to create some distance between herself and any unwanted associations. The music suddenly seemed too loud, the bar cart condescending and judgmental, the room cramped, the company unfamiliar and blessedly ignorant. For a hot second, a blade of resentment sliced through Avra while Karly—her parents upstairs and still married and probably not wasted—giggled

across the packed room, and Tati passed out what was left of the
Jell-O shots. Avra glanced toward the kitchenette. *Safety.* She could
get some water, get a break from the music, escape the game and the
straight people everywhere, take a deep breath, maybe stop thinking about her mother and Jack Daniel's and a broken lamp in the
living room and Mom lying, saying they'd been robbed to deny
the obvious truth that she'd smashed up more furniture during yet
another unmedicated manic episode.

Avra's benign smile slipped as she considered the bar cart and
chewed her bottom lip. She could sense Kieran's eyes from the
couches and was too tipsy to maintain neutrality, too tipsy to feign
apathy. When she looked back to meet his gaze, his eyes were on
her mouth. They stayed there for a stretched, simmering lapse. Avra
counted the seconds. If she could shrink down to the size of a flea
and crawl into one of Kieran's ears and burrow into his brain tissue
and eat her way toward reading his mind—something she, sickly,
had always wanted to do—Avra would know how Kieran hated
when she bit her lip, hated thinking about her mouth, because his
brain would get stuck and skip like a record. *Her mouth her mouth
her mouth her mouth. It's pretty it's pretty, her mouth her mouth.* She
nearly stuck out her tongue, but considered the *whub-thump* of
speaker bass, the pulsing opportunity here, and licked her bottom
lip instead. Kieran shifted; he glanced up at her eyes and then back
down, like he couldn't help it. Avra, pleased despite herself, worried
her lip between her teeth, half intentionally. Kieran watched.

Avra's low belly flutter gathered momentum. She forced herself to tear her eyes away from Kieran's keen expression, instead
assessing the scene around him. Will was sitting next to Grace (the
glittering irony of their paired names always made Avra want to
laugh), adjacent to Kieran, who Avra knew must have hated this,
must be twisting at the flagrant heteronormativity. She would have

hated it, if it were Isabella and some guy, Isabella at this party acting like a straight person. While Avra watched, Grace wrinkled her nose adorably, giggled at something Will said, tilted her head, and placed her small hand on Will's thigh. Will leaned closer, whispered in Grace's ear the way that boys do, and Kieran abruptly moved to rise. Avra, caught staring at the group, a little embarrassed for it, darted toward the kitchenette. Kieran, provided the option of something heady, something new, something the fuck else, followed.

When he entered the kitchenette, Avra was standing at the sink around the corner. There were water droplets on the side of her face, pink and flushed from cold; she had just splashed it. Her hands were wrapped in a dish towel, which she placed down on the counter next to a collection of cut limes, shot glasses, and a half-empty bottle of tequila, left abandoned by someone—probably Garrett. She turned at the sound of Kieran's entry and looked entirely unsurprised to see him. Internally, Avra marveled at Kieran's uncanny gift of finding her whenever she felt most unsettled, most vulnerable. A bead of water rolled down her cheek to her throat. She wondered whether it was visible, whether Kieran was tracking it toward her collarbone. The room steadied as she stared at him. Kieran always forced Avra's mind to the present—old protective habits die hard.

Kieran, perhaps emboldened by four beers, three shots of liquor, or the rage of watching Grace giggle next to Will, spoke first. "Why are you hiding?" Annoyance bubbled in Avra's recently fluttering belly. It seemed *rich*, from Kieran, to accuse anyone of hiding anything at all.

"I'm not *hiding*." She let the word drip.

"Yes, you are."

"The fuck does it matter if I'm in here or out there?"

"Maybe you're scared of something," Kieran suggested. A swoop of anger, then, steely and brittle, at the utter hypocrisy. Avra glared at him, pursed her lips, and enunciated her retort, landing on every consonant.

"At any fucking moment, on any day, whether I'm scared or not, we both know I'm still braver than you." She said it the way she said most things—bold, direct, and straight to Kieran's face. She never did pay much mind to consequences, and besides, it was true. Avra half expected some mighty defensive reaction, but none came. Kieran paused, eyes searching her haughty, freckled visage, before acknowledging her challenge with a shrug.

"Suit yourself," he muttered passively. Avra turned her body away from him, and glanced down to the cut limes, the saltshaker knocked on its side, granules scattered across the countertop. "Tequila shot?"

Avra didn't look up at Kieran's olive branch invitation. She just swallowed and said baldly, "I'm not sure how. Like, the order. Never taken shots. Never really tried anything before tonight." The fight was draining from her, as quickly as it had flared. She didn't know why she was telling him this. There was a note of pleading in her words. *I want to fit in. This is me trying.*

Kieran's voice was quieter now. "I'll show you." The offer sounded so generous to Avra that gratitude bit at her heels. She mentally kicked it away.

"Yes. All right."

He walked toward her, stood before the counter like a butcher, and reached for a shot glass. Avra took a step back to give Kieran more room, and he moved naturally into the vacated space. He smelled like something malty. The sleeve of his T-shirt was ripped. Avra watched his hands as Kieran carefully poured an ounce of tequila—the bottle had a blue label, Camarena, she'd remember—into a smudged glass. The part of her that would normally insist upon a clean one was soothed by the alcohol still buzzing through her veins.

"Where's Will?" Avra inquired innocently, trying to keep her tone as neutral as possible.

"Hanging with Grace," Kieran responded, seemingly trying to match her tone but still sounding petulant. At this, Avra—decidedly tipsy, stricken once more by the ridiculous heterosexuality play—cackled. It was not a feminine sound, but abrupt and witchy and bright, and it went on for a long time. Kieran waited.

"Will and Grace," she said amusedly, through sharp little bursts. To her surprise, Kieran actually smiled, apparently placated by Avra's recognition of the stinging irony. Avra sensed that this was something they both found absurd; that he'd laugh too if he weren't hurting. "Want to chat about that?" she asked mildly, once she'd stopped chuckling.

"Not even at all," Kieran replied, brushing salt onto the floor while he righted the shaker. His timbre shifted a bit, guard climbing up, and Avra reached unconsciously toward him before realizing what the fuck she was doing and stilling her hand. Kieran pretended not to notice. Or maybe he simply hadn't noticed. Avra couldn't tell.

Kieran licked his own index finger to dampen it, and Avra felt a pull in her belly entirely unrelated to either anger or amusement. His tongue looked very pink. Avra had a frantic, momentary urge to coax it back from behind his lips and bite it. Eyes dark with concentration, Kieran shook salt slowly onto his index finger, where it clung to his spit-dampened skin.

"Tell me the order," Avra said, her voice softer than usual, as she watched his ministrations with poorly concealed fascination.

"Salt, shot, and then lime," Kieran replied easily, as if he'd done this a hundred times. Maybe he had. Avra *hated* not knowing things, hated even more having Kieran instruct her, but the discomfort of asking felt modest compared to the potential humiliation of getting it wrong and, god forbid, retching or coughing or somehow not

taking it like a man. Avra allowed herself a small smile at thinking that phrase—*taking it like a man*—in Kieran's company. If
they were friends, she might have shared the joke, queer recognizing queer. As it was, she maintained false casualness. Salt now set
against his index finger, Kieran balanced it and citrus in his right
hand, a to-the-brim shot glass in his left. Avra expected a demon-
stration. She did not expect what happened next.

Kieran turned his eyes back toward her face—she thought
they'd have spent more time there, if he were braver—and moved to
stand in front of Avra, directly in her space. It had been a long while
since he'd had an excuse to be close to her like this, to be *invasive,*
and he looked comforted, satisfied. It must have been relieving to
feel powerful around Avra, who had a knack for suggesting that
everyone was weak and scared and stupid without having to say it
out loud, though she sometimes said it out loud. Tonight, Avra was
out of her depth, whereas Kieran had been swimming laps in this
pool for years. She didn't know what she was doing, and Kieran
did. She needed to ask for help, and Kieran didn't. It was glorious,
intoxicating in a different way than the booze still rolling sluggishly
through their bodies.

Avra was grateful for the two hours she had spent getting ready.
She hoped she looked pretty, and that Kieran noticed. Her shiny
brown hair was tumbling around her shoulders, tamed into submission by a curling iron. The all-black clothing suited her, she thought,
as did the red lipstick, intended to make her mouth look plush and
tempting. Perhaps this explained Kieran's earlier gaze, his fixation,
again and again. She was pale beneath all her freckles. She wondered vaguely whether Kieran would like her even better smudged
up, dirtied. He liked disheveling Avra, always had. She could tell
from his pleased expression after slamming a locker next to hers
or jostling her backpack, like he'd accomplished a task, checked

something off a spitefully titillating to-do list. She was so good at fucking with him, setting him off-kilter, it seemed only fair for him to shove back where he could. And Will was sitting on the couch with Grace. And Avra was in front of him, a little self-conscious, uneasy at the avidity of Kieran's expression.

Kieran took another step forward, and Avra had a sharp sense of locker-pressed déjà vu as her lower back hit the ridge of the sink. "Ready?" The word was soft with provocation, the silky lilt of suggestion strung along the finishing upspeak. Another half step, and Kieran's hip pressed firmly against the soft fabric of her skirt. He held her still against the sink, lime and salt next to her left cheek, tequila by her right. In the rush of power, taken or exchanged, intoxication hit Avra with a brute force. Kieran's cheeks were red, there was a searing flush rising along his neck, and he ground his molars to regain control. He was in charge, at least for right now, and Avra—confident queer girl, condescending, ballsy—was not. Her hazel eyes were wide and nervous, her lower lip wet, mouth slightly open, breath coming quick enough that the rise and fall of her chest moved the fabric of Kieran's shirt.

Avra was warm all over, and furiously turned on. She tried frantically to replace the blaze of her arousal with rage. She hated him for this. For her thighs, which pressed together to steady the adamant thrumming between her legs. For her nipples, which were hardening against her top. For her stupid traitorous brain, which had never thought less about women in her whole gay life.

Kieran lifted the finger painted with salt to Avra's mouth and rubbed gently, smoothing his knuckle over her lipstick, willing it to smudge. "Lick," he said, husk in his voice reinforcing the certain command. *Fuck.* Avra complied, immediately. She flicked her tongue to chase the salt and tasted something unfamiliar beneath—it was a second before she realized the new flavor was Kieran's skin. "Hold it on your tongue. Keep your mouth open." Avra licked the salt again (tasted Kieran, shivered) and let her tongue rest at the bottom of her mouth, still open, saliva gathering slowly. Kieran, a look of rapturous captivation on his face, rubbed his fingers against her bottom lip until it was spit-slick and almost dripping. Avra imagined his fingerprints leaving their signature in her lipstick. It felt wonderful, the gliding pressure, like sparks and slowed time and some sensuous, unlanguageable thing. Her mouth was sensitive. She wanted his thumb to press down on her tongue, his fingers to explore the inside of her cheeks, for him to smear her spit across her jaw, over the side of her face. A dozen scenes of filth played across Avra's imagination—active, vulgar—as Kieran held his lipstick-pinkened finger against her mouth and she drooled prettily. Then, coming back to himself slightly, Kieran raised the shot glass and, like a priest offering the blood of Christ at mass, fed her the tequila. He made a mess of it, spilling it over her bottom lip. Avra suspected this was on purpose. The liquor dripped obscenely onto her chin, which Kieran pressed upward with his thumb, encouraging Avra to close her mouth. She did, obediently.

Avra swallowed. Any tequila that hadn't been lost burned on the way down, sensation made more pleasant by the taste of salt, of Kieran's skin, and the elongated rush of this tightrope moment. Avra wanted to whimper, to tug at him, to writhe and drown. The spirit hum in her blood was ritualistic, preordained. Her eyes were heavy-lidded, jaw slack, hips pressing forward toward Kieran. She could feel the swell of his erection warm against her thigh and was comforted, relieved, that she wasn't the only one so affected. She felt completely wrecked, entirely devastated, all reason burned to ash and dead on the linoleum. Avra momentarily considered demanding that Kieran lick off whatever tequila remained on her chin, but her voice was gone. For once, she had no order, no retort.

Powerlessness was refreshing, Avra thought vaguely as she watched Kieran watching her mouth. The moment clung to a knife edge of something so dastardly, so wicked, it was sliding pointed fingernails down Avra's spine, carving her open.

Kieran's fingertips were on her neck, applying barely there pressure, and Avra knew instinctively to open her mouth once more for the lime, which Kieran held salaciously against her bottom lip for several long seconds—during which Avra tried her hardest not to whine—before feeding it to her. As it slid past her teeth, Avra bit down. The burst of citrus chased the flavor of salt and Camarena off Avra's tongue. When he pulled the lime from her mouth, Avra licked her lips unconsciously, and Kieran made a furious noise, dragging his slickened thumb over her top lip this time, watching the red lipstick smear like a punch beneath her nose. Gorgeous. Gruesome. Indecent. As if deciding something, Kieran lifted his eyes to Avra's, raised what was left of the lime slice to his own mouth, and licked it slowly, over both sides, and then his own lipstick-stained fingers, tongue moving wetly while Avra's eyelashes fluttered and her knees buckled slightly and she was trapped between Kieran and the sink, his erection and the steel, the heat of his body and the cold, hard surface. It was almost threatening. It was brutally erotic. The shot was gone, and Kieran had not moved away. He dropped the debased lime onto the countertop behind her and lifted his fingers to hold the line of her jaw. He hooked his other hand, still holding the shot glass, over her collarbone, one finger pressed to the notch just beneath Avra's throat, possessive and certain. They stared at each other for several long, tremulous moments, her pulse jumping frantically, their roles reversed—Kieran mighty and dangerous, Avra entirely hypnotized, her pale neck fragile as a bird in his grasp.

Avra thought fleetingly of what people said about boys with long eyelashes—that women will use glue and falsies and oil and

serums and still never have half the length as some fifteen-year-old
Brad on the soccer team—and nearly laughed, boozed brain casting
around for a hold. Kieran, starting to buckle under the weight of his
half-dozen drinks, caught the almost-laugh and drunkenly misin-
terpreted. His eyes grew overcast: confused anger, arousal. Kieran
made a noise of frustration in the back of his throat, and Avra
couldn't have moved even if she wanted to, and Kieran's mouth
was half open, and she wanted to crawl inside of it, close his teeth
behind her like a trapdoor.

With all the intention of an executioner, Kieran dropped the
hand holding her jaw and wrapped his (long, elegant, strong, beautiful, damn him) fingers around Avra's wrist, tight enough to ache.
The other hand abandoned the shot glass with a *clunk*, dragged
slowly across her sternum from her neck. It flattened between her
breasts and down over her soft belly before sliding around her waist
and curving onto her hip. Kieran held Avra steady, thumb pressing
into her hip bone hard enough to bruise, and Avra hoped it would.
She wanted to watch it bloom over a day or two: evidence that this
actually fucking happened.

Kieran lowered his head toward her mouth, their faces inches
apart, and Avra was once again unsure of what to expect, unsure of
anything. Kieran was watching her lips, and Avra did not move, did
not inhale or exhale. Lack of oxygen was making her woozy. When
Kieran spoke, Avra heard the question like an echo in her head, as
if she should have known it was coming.

"Do you think I'm a faggot?" He said it so quietly, the sound of
her breath would have obscured the words. They hit Avra like a violent pleading, a dare, anything but a joke. Avra lifted her chin and
stared directly into Kieran's handsome face, twisted with a drunk,
defiant hurt she could feel beneath her ribs. A hurt she had carried
in a small cage within her chest since she was six years old and had

her first crush—some Disney princess, some heroine. A hurt made of mirror glass, reflected in each other, in the warm press of their bodies, seeking intimacy, sensation, the comfort of a counterpart.

Kieran dug his thumb a bit harder as he awaited her response, and Avra squirmed, certain this was a question Kieran never should have had to ask. "I know you are," she said, too strung out to brace for a reaction, "I know it. And I'm a *dyke*." The last word was a rebuke: *How dare you ruin this*. Kieran did not let go, did not drop his hands, did not let up one ounce of pressure. His face did not fall. He did not cry, or whimper, or beg for a different response, or tell her to go screw herself, or kiss her, or hit her, or do anything at all. They stood, barely breathing into each other's faces, eyes locked and furious, hating each other for the mutual knowing, and for somehow wanting this, too. Hating each other for being the ones to bear witness. Hating each other for the confirmation of a kinship neither had sought, that neither wanted.

And then Karly came twirling into the kitchenette, happily seeking the Camarena and Avra and a public trial of Darren's pussy-eating skills, but stopped abruptly at what must have been a frightening scene. Avra expected Kieran to release her as if he had been burned, to back away stammering explanations, but he didn't. He dropped his hands from her wrist and hip slowly, letting his fingers drag along the parts of her he could touch, reluctant to break whatever fragile connection had just formed. Karly's face fell slightly at his delay, an eyebrow arching in confusion, but Kieran didn't offer any insight. He merely stepped back from Avra (again, she mourned the lost contact, mourned his hands), said a quick "All right, then," and turned to leave. Avra stood frozen, grounding to the indifferent press of the sink, still preoccupied by the pain in her hip bone, which was fading slowly. When Kieran was around the corner, likely out of earshot, Karly approached with some caution.

"I didn't realize he was still doing all that."

"Doing what?"

"Hassling you."

"Oh, he wasn't—that wasn't—it's not . . ." But Avra didn't know how to explain, and found she didn't really want to, and besides, Kieran had tormented her for years. This was a reasonable conclusion to which Karly could jump. "It's okay," Avra said instead. "He's just drunk."

"Want me to get Matt to kick his ass?"

It was a generous offer, and Avra laughed, "Could you even do that?"

"Well . . . well, no, probably not. Matt's his friend. But Garrett might go for it, if he thought it meant you'd go to a game or sit on his lap or something." Karly licked her teeth while Avra made a "no thank you" face, trying to pull her mind from someplace very far away.

"That's all right, I don't think it'll happen again." She prayed it would. Karly, who had all the social graces of head cheerleader and homecoming queen, dropped the subject.

"As long as you're okay. Come on, Darren's waiting for a performance review." They left the kitchenette behind. Avra rubbed the back of her hand over her mouth. It came away pink from lipstick and spit, gritty with salt. As she turned out of the room, Avra cast her eyes toward the lime, which still had marks from her teeth, still held the saliva from Kieran's tongue—proof that she hadn't dreamt any of this. Proof that it was real.

CHAPTER 6

OCTOBER 2010

In the fall of Avra's senior year, the theater department chose to put on a genuine classic: *Hello, Dolly!* It was an ambitious selection for a public high school of about three hundred and fifty students. As one of a handful of Jewesses currently living in Ridgefield, Avra was determined to land the lead. The thought of this canonically Ashkenazi role going to a WASP-y non-Yid scene-stealing shiksa boiled her blood. This was *Streisand*. This was socialist-adjacent *shadchanit* excellence. This was Golden Age, widow-wins-a-millionaire, yenta-runs-Yonkers, big-hatted Hebraic camp. This was Avra's—period.

She sang "Don't Rain on My Parade" for her audition, and she crushed it.

The pressure of upcoming college application deadlines had impelled an unanticipated crew to audition. The Ridgefield High School jocks, basketball and football and baseball players alike, decided that a creative endeavor might stand out impressively on applications otherwise heavily featuring running, jumping, hitting, catching, and throwing. To Avra and the veteran theater kids' bemusement, many newcomers were cast in ensemble roles—Kieran and Will, Matt, Darren, Jacob and Ethan from the baseball team, and even a couple cheerleaders. Karly and Grace had auditioned mostly to spend more extracurricular time with their now-official boyfriends. They were promptly cast as dancers. The director was delighted ("A treat! So many new faces!"). He rounded out the cast with frequent fliers from choir and techies borrowed from band, and rehearsals were two evenings per week, several hours every Sunday.

The newbies took to thespian culture with genuine, albeit slightly delayed, enthusiasm. After a smattering of self-conscious "jokes," which did not garner the typical peals of laughter (theater kids don't make it a habit to indulge the comedic stylings of athletes), not-so-wisecracks were replaced with tentative curiosity. Avra watched these almost-men she had known since early childhood suddenly forced outside of their element. Far, far outside. They learned to sing, examined sheet music in black binders, participated in scales and warm-ups. They learned to dance, and drilled the choreography, and drilled it again, and approached the girls for help, and asked questions:

"Wait, are we starting on the right foot or the left?"

"Hold on, what's a *pas de bourree*?"

"Can we run it once without the music?"

It was *astonishing*.

Avra, who had initially fought annoyance at their presence, felt steadily mounting gratitude at the opportunity to observe this chronic, stunning violation of norms. She loved capital-D Drama for the gender anarchy, the pursuit of perfection, the utterly predictable showmances (at least two love triangles, always), the space to be silly, to take on a character and bring them to life, to change outside and inside, to learn from a role. Over the years of borrowing other personalities, Avra had learned to keep what she liked and to leave what she didn't. Watching the athletes soften into this (decid-edly queer) culture was a complicated tonic. Despite the joy, the infatuation, the newness, Avra could sense an ambient grief from the boys; boys who had only now learned that a community such as this was even possible. They could have been happier, safer, fuller, and free. It was something like falling down the rabbit hole, or discovering Narnia, or receiving a Hogwarts letter when you were already grown: too little, too late.

While Avra watched the athletes adapt, she did her very best to impress. She knew she was impressive in this particular arena, not narcissistically, not cruelly like she could be in a classroom, but joyfully, truthfully. Theater came as naturally to her as crying. She was skilled, and passionate, and entirely worthy of the spotlight, and she wanted Kieran—who occasionally gawped at her during rehearsals—to agree. She could belt, higher and higher. She picked up choreography with almost as much ease as the cheerleaders. She took director's notes seriously, took her role seriously, took her stage time seriously, and—despite their newness and their giddiness, despite the fact that she had every right to defend this sacred space with bared teeth—took the rest of the cast seriously.

Avra was kind and supportive. She led the group through vocal warm-ups, prompted them to stretch, gave them cleverly sand-wiched feedback (a compliment, a gentle correction, another kind word). She tried to be charming, to be wonderful, to revise Kieran's initial appraisal of her. Avra knew this was working; Kieran's eyes landed on her *differently*. He stood quietly as she sang her solos, refusing to participate in stage-side chatter. He took long drinks of water when she urged the cast to hydrate. He huffed—impressed, not annoyed; a new sound—when Avra learned an eight-bar of solo choreography in only several minutes of rehearsal time. He attended to her excellence, reluctantly accepting her ability to defy expectations. She was not the snarling, discomfited, prickly Avra of the locker bay or an advanced placement lecture. This was very clearly her home turf. She presided over it with ease, humor, generosity, and grace.

All this effort left Avra optimistic that Kieran's understanding of her could round its edges. She did not expect the rest of the cast to be so easily beguiled. Their sudden and shocking affection was such that, on Avra's eighteenth birthday, the ensemble surprised her with a cake. Karly had baked it.

"From a box," she said. "Don't make a big thing."

The icing traced the outline of two large, round breasts. Candles came out of the nipples. Clearly, no member of the faculty had been approached for approval. Avra fought back stunned laughter along with grateful, overwhelmed tears while the group pelted her with a rousing chorus of "Happy Birthday," harmonies and all. She beamed through the entire first half of rehearsal—at the sincere warmth of the cast, at the praise from her director, at the many offers of piggyback rides from Will and Matt, who switched off carrying her to marks. Even the accompanist clucked merrily as Avra stood in bafflement, intermittently laughing, intermittently blubbering.

Kieran withdrew as rehearsal moved along. He shifted his weight when Avra clung to Matt's broad back, winced at Avra's grateful tears, and flared his nostrils when Avra beamed around before blowing out the glowing nipples on her birthday cake. She tried to make sense of it. She had garnered the sudden allegiance of Kieran's very own social network—maybe this was the source of his discomfort. On the other hand, perhaps Kieran was simply grappling with the absurdity of his own cruelty, with his *guilt*. He had tormented, mocked, shoved, bruised, insulted, spun, stalked, frightened, and humiliated Avra, for years. He had been forced to observe her talent, her gifts, her profound aptitude, for weeks and weeks. He had seen, now, how she could be sweet to his friends: encourage their ensemble, give specific praise, arrive to rehearsals early, and remind folks to rest. Perhaps this was simply shame at watching the woman who had withstood years of his viciousness finally break, finally cry, at something as soft as kindness.

About halfway through rehearsal, while the ensemble practiced their choreography, Avra asked for a short recess. She often felt the need to hide after receiving warmth—wanted to give it the time to sink in, to privately whisper her permission for it to stay. Emotional generosity made her think of her mother, who could provide loving praise one moment and steal the cash from your wallet the next. She hadn't seen her mother in eight whole birthdays.

One of the practice rooms was free, and Avra sank onto the bench in front of the piano, her legs a bit sore from piggyback-ing, her teeth still tasting of store-bought frosting. Why did things always get so good immediately before you had to leave them? The show would go up in less than a month. Avra would leave Ridgefield High in just over half a year. The anxious urges to stand still and to count down warred inside her.

Kieran pushed open the door. Of course he did. Avra looked up from her seat on the keyboard bench and smiled at him, gratitude surging unexpectedly from somewhere behind her lungs. She had forgotten to raise the drawbridge today, or maybe the pulls were just broken. As the door closed behind Kieran, Avra noted to herself that, more and more often, he was seeking her out. The power they tugged like a rope between them was shifting. Where she went, he would follow. Like in the lounge. Like at the party. When Avra permitted herself space for more detailed fantasies, he followed her out of Ridgefield: to college, to some strange city, to an apartment with vining plants and a king-size bed, to the dark corners of gay bars, where he kissed boys and she watched protectively, making cooing, encouraging sounds.

Kieran approached solemnly and sat beside her on the bench, closer than entirely necessary. Their thighs pressed together from knee to hip, and Avra shifted toward him subconsciously, planetary gravity between them, insistent yet gentle.

"Happy birthday," said Kieran simply, staring at the piano keys, not looking at Avra.

"Thank you." Avra noticed Kieran's unease, his body held still, shoulders bracketing his chin, but she did not inquire. They sat in silence for a few long moments, the drifting sounds of dancing feet coming in underneath the closed practice room door. Avra drummed her hands nervously on her knees, clacked her fingernails, pitter-pattered her fingertips. Kieran watched. Avra had shorter than usual fingers, butter-soft skin. There was peach fuzz across the backs of her hands. She was self-conscious about this, wished—as so many girls do—for an impossible hairlessness. The intrusion of each fine strand was offset by the stark blue of her veins, glaring and slender and feminine. Avra and Kieran stared at her hands, wringing and fiddling, and Avra wondered if they were each remembering the press of her thumbs on the back of his neck, his arms, his shoulders, pushing against his chest while he cornered her against a locker, years ago now. Avra, feeling the pins and needles of Kieran's contemplation, turned to look at him. Caught, Kieran glanced quickly back toward the keyboard.

There are times when you know something is coming and that it will not be rushed. Waiting is your only option. The moment stretched between their bodies, tugging Avra's earlobe, curling around Kieran's spine, and the heat of Kieran's thigh against Avra's thigh burned hot as a brand. She imagined his initials on her hip, for a brief, reckless second. She thought about some permanent marking, some acknowledgment of whatever the fuck this was.

"I wish I had known it would be like this," Kieran admitted.

Avra took the opening. "That what would be like this?"

"Doing a show. Doing something that wasn't . . . that wasn't basketball, or—I don't know. I just didn't think . . . like, something a little more creative, or expressive, or—"

"Gay?" Avra cut him off, noting the rambling of someone struggling to reach a point.

"Shut up." Kieran didn't stiffen or move away, and there was no fight in his tone, no anger. A reflex, absent ire.

"I don't mean it as a bad thing."

Kieran looked over at Avra, at her striped T-shirt, at the rainbow pin stuck just above her right breast—a few weeks ago, she had handed out these pins in the cafeteria to celebrate the one-year anniversary of Ridgefield High School's first Gay-Straight Alliance. Avra tried to demonstrate her earnestness, noticed the defensiveness crawling in. "Highest praise I could possibly give something, calling it gay. I would hope you'd know that about me by now."

"I didn't mean—"

"It doesn't have to be an insult, you know." Avra's hastening pace, quickening pride.

"I know."

"Just because your *friends* use it like a dagger."

"I *know*."

"Just because *you've* thrown it around like nothing." The heat in Avra's face and voice was rising, matching her speed. This wasn't the moment she wanted—not some discussion about how theater was unexpectedly fun, despite the freaks (of which she was most certainly one). She still felt off-kilter from the day's early kindness. She was caught in a cogitative loop: the conspicuous absence of her mother on her eighteenth birthday. And sometimes when Avra tried to let her guard down, her fists came up. Kieran, appearing unsure how to soothe her, how to circumvent her rising frustration, placed a careful hand on Avra's thigh, as if hoping earnestly that the touch would calm her.

Her tirade halted immediately. She looked at the hand on her leg—the spider-long fingers, raised knuckles, cut nails, thicker dusting of dark hair—and it did not look like the hands of the girls she had dated before, or kissed at two a.m. during sleepovers, or held gingerly. The shock of it was enough to soothe the tension, which crawled apologetically out from under her skin. She blew a slow breath and counted down from ten, although she didn't speak aloud. Kieran moved his thumb in slow circles, grazing the outside of her knee, and Avra pressed her thigh against his in recognition. His strategy had worked quite well.

"That feels nice," Avra said simply.

"All right." Kieran kept his hand there, his thumb brushing steadily, acknowledging the praise.

"I miss being touched." Avra was always bold, always honest. Kieran had hated that about her, once.

"I don't know what you mean."

"Well, I've been single since Isabella, and we aren't exactly the cuddliest family. Mom was the one who—" Avra cut herself off. *He doesn't need to know this.* Kieran followed the thread, his thumb continuing its quieting circles.

"What about your mom?"

Avra stared at Kieran for a moment, as if considering, and must have found the *thing* for which she was looking. She plunged forward, "She was the affectionate one in the house, I guess. When I was a kid, she'd play with my hair, or tuck me into bed. She was always the one who . . . Well, she was a hugger." Avra gave a small, rueful laugh. "But I'm eighteen now. Guess that means I'm an adult.

No more hugs for me." Her tone was oversteeped tea—full, bitter.

"My mom hugs, I guess. Not like yours, maybe, but like—I can think of the last time she hugged me. My dad? Not so much," Kieran said, and then blinked, apparently surprised at his own disclosure.

"When did she hug you last?" Avra asked, genuinely wondering, her tone gentle.

"When I got cast in the show, actually," Kieran replied with a wry half-grin, like this was ironic. Avra wondered how his dad felt about him doing theater, thought she could probably guess, but did not ask.

"I haven't seen my mom in like . . . eight years?" Avra said, hesitating though she knew the exact stretch of time, had perseverated on it all day: eight years and two months. Mom had moved away—disappeared with the spectacular efficiency that only she could—shortly before Avra turned ten. On her sadder days, Avra asked herself if a full decade together would have made any difference.

Avra felt Kieran shift, watched him raise the hand that had been set on her knee. He drew his arm around her slowly, cautiously, with all the deliberation of a shelter crew approaching a feral dog. He moved like an astral projection, and Avra matched his unreal quality—hovered somehow outside of her body, watching all of this happen from several feet away, sensations dreamlike and liquid.

It wasn't quite a hug, more a side-squeeze, the half hold of a hockey coach comforting the losing goalie. Avra leaned into him immediately, sinking gratefully into the touch.

A wave was coming. The shoreline in her belly pulled, and the tide rolled over itself, and the water whispered *patience* as it dragged along a million grains of submissive sand.

Avra laid her head on his shoulder, strands of her hair tickling Kieran's neck above his shirt collar. She wondered whether he could smell her perfume—something vanilla and vaguely spicy. Her little sister had handed the bejeweled bottle to Avra in a wrapped box that very morning, thus proving for the approximately six thousandth time that she had an elegance Avra might never achieve despite her additional twenty months of life. Avra wondered what Emerson would say now if she were a fly on the wall. Wondered if she'd be buzzing frantically around their heads, or scoffing a minuscule dipteran scoff, or covering her many wide buggy eyes with her many tiny insect-y legs.

The cadence of Kieran's breath returned Avra to the shock of their paired gentleness. It was so much sweeter than the last time they touched (Kieran's thumb against Avra's hip bone, fingers around her wrist, face inches away from hers, the memory clear as glass). Avra assumed Kieran's earlier position, dropping her hand to his knee, fingers brushing idly over denim. Kieran's legs fell open immediately, invitingly, and then she was tilting her head up to look at him, her expression resolute and a little needy, hazel eyes as big as moons. The air shifted between them, and Avra knew what would happen next, as certain as if watching a birth on a screen, inevitable as gravity.

He turned his handsome face toward her, dropped his head slightly, and Avra's intake of breath was audible. She was warm against his side, he was warm under her palm, and the sounds of their castmates were muffled, far away, nonthreatening. Avra's pulse was quick and urgent and she hovered over the precipice of some enormous chasm in her own insight, unraveling, weaving something new. *Take another step toward me. Follow where I go.* Kieran let his arm fall from Avra's shoulder, linger against her shoulder blade, the small of her back, and hooked his fingers around her waist. Avra squeezed his knee, encouraging. Her hands were trembling. Kieran's mouth looked impossibly pink.

Kieran brushed their noses once, then again, and the autumn leaves outside met the welcoming ground, landing with an equal, even softness. Avra's eyelashes fluttered closed. She could feel the bone of his kneecap under her pointer finger, the flush atop her own cheeks; imagined she could feel the matching friction of their freckles, dark, complimentarily patterned.

He kissed her. It was a simple brush of lips, almost chaste. At the end, they lingered, mouths millimeters apart, each unwilling to pull away. The thread between them continued to shudder in the air, the moment vulnerable to any sharp and slicing influence. Kieran kissed her again, his bottom lip held just above her own for full seconds longer. Avra could taste their breath, sugared by frosting. She pressed the kiss back, mouth opening slightly, and Kieran's exhale was on her tongue, and she wanted to lick into his mouth, and she was holding as still as she could.

When she spoke, Avra's lips brushed enticingly over Kieran's with each word. Her eyes were still closed. "Do you wish I was someone else?" Her voice was low and would have been expressionless if not for the wobble on "else." She imagined Kieran flipping through his catalog of alternatives: Will, muscular boys in jerseys, superheroes, firemen, priests, saints.

"No," he replied. Her pulse tripped over itself. Kieran's top lip caught Avra's as he returned the question. "Do you?" Avra shook her head, sliding their mouths together fervidly, and the barely there pressure, the erotic tug of waiting, stirred in her belly.

"No," she reiterated. Kieran made a small, approving sound, and Avra nipped more confidently at Kieran's bottom lip, flicked out her tongue briefly to drag along the corner of his mouth, and the memory of his gliding, spit-slick thumb, of a lime on the counter, of her drooling as he told her to hold her mouth open, crashed into them hard as a tsunami wave, core-deep *want* sharp enough to cut diamond. He brought the hand that wasn't around her waist up to tangle in her long, wavy hair, closed his fist slowly against the nape of her neck, and tugged lightly, pulling just enough to tilt her head back.

Once, at a girls' night, Avra had demonstrated proper hair-pulling technique, which she had learned from a BDSM-oriented fanfiction—grab a large fistful of hair, always pull from the base of the head and close to the scalp; start gently, just closing your hand to tug, and check in. Word of this tutorial made it through school in under a week. Students had practiced in the hallways and laughed and yelped. Avra wondered whether Kieran ever practiced on Will, but then he was tightening his grip, tilting her head back further, sliding his tongue wetly over her cupid's bow. When she opened her eyes, he was looking at her face, carefully gauging her responses, and this—the purposefulness, the hypothesis testing—was somehow even hotter than the rest. Avra actually *whimpered*, dragged her hand to the top of his thigh, hooked the other desperately around his elbow, and retaliated with a bite, her fingers a vise on his arm.

They kissed in earnest, then, mingled breath coming in small gasps while Kieran maneuvered Avra's head and she gave, sighing eagerly, responding instinctively, matching what she hoped he wanted, struggling a bit, playing, pressing back into him. Currents. Opposing forces. Lunar and solar synchrony. They closed their eyes, and then opened them, watching each other, and watching each other. Filing reactions away for later. They tasted like her birthday cake. Avra grabbed at Kieran's shirt, his biceps, the back of his neck, letting her fingers card through the short, soft hairs at the nape. When she licked into his mouth, he groaned softly.

"Jesus." His voice was disbelieving.

Avra, emboldened, ran her tongue hotly over his bottom lip and whined again, trying to pull him closer. The tone, the shock, went straight to her spine and made her shiver, deliciously. He dropped his hand from her hair, returned it to the inside of her knee. Avra shifted her legs open in turn, panting softly against Kieran's mouth, and Kieran dug his fingers cruelly into the flesh of her inner thigh. The grip was bruising—angry and swift—like he wanted to hurt her, to make a mark. Avra pulled his hair then, warningly, and Kieran growled against her mouth. When he sucked her bottom lip between his, rolling his wet tongue over the already well-bitten flesh, Avra practically purred her submission. Kieran swallowed her noises, hungrily triumphant.

He moved his fingertips carefully up her inner thigh, dragging his nails, leaving little trails of reddened skin beneath them, and Avra was wet, squirming on the bench, her clit pulsing in time with her breath.

"Slow," she murmured, shifting away from Kieran's lips to nip at his jaw before tugging him back. She liked being touched slowly, being forced to anticipate.

"Always so bossy," he retorted, a smirk in his voice—the *even like this* was implied—and Avra giggled frantically, the sound meeting Kieran's cheek in happy puffs. Her skin felt like glitter, stunning and reflective. Kieran's erection pressed unforgivingly against the zipper of his jeans. Avra could see the raised outline when she chanced a glance down. She squeezed her eyes closed tight again, as if she had done something without permission. One of Kieran's broad hands was sure but shaking on Avra's waist, the fingers of the other still tracing an excruciating path up Avra's inner thigh as she hooked one leg over Kieran's knee. She wasn't above begging, if it came to that.

As if on cue—*Why the fuck can't people just leave us alone?*—a knock sounded against the door. They both froze, eyes snapping open, mouths and hands stilling on one another.

"Avra, come back to the stage! We're running the parade." Avra's body was pulled taut, her clit throbbing furiously. She expected that Kieran's erection felt heavy and demanding between his legs. She wanted him a mess, like her. Wanted his knees to buckle should he try to stand.

"Unbe*lievable*," Avra huffed petulantly against the side of Kieran's face before licking it in playful annoyance, and he laughed openly, pulling away. Her thigh slid off his, landing back on the bench with a disappointed *thump*. Their hands returned to themselves, bodies returned to themselves, earth returned to its axis, universe returned to logic, one inch of space—then five—emerging on the bench between them. The air in the room seemed to cool by several degrees as reality came hurtling back. It was stupid, this interruption. Avra tried to label the voice outside the door. Darren? Ethan? She hated him, whoever it was.

After a handful of seconds, in which Avra and Kieran attempted to allay the arousal still crawling along their spines, Avra spoke, her voice a little breathless. "Talk to you in another few months, then?" She meant it as a partial joke, but her guard was climbing up, reinforcing itself as she straightened her clothes, tucked her slightly mussed hair behind her ears, took a few breaths and scanned the room, no longer looking at Kieran. As she oriented to time, place, and situation, Kieran watched. The humor faded into sobriety. Avra wished she could read his mind, beyond cataloging each subtle shift in expression: the tight corner of his lips, the pulse by his temple, a fractional movement of one eyebrow. She wanted to know what he was thinking, while he hesitated over her face, her eyes, her mouth: that she was pretty. That he had missed how pretty she was. That it was her birthday. That she kissed like drowning, like a death sentence.

She hoped he was still hard.

"Something like that, sure," Kieran replied. Avra turned swiftly around on the bench and rose to stand. She was wet, uncomfortably turned on, her underwear sliding slickly between her thighs, but now it was distracting in a less pleasant way, borderline shameful. Her cheeks flared softly. She'd have to sing through the embarrassment. Sing, and pretend she didn't just have her thigh across Kieran's knee, her legs open while she made wanton noises against his mouth and his fingers slid fiendishly, and up, and still further. He had been so close. Kieran remained on the bench, unmoving, persistent erection pressed visibly against his zipper, hands curled into fists on the tops of his thighs.

Moving toward the door, Avra paused momentarily and turned to face Kieran again. Noticing his posture, his look of confusion, the set of his teeth, she reached out a hand instinctively to comb through his hair, from the nape of his neck to the top of his skull. He pressed back into the comforting touch automatically, eyelids fluttering closed, and Avra unfurled something in her gut that she had been holding. She leaned down toward Kieran and kissed his cheek. She wanted to lick a hot stripe from his mouth to his ear, to bite down again, to claw at him, to mark him up, to crawl into his lap, straddle him and grind down against the denim stretched over his erection, spread her thighs, and see what noises she could wrest from his throat. She wanted several days and nights in a room alone with him, just to see how shattered and satisfied they'd be once they emerged, to experiment, to learn. She wanted to tell the director to fuck off, she was *busy*. In place of these superior options, she lingered momentarily, her lips petal-soft against his aching skin.

"Bye." She left.

CHAPTER 7

JUNE 2011

Their graduation robes were cobalt blue, and the marking tape on the stage was black, and the tassels on their caps were white with small metal Rs attached. Avra wore red lipstick, and Kieran's gray sneakers under his regalia clashed magnificently with the pomp and circumstance. Families packed into the local theater and sweated merrily next to one another in the rising auditorium heat. Avra tried to wipe at the perspiration around the base of her graduation cap as discreetly as possible, but all she managed to do was loosen one of her hair clips. She wondered idly—as names were read one after the other after the other and different regions of the audience clapped—*how* so many people looked coolly sweat-free.

A few things stood out to Avra as she crossed the stage: Karly whooping exuberantly as she received her diploma, her aunts' faces in the audience beside her father, the fear of twisting her ankle on a pair of high heels, the worry that she might have lipstick on her teeth. Avra was sure these were the pieces she'd remember most— the crunch of anxiety, the efforts to steady.

When it was Kieran's turn to walk, Avra watched him go with

a small admiration-adjacent tingle. Kieran's firm grasp of the principal's hand displayed all the confidence of a varsity athlete. He flashed a dazed smile to the gathered crowd, and even waved—suddenly boyish—to his mother. His friends jostled him as he returned to the bleachers. He seemed to have aged backwards—sixteen again, swinging imaginary dicks in English class, soaking up the last few moments of juvenility. But then, men are always allowed the latitude for at least some juvenility, so perhaps he was safe. Avra peeked back over her shoulder, looking at him, and observed Kieran's open face, a combination of relief and reservation, scanning the back of his classmates' heads, looking for her. There she was, waiting eyes, matching recognition: *Hello, yes, I see you.*

They had not spoken since sometime in December, when Avra went on a date with Sarah, an introverted junior girl in AP Art. Karly had presented a dramatized version of the date to an entire crew of rapt senior lounge listeners, adding several full minutes and a lot of tongue to Avra and Sarah's first kiss. Their classmates catcalled hideously while Avra huffed and thought about correcting the record but didn't. She sent a quick apology text to Sarah instead, for the inevitable gossip wave, and Matt tried with little success to close his gaping mouth, and Kieran promptly stopped acknowledging Avra's existence.

In February, around Valentine's Day, Avra ran into Kieran's younger sister ("Brigid!" she introduced herself with an enormous smile, thrusting her hand forward for a surprisingly formal handshake) in the school hallway. Brigid was a freshman, a year below Emerson, and seemed to take up the space that Kieran left vacant. In fact, she seemed to be doing so very much on purpose, with a nosily intervening energy that Avra found sweetly comforting. ("You were excellent in the play, I meant to tell you!" Brigid had professed a few weeks later, not-so-subtly inserting herself beside

Avra in line for the vending machine, before going on: "I'm not surprised, though. Kieran talked for like *two straight weeks* about how talented you are." She then paused for a second to stare at Avra's face and finished with a performatively apologetic shrug, a twitch of her nose: "I probably shouldn't have told you that."). Brigid navigated the halls with obvious confidence that nobody would *dare* refuse her friendship, and Avra wondered if her abundance of elder siblings had simply spoiled the intimidation factor of high school. She turned out to be a precocious little proxy, a Senior Spring blessing, Avra's imaginary go-between, her connection to whatever she had lost. Avra was careful to greet Brigid with familiar looks in the school hallway, as if they were sharing a joke—as if this were some ordained connection, an eventual friendship, a certain but delicate filament, thickening over weeks of happy nods, biding its time. Brigid returned them with confident confirmation. Like *absolutely*. Like *obviously*.

Avra still caught Kieran looking at her. She missed him and tried not to. Craved his attention like a rock in her shoe. Some nights, she was plagued by the kiss in that practice room back in October, and if Avra occasionally saw Kieran's face swim across her mind on those trembling evenings when Sarah felt under her shirt and bit down on her lip, she pushed the image resolutely away and told no one. Avra had attached a new flag pin to her backpack. Pink, purple, and blue—bisexual pride. Nobody ever asked. Avra never explained.

A sudden bubble of audience laughter jolted Avra back to the valedictory speech—a pop culture reference, some easy joke about teenagers—and Avra looked forward again, ice in her belly, pressure in her ribs, the distance between them hurting and hurting. Where he had been a king, Avra had been caged, high school forcing her to shrink. But then, kings aren't usually called names by their subjects, she supposed. A shitty crown, no real protection from the mob. And hadn't she fought back? And hadn't he gone quietly?

After the ceremony, once the recessional had spilled out into the front hallway and the lawn, Avra tried to find Kieran without looking as if she were looking. She browsed their blue-clad classmates until she found his neck, a lone lock escaping from beneath his graduation cap. She could see a light sheen of perspiration along his hairline, matching the sweat on hers, and was seized with the kind of desire that can only hit at closing time; the opportunity window narrowing, the two of them destined for different college campuses. As cobalt roved around her, Avra spent a succulent several seconds imagining Kieran grabbing her wrist, dragging her down a private hallway, crowding her against some corner, burying his face into the curve of her neck and licking brutishly, smearing his sweat into hers. Smelling her just below her jaw, roving his tongue below the collar of her robe. In short, celebrating.

Shaking out of her reverie, tearing her ravenous eyes from the precise meeting place of Kieran's robe and his bare skin, Avra grinned frantically as she caught Karly's impending approach. Closing the distance between them in three buoyant leaps, Karly tossed herself into Avra's arms, squealing dramatically. Several minutes later, Deirdre moseyed along to offer a subdued congratulations—a belated truce. Avra glowed from joy as much as sweat. She was getting out (a liberator leaving unfortunate prisoners behind), and Kieran would have to watch her leave. It was an honest, wonderful thing, and it wrapped a claw around her throat. She hoped—as she resumed her observation—that he would notice each long beat of her absence.

Kieran's mother fussed and cried over him. His father was flip and insulting. ("Wasn't sure you'd make it, boy-o," a single pat on the shoulder, a loud joke at Kieran's expense, a flush on his face that was likely more liquor than pride. This version of Kieran's father was universes apart from the man who had, in fact, attended the school play last semester. Avra had been shocked when Mr. Monahan sat in the front row, beamed through the group numbers, and was among the first parents to gift the cast a standing ovation.) Kieran's brother stood in a group of graduates' siblings, already finished with college, seemingly too cool for the spectacle. Kieran's sisters crowded him and flicked the tassel on his cap and gossiped eagerly about which family members had fallen asleep during the reading of the names, while Avra nodded at Karly and nosily eavesdropped. ("But there were only, like, seventy people in the whole class!" Kieran reprimanded. "Exactly!" Brigid hooted, endorsing his scolding, rolling her eyes accusingly toward their grandparents.)

Avra watched Kieran's mother hug him for the fourth time and tried to ignore her own mother's hideously obvious absence. *It doesn't matter, she'd have shown up trashed, she'd have been so embarrassing.* Her dad was wholesome and charming, clapping other parents on the back, only tearing up a little at the sight of his queer, sensitive, defense-darkened elder child all decked out in regalia. Emerson grinned with compassionate relief, calling Avra by the name of her soon-to-be college, pinning a few strands of sweaty hair back into Avra's bun, greeting Karly with surprised pleasure when Karly remembered her name. Her aunts were happy—"proud"—and Avra inflated beneath their graceful, measured praise.

Before leaving to seek cars and parties and Avra's graduation cake (German chocolate, baked with family care and sitting in the fridge at home), Avra excused herself to the restroom. She expanded the periphery of her attention, a determined lasso. Kieran—who must have been watching and waiting, though Avra wasn't certain of this, could only have wished it—pushed his siblings back, ribbed his mother for crying ("It's enough, Mom, come on"), and quickly made a paralleled escape. And then he was ducking around the corner, following Avra. Ducking around another, and somehow, miraculously, the hallway was empty save their resonant steps, and Avra was turning at the sound, expecting exactly what she saw, and he was walking, still walking, coming right up to the barrier of her space (two feet away, maybe), and she was looking up at him again. Tilting her chin to take in his height, grinning loopily at the non-coincidence. Today was too happy a day for grudges. Avra was getting out. Kieran had followed her. They were alone, like she'd wanted, like she'd dreamed and dreamed. She spoke first.

"Congratulations, Kieran," she said his name, and it echoed a little throughout the empty hallway: *Kieran, Kieran, Kieran . . . Congratulations, Kieran.*

"Thanks. You too." Something pained and precious passed between them, a wrinkle in Avra's eyebrow, a jump in Kieran's cheek. Her grin threatened to cleave her face.

"I used to hate you, you know." It was admirable, how she always just came right out and said it.

"I used to hate you, too," Kieran offered back, nonchalantly.

"I don't anymore."

"Good. Me neither." A mutual pause.

"You haven't spoken to me all year," Avra began. "Not since—"

"Sarah—" Kieran cut her off.

"October—" Avra finished her thought.

Kieran scoffed, eyes suddenly on the floor. "I've talked to you since October."

Avra backpedaled, smile faltering, eyebrows floating up. "Sarah?" She wondered if he was about to confess, to hold something out between them, and waited.

Kieran flushed, scuffed his sneaker against the linoleum tile, and shrugged, all without looking up.

"You went on a date." He said it to the tile and as if it were any sort of explanation.

"I went on a date," Avra confirmed, hoping the simple repetition might force him to expatiate.

"After the practice room, I thought—" he broke off, sighing. There was frustration in the hold of his shoulders, sheepishness in the downcast of his face. "I haven't been on any dates, is all."

Avra considered this. She would have noticed if someone had mentioned Kieran dating. She would have cared. She hadn't heard anything about his love life in the last half year, but then, she hadn't expected to.

"I thought you were in love with Will."

Kieran made a small, choked sound. "Will isn't—That's not— I'm not talking about—"

"You don't even talk to me in front of other people."

"I talk to you sometimes!" It was proffered with a bit of a whine, and Avra pursed her lips to repress the grin threatening to return. Kieran lifted an abashed face, as if belatedly realizing *I talk to you sometimes* was hardly a swoon-worthy plea. They stared at each other in a moment of shared imagining, which spun the possibilities of the last year into the preferable yet abandoned chapters of a Choose Your Own Adventure.

"Guess it doesn't matter now," Avra said with a cool, practiced calm that she didn't feel.

"Not here for the summer, then?" It was brave. One of the bravest things he had said to her, Avra thought. She had to give him credit. He caught her pleased expression, smiled sheepishly in invitation, and Avra felt the core of herself vibrate with possibility. She couldn't help it. This absurd relief was like post–rain puddle reflections, a flood of light breaking over a departing cloud, and what horrific clichés. Terrible. Despicable, how he did this to her.

"Here for a bit," Avra replied. She wanted to laugh at how brutally predictable this was. Him, catching up to her right before the runaway. His cowardice over the past six months, his woeful gutsiness in the last six minutes. They knew each other, like ghosts haunting the same house, vultures circling the same carcass. Avra, aware again of the cruelty of time, experienced a stab of familiar bitterness: too little, too late.

"You'll have different opportunities at college." The double entendre was obvious. "And basketball, right? You're playing."

"D-Two."

Avra was tempted to make an R-2 joke but figured this, like so much of her high school cleverness, would be lost on the audience.

"If you'd like some unsolicited advice, maybe experiment beyond athletic extracurriculars. Something a little gayer. And try not to miss me." It had the same needling cadence as "Try to make it to class on time" or "Try not to forget your shower shoes."

Kieran laughed, then, mouth showing both rows of teeth. A shark with no shiver and no blood in the water.

"I promise not to miss you." He might never see her again. He would miss her if that happened, Avra thought. He was lying. He wouldn't say so.

"Me neither. I promise not to miss you. Won't stay in touch. Definitely won't make fun of the first idiot in an English class." They were smiling in earnest now, faces matching a kind of sardonic appreciation for the other, for the gaps in their speaking, for the loud things kept lidded. This was *connection*, Avra thought, as Kieran moved toward her again, as he had so many times before, and she stood her ground, never fearing him less. Fuck, she *had* missed him. Six months away from someone who knew which buttons to press was a long time. Neither Sarah nor Isabella had ever towered over her like this, or read her silences with such simple acuity.

Kieran reached out a steady hand, curled the tassel of her graduation cap around his finger once, then twice. Avra watched his nimble fingers and thought sharply of their slow drag up her inner thigh. Smile dropping from Kieran's face, he lifted the tassel in a rainbow arc over her head and laid it flat over the opposite side of her cap.

"There. Graduated." Mortified, Avra realized that her eyes were burning, as if her body had finally caught up to the reality of parting. Quite suddenly, the moment of joyful camaraderie was gone, and Kieran's chest was right in front of her eyes, and the horrible polyester strands of his blue gown were blurring as she blinked back intrusive, shocking, awful tears.

Avra stood on her tiptoes, reached over Kieran's tousled head, and returned the gesture. He watched her face as he always did, and she could smell his cologne (something new she didn't recognize), and her lips were pink from that habitual biting, and he stared at her mouth with a resentful kind of wanting.

"Bum, ba da dum, bum bum. Bum, ba da bum bummmm." Avra sang several tremulous lines of the traditional processional as his tassel and its gold charm swung lazily on the opposite side of his cap, next to the sharp jut of his cheekbone. Regardless of the symbolism, Avra knew, with a fierce knifepoint of empathy, that Kieran would be stuck in this town no matter where he went.

She lowered her heels back to the floor, and Kieran's face was a foot away, wearing a blazing expression, his teeth clenching anxiously, his neck corded. Avra tried to return the intensity of his gaze—*I get it, I know, this is perfect, this is awful*—the shimmer of tears clinging to her lower lashes. Kieran placed a large hand on the side of her neck, one finger coasting a warm path beneath the line of her jaw. Avra—shivering slightly at the touch, leaning into it, taking a small and savoring breath—tilted her head back to look at him. Words spilled forward, reckless, impulsive, as usual.

"I promise not to tell."

"I know," he replied, soothed and soothing.

"And I promise not to make you say it if you don't want to."

"Thank you." He meant it.

"And I promise to never, ever call anyone 'faggot.'" Avra knew this one was an anvil.

Kieran's hand stilled above her throat, his expression shuttered, and Avra felt more than saw him tug the sleeve of his gown with his free hand. Little lost boy in mom's dress. She took another step forward, and this time it was Avra crowding into Kieran's space. She wrapped one comforting arm around his back, pressed her small hand flat against his spine, and pulled him in for their first full, actual hug.

It was surreal. It took a moment for his arms to come up to hold her, as if he was confused by the working organization of his limbs, and Avra wondered—with a prickle of anger at the injustice of gender—when Kieran had last been hugged, been held, by anyone but his mother or sisters, and whether he would be hugged at all in college, and she knew with a sad surety that the power he'd held in the gladiatorial arena of a small-town high school would inevitably wane. For her, it would accumulate for the rest of her life. In college, being queer was cool, and maybe straight kids were just . . . boring. In college, Avra would be free, and Kieran would be trapped for a long, long time.

"Do you promise not to call anyone 'dyke'?" she asked it into his chest, her cheek against the scratchy polyester, her graduation cap probably poking Kieran somewhere along his collarbone. Upon his gruff reply—"I'll never say that word again"—Avra pulled away to look once more into his handsome face and knew immediately that he was telling the truth. Unbidden, an embittered fury rose in

Avra that twisted her stomach. She swallowed the urge to shove him away, to kick him in the shins, to scratch at his face, not quite knowing where this came from, this residual rage. She took a soothing breath, which Kieran felt against his neck, and tried not to love him in her spiteful, afflicted, obsessive, petulant way—in the only way that he could match.

It was another one of those tightrope moments, and Avra's heart hurt, and her head was aching slightly, and Kieran was leaning forward, his lips parting, his hand tilting Avra's face up. Their graduation caps sparred, and Avra could feel one of her hair clips clinging to a single strand in a way that stung. Their noses were touching, sliding along, and his top lip was warm against hers, and she could almost taste his mouth.

The sound of the swinging bathroom door made Avra leap back, separating herself from Kieran with a protective instinct grounded somewhere near *He can't be seen with me*. She'd recognize the self-loathing in it eventually. The new arrival was one of the golden girls of Ridgefield High. She was pretty, blond, tall, thin, straight, with a voice like a needle. Years later, Avra would not remember her name. While the intruder looked confusedly at the scene, mild disgust twisting her perfect ski slope nose, Avra internally scolded herself for the moment of trust, of vulnerability, in this town where so much felt like a fox trap. She hoped wildly that the girl had noted the dampness of her lashes, which may have suggested some confrontation related to angst and antipathy, certainly not the heartbreak of an unpracticed goodbye.

Kieran and Avra broke eye contact and cleared their throats. Neither acknowledged the invader, nor the other. They simply turned their backs and parted. As Avra entered the restroom— as she stood before the mirror and dabbed a tissue to catch the smudging mascara—she thought of Kieran's hands following her throat and her waist for a desperate second. Like a child grasping at bubbles, steam, the light cast from a suncatcher: something it can never truly hold.

CHAPTER 8

AUGUST 2011

They did not see each other that summer after graduation, or the ensuing fall. Avra—convinced of her power—held herself back, a much-desired treat in a closed palm. Kieran stayed leashed to Ridgefield nobility like a hapless, abused little dog lacking either a tracking nose or object permanence. Avra tried in vain not to be furious, or disappointed. She tried very hard to feel nothing about Kieran at all. When he posted a picture in cap and gown, she rolled her eyes and made several dissatisfied noises before saving it to the photo album on her computer she had considered deleting but instead labeled "Probably Fucked Up." It already contained a picture of Kieran from a senior-year basketball game (stolen from the local newspaper), the one that Karly sent her, and a handful of favorites from various social media accounts. Avra knew this was unhealthy, bizarre behavior. She compartmentalized.

Devastatingly warm and boring months passed under the stale pall of unfulfilled promise. As the ache of her addiction slowly eased and her freckles darkened, Avra left for college with a shiny new driver's license, her father's broken-in Prius, and a rainbow flag for her dorm room. When she arrived and began to unpack, her new roommate, Ellie, unfurled its match. They laughed themselves into the appropriately euphoric tears of two rural queers attending liberal arts college in a city that hosted an annual pride parade. This must be gay excellence, or maybe bi femme predictability, or perhaps queer lib had become unnecessary: presumed and commercial and banal. After brief deliberation, they decided to display one on the wall over Ellie's desk and to hang the other out the window, facing the quad. It was all a bit much. The political whiplash did its best to drive Avra to fits of grateful hysterics. When she attended her first English class and saw that the only dark-haired boy with a collar-popped polo had a looped-italics "ally" sticker on his laptop, she smiled so desperately that her teeth may have cracked.

Several months into the semester, Avra met Naya—beautiful, sophisticated, Black, cooler than Avra, and really fucking gay—at an off-campus party. Naya was a junior English major, cutting a broad and handsome swath through the competitive honors program. She was planning a thesis on feminism and embodiment in 1970s anti-carceral literature. She wore pleated slacks with a "wife-pleaser" and drank whiskey, neat, and made quick and grinning jokes about caucasity. She quoted Malcolm X and Angela Davis. She spoke about Kathleen Collins's seminal short stories with worship in her throat. Avra stood in the corner and clutched a Solo Cup and nodded rapturously at Naya's smooth sermon and did not admit that she had never even heard of Kathleen Collins. Instead, she googled the name after getting back to her dorm at four a.m., her own mouth still tasting of Naya's Chapstick. The next morning, Avra drank sludgy gasoline coffee to combat her railroad-spike headache and read that one essay about the woman whose husband leaves, so she goes into the woods to grieve and heal and play her violin and her cabin burns down with the instrument still inside. All that luscious prose, all those themes of antipatriarchal liberation and punishment and loneliness and intimacy, left Avra vulnerable to seduction, eager to recognize Naya's authority on queer culture, and frantic in her effort to be just cool enough for a Black butch lesbian who wore slacks and lectured in dark party corners and drank whiskey, neat, and read Kathleen Collins.

The gold-star social justice warrior, ignorant-but-trying white girl practice of dutifully acing her classes and reading intersectional feminist theory on the weekends and hanging on to Naya's every brilliant anticapitalist pronouncement in the evenings strengthened Avra's resolve not to speak to Kieran. She recognized, wisely, that he was the embodied antithesis to everything she was learning in college. Closeted, self-loathing, cis, white, toxically masculine, privileged in a wealthy Connecticut way, an only possibly reformed bully, and the traitor of her past summer? He was simply *not a values-aligned choice*. Avra tried perfectionistically to justify her prior attraction to him—along with her persistent fixation on what he was up to and whether he was thinking about her and if he regretted his own cowardice—as "compulsory heterosexuality," a new term Naya taught her. She examined the phrase like a pinned butterfly. Avra contemplated whether she should still call herself bisexual, or just gay and "struggling with a social norm," and she resented that (glorious) kiss in the practice room, and she was falling in love with Naya, she really was, and she craved freedom from patriarchy with such a burning fervor that she refused to masturbate to any pornography featuring a penis.

The precarious balance of their—sometimes steamy, sometimes intellectually exhausting—student-teacher dynamic was sabotaged at Avra's seventh (eighth, maybe?) post-party mention of Kieran. She and Naya swayed tipsily back to Naya's apartment. It was frigid. February. There was snow on the ground. They had been *officially* dating now for about four months, and Naya had been surreptitiously keeping track of each and every Kieran mention since their first date. This time, she interrupted Avra impatiently, stopping the tracks they were carving messily through the quad.

"God, Avra, this is the type of shit I'll never understand about bi girls. Why do you all want to fuck the men who were mean to you?" Naya had paused beneath a frozen-over crabapple tree, which dripped twinkling icicles. Avra noted the appropriateness of the setting. Sour. Cold.

"I don't want to fuck him." Utter crap. The words felt thickly dishonest in her mouth. She had taken shots. She was a clumsy liar.

"Yes, you do. It's just so . . . pedestrian. Classic bi-girl shit. You *know* fucking them isn't actually getting back at them, right? It's . . ."—Naya's use of ellipses was always for dramatic effect—". . . role fulfillment, is what it is. Comfort. The relief of abandoning the fight." Avra thought internally about what it would mean to abandon such a Sisyphean task as feminism, and felt wretchedly traitorous. "And there's just no power in that for you. It means he gets what he's always wanted—to use you as some *hole*. Some confirmation that he's a *real man*. And if we're going to be honest right now . . ." Naya was getting louder. She was drunk, and certain, and emboldened by both. "He's already *been* fucking you. For *years*."

Avra imagined briefly letting down the boulder. Being *penetrated*—manhandled—by a rough and angry man with a *penis*. It sounded amazing. She would never, ever say that out loud.

She said instead, "Women, not girls."

Naya was caught off guard. "What?"

"Bi *women*. Nobody ever says 'lesbian girls'—why is that, d'you think?" Somewhere under the blur of too much booze, Avra was convinced that this was a good point.

"Because liking dick is juvenile." A pause. Naya meant it. And

Avra knew that she meant it, even if it was an ugly slip of the tongue, even if it wasn't exactly radical or inclusive. Sometimes Naya said things like that.

The windchill was getting to Avra. She began to shift within the cocoon of her coat and could feel her nose pinkening. The shells of each ear burned. It was maybe two o'clock in the morning. Naya reconsidered. "I didn't really mean that. I mean, dick is gross, anyway, but I didn't mean *that*. Playing these ridiculous *games* all the time is juvenile. Not knowing *what the fuck you want* is juvenile." She sighed, long-suffering. "I'm not saying you've got to choose a side or whatever, but I cannot hear the name Kieran again, Avra, I swear to God. I just can't."

"You're dodging," Avra retorted, dodging herself, and Naya was very smart, and Naya did not abide avoidance, and Naya called her out.

"So are you! What kind of strawman bullshit is 'bi girls' right now? When you've just brought him up, *again?* How many times have we talked about this?" They had, indeed, talked about this. "When are you going to get over the fact that this guy is *never going to actually fuck you?* Maybe he'll fuck *with* you. Might fuck you up, or fuck you around, or fuck with your feelings. He just doesn't give enough of a shit about you to *actually* fuck you. You know who fucks you?"

Avra was bouncing on the soles of her feet to stay warm, and she was looking at the ground to avoid Naya's oft-on-the-money inspection. She barely registered Naya's advance, her confident forward reach, the gleam in her wide brown eyes. Naya hooked her mittened hands around the back of Avra's neck, behind her jacket hood, and tugged her closer, toward the crabapples and the icicles and her whiskey breath.

"I fuck you." She kissed Avra once, twice, and Avra parted her lips acquiescently, endeavoring against her own jolt of defensive anger. Naya was good at this, had always been good at garnering Avra's allegiance.

"I fuck you," Naya said again, and Avra thought of the pink silicone dildo that they bought together to fit Naya's vegan leather harness, made from recycled bicycle tires.

"I fuck you until you're panting after four orgasms." Naya played with Avra's earlobe between two cold fingers. "I fuck you with a strap and without one. *I* fuck you and you like it." It was true. Avra liked it. She liked learning, and she was good at it, and Naya was so mature, so knowledgeable and experienced, and Naya had never, ever had a Kieran. Naya was still talking.

"And I love you. It might be *reckless* to love you, might be *stupid* to love you, but I'm doing it. My friends told me not to date a bi girl and I said fuck that, because I knew I could love you if you were ready to let me." It was all so self-indulgent, praise dripping with condescension. She was a tragic hero about it—the lesbian martyr taking a chance on the inadequate, confused little *bi girl.* Even in this liquored haze, Avra hated being referred to as a reckless choice. It was degrading, holier than thou; the monologue taxing, tedious. She was still being kissed, her mouth held open like a hooked fish's. Her lips cracked from the cold and she tasted blood. She wanted her own Chapstick, and to get back to her dorm, and to crawl into bed. She wanted a hot shower. She wanted, momentarily, to cry.

"Just don't say his name again." Naya kissed both of her cheeks, decorating her constructive scolding with two punctuation marks. "Tell it to your therapist, or your sister, or anyone else. Not to me. I don't want to hear it."

Two weeks later, Naya dumped her. She didn't bother with the comforting platitudes. No hint at all of "It's not *you*, it's *me*." Instead, she looked shrewdly into Avra's face and said, melodramatically, "It really sucks to be in love with someone who's in love with someone else." Avra didn't bother arguing. She sacrificed the toothbrush and sweatpants at Naya's place to the breakup gods.

Pictures of Naya disappeared from Avra's Facebook. The one of them laughing at that January costume party, and the one of Avra kissing Naya's warm cheek, the one of their clasped hands that day they picnicked in front of Jefferson Hall. It felt important in the context of a broad campus with so many attractive single people to broadcast her new relationship status.

Avra called her dad with the update, and he *aw, shucks'ed* sympathetically. David was always supportive of Avra's flings with this or that woman because, as he'd told her when she came proudly out at thirteen, "No pregnancy! No pregnancy!" He had followed up this outburst by singing a little impromptu "No pregnancy!" jingle and dancing a ridiculous single-father-of-a-gay-daughter jig around the kitchen, after which he'd given her a thumbs-up, and then a high-five. It was fairly excessive, Avra had thought, both overwhelmed and overjoyed. Noting Avra's expression of gratitude, her watery eyes, her father had given her a real hug, thanked her for telling him, fixed her with a shrewd, parentally aware expression, and asked, "Does this have anything to do with Willow?" Willow was Avra's seventh-grade crush. She spent the next hour dishing to her father, who helped her analyze whether Willow holding her hand on the bus was as, like, "girl friends" or "girlfriends." She gave him more regular updates after that.

A few days after the Naya breakup phone call with her father, Avra texted Emerson, who texted back "boooooo," though it was unclear whether she meant boo to Naya or to the breakup itself, and

Avra didn't want to seek clarification. She thought either option would mean a longer conversation, and she was feeling prickly, and self-conscious, and avoidant.

Despite staying away from a longer conversation with Emerson, Avra took to checking her phone for contact from Naya at fifteen-minute intervals, more out of habit than any desire for reconciliation. Naya never texted her. They ran into each other sometimes in the cafeteria, and Naya would give her this pitying look that made Avra itchy and short-tempered. Ellie, wholeheartedly embracing her post-breakup roomie responsibilities, shepherded Avra from the cafeteria with an extra serving of Lucky Charms squirreled away in a Ziploc bag and reminded her to hydrate and invited her to join her almost nightly tradition of *West Wing* marathons. They ate popcorn on Ellie's twin bed and pointed out the best of Aaron Sorkin's dialogue and made room for Ellie's new boyfriend, Nico, who was a reformed Republican.

"Doing my penance," he'd joke with Ellie's bare feet in his lap, as he gave her "another—he's just so generous!" foot massage. At first, Avra cynically suspected that Nico had a foot fetish. Naya's warnings that "guys are pretty fundamentally self-serving" echoed in Avra's head. But still, they were sweet. And really, Avra thought, four months into watching Nico pamper Ellie from dawn till dusk, she had no proof at all for the foot-fetish thing.

Ellie had been very careful to cheerlead Avra and Naya during the early relationship. Now that they had broken up, however, Ellie revealed a laundry list of concerns that she had previously neglected to share.

"She just seemed too old for you."

"Gee, thanks."

"I mean that she really seemed to think she knew *more* than you about stuff."

"Well, she usually did," Avra admitted. There was some truth to that.

"Sure, fair—"

"—ouch—"

"—but not about *everything!*" Ellie went on. "And the constant biphobic shit? Like, what was that about?"

"What do you mean?" Avra paused halfway through wrestling her fitted sheet around the corners of her extra-long twin. Ellie scoffed.

"Oh, c'mon, Avra—that night we went to the baseball house and she made that gross fucking joke about the D-Three guys railroading you? And called herself Gold Star all night, and you Silver Star because you kissed a guy *literally one time* in high school? And the time she told her friends that you owed a ritual sacrifice to Sappho?" Ah, right. That was maybe the fourth night Avra had mentioned Kieran. Naya had been very drunk and spent about an hour asking Avra to recite queer poetry—"as amends"—which Avra did, before doing another shot and bringing up Kieran's hopelessness with Shakespeare, which set Naya off again. Neither of them would let it go.

Avra, for her part, couldn't seem to eliminate that chronic desire to press, to navigate around set boundaries, to get under people's skin, to *test* them, to see what they could take before they simply had *enough*. She was learning, one departure after another, that nobody scrapped back the way that Kieran had.

Nico piped up: "Remember the day she came around when Ellie was out and asked why we were chilling alone?"

Ellie continued: "And the time she told you her ex-girlfriend thought you were a downgrade and that she should return to 'the lesbian folds'? Folds, plural? Like, other *pussy people?* For real, it was fucked up."

Avra, who hadn't realized Ellie and Nico even paid attention to those things, grinned appreciatively and resumed her bed-making.

"Quite a list. Anything else I missed?"

Ellie opened her mouth to respond at the same time Avra's phone pinged softly from the bedside table.

"Hold that thought," Avra instructed, releasing the sheet around the final corner with *phwip*. She raised one finger in a "hang on" motion as she leaned over. The screen showed a new text. It was from an unknown number.

hey

"No idea who this is," Avra said by way of an update, while Ellie and Nico turned their focus back to the little laptop screen.

"If it's Naya, tell her you're being satisfactorily fucked by me and Nico," Ellie replied with genuine glee.

"Satisfactory is hardly a standard," Nico rebuffed.

"Well-roundedly?" Ellie offered.

"Best of both worlds," countered Nico, nodding. Avra tossed a throw pillow at them. Ellie dodged. It hit Nico on the chin. He tucked it behind his head.

Sorry, don't have your number saved :/ who is this?

An ellipsis bubble—typing in progress, Nico quoting along to some snappy Bradley Whitford line—and then,

kieran

A few seconds later:

karly gave me ur #

Avra's stomach had erupted into a full migration of butterflies. Of course he abbreviated "your" to "ur." She smirked at her own lack of linguistic surprise, at the still-crashing waves of relief, at the immediate sense of familiarity, and watched another bubble appear.

how r u

"Okay, who is it?" Nico, an unabashed gossip, had paused the

DVD. Avra realized she hadn't spoken (or indeed moved) since checking her phone, and that she was chewing her bottom lip in gleeful, twisting anxiety.

". . . It's Kieran."

"Shut *up*. Are you *serious?*" Avra loved Ellie so much. The way she always knew what was important and when to get invested. She was reliably reactive the way a real friend knows to be reactive in those moments truly worthy of reaction.

"Fully serious," Avra said, leaning toward them and tilting her phone screen so they could read the chat.

"I'm missing something," Nico said, wheedling. "Who's Kieran?"

"The guy who ruined Avra's lesbianism," Ellie joked.

"High school dude?" Nico prompted, as it rang a bell.

"High school dude," Ellie confirmed, looking indecently Cheshire cat as she waggled her eyebrows.

"You two know entirely too much about me," Avra said to Ellie's still-dancing brows.

"What are you gonna say?" Nico, always asking the hard-hitting questions. The sweet, sweet boy had zero chill.

"Give a girl a minute, damn." Avra retorted. She returned her attention to her phone.

Oh, hi!

The exclamation point was too much.

Oh, hi :)

The smiley face was too much.

Oh, hi

She hit send, and immediately worried the message read as unenthusiastic, bordering on rude. She began another.

School is amazing, honestly. I love it here.

Another momentary debate. Then,

Glad Karly passed along my number. How are you?

Kieran was sitting in his own dorm room about seventy-two miles away. Avra had mapped the distance between their campuses, once upon a time, just in case. She imagined him smiling his matching relief into his screen. Maybe he'd be saying the same things to himself—that he should have known Avra would text with full grammar and punctuation. Or maybe Avra had this all wrong, was projecting, interpreting through the halcyon whirr of her own attachment chemicals. Maybe Kieran was simply bored, playing another little game, from afar this time, the "catch me if you can" version of flat-tiring her shoes, a long-distance torment. The rippling unease that had gripped Avra as she awaited a response relinquished its grasp when the phone pinged again.

good, he had fired back, no exposition.

Playing any sports?

basketball. great first season

Avra couldn't tell if he was kidding. She had always been the gym-phobic type; she had never gone to one of his games. She watched the ellipsis bubble as Kieran, about a ninety-minute drive away, she guessed, continued typing.

frosh live on the bench, he clarified.

Avra rolled her eyes at "frosh." So predictably bro-y. He had probably joined a frat.

Who was she kidding? She regularly checked his Facebook. She knew he had joined a frat.

Thought I told you to try some gayer extracurriculars.

Avra tried to sink into the ease of their repartee, tried to return to the core of them. She texted like she spoke, still ballsy enough to hammer his buttons, diving directly into their first conversation in almost nine months.

i didn't listen

What, not even a little?

Avra wondered if Kieran would name whatever had inspired him to reach out. He could semi-safely assume she was mad, or hurt, and playing it off. Almost a year without contact. A full June, July, and August sharing their hometown main streets without so much as a clandestine make-out by the lake, or a midnight "u up?" message, or showing up at her front door with chocolates and flowers and his stupidly beautiful face. Avra *had* been both mad and hurt. She had spent every day the prior summer strangling the fantasy of Kieran's confessional. She held her thumbs over the keyboard, waiting and waiting, and then:

sorry abt last year

"Shit," Avra said aloud, genuine surprise coloring her tone.

"What'd he saaaaay?" Ellie this time, but Nico paused the DVD again.

"He's . . . apologizing, I think. For blowing me off over the summer."

"Shit," Nico echoed, scratching the back of his neck thoughtfully and repositioning the pillow. "Bet he missed you."

"You don't know that," Avra retorted automatically, a recognizable insecurity sneaking back in. Kieran never talked to her in school. Kieran only kissed her once. Kieran had failed to follow up. Kieran had waited almost a year to even get her number. The rumination was gaining momentum.

"He *definitely* missed you," Ellie said confidently, as Avra's phone pinged again. "Poor guy."

i should have gotten ur # at graduation

Then,

was being stupid.

What a monumental change for you, Avra replied, momentarily bitter. But then, *:P*

when r u coming back to the 860

The reference to their shared area code whipped up an internal dust bunny of nostalgia, and Avra bit back a grin. She considered lying, considered saying something threatening and silly like *I shall never return* or *Not till I'm invited.* Unsure how Kieran would reply, Avra opted for truth.

Our spring break is at the end of March—taking that week off. Then I'm back like two weeks later for Passover. Will you be home?

Her palms were tingling slightly, body acknowledging a possessive little hum. Her axis was shifting back, back, tilting into habitual orbit.

ill be home

Twenty minutes later, Nico asked her to please silence her cell phone, as it was screwing up the percussive flow of Sorkin's dialogue. He said it in a goofy movie theater announcement voice, to soften his irritation, but Avra could sense his annoyance and quickly complied. Two hours after that, Ellie, in full pajama-set Mama Bear mode, reminded Avra of her nine a.m. class and urged her toward bedtime. "He'll still be textable tomorrow." She flipped off the lamp light. At around three-thirty a.m., phone sitting warmly in her palm, a *good night* message glowing blue on the screen, Avra fell asleep.

CHAPTER 9

FEBRUARY 2012

The five weeks until spring break were punctuated with the thrill of Kieran following her back on Facebook. Every week or so, he'd like a photo—"but, like, the ones from high school, so I know he has to scroll a bit to see them," Avra informed Ellie. The latter listened with a Renaissance-era appreciation for the drama of the court. Avra brainstormed strategies to counter Kieran's carefully measured attention. "Is it too weird to poke him?"

"Yes," Ellie replied, fishing one of Nico's shirts out of their— now basically shared—closet.

"Too forward to send him a Facebook message?"

"Why don't you just text him again?" Nico, earnest as ever.

"Because he's not texting me."

"That's a silly reason," said Ellie, who was tossing under-wear haphazardly into a duffel bag. "You could literally see him tomorrow."

"I texted him like two weeks ago!"

"Saying what?"

"Asking if he'd be going to this spring break party Karly is

throwing." Avra had not stopped thinking about this party, the possibility of her and Kieran huddled in that same kitchenette, since
Karly had invited her.

Ellie bristled at Karly's name—she had that college roommate
sensitivity about high school best friends.

"And what did he say?" Nico asked, while Ellie said, "Remind
me again before you leave that you love me more than her."

"I love all my children equally," Avra chided, hopping off her
bed to smack a kiss onto Ellie's cheek. "And he said yes."

"So why are we even talking about this?"

"Because he just liked a photo of mine from *2010* and I have no
chill way to give him an approximately equal amount of attention
without looking like I'm either copying him or am a forty-year-old
Facebook mom and I just don't . . . know . . . how . . . to do this." The
last string of words was accentuated by Avra jumping up and down
as she tried to reach her suitcase, stuck resolutely on the top shelf
of her own closet.

"I've got it," Nico offered, coming around the corner to reach
for Avra's luggage.

"My hero," Avra said, swooning cartoonishly.

Ellie rolled her eyes. "This boy needs no more praise—please
do not give him any."

Nico pouted. "On the contrary, please give me all the praise.
I thrive on praise."

"There's a 'good boy' joke in here somewhere," Avra responded,
grinning, as Nico handed her the suitcase.

"As part of my 'good boy' duties, then, let me give you some
advice." Nico walked over to Ellie as he spoke, wrapped his arms
around her waist from behind, and rested his scruffy chin on the
crook of her shoulder. Ellie leaned into his hold, tilting her head
automatically to accommodate him, and Avra felt a warm little

hum of affection for these two very kind, very charming people who
shared love like it was easy, like anyone could do it. "Chill is bullshit.
Don't pretend to care less than you do. It isn't like you. Poke him on
Facebook—it's funny. Comment on every single one of his posts.
Go see him at the party. The dude just liked one of your pictures
from 2010. If he's not being chill, why should you be?"

"Because the last time he liked one of my photos was . . ."—
Avra did the mental math—"nine days ago."

"See? *See?* Why do you know that? *Why* were you able to tell us
that without even looking at your account?"

"No chill," Ellie agreed, nodding sagely.

"I really think—and I am literally vomiting in my mouth as
I say this—you should *just be yourself.*" Nico meant it in the way
someone who had truly never been bullied could mean it.

Avra looked away then. Something about the "arrive authenti-
cally" advice gave her the strong urge to hide her face, find someplace
little and dark, and go to sleep there. She opted for a change of
subject.

"You know, I think I'm actually going to miss you two this
week."

"Back atcha, baby." While Ellie and Nico turned toward their
packing, Avra pulled open her laptop and navigated to Facebook.
When she entered a "K" in the search bar, Kieran's profile popped
up as first on the list. She clicked it, lingered for a second on the
tiny icon of his picture, said a quick mental *fuck it* to herself, and
hit "poke."

The text came in about thirty minutes later, as she wrestled
a pair of jeans that she probably wouldn't wear anyway into the
remaining four cubic inches of her suitcase.

It just said *lol.*

"At least it's not a filler 'haha,'" Ellie said, soothingly.

"I hate those." Avra hated those.

Another thing Avra hated was the self-conscious, body-bending shame that accumulated uncomfortably as each lethargic minute ticked by. The brutal, snappish response to her own desperation for something—*something*—from Kieran. She had taken to keeping her phone volume on, just in case. She had taken to checking his Facebook first thing in the morning, curved over her laptop screen like a gargoyle; viewing his Snapchat stories within a few minutes of his posting; googling his name when there was nothing new. She had taken to writing his name in the upper right-hand corner of her notes during class, just to see those letters all in a row. Her illusion of power had gone, and here she was, grasping at smoke. Here she was, furiously reminding herself that *he had reached out first*, he had started this all up again, while their contact became less frequent (less frequent than she'd like, anyway) and she scrolled through week-old Facebook notifications to tally up proof of his interest. One, two, three, four likes, two text messages, one she had left unanswered as punishment for six full days of silence. Avra didn't know why, but she was taking screenshots. It felt important, somehow, to collect this evidence. For weeks, she had been meticulously compiling everything they said to each other, even starting a Word document on her laptop for storage. The haunting trauma of high school peer cruelty reinforced Avra's belief that all this could be damning for him: If the Ridgefield elite knew how he liked to keep in touch with the freak, the queer, *something terrible* might happen.

Avra had that bad habit of anxious people—assuming others thought of her much more frequently than they did. Rumination spiral underway, Avra's petulance settled onto her like a shroud. Maybe she *would* see Kieran tomorrow, or the next day, and maybe he would laugh in her face, push her latte off a café table, smack her backpack out of her arms, sneer in that way only he could. She wrinkled her nose at the *lol* and put her phone down on the desk.

"Are you going to text him back?"

"No."

Ellie's pointed neutrality seemed effortful. "Why not?"

"Because 'lol' is not a conversation opener."

"Maybe it is for him," Nico said, as if guys were really *different*, as if Kieran were trying to *connect*, and Avra suddenly felt too impatient for this conversation.

"Then he's boring."

"Seems a bit extreme from someone who has stayed up chatting with him until like three a.m."

"Not for weeks, though."

"Sure, but you poked him on Facebook and he responded with a text. I mean, that's *something*."

"Why are you defending him?"

Ellie blinked. "Defending him from what?" Avra paused at this. Ellie and Nico hadn't shared their high school halls. They hadn't heard Kieran's jeers or taunts, hadn't seen him slam Avra's locker just beside her face, hadn't noticed him freeze with his fingers on her thigh, hadn't felt his dangerous vise grip on her wrist while tequila dripped down Avra's chin. They had missed the ways Kieran could be nasty and violent and ashamed of her. They had missed his stupid, absurd cowardice.

"Nothing. Never mind," Avra blew out a heavy breath. "Sorry, I think I'm just stressed." Ellie, who hated confrontation no matter how mild, shrugged and returned a cool silence. Nico, always the peacekeeper, walked by and ruffled Avra's hair.

That night, Avra slept with her phone on silent. She dreamt of Kieran on a stage. She dreamt of his cut-glass cheekbones underneath her fingernails, of his too-red mouth between her thighs. She dreamt of sucking him through a straw, of breaking his bones, and of him lashing back, wrapping his fingers around her pale throat, biting her until she was bloodied, hurting her. Even asleep, Avra's body thrummed responsively. It was savage. It was not a nightmare. She slept through the pretty promise of chaos. He was gristle in her teeth. A fading bruise. She woke with the urge to press on it. Hit it with a mallet. A hammer. Get it to stay.

<hr />

Three days later, Karly had her party. Avra tried on seven outfits before deciding on a pair of tight jeans with a high, clutching waist and a crop top that showed off the freckle above her belly button. She didn't wear a bra—"boob cages," Ellie called them. Besides, Avra had come to embrace the postmodern feminist ethos of reclaiming sexuality in a way that was *totally empowering* but also approachable and still conveniently marketable. In this ethos, nipples were, like, accessories. She stood in her childhood bedroom examining the shadowed outlines of her areolae through her top in the full-length mirror hanging on the back of the door. The sounds and smells of her father's cooking floated upstairs. A pan slapped on the stove. A thick, buttery sizzle promised a high-calorie hangover food—she'd eat the leftovers tomorrow morning, maybe even cold. It was all so asymmetrical: Avra, an adult, stylish, sexy, in a room where she'd once read Panic! at the Disco fanfiction, while her father cooked a meal just downstairs. Avra, ready to go party, to *drink*, while her little sister chatted on the phone from one bedroom away. The sound of heavy tires crunching along the driveway interrupted her reverie: Tati, here to pick her up.

On her way out the door, Avra reminded her dad assertively, "I am in college now. Curfews are a high school thing."

"I wouldn't want you driving anyway," he said, turning to her in an apron that read: HI, HUNGRY, I'M DAD!

"Smart man. Responsible," she said, and then, gesturing to the stove, "Smells awesome, by the way. Save me some?"

"If you're lucky!"

Then Avra was gone, the front door closing behind her with a definitive snap.

When she slid into the passenger seat of Tati's intimidatingly large and leathered SUV, Tati *ooh*ed and *aah*ed appropriately over Avra's outfit, while Avra tried to ignore the fact that this car probably cost a full year of university tuition. They exchanged a one-armed, over-the-console hug before Avra buckled her seat belt (smart, responsible) and clocked the twenty-four-pack of beer and two handles of vodka in the back seat. How Tati always managed to secure booze when Avra had never managed to pick up a single time in her life was a mystery. As the SUV backed authoritatively out of the driveway, Avra almost asked where the liquor had come from, but when she looked toward the driver's seat, she noticed the expression on the younger girl's face. Tati was smiling that manic high-school-girl-partying-with-college-kids smile, and Avra was suddenly a little embarrassed to be the one riding shotgun. Before Avra could speak, Tati held up the hand that wasn't on the wheel in a "wait, wait" gesture. "I want to hear absolutely everything about college." The word dripped with an escapist reverence. *College.*

"In short? Nothing like high school."

"I bet! Except Karly says some girl dumped you again." Tati made a convincingly sympathetic pouty face.

"She did."

"Ugh, that sucks."

"It really did."

"But you're home now and we'll take care of you. Wonder

which lucky girl you're gonna turn tonight." Tati was grinning, and Avra felt her "token queer" energy bubble. She practically puffed out her chest.

"Okay, I guess some parts are like high school."

"Karly also says that Kieran asked for your number." Tati's grin stretched by a few invitational centimeters.

Avra paused. The SUV's blue-tinted headlights were illuminating the familiar roads of her hometown, the nostalgic drive to Karly's den of debauchery. Maybe it was the can't-be-a-new-person-in-an-old-place logic, the routine of adolescence clicking back into focus, but Tati's remark felt dangerously suggestive, the way it might have when Avra was sixteen, guarding her bookbags and checking around corners.

"No comment." To avoid the inevitable follow-up, Avra posed a question of her own: "I heard you were going out with Garrett." She trusted Tati to elaborate.

"In honor of a classic: *as if.*" Tati snorted when she laughed, and Avra thought it made her seem more human, took some of the sparkle away. It was charming, pleasant. "We hooked up one time— ONE time—the last weekend he was home and he didn't even try to get me off. And then *he* told *me* that he actually wanted to see college girls. Can you imagine? Like I would *ever* want to fuck him again!" Her voice was pitched high, and she was proving her status, defending her status, her eyes saucer-wide. Avra felt that familiar pang she did so often when she interacted with Ridgefieldians. They had no idea they were in the trap. Avra herself felt the pull of it, the waist of her jeans digging into the soft skin of her middle, lip gloss sticky on her mouth, hair blown out even though she wore her Ashkenazi waves to college. It was a box she could recognize, all the walls painted the same pretty, fuckably femme colors. She had even done her nails. Pink.

They pulled into Karly's driveway while Tati detailed her winter holiday fling with the "literal, actual son of a farmer." He was six-foot-four and had outrageous forearms and went to the rural school a town over, which had an agriculture program and made Ridgefield look positively metropolitan. She was still describing him when they walked inside, and Karly careened up the stairs from the basement to tug them both into tight, bouncy hugs.

"Oh my god, you're here! You're actually here!"

"We're here!" All three girls were smiling, and Avra felt for a minute like a soldier on leave. Like maybe the battle was all of the other stuff. Besides, how do you even fight a box?

"The guys are downstairs! Grace, too, and my friend Sophia—you'll love her—and wow, it is just *so good* to see you." Karly tugged Avra's hand as she spoke, and Avra let herself be steered obediently toward the basement staircase. "Kieran's heading over in a bit."

Avra's stomach clenched momentarily, but Karly's dark pony-tail was swinging in front of her, and Tati was already chattering about the party games she was going to have them all play.

("Your choices are Never Have I Ever, Truth or Dare, or Seven Minutes."

"No one plays Seven Minutes anymore!"

"They do if they're me!")

The next hour and a half passed in a blur of Solo Cups and catch-ups. Matt stumbled downstairs with a crew of polo-clad bros at around nine thirty and flung a large arm around Karly, who pushed it off with a laugh. Context clues told Avra that they weren't officially dating anymore, but they weren't *not* dating, either. That liminal space seemed to be contagious. Garrett was following Tati from one corner of the room to the other, helping her pass out shots and talking loudly about how none of the girls at his college had been able to "hold his interest." Avra gagged internally. Tati rolled her eyes and barely concealed a self-satisfied smile. Will and Grace had stuck it out, somehow. Grace fiddled with the sleeve of Will's henley. He kept a comfortable we've-been-doing-this-for-a-year hand on her lower back while she and Sophia bonded over their shared interest in the *Twilight* series (both were Team Edward).

By ten thirty, the basement was full of friends, and friends of friends, and Karly was playing warm hostess. She encouraged people toward the bar cart, pulled herself off Matt's lap over and over to give hugs, showed already-tipsy guests to the cooler out back, and reminded Tati (swaying, selecting moody playlists) for the third time to please pace herself. Tati cheers'd in response, raising her cup, a bit of punch sloshing over the edge onto the carpet ("Whoops!"). For her part, Avra felt inexplicably . . . well, popular. Two junior girls—petite, pretty, one with a pierced nose—came over to tell her they had joined the Ridgefield GSA this year, "as allies."

It wasn't like her college parties. Nobody was preaching about justice and equality to nodding heads. Nobody drank whiskey, neat. Nobody even tried to mention assignments, or their thesis, or any local band. Instead, they gossiped jovially about Ridgefield hook-ups and breakups. They spoke in scandalized whispers about the social studies teacher who had recently married an ex-student. They played beer pong for the routine and an excuse to drink quickly. Avra got the sense that this homecoming was universally reassuring to the college kids, who had just spent their first semester and a half as freshmen and ached to be back on top of the social hierarchy.

Kieran came down the stairs shortly after eleven. The low thumping bass from the expensive corner speaker obscured his greeting to Karly, Matt, and Garrett. Someone yelled a hello from across the room and he raised his hand in a casual greeting, looking precisely like someone who had just stepped out of a Hollister catalog. Jeans, white undershirt, unbuttoned green flannel, hair waving across his forehead, broad palms clapping backs and high-ing fives. Avra inventoried the image as Kieran laughed at one of Matt's comments, scanned the room, caught Avra's eye, and did absolutely nothing.

He didn't even nod, just looked right past her toward Sophia and Grace.

A stinging confusion hit Avra in small building waves. Their reunion was meant to be epic. Time was supposed to stop. Kieran was supposed to cross the room—part the seas—to reach her. He was supposed to pull her into a room alone, sink to his knees, and apologize for his many years of cowardice. He was supposed to hold her face in his long-fingered hands and thank the universe that they were back in the same place, with boozy lubricant facilitating their willingness to say all the unsaid things. Instead, Kieran leaned toward Karly, who pointed him toward the French doors, the slop-ing lawn, the ice-cold beer. He went, probably to retrieve a can of something hoppy, and Karly made significant eye contact with Avra, who only then noticed her own mouth was open, indignant. *Fuck* that guy. Avra felt a pit in her stomach—nothing had really changed, except this time, at this party, she already knew how to take tequila shots.

Tati sidled up to Avra with a bottle of something clear and a bag of sour gummy worms. At Avra's wry grimace, Tati tilted the bottle toward her invitingly. "For the nerves," she said, tipping her head significantly in Kieran's direction—and what the fuck? How did people even know?

Karly arrived at their sides half a second later, saying with an impatient sigh, "I give him five minutes before he's come up with some excuse to talk to you." Avra shrugged, took several long pulls from the bottle, and felt her belly warm.

"Boys are so stupid," Tati said, taking the bottle back and holding out a gummy worm.

"*So* stupid," Karly agreed, as Avra bit down. The sour-sweet made her mouth water, and she thought briefly of a lime pressed against her bottom lip. "It's not like we don't all know he's obsessed with you." This was a surprise, but Karly said it with certainty, and Tati was nodding seriously, and it wasn't so much a question. Avra—tired of the denial, and tipsy, angry, and hurt, opted to confirm.

"That dude is the human embodiment of pulling pigtails." It felt nice to have her frustration validated. Tati was practically vibrating with empathetic fury, as if her own annoyance on Avra's behalf couldn't be held by her tiny body.

Karly tucked a lock of curls behind Avra's ear maternally, but her smile was wicked as she said, "There's always time to change your hairstyle. Make it a bit easier on the boy."

"Handlebars," Tati said, giggling. Avra had never heard of pigtails referred to in this way, but knew she'd remember the comparison. She grabbed the bottle back from Tati, took another swig, and shuddered.

"In lieu of that, I'm just going to drink the pain away."

"No," Tati countered, moving toward the couch and glancing back over her shoulder to make sure Avra and Karly followed, "you're going to *play* the pain away." Karly's hand was warm in Avra's and the room was shimmering a little after what was probably at least three shots of something eighty-proof. Avra could feel the promise of a hangover and didn't care. She shook off the subtle worry that perhaps she and her mother had this apathy in common.

It took Tati all of two minutes to gather a crowd for Truth or Dare. She could be convincing, that Energizer Bunny enthusiasm beguiling and infectious. Some people made the requisite sounds of reluctance—they were *college* students now; they were too *mature* for this nonsense—before settling gladly down in the circle. The collective eagerness was palpable, the performance of hesitation transparent, and Avra wasn't someone who normally endorsed token resistance as a phenomenon, but here were six women blushing nervously while the guys scoffed their boredom and Tati, bravely and accurately, insisted that they all just shut up and let themselves have some fun, Jeez.

Kieran joined the circle with an unbothered expression, though the flush high on his cheeks told Avra that he might be drunk already. Avra noted her own level of drunkenness—four out of ten, approaching a five—and perched on the right side of the couch. She reached for Tati's bottle of mystery booze, and Tati handed it over. Karly sat directly in front of Avra, her back against Avra's shins, and the affection was welcome. Karly's long ponytail spilled over Avra's knees, and Avra ran her fingers through it, gently combed out the few knots. Will settled to Avra's left, Grace beside him, and the couch cushions sank squishily. Avra could tell Will was stoned. His eyes were rimmed red and his hand was in Grace's lap. Grace may have been stoned too—her fingers painted soft little lines down Will's wrist, and Avra watched out of the corner of her eye as Will glanced across the circle at Kieran, who was seated on a large tan pillow Tati had set on the floor. As Will watched Kieran, Kieran picked at the threadbare center carpet, shifted his shoulders back as if removing a jacket, and pretended not to notice. They were joined by Matt, Garrett, Darren, Sophia, a timid junior named Alison, and one of the GSA girls.

Tati began the game with a swift smile at Grace, who picked truth, and soon admitted that she and Will once had sex in the White Memorial Woods. Matt picked dare and Grace instructed him to take his shirt off, pour a shot on his chest, and select a girl to lick it off. Karly was across the circle in an instant, her absence leaving Avra's shins cold. Matt asked the new girl (GSA Ally #1) which guy in the circle she'd most want to date. With an apologetic shrug to Grace, the girl pointed at Will ("Sorry! I don't remember your name"). Will took the compliment by giving her a thumbs-up before placing a comforting arm around Grace. When he was dared to give a lap dance to a person of his choosing, he gyrated his hips awkwardly in front of Grace's face while she hooted and hid behind her hands. She was still wiping tears of mirth off her cheek when Will sat triumphantly back down beside her. The whole circle was buzzing with drunken exuberance. Tati handed around another big bottle of something brown and a bit smoky. Avra didn't even read the label before taking a large drink. Kieran was rocking slightly to the bass line of whatever song had started. Karly was on Matt's lap once again. Darren was joking expressively with the other GSA girl and a guy Avra didn't recognize. Alison was watching Karly on Matt's lap with a near-invasive curiosity. The room was turning slowly, and Avra had to blink once to focus.

Will burped politely, took another drink, and turned purposefully toward Kieran. "Truth or dare?" Avra's blood hummed as she tried to watch Kieran's face without looking too invested, too interested.

"Truth." Kieran's practiced nonchalance was frayed a bit by his obvious inebriation.

"Been seeing anyone at school?"

Kieran hesitated for a long moment, finally looking back at Will, and Avra suddenly wanted nothing more than to shove Will off the couch. Fucked up, to put Kieran in this position. Her protective instincts sharpened their stakes.

". . . No." Kieran paused again before saying, "A few hook-ups, but no." Avra felt her fingers flex responsively, the thought of Kieran squirming under some strong, tall basketball player forming

hazily in her mind. She pictured him with someone a little controlling, a little aggressive, masculine, sarcastic, definitely closeted,
and the image made her lick her bottom lip, piqued her interest so
sharply that she didn't quite catch whatever ribbing comment Karly
made in response. When Kieran looked self-consciously toward the
French doors, however, Avra stepped in, hoping Kieran wouldn't
make some beer-oriented excuse to leave.

"What's next?" Avra prompted, raising her eyebrows encouragingly at Kieran. She didn't say "Please don't go—I never get to see
you." She didn't say "Dare me to drape myself across you like a flag,
claiming my goddamn territory." Maybe it showed in her expression, or her tone, because Kieran cracked a small, rueful smile (his
first smile at her in almost a year, and she felt it like an arrow, point
dulled only a bit by intoxication—she was now at a six) before turning to Darren. Kieran, emboldened by his own buzz, dared Darren
to hold a plank while describing a sexual fantasy. Darren's soliloquy
was so creative, so filthy, so unencumbered by the inhibitions of
sobriety, that the partiers whooped their praise.

Karly, jaw practically on the floor, purred across the circle,
"Baby, I *underestimated* you," while Matt went surly. He hated when
Karly paid attention to other guys. Not ideal, Avra thought, for
a man whose (unofficial) partner was the most outrageous flirt their
hometown had ever seen. Darren pushed himself back into a seated
position and preened under Karly's encouragement. He directed his
"Truth or dare?" toward her. She selected dare with an immediate,
wolfish smile.

"Give a hickey to the person in this circle you'd most want to
sleep with, besides Matt." Matt made a furious noise, Darren guffawed, and Karly laughed brightly, delighted. She lifted herself off
Matt's lap and pointedly ignored his protestations.

"Will, sweetheart, I'm going to need you to move." Her voice was a pastel coo. Avra, face burning, somehow knew what was coming, because this was just like Karly. What an opportunity for a show—something that would be talked about for weeks, maybe months. What a way to keep Matt in the circle, to keep them all locked in and reeling from the soft-core scene, made possible by low lighting, loud music, laughing peers, and abundant liquor. Karly cozied up next to Avra on the couch and said with a small huff, "I apologize in advance for the excuses you're going to have to give your dad tomorrow." Avra visibly cringed, mouth tightening into a reckless little grin, before Karly kneeled against her side, brushed her long hair over her shoulder, and licked a hot stripe across Avra's neck.

Karly made a show of it—nibbling Avra's throat, scraping her teeth gently below her ear, breathing warmly over the wet skin, before sucking hard. Avra's neck and shoulders erupted into goosebumps, her eyes fluttered closed, and she felt the alcohol pulse impetuously through her body. Karly made light, eager sounds with all the relish of a woman who had never gotten to fuck another woman, a woman whose curiosity was emboldened by the male gaze. It felt, honestly, *very* good. Languid and indulgent. Avra kept her eyes closed and tilted her head slowly to give Karly a little more space. She could feel the pace of her own breathing increase, feel Karly's manicured hand in her hair, thumb rubbing a comforting line behind her ear, and Avra couldn't help but smile at the utter ridiculousness, the sensuality, the spectacle. If this was a circus act, Karly was certainly the ringleader.

Garrett whistled low and loud across the circle. Tati just said "Oh my god" as the moments stretched luxuriously in a haze of warm, wet kisses. Avra could feel her capillaries bursting below the skin. The air was thick. She was certain that Karly's red lipstick was smeared across her neck at this point. Certain her nipples were hard and visible against her top. When she opened her eyes, Kieran was staring openly at her, eyes roving across her neck, her collarbone, her chest, her belly. Avra resisted the urge to suck in, instead noting Kieran's hungry expression with satisfaction. Kieran's chin was squared, face furious, eyes darkly possessive, and Avra herself was so turned on it was almost uncomfortable. She wanted to squeeze her thighs together and grind against the couch. She wanted to shift toward Karly's mouth just to see what Kieran would do. Wanted to preen and sigh. She hadn't thought of herself as an exhibitionist before. Had always preferred the privacy of a soft bed and a closed door, but even from across the circle, Avra could tell Kieran's pupils were blown huge, and she liked that part. Karly licked another slow line over Avra's neck while Kieran shifted, annoyed, and Avra let her eyelids flutter responsively. She breathed slow, into her belly, and felt a pulsing heat unfurling between her thighs. When Kieran's eyes finally locked on to hers, Avra's breath hitched obviously. Karly, seeming to suddenly notice that the game had shifted from "harmless homoerotic play" to "decidedly, actually gay," returned to her senses. After a final soft bite, she pulled away from Avra with an impish tug on one of her stray curls.

"May have gotten carried away there," Karly said at the enormous bruise forming on Avra's neck. Then, almost as an afterthought, "You taste good." Avra watched Kieran's eyes widen, barely perceptibly, and was suddenly quite grateful for the soothing effect of liquor. She wanted to laugh, to pitch herself into a rolling tumble down the sloping lawn. Instead, she straightened the scooped collar of her shirt and wiped slowly at the damp spot on her neck with her palm. Her hand came away sticky and pink with gloss.

"Thank you for your service," Avra said, joking, as Tati—looking scandalized and fascinated and left out—passed over another gummy worm. Avra couldn't look away from Kieran, who appeared to be trying to calm himself via long, slow breaths. His nostrils were flared. His forearms even looked corded. His eyes were boring into hers, excavating whatever residual crystals of queerness had gone momentarily un-mined. Avra grinned, ran her tongue over her teeth, and tilted her head. Her pride was elastic—warm, pulled toffee—as she considered the effects of this scene. *That'll teach you to ignore me*, she thought, waspishly, before biting the candy in half.

The game wasn't over. Karly had already settled comfortably back on Matt's lap. He was shifting, hands on her upper thighs, holding her down as if he meant to staple her there. Avra was sure he was turned on from watching them, wondered if Karly could feel him half hard against the back of her thigh, and maybe Kieran was thinking the same thing. Avra was still watching his face, Kieran returning her gaze fiercely. The aphrodisiac pulse of this moment— the one just after the last and before the next—left Avra wanton. Karly made a valiant attempt to wipe the lipstick off her chin using her forefinger and thumb, as if she'd done this a hundred times. She arranged herself into a dignified position, one leg tucked neatly over the other, and shot so dazzling a smile around their circle that Darren actually laughed out loud.

"Okay, Avra, sweetheart, truth or dare?"

Avra pulled her eyes from Kieran's face and blinked at Karly. She pursed her lips a little, considering, and felt the buzz of arousal and alcohol encouraging her toward audacity.

"Dare." Of course. There was no other choice, really.

"Kiss Kieran, then."

Avra waited for the inevitable reaction with all the patience she could hold, because the same shrewd voice that told her to make room for Karly on the couch—the one that could predict the future, could read the room—was telling her to please, please play it cool. The fascination with an old high school rivalry ricocheted through the circle as Grace said, absolutely scandalized, "For heaven's sake!" and Garrett said, "About fucking time," and Will said (annoyingly, Avra thought), "Neeeeever gonna happen."

Kieran was quiet in that way he got when presented with a choice. Considering, curious. Avra turned her focus back to his face—the drawn brow, the muscle jumping in his cheek, the red mouth, the eyes molten with heat from watching Avra's head tilt back, watching her eyelids flutter helplessly, watching her breath come quick and shallow while Karly kissed her neck. Avra waited another long moment, and Kieran made a gruff, impatient little noise. *There.* She wanted to shout her triumph. Instead, she bit her lip, performing a coy nervousness she didn't truly feel.

"Only if I have his consent."

"Classic Avra," Karly interrupted, "asking for consent in a game of Truth or Dare."

"It's responsible!" said the girl next to Darren. She was earnest and loud and very clearly drunk.

"So, so responsible," Tati said with a smile and a roll of her eyes.

"Of *course* he consents," Garrett said, as though no man had turned down a kiss during a game of Truth or Dare, or in any context at any time ever at all. Avra was enjoying making Kieran wait, enjoying the absolute certainty of his yearning the way she could feel her own—deep and bruise-dark and squirming under the skin.

"Well?" Avra prompted again, while Will glanced repeatedly over at Kieran in a pathetic, beseeching, passive, heinous way. Once more, Avra had to resist the strong urge to kick him. Kieran, however, was not looking at Will.

He cleared his throat—unclenched his fists from where they had been curled on his thighs—before saying, direct and deadpan, "You have my consent." A shiver of anticipation moved through the group. Avra recalled the way their classmates used to pause when they were in the hallway together, or in the cafeteria—onlookers poised and ready for the dogfight. At her accumulated hesitation (she tipsily debated whether to part the circle to get to Kieran or to beckon him to the couch), Kieran's annoyance broke through the space between them. His voice was just this side of reproachful, thickened with wanting, when he finally snapped, "Karly was literally *sucking on your neck* a second ago, for fuck's sake, just do it." The command in his voice was sharpened by his envy, and Avra wanted very suddenly to obey.

Taking her cue, Avra rose from the couch as if in a trance. *Do this right*, she internally admonished, trying to fit the role of coquette before dropping to her knees. Arching her back a little for the effect, Avra leaned forward onto her hands. The coarse weaving of the carpet would redden her palms. When she licked her bottom lip subconsciously, she thought she tasted lime and salt, thought she could see Kieran's expression go keen and hungry, thought she could see his throat dip in a swallow as she began to move.

She crawled across the circle toward Kieran, slowly and deliberately, and it was despicable—as crass as a stupid, early-2000s high school movie, as contrived as pornography. She was sure Kieran could see down her shirt. Was sure the people on the couch behind her were watching the curve of her ass in her jeans. The circle had gone all hush-quiet now, as if nobody could really believe what was happening, and Avra's mouth was watering. She could feel a dozen sets of eyes on her, and Kieran's gaze on her lips, and the space between them was closing but not quickly enough. Her body was two feet away from his. One foot away. She could see where the flush began on his cheeks, could see his eyes widen a fraction when she reached out to steady herself on his thigh, and suddenly he was reaching for her before she even had the chance to settle herself. He was reaching for her like she was taking too damn long for his liking, which was her body closer to his, and more quickly than this. Kieran cupped both hands around the back of her neck, cradled her skull with those perfect tapered fingers, dug his thumbs punishingly behind her ears—a *how dare you* and *get the fuck over here* all in one—before dragging Avra forward for a bruising, heady kiss.

It was messy. It was ecstatic. Kieran bit her lip possessively, ran a wide palm over the front of her throat while Avra whimpered a little louder than she had intended, licked his top lip and then his bottom lip twice before carding her hands through the hair at the back of his neck and pulling him crushingly forward. They moved with the rhythm of a snake coiling deliriously around its prey, each killing or being killed. Avra noticed with a burning knife of want that Kieran was pulling her toward him, more, more, until she was stretched obscenely across his lap and straddling his thighs. He ran one hand down her spine, palmed her ass to drag her forward, and Avra made a greedy noise of approval into his mouth before losing herself in the kiss again.

Her hands were everywhere—gripping his shoulders, scratching little pink lines across the back of his neck, thumbing his jaw so that he'd lift his chin, and Kieran was responding with equal fervor, grabbing Avra's hips and pulling her down so that she could feel his trapped erection while she straddled him. They were panting, making furious sounds against each other's mouths, and Kieran's hands were in her hair, on her waist, ghosting a warning over her throat. The next time their tongues slid wetly together, Avra pressed her hips down automatically, grinding to relieve the ache between her legs. Kieran murmured a dazed, broken "fuck" against her mouth, quiet enough that Avra could only taste it, before tangling his hand in her hair and closing his fist slowly in a sensual, encouraging tug. Avra felt the strands pull against her scalp pleasantly. She felt her blood as if it were boiling.

The seconds were liquid, each moment dripping and dripping onto the next. Avra wanted Kieran to demolish her, to swipe his thumbs lightly over her nipples through her shirt, to pull her absolutely useless, ruined underwear down over her thighs. She wanted him to spread her legs and bite red and violent bruises over her raised hip bones and demand that she fuck herself on his fingers. She wanted to ask politely for his mouth, and to whine prettily if he made her wait. She wanted Kieran to order her to describe, in full sensory detail, every filthy little thing she'd ever hoped they would do together. Avra wanted to watch his jaw slacken, watch his eyes roll back, while she impaled herself on his cock. She couldn't remember—as her thighs ached from being spread in a straddle, as Kieran pulled away from her mouth to lick over her hickey, as if to reclaim his territory, as if to replace any ounce of Karly's spit—ever wanting to ride anyone. The silence in the room around them was becoming a parody of itself. Avra could hear her own breathing and Kieran's breathing. She thought she could also hear his skin humming contentedly under her fingers, and nobody else was speaking, or moving a muscle, but the short pause in which Avra noticed the lull was enough to break whatever bewitchment had held their tongues.

"...I knew it. I fucking knew it." It was Garrett, sounding half impressed, half enraged.

"Knew what?" Kieran spoke almost against Avra's face, both of his hands back on her hips as she turned in his lap to look at Garrett. Her hands were still on Kieran's neck, fingers automatically smoothing themselves over the tiny hairs at the base of his scalp. They touched each other for grounding, on autopilot, as they awaited Garrett's commentary.

"This is so not the first time you two have done that."

From the couch behind her, Avra could sense Will rise. She knew without looking that he was heading toward the double doors, leaving Grace confused in his wake. *You could have had this,* Avra thought in Will's general direction. She wanted to judge Will for fucking up whatever shot he may have sabotaged with Kieran, but her gratitude wouldn't let her. Kieran's cock was hard under her body, his hands warm on her hips, his hair soft under her fingertips, and Will was a fucking idiot for losing out. Avra, however, was patient and determined and *entitled to this*, she thought, after years of torture, and, after all—to the victor goes the spoils.

Kieran's voice was a little slurred with lust and booze when he responded, impulsively, "We made out in the practice room once during that show."

"Wait, really?" Tati sounded disbelieving—a piece of gossip right under her nose? How had she missed it?

Avra felt a bubble of unexpected pride—thought fondly back to Kieran's fingers inching up her inner thigh while she mewled on the piano bench beside him—but then Kieran said, as if thinking better of his confession, "No." The bubble burst as quickly as it had inflated. Avra knew that she had been dismissed.

Kieran wasn't watching Avra anymore. His eyes were trained defiantly on Tati, the assertion that his sex life was *none of anyone's business* scrawled across his face, but Avra thought he might also be noticing Will's absence and realizing feelings had been hurt. He could be slow on the uptake, obtuse the way that guys are often obtuse. Kieran took a deep breath before lifting Avra off his lap with both hands. It seemed too easy, and Avra once again grieved their loss of contact, like something wrested by a thief. Each moment spent not on top of Kieran was a moment robbed.

Pausing to collect herself, Avra rose—not quite steadily—to stand. Her hands were shaking. She could taste Kieran's mouth, his spit, his sweat, and licked her lips as she cast around for something to say. The room felt so full all of a sudden. She opted for a team effort.

"Nothing ever happened in the practice room, Tati. I'd have told you."

Kieran looked relieved, Tati soothed, Karly concerned as Avra turned toward the bathroom, leaving the remaining members of the circle to gawp at her retreating back, at the strip of skin between her crop top and the waist of her jeans, still warm where Kieran had touched her.

CHAPTER 10

MARCH 2012

When Avra emerged from the bathroom after splashing her face and taking a few soothing breaths and cursing her own panties and sipping two handfuls of water and hating Will—Kieran was nowhere to be found.

"He's outside." It was Grace, waiting by the bathroom door. She looked out of place without her dutifully present boyfriend. Grace sighed thoughtfully as she scanned the room. Avra suspected the other girl's suspicion for a moment. "My turn, then," Grace said. She ducked into the bathroom behind Avra and shot her a rueful grin—could that be sympathy? empathy?—before closing the door.

Avra wasted no time. She marched—drink-emboldened and just this side of furious—toward the double doors, but was intercepted by Karly.

"Sooo, that was hot. Who knew you could get that far down with your bad self?"

"Either *thank you* or *ouch*?" Avra was drunk, but still quippy.

"No, I mean it." Karly smiled, but that familiar pity was back on her face. The I-can-see-you're-not-getting-what-you-wanted condolence. Avra always hated that look.

"Well, women are excellent tutors. Rare treat to kiss a guy who knows what the fuck he's doing." Avra was loath to give Kieran the compliment. She also wasn't wrong.

"Okay, yeah, that's another thing I didn't know! I thought you were an all-ladies kind of lady. When did you get bitten by the dick bug?"

"Gee, really grateful for that image." Avra cringed as her brain, blurred by booze and moral injury, conjured an impressive matching visual.

"For real, though. I knew you and Kieran had this . . . morbid, fucked-up mutual obsession back when, but I figured it was a stupid high school thing. When did you start fucking guys?"

"I've never fucked a guy."

"Oh. Well, do you want to?"

"I—" Avra paused, aware of the way the room was tilting, of the fact that Kieran had followed Will outside. "I'm not sure."

"I can't imagine never having fucked," Karly mused.

Avra bristled. "What do you call what I've done with allthose-women, then?" It came out as one word—allthosewomen—like proof of a whole life outside of this party, far away from Ridgefield.

"Right, you're right. Sorry. I just mean I can't imagine, like, not having a dick involved."

"I've got a harness in my dorm room and an adorable, chic, respectably girthy pink dildo that could change your mind." Avra didn't mean for it to come across as an invitation, but Karly's hickey was still on her neck, and Kieran was outside with Will, and superficial flirtation was a comfortable alternative to the envious, insistent nausea curdling in her gut.

"Matt doesn't like competition." Karly grinned earnestly this time, parrying the flirt with a kind surrender. Avra glanced across the room at Matt, who was watching her and Karly with his characteristic concern.

"No, he does not." Avra took a deep breath as the room suddenly lurched, and her stomach followed. "Mind if I head upstairs to crash?" And if she wound up having to puke, it would be nice to do so away from judgmental, non-Ashkenazi, BAC-tolerant Ridgefieldians.

"Sure thing, babe. The guest is open. Tati is staying in with me."

"Perfect." Avra turned toward the stairs just as Will came back in through the double doors. He made an unintentional show of it. His face was pinched, his shoulders drooping with disappointment. Will found Grace across the room and dropped his head to murmur something soft and serious in her ear. She kissed his cheek, smoothed his shirt collar concernedly, and Avra read her lips as she promised to grab her coat. Interesting. This was interesting. Avra's stomach lurched again, and the moment of interest was replaced with acid urgency.

A few moments later, Kieran—tossing his hair, falsely casual—rejoined the party, which was clearly trundling to a close. Darren was yawning in the corner. One of the blond girls was curled up on the left side of the couch, her foot resting against someone's discarded beer can. Kieran approached Karly and Avra. Avra swayed as the night's drinks hit her system all at once.

"'M heading out," Kieran said, pulling Karly into a one-armed side hug. *Men.*

"Now?" Karly looked between Avra and Kieran, but Avra's stomach was roiling bitterly, and she didn't care so much if Kieran left, because it was probably better than him sticking around to watch her be sick (an inevitability—she knew the sadistic promise of this feeling).

"Great party," Kieran said, by way of an answer. Then, to Avra,

"Good to see you."

"Same," Avra said, not trusting herself to speak any more than necessary. Her mouth preferred to be closed at the moment.

"Well done with the reconciliation make-out, you two. Tens across the board." Karly spoke in an exaggerated "proud auntie" tone. Kieran cracked a smile and ducked his head in what must have been embarrassment.

"Couldn't have done it without you, K." It was sweet, watching him be soft with someone else. Karly had that way about people—she could make them gracious even in their shame.

"Sure you're okay to drive?"

Kieran rolled his eyes, moved past Avra with a quick hand against her lower back (she pressed into the touch automatically, chased the contact even as her body insisted she go find cool bathtub tile and hold her forehead against it). "I'll be fine."

"Text when you're home."

And then he was gone, up the stairs without so much as a "Goodnight" to Avra, who watched him leave resignedly. A tiny, niggling sense of humiliation was starting to work its way through her, past the alcohol and the rageful tummy. A pouty voice saying, "You kissed him—well and thoroughly—in front of a whole room of his friends, and he still can't bring himself to treat you like a person."

"Figured for sure he'd be trying to crash here," Karly sighed, turning back to focus on Avra. Her eyes widened as they landed. "Shit, babe, you okay?" Avra thought she probably looked gray, the way party girls do before they excuse themselves to go lie down on a shower floor.

"Excuse me," she said. "I need to go lie down on a shower floor." Karly churred with some compassion before shooing her upstairs.

Avra spent the next forty-five minutes turning completely

inside out. She was curled miserably next to a we-have-a-house-keeper pristine ceramic toilet when the text came through.

coffee tomorrow?

Avra groaned quietly in a combination of relief and surprise and gratitude at Kieran's having left before seeing her in this state. She shot back a *Sure*, and then, *afternoon or later, please* before promptly throwing up again.

Avra woke the next morning in Karly's guest room with her hair still wrapped in a fluffy towel. She had commandeered it in the wee hours of the morning, sometime after dragging herself off the bath mat and into the shower. Groggily, she checked the time—11:17—and sent off a text promising to meet Kieran at a local coffee shop at two o'clock.

Karly and Tati were at the kitchen island sipping Bloody Marys when Avra came downstairs.

"Hair of the dog?" Karly asked, raising her glass, which was piled high with olives and some bacon and celery. Hot sauce sat mockingly on the table. Avra grimaced and shook her head, her hand flying comfortingly to her still-fragile stomach.

"Big no." Then, "My teeth are filmy."

"Hate that feeling." Tati was kicking her feet from the elevated stool, her hair curled and wet from a shower that hadn't cleared the dark mascara rings from her eyes.

"Free to drive me home in a bit?" Avra asked, comforted by the mutual humility of next-morning makeup smudge.

"Sure thing, babe," Tati replied, taking a dainty bite of her own booze-soaked bacon before asking, "You in a hurry?"

"Meeting Kieran for coffee later."

Karly snorted. "Course you are."

Tati chatted the whole way home, about the size of Avra's hickey and the way Will scurried out so abruptly and how Garrett

asked her to leave with him: "at least three times, it was *so sad*." She
beamed. "I'll see you again before you head back to school, yeah?"

"Yeah," Avra promised as she hopped out of the (expensive,
lifted, leather-clad) car. Her stomach turned over once and she
resolved not to hop for the rest of the day.

It took her an hour to brush her teeth, swish with a too-minty
mouthwash, shower for the second time in half a day, pick an outfit,
then another, then a third, settle on the first, and worry over her
shoe selection. She ran a brush through her damp hair, attempted
to style it, gave up, tamed it into two braids, and clumsily applied
hangover-hiding makeup. It took three thick layers of concealer to
barely obscure the hickey, which sat proud as a beacon on her neck.
Begrudgingly, Avra wiped the concealer off with a towelette and
opted for a preppy little scarf not at all her style. She bounded into
the kitchen with twenty minutes to spare.

"Cool if I borrow your car? I'm late on an oil change."

Her dad was washing dishes. The soap was halfway up his thick
arms and spilling over the countertops. The man knew how to make
a mess, which partially explained Avra's preference toward the tidy.

"You didn't touch the leftovers." He sudsed as he spoke.

"An enthusiastic 'no thank you' to food at the moment."

"Hope you were safe last night."

"I'm here, aren't I?"

Dad grinned wryly at the cheek and gestured with a dripping
sponge toward the fridge. "Don't worry about the food—I finished
it for you."

"Many thanks. Car? Looking for a yes or a no or some
bargaining."

"Drop your sister at Hannah's when you go?"

"Can do, will do!"

"Just for that, I'll handle the oil change." He was munificent that way, consistent the way her mother never had been. Avra had expected the offer.

"A gentleman and a scholar." She turned the banter down for just a moment to deliver an earnest "Thanks, Dad." He had the dual-parent role down to a fluffy, exuberant art.

Emerson was down the stairs a moment later, a handsomely bruised Italian leather bag slung across her shoulder. She had impeccable taste. "Nice scarf," she said, with sisterly acuity. The "What are you hiding?" was implied. Avra sucked her teeth and made for the front door. Emerson and Dad exchanged shrewd matching smiles as Avra, neck burning, walked out.

It helped to have Emerson for company. She asked reasonable questions about the prior night's festivities and college coursework, fiddled with the radio dial so neither was subjected to the local country station, respectfully avoided the scarf subject, and filled Avra in on her many extracurriculars. The minutes before two o'clock moved with a satisfying quickness. As Emerson slid out of the car, Avra couldn't help noting the distinction between Tati's SUV and the second Prius in their family. Eco-friendly. Practical. Appropriately progressive. Cheap.

When Avra pulled into the parking lot of the little town coffee shop, Kieran was standing outside. He flipped through his phone as Avra parked. She checked her face discreetly in the mirror before approaching.

Kieran's hair was picturesquely rumpled. His shirt smelled vaguely of an herbaceous men's deodorant, and he had a scruffy chin shadow that suggested a morning inability to shave. Avra's stomach responded with something very different than disgust.

"Hi." His voice was morning-rumbly, despite the time of day.

"Hey."

"We've got options."

"Say more?"

"Coffee," Kieran said, gesturing behind him, "or cocktails." He pointed across the upscale little plaza toward what seemed to be a bookshop.

"That's new," Avra commented, grateful for an easy topic of conversation. "And looks like books?"

"Bookstore bar. This town is getting cooler without us."

"The effect is mutual," Avra returned, before doing a quick mental assessment of her hangover—mild, fading, and perhaps booze would be a helpful lubricant, books a useful buffer. "Can we even order drinks?"

"Not if anyone inside knows us, but Darren told me he came here over the winter break and they didn't card. Do you have a fake?"

Avra tucked her hand into her jacket and pulled out a wallet. Inside was a false ID that Naya had procured for her. She passed it to Kieran.

"Nice to meet you . . ."—he checked the name—"Bailey?" He fished in his pocket and handed a slim card to Avra, who flipped it over.

"Oh, this is adorable." It was his brother's.

"Gave it to me when I started college." Kieran shrugged like this was a fraternal rite of passage.

"Quaint little family tradition." They paused for a moment, holding each other's manufactured identities, before Avra broke the silence. "Try something new?"

The metaphor was lost on neither.

They crossed the street, Avra taking three steps for each of Kieran's two long strides. She silently cursed his elegance.

The bookshop was empty save two forty-somethings sitting in the back booth, each engrossed in their novel of choice. The bar counter was set on the wall opposite a row of heavily curtained windows. A tall, packed bookshelf intervened somberly between the smooth, oiled bartop and the luster of natural light. Thick wood slabs bowed perceptibly under the weight of cocktail mixing manuals, international cookbooks, and illustrated spice instructionals. Despite outside's midafternoon sun, the dim golden glow of the bar created a cozy evening illusion. Pastries were piled enticingly behind cut glass. The countertops were scrawled with Sharpie; a set of fresh markers sat stacked in the corner, next to a printed paper invitation to sign your name. Avra was delighted at this charming addition to her hometown.

"Cute," she commented, hanging her jacket on a waist-level hook before sliding onto a barstool.

"Thanks," said Kieran.

Avra rolled her eyes over a reluctant smile. "Not you."

"Respectfully, I disagree."

The ease alone was unsettling. Avra had mentally prepared for raised hackles, moodiness, barbs, and discomfort. She had expected a careful navigation of half a decade of angst. These clever attempts to charm each other, the effort to be gentle, felt more awkward than the alternative. Cruelty and salt they knew. This? They had never learned how.

Avra reached across the counter for a drink menu, stretching her hand over the moment of silence. Kieran slid onto the stool beside her, his knee six inches away, and Avra cataloged the closeness for future exploration. Even with elbows on the bar, he was a full head taller than she was. His body next to hers felt like foreshadowing. She scanned the menu and tried to focus on the drink options as the scent of Kieran's deodorant drifted over her right shoulder. Something with rye. Something with gin and lavender. Something with vodka and mint. Something with tequila and elderflower.

"Are we really going to do this midafternoon on a Sunday?"

Avra asked, as she surveyed the menu.

"Hair of the dog, right?"

"You know, Karly said the same thing this morning."

"And we know her judgment is *excellent,*" Kieran countered.

The bartender moseyed over to take their orders. She didn't prompt for ID. Avra fought the temptation to let out a sigh of relief while Kieran ordered an old fashioned.

"I have this hypothesis," Avra said, before selecting the St-Germain mezcocktail and turning back to Kieran, "that men always order an old fashioned to look macho and sophisticated and not because they actually like the taste."

"We'll see, I guess." Kieran was softly pink around the ears, and Avra hated how it warmed her. The bartender smiled before walking away. Kieran lowered his voice. "I don't like clear liquor." He paused. "And I wasn't sure what to get." Vulnerability. It was nice.

The scarf was starting to feel tight and uncomfortable. Avra reached up instinctively to remove it and remembered the hickey. She stilled her hands, returned them reluctantly to her lap, and turned to face Kieran on her stool. Their knees brushed and a thrill sparked promisingly along the base of her spine.

"You must be a mess from last night."

"What?" Avra thought about her legs splayed across Kieran's lap, about Kieran's hands holding her firmly in place as the room swam. She thought about the taste of his tongue, the eager sounds he made into her mouth. She pulled herself back to the bar with some difficulty as Kieran answered.

"The hickey. Karly practically destroyed you."

Ah, that. "She . . . left an impression."

"Let me see?" It wasn't a question. Kieran was already reaching across to untie Avra's scarf. His eyes were focused, his hands sure. As he worked the small bow free, his knuckles brushed Avra's throat beneath her chin. She held her breath, both surprised at Kieran's forwardness and unsurprised. He broke the touch barrier faster and faster each time they saw one another, and Avra straightened her spine as the scarf was pulled tenderly away.

"Jesus." Kieran stared at her neck, knuckles tightening around the scarf in his hand. He looked as if he had tasted something he wasn't certain he liked. "You bruise easily."

"I do."

"It's really fucking dark."

"It is."

"This isn't you." He waved the scarf a little before placing it on the bar.

"Too preppy?" Avra asked, aware that Kieran's eyes had not left her neck.

"Too Ridgefield."

She grinned at the rejoinder. "Thank you. Or, I suppose I should ask—is that a compliment?"

"Well, it isn't an insult." Kieran was running one finger over the soft fabric of the scarf when the bartender returned, their drinks in hand. Her ink-lined eyes darted to the scarf on the bar top, Kieran's transfixed expression, and Avra's bruised-plum neck. The drinks quivered a bit in her hand as she placed them down, cleared her throat once, and turned away. Avra watched her eyes widen, scandalized, as she departed.

"Bet she thinks I did that to you," Kieran noted, turning toward his drink. His voice was gruff, self-conscious. As he moved to reach for his glass, his knee brushed Avra's again below the bar. She felt a flutter of both flattery and pleasure at the comment, at the contact. It was dizzying, that someone might assume the two of them a pair. She had never considered herself conventionally attractive enough to be presumed Kieran's match, although she had grown out of her self-deprecating awkwardness several years ago. Somewhere behind her urge to plume she felt a tiny sting that the bartender might label her straight, might not know this hickey came from a woman, might not understand that Kieran was the *exception* rather than the rule. The complicated internal war— between compulsory heterosexuality and the insidious judgment of queer betrayal—must have shown on her face. Almost comfortingly, Kieran pressed his knee against Avra's more firmly. The scratch of denim coasted along her bare skin below the hem of her short, femme skirt. Avra squirmed a bit on the barstool. She was already wet.

"Genuinely never would have believed this a few years ago."

"What, us having a drink?" He was still focused on his glass and taking small, thoughtful sips as the ice clinked jovially.

"You, being seen with me." She hesitated before plunging on: "Especially after last night. It's just kind of surreal." Kieran didn't answer. He stared into his glass with a frozen, guilty expression. "Not bad, though." Avra tried again. Kieran looked as if the liquor was chastising him, and Avra wanted very much to ask about the prior evening, about his conversation with Will, about why he had left so suddenly. Never one to hold her tongue, she pressed forward. "Want to tell me what happened last night?"

"What do you mean?"

"You pretty much ran out after talking to Will."

Kieran shifted in his seat, his right hand rubbing a soft line over the scarf on the bar top, his left hand clutched around the rocks glass. "Will always gets weird when I talk about my . . . friends from school." His voice caught on the word "friends," and Avra knew to follow up.

"Like he's jealous?"

"Something like that."

"My roommate, Ellie, hates when I bring up Karly. She feels threatened, I think, like I'm automatically going to love my high school friends more than someone I met through a dorm arrangement." Kieran shrugged. His knee had retreated from Avra's. She continued: "But then, Karly was sucking on my neck last night, and there are some lines Ellie and I just won't cross." Avra knew, somehow, to tie the threads. She did so clumsily, impulsively, brazenly, and on purpose. "Maybe Will just wants to hear that you aren't sucking on these guys."

Kieran choked on a sip of his drink with spectacular comedic timing. "You really can't help it, can you?"

Avra ignored him. "So, who is he?"

"There's not an anybody." His tone was tight, defensive.

"Oh, please."

"Can we drop it?"

"Sure, right." Avra's words landed heavily over Kieran's boundary, disregarding it, ignoring it. "You and Will were just having some casual private outdoor chat about a *totally platonic* dude-bro-friend-guy from one of your myriad straight-boy sports teams, which is why Will left in such a huff and you practically fled the scene."

Kieran had had enough. He snapped, turning toward Avra with a look of simmering frustration. "You always think you fucking know everything." He downed his drink in two gulps and placed it back onto the bar rather harder than intended. It skittered a few inches. The bartender's head snapped up, and she scowled across the room in alarm. "Did you think even for a second that Will might have been bothered by something else last night?"

"Like what?"

"Like *you!*" Kieran's voice had lowered to a hiss.

"What about me?"

"Like you on top of me, us kissing right in front—"

"But I'm not any kind of threat to *him*," Avra spluttered at the suggestion.

"Why not?"

"Because he's *Will*. He's your . . ."—she cast around for the language— "He means something to you. And I'm just . . ." She trailed off, realizing what she had meant to say.

"Just a girl?" It hung in the air, scintillant and precious. Avra reached for her drink and took two long gulps. It burned her throat on the way down, smoke and citrus.

"I'm not your type," she finished, anticlimactically. Kieran laughed, charmless and frantic, his own confusion tumbling across every "ha."

"Then what the fuck are we doing here?"

"You know," Avra said, dodging the question expertly, "you get unpredictable when you drink." Kieran rolled his eyes, took another swig—impertinent. "Unpredictability isn't sexy."

"No?" He turned toward her on the barstool, placed one hand menacingly on her thigh, and Avra took a sip of breath. Unpredictability, as they both knew, could be sexy. Kieran's hair was flopping into his eyes, his fingertips chilled and a little damp from condensation. He looked fit to shake her. They weren't quite causing a scene, but it wouldn't be long. Avra placed her hand over his, her palm warming his fingers, and gestured across to the bartender for another drink. She smiled winningly to make up for Kieran's gust and bother, and the bartender appeared placated. Avra considered, for a moment, what it meant that she wanted Kieran a bit tipsy, spun out, off-balance. She wanted power. She knew, core-deep, that she could get it. She pushed the unsettling thought away.

"I should have known we'd just end up arguing." She selected a new button to press. "It's not as if we're friends." His grip tightened on her thigh, and she flashed back to his earlier comment on the ease of her bruising.

"No, we're not *friends*." He spat the word, and it stung, but Kieran's hand was thawing on her thigh; his fingers intimidating, printing into Avra's flesh.

"If we *were* friends, you'd tell me what you said that bothered Will so much." Avra took a dainty, condescending sip of her own drink. "You'd already have told me about college guy."

"Why should I tell you anything? What about you? Fucking any ballerinas? Scissored anyone good lately?"

Avra laughed witchily at the reference to Isabella, at the crude misunderstanding of lesbian sex, and—mostly—at the utter madness of having this conversation within the zip code boundaries of Ridgefield, Connecticut. The bartender approached and left a second sweating, clinking drink in front of Kieran. He looked up, surprised. Avra was grateful for the bar top, for the concealment of Kieran's fingers on her skin (just beneath the hem of her skirt, suggestive, immodest). She nodded her thanks, wondered briefly if Kieran had even liked the first old fashioned, and waited until the woman retreated far enough out of earshot before replying, her voice calm and easy.

"You know queer women don't actually fuck like that, right?" She meant it as a chastisement. Kieran took a drink as he considered this, his expression shifting vaguely from surprise toward interest. It was a safer topic for him. A new topic. A learning opportunity.

"How do women fuck, then?"

"What?" Avra paused. She knew a dare from Kieran when she heard one. Knew a distraction, too, but didn't care. Kieran was downing the second drink, flexing his palm against the soft hull of her, and Avra's body thrummed reactively. He dug his fingernails into the flesh above her knee at her hesitation, and she pinched the skin between his thumb and forefinger in retaliation.

"How do women fuck?"

"Do you actually want to know?"

"I'm asking, aren't I?" Two dark pink spots arose on his cheeks as he leaned back, removing his palm from her legs. Kieran was looking resolutely at Avra. He sat still and focused, as if entirely prepared to memorize her response. Avra finished what was left in her glass—the cool syrup clung to the corners of her mouth, and she licked thoughtfully as she planned her reply. Kieran's eyes dropped to watch. He shifted in his seat. *Good.*

"Well, it's not all about penetration, for one."

"Obviously."

"Is that obvious to you?" The surprise might have been insulting.

"Well, yeah. It's not all about penetration for men, either."

Avra rolled her eyes. She couldn't help it. "I mean, there's just so much *more* to sex with women. Or, I guess I mean, there's more nuance. It's about . . . about honoring the clitoris"—she said the word with stars in her eyes—"and knowing how to eat someone out. Being willing to stay between her legs for thirty, forty minutes. An hour." She considered, revised her estimation for maximized pleasure, and corrected. "Over an hour." She went to take another sip of her drink, remembered it was empty, and sighed before continuing. "It's about consistency, and finding which pattern she likes, keeping your tongue flat and wet and not switching it up so goddamn much. My friends are always complaining about men changing up the pattern and going so fast and being too rough. Like, you can be *enthusiastic* without being all quick and haphazard about it. It's about taking your time, really. Being slow. Being gentle. Softer than you think you have to be. Making her wait, making her reach for it a little." She was blushing, but not enough to stop, and in no universe would Avra have given up the opportunity to instruct Kieran in this arena. It was a chance she'd never expected to have. "I refuse to enter a bedroom without a vibrator, you know. It doesn't matter who I'm with. I will not compromise on my best bet to have an actual orgasm." She was wide-eyed, earnest, and Kieran was still listening. "I'm not going to neglect my pleasure just because an ego might get hurt, and I know a rumbly wand vibe is reliable for me. It's foolproof. Most women don't actually prefer those stupid, tinny bullet vibes." She shook her hand as if banishing an irritating fly. "Complete mystery to me how those got so popular. Probably bigger vibrators make men nervous, or embarrassed, but whatever." Her tone was shifting—the erotic crackle in the air had been replaced with a rebellious kind of urgency. "I need something with an engine. There's research on that, you know—on the quality of vibration that women prefer from a toy, and it's not a high-pitched buzz. It's more like . . . like a motorcycle." When Kieran blinked, said nothing, Avra continued. "And from what I understand, straight people are, like, *obsessed* with dick size and tit size and all of that bullshit, but I've been fucked by my fair share of strap-ons and an array of dildos and I'm serious: four to six inches will get the job done, seven inches will stretch, eight inches will *hurt*. Any more than that, I'm probably out." Avra summoned bravery through her blatancy, through the pace and velocity of her speech. She tried to lean into obscenity like she wasn't the slightest bit self-conscious. Kieran was watching her teeth as she spoke. "And women have limited refractory periods. Men get worn out so fast, one or two orgasms and they're done, but my last girlfriend set a goal of five per session, for each of us. The most I've had in a day was twelve, I think, and I probably could have had more, but I just got so tired." Kieran cracked a smile at this. He turned to wave down the bartender. Avra, on a roll, nodded encouragingly and pushed her empty glass toward the other side of the bar. "I just don't understand why, even among sex-positive people, pleasure-positive people, the conversation about pleasure equity is focused on the orgasm gap. That's what my professors call the phenomenon of men, on average, having more orgasms than women: the orgasm gap. And, like, closing the orgasm gap via a one-to-one balance is somehow the focus of work on establishing pleasure equity, but that's so *silly*. It's so shortsighted, and it's *still* all about minimizing the amount of effort we demand from men." She was annoyed now. "The expectation of an exactly equal ratio, especially among straight people, is genuinely absurd. Like, my pleasure potential is three times, four times, maybe *more* times that of a person with a penis." The bartender was standing nervously in front of them, clearly trying not to listen. Avra turned to her, said, "I'll have another, please," and faced Kieran again. He laughed softly at her momentum and put his face in his hands while the bartender walked stiffly away. "Like, why would I have a one-to-one orgasm ratio with a guy if my refractory period doesn't demand it?"

She was looking expectantly at Kieran, who said from between his hands, "You wouldn't?"

"You're goddamn right I wouldn't."

"A warrior of the people." He scrubbed a palm over his chin.

Avra went on, "And I'm not even really covering all of the . . . variety. The diversity, I mean. Like, some women have penises, and some men have vulvas, and gender is a whole spectrum, and *we haven't even gotten to kink yet*." Somehow she had moved from *women* fucking to the *menu* of fucking, something Naya had explained to her, something she and Ellie had discussed in detail after their first Women and Gender Studies class. She briefly recalled the game they had played about halfway through the semester on challenging phallocentric sexual scripts, and how her professor had used the word "vibrator" without flinching. The bartender returned with her second drink, and Avra reached for it with a small, satisfied smile.

"Thank you," she said, letting the cocktail glass rest against the side of her cheek as she thought. She was already far gone. She hadn't eaten today, hadn't hydrated enough, and the familiar comfort of tipsiness was encouraging her onward. "I'm not sure if this is fetishistic, or fucked up, but I've really always wanted to fall in love with a trans woman who didn't want bottom surgery. Because I think, like, along with loving women, I'd really, really like to experience a penis without having to put up with a man, or the performance of binarist masculinity." Kieran coughed, but Avra wasn't deterred. "I mean, you get all the perks of being with a woman—the visceral understanding of oppression, the feminine energy, emotional intelligence, the ability to empathize, the experience of fighting on behalf of a marginalized identity, the shared trauma of contending with cis guys and queerphobia, all of that—without having to deal with the hassle of a strap. And actually getting to feel her body respond to me and what I'm doing, instead of plastic or silicone . . . I mean, it sounds really nice." She trailed off, realizing she may be overexplaining.

"I don't really know what you're talking about," Kieran intoned, slowly, "but I'm going to be honest—that does sound a bit fetishistic to me."

"Yeah, it does," Avra said, blowing a raspberry and taking another sip of her cocktail. "I know it does. I never usually say anything like this. Not out loud. But I mean, like, if I'm not going out *looking* for a trans woman with a penis—if I just happen to fall in love with her, and appreciate the way my desires are compatible with her decisions—is it still fucked up?"

"I'm not the person to ask," Kieran replied. "But maybe."

"Damn." Avra realized how low her inhibitions had fallen, mid-tirade. She was eager, and honest, and trying very hard to make Kieran understand. She had to make him understand. "I know I'm supposed to be explaining how women fuck," Avra said, trying to rediscover the thread, "but I just want to say, this community is gorgeous."

"This community?"

"Queer people."

"Queer people are gorgeous." He said it flatly, but without malice.

"Yes," Avra said, and she felt her eyes water at how much she meant it, at saying this out loud in her hometown, staring down a man who had once called her a dyke. "We are gorgeous. And so different from what people expect, probably different than what you would expect." She knew she was being condescending, being pretentious, but she couldn't quite temper the tone, and Kieran hadn't told her to shut up yet. "So . . . brave, and interesting, and sexy, and we make opportunities for the newness. We create things that nobody thought about, we fuck differently, we even kiss differently."

"What's so different about it?" Kieran asked, but there wasn't any skepticism in his voice—just an open, tentative curiosity that made Avra want to pour queer wisdom into iridescent shot glasses and feed them to him one after another after another.

"Well, for one thing, we have spectacular touch intuition."

"Which is . . . ?"

"It's . . ."—she considered her definition with worshipful care— ". . . it's knowing instinctively what will feel good. Being able to guess what will be physically pleasurable for another person. I think it's something queer people have more than straight people."

"Why?" Kieran leaned forward, head tilted, eyebrows up, like he really wanted to know.

"Because we aren't allowed to touch the way we want, for a long time. You spend years in the closet imagining how you *might* want to touch someone. You spend years holding yourself back from the affection you want, being refused the kind of affection you want, and imagining how you'd like other people to touch you. You spend years *afraid* of it, terrified of what it would mean to you, of what it means *about* you. You fight it, and it intrudes. You embrace it, and it intoxicates." Avra was practically singing her description. Kieran nodded automatically, locked in by the way she spoke, the way the cadence of her own voice could carry her away. He could have reached out—an anchor, a port. He didn't. "A lot of the time, you assume you're never going to get it. Never going to get to have that thing where someone kisses you and it's so good, so beautiful, it makes you want to die." Kieran's foot was shaking, tapping the leg of his barstool, and Avra wanted her words to cover him like a blanket, the sympathy was so fierce, so tangible. They didn't have to name the shared understanding. It was held like a bird between them. "So, instead of touching, you fantasize about touch, down to the detail—precise and painstaking—to make up for what you're afraid to miss. Queer people have such rich fantasy lives because we don't necessarily get to live what we want. We're forced to live it in our heads. All that daydreaming, the desire that might not be ful-filled; it makes things better when we finally *do* get to reach out, to hold each other, to feel. I think it makes us more thoughtful lovers." Avra realized she had switched to the plural. Kieran hadn't cor-rected her. "And we have to fly without a script, you know? There's no Hollywood movie telling us, okay, *this* is the way women fuck. No porn that really gets it right. No repetitive Hallmark bullshit about the tropes and the pitfalls and the happily ever after. And the few films that do *dare* depict our sexuality are directed by men, and written for the male gaze, and just trying to mimic straight sex so that queerness can be more easily commodified and consumed and objectified. So that men feel like they're doing it *right*, like they have lesbian approval. So that queer women are still perceived as fuckable and sexually available to guys. They just don't really teach you anything. And then, all of a sudden—because it always feels sudden—you're in a room alone with someone, some girl you've wanted because of the way she smells or how fucking smart and cool she is, and there's no guidebook. There's no schema telling you okay, touch her here, use this many fingers, call her these names, lick her this way." Avra sighed deeply, took a long sip, and blinked twice at Kieran, who blinked back. "The only reference point you really have that you can trust is what you know you'd want for yourself, what you've tried with your own body when you're alone in the dark, what you've envisioned doing for years, what you've craved in your sleep, what you've imagined when you've seen them in the halls or in the cafeteria or at that party. You just sort of have to play, and ask questions, and figure it out. You have to go slow, and check in. It's . . ."—she grinned in anticipation of what she was about to say, impressed with herself, with her articulation of an experience she'd never seen put to words—"it's an iterative process. A creative process. You're really . . . building something with that person. It's not just being fucked. It's—and I know this is a lot, and maybe ridiculous to say—it's making a dream come true, in real time, while the other person is there, doing the same thing. It's generating something new, bringing something into existence that you've never seen before, that nobody has taught you. Having queer sex is the closest thing I think I'll ever experience to being a God."

Kieran's eyes were bright, his mouth a white line on his face, which looked aggrieved, and enthralled. Avra tried to gentle her tone, but probably it wasn't enough, and she wouldn't have known how to put any kind of bow on this conversion regardless. "And just for that, I think you'll fuck a guy someday. I'm sure you will. Because I think you know I'm right about this." Kieran swallowed. "And, more to the point, who is he?"

Avra had reached her intended conclusion, and then pivoted so fast, so aggressively, that Kieran's brain seemed to take a few moments to catch up. His face didn't fall, and he didn't shove away from the bar, but something behind his eyes shuttered as the question landed—invasive, inconsiderate.

"I'm not . . ." Kieran trailed off, and Avra wasn't patient enough to wait.

"Maybe I'm pushing too hard." Her second drink was half gone. "But honestly, I don't care. I know there's a guy. Why won't you tell me?" She could see the wheels turning, and Kieran's face heating from shame. He probably felt stupid, or ignorant, but Avra hadn't the latitude for gentleness. She wanted him to know what he didn't know, which was everything. He was a fucking baby. He was a fucking baby, and he was missing out.

"I told you," Kieran said, voice apprehensive, as craven as the rest of him, "we aren't friends." It was enough. Avra felt the words like a blow, and her teeth snapped shut. It was a rejection, not just of her but of their community, and she was done with him. Done with the conversation, the pretense of his straightness, the bullshit performance she had seen directly through for three stretching, aching years.

"Fine," she said, after a moment, and she took her scarf back impulsively. "Okay," she said again, reaching into her wallet and pulling out enough cash to cover her drinks. She threw two twenties on the bar, swigged the remainder of her cocktail, tossed her braid over her shoulder, and rose to leave. She expected, optimistically, Kieran to stop her, or to say something.

He was silent. That was worse.

She had tricked herself into the illusion of *knowing* him, years of high school obsession and pining and fantasy colliding chaotically into a mirage of familiarity that they'd never actually had. She had been wrong, she supposed, to waste her breath. She grabbed her coat and headed toward the door, leaving Kieran alone on his stool, staring at her retreating back.

She was a few strides from her car, blinking rapidly against the unexpected afternoon light, before he caught up with her. The parking lot was empty, for which Avra was grateful. She felt angry enough to cry. At the sound of fast footsteps, Avra wheeled around, fight-or-flight instinct twisting her insides. She had learned the lesson most women learn—men running after you is never a good thing. Danger. Danger.

She was right to turn. Kieran, body large and hard, was crowding into her space, walking her four paces back against the side of her car, one hand on her arm, the other on her hip, as if to shake her, as if to plead or punish. His effort to be domineering was whiplash-vivid and contrived. It was nonsense. Kieran's brow was furrowed, but he looked lost in the lines around his mouth, baffled and hurt. Avra wasn't having it. She shoved him back with both hands, turned the two of them around, pressed Kieran up against the car door, and placed her palms squarely on her hips, blocking an exit path.

"*What?*" The word cracked like a whip. "What the *fuck* do you want? You're right. We're not friends. How could we be friends?" Kieran's hands were shaking in time with the tremble in Avra's voice. Unmoored, he was reaching for her again, fisting one hand in her shirt, knuckles against her belly. She breathed fast, angry, panting with the weight of her own injury. "I've always been braver than you," she said, and Kieran nodded as she raged, as the sun shone down on them both. He pulled her shirt. She could feel the little hairs on his knuckles against the soft flesh of her navel. She stepped closer, acquiescent in spite of herself, disgusted with the momentum, certain of what was next, as usual. "I've always been smarter than you." Again, he didn't protest. Avra's eyes bore into his face. They traced his freckles, his stubble, that absurdly red mouth. She wanted to see it bleed. "I've always been fucking ballsier than you. And as much as you might hate it, I *do* know you."

He had settled his trembling fingers on her waist now, below the strip of her shirt, mimicking the memory of Isabella as if he could ever replace the way a woman would touch her, as if he would ever know how. He breathed hard against Avra's forehead, and Avra clung to his jacket like a lost thing.

"I *know* you," she said again, "like I know how badly you want what I've always had, like I know there's some guy at college you're not telling me about, like I know that's the reason Will left last night, like I know you're too . . . too ashamed to say because you've never been able to sit in your queerness without running away for a *single fucking minute.*" Avra shoved his chest again, hard, and he gripped her waist fiercely. She willed the bruises, willed the evidence, willed him to snap again, wanted to see him break. "It's *pathetic.*" She spat the word. Kieran flinched, and his hands twitched, but he didn't shove her, didn't resist, and something inside her howled, furious at his complacency. "I know all about you, Kieran." He was barely off-guard, responding to her fury like he expected it, like it was all part of the game. He absorbed each shove, each press, with acceptance— the price he should pay for his cowardice. "I know *everything.*"

Kieran nodded even as he lowered his face to hers, ready to catch whatever she would throw. He was still nodding when he kissed her, his tongue hot against her bottom lip, her mouth melting open beneath an onslaught of shared grief and wanting so sweet, so vicious, it made bloodhounds of them both: each starved for likeness, each finding it.

CHAPTER 11

MARCH 2012

At the sound of tires rolling across the parking lot, Avra broke away from the kiss. Her heart was fluttering along an unfamiliar time signature. She was sure her cheeks were red, her pupils enormous. It was embarrassing how quickly Kieran could sabotage her composure.

"Stop," she said.

"Why?" Even in a one-word question, Kieran sounded disoriented.

"There are people."

Kieran's thumbs were settled in the wanton flesh above Avra's hip bones. His mouth looked well-bitten and wet. She wanted to slide her fingertips across it just to lick off his spit. She wanted to drink the sweat gathering along his temples. She wanted to dig her hands into his chest and come away with layers of skin cells buried beneath her fingernails. The humiliation of it crackled. She glanced toward the cars. Kieran jostled her gently to bring her attention back.

"There were people last night too," he said, small and quiet.

"I was drunk last night."

Kieran rolled his eyes, understanding Avra to be an exhibitionist in or out of intoxication. "You're drunk now?" Another question.

"No, I'm—" Avra paused, considering. "I'm tipsy." She ran the nail of her forefinger across Kieran's neck just to watch the skin pinken, and the satisfaction that crawled her bones felt dangerous, degenerate.

"I guess that means it would be a bad time to take you home." Kieran's height was blocking the light, but Avra still had to blink to look into his face. He was framed by midafternoon sun. He was Herculean and Thesean and Odyssean and still a coward and at least a little gay and definitely also hard. She wanted to drop her palm and rub, flat and slow, over the bulge at the front of his jeans. She wanted to drop to her knees in the parking lot and lick over the seam, the zip, until Kieran was distraught, pleading. Instead, she made an offer.

"My house is free."

"Oh?" He was taken aback.

Avra was optimistic about their chances for privacy. As far as she knew, Emerson was spending the day out of the house and Dad was off getting the oil changed. Inevitably, this would lead to at least a few hours of miscellaneous errands, and a mercifully empty second floor, and besides, she was in college now. She considered how to frame this proposition.

"I'm . . . I don't like you very much right now."

"You never do."

"But I like kissing you."

"That's something, then." His hands were still on her hips. She could smell the elderflower liqueur on her own breath.

"And I want to be horizontal with you," Avra went on, "somewhere strangers can't see."

Wordlessly, Kieran pushed away from the side of the car, pressed Avra back a pace, walked around the front of the Prius, and stood by the passenger-side door. He stared over the top of the car at her, expectantly.

"Okay," Avra said, confirming, before getting into the driver's side.

The ride back to her house was silent. The smoky aftertaste of tequila reminded her impishly that she probably should not have been driving. This was reckless and shortsighted. She tried to justify the trip via a lust-addled cost-benefit analysis. She kept her eyes on the road. Kieran kept his hands to himself, didn't look across the console, didn't fidget, and barely breathed. His long legs took up all possible space, but he didn't adjust the seat. The air inside the car was sticky and sun-warmed, and the taste of Kieran's mouth—bourbon and orange and something distinctly *him*—was still on Avra's tongue. She worried she might drool if she thought too hard about it. He reached over, once, to drag his finger along the scarf now looped loosely around her neck. By the time they pulled into the empty driveway of her childhood home, Avra's pulse was thick and heavy, her thighs slick from sweat and a vindictive, heedless want. Her legs shook as she got out of the car. The sound of the passenger-side door closing, of Kieran's footsteps behind her on the path, built an anticipation that tugged insistently between her shoulder blades. She could feel Kieran's eyes on the nape of her neck as she led him inside. She had never had better posture in her life.

They made it a few paces into the front hall. Avra opened her mouth to speak, but Kieran was already crowding into her space, already tilting her face up for a kiss, holding both ends of the scarf, then her jaw, then her shoulders, then her waist; he touched Avra with a fleeting, erratic confusion that caught her off-balance. She fought back the impulse to shove him, to snap, to press him up against walls and windows. Instead, she gripped his chin in her palm, fingers splaying flatly over his mouth. She licked over her hand, and her tongue slid obscenely over her own fingertips and the parts of his lips that it could reach.

"I hate the trope," she muttered, breath coasting sweetly over her own fingers, over Kieran's mouth, "where the guy kisses the girl before she has a chance to say something." Kieran pulled back to look at her, his gaze perching upon the hickey half-covered by her scarf. He brushed his fingers over it distractedly. It appeared to be taking his total concentration to remain upright. Avra pulled her hand away from his mouth and settled both against his chest. She could feel his pectorals beneath his shirt, hard and very unlike breasts, and recognized with a small thrill that Kieran was a man, and that she had never done this before. His fingers skated against the bruise on her neck again, again, again.

"What," he asked blankly, running his free hand haphazardly through his dark hair, "could you *possibly* want to talk about right now?" Avra shivered at the ghost of his fingers over and over the hickey, feather-light and unceasing until the skin was sensitive, singing.

"We should probably talk about what the fuck this is," she said, dropping her head to the opposite shoulder to give him more space. She didn't really mean it, but it seemed like a mature proposal. Responsible, or whatever.

"I've never known what the fuck this is," Kieran replied, tugging the scarf out of the way. He was impulsive, pushy, and Avra was reminded for a moment of a puppy being refused a chew toy. Before she could respond, Kieran lowered his head to her neck and sealed his mouth possessively over the previous night's bruise, sucking hard. Avra gasped, not expecting the strong, capillary-bursting pull over flesh already raw and sensitive. It was intense, and uncomfortable, and forcefully lascivious. Finally, evidence. She would photograph it. Frame it.

"Watch it," she warned, not meaning it for a second.

"I will not," Kieran rebuked. "It felt fucking wrong watching someone else do this to you." He said it as an aside, hardly audible. The words twisted themselves into a core memory.

"You're just mad I get to be gay in public." Avra wanted the upper hand. She did not have it. Kieran dragged his tongue punishingly over the bruise, bit down hard, and Avra made an involuntary noise of pain. Kieran laved his tongue over the mark again, sucked a darker spot along one of the edges, Venn-diagramming the bruise with daggered focus, and Avra felt the sensation move liquid-hot along her spine. He walked the line of not-enough-too-much expertly. He must have experience. Avra didn't know with whom. She hated that.

"You're a showoff," he replied, tilting her head back practically as he peppered a stinging constellation of marks under her jaw. It was efficient, in service of possession more than pleasure, and Avra knew covering these up would be hopeless. She didn't care.

"Just because I'm braver than—" He actually put his hand over her mouth this time, and Avra wanted to bite him. She resisted.

"I know, I know, you're braver than I am. You're queer and experienced. You're smart and informed. You understand me better than I do. You understand *everything*. I get it. Before we dive back into you . . . shaming me for making different choices than you've made"—he had a point—"I think you mentioned something about being horizontal?" He lowered his hand from her mouth and rubbed his thumb lazily over Avra's bottom lip, which tingled with nostalgia for salt, cut lime, threats and tequila. Want burst in Avra's belly so quickly, so intensely, she nearly broke, nearly asked him to fuck her wet mouth with his fingers, nearly offered to crawl across the carpet.

"Upstairs," she said instead.

Avra led Kieran up the creaky, narrow staircase and down the hall to her childhood room with the band posters and her twin-size trundle bed. The juvenility was a sharp contrast against Kieran's large, warm body, which pressed up against her from behind as she walked into the center of the room. As she kicked her shoes off haphazardly—they thunked dully against the closet door—Kieran positioned himself behind her with a kind of possessive invasiveness. She could feel his erection against her lower back, just above the swell of her ass. The pressure lifted her little femme skirt an inch or two higher, and she squeezed her thighs together unconsciously to alleviate the dull, thrumming ache between her legs.

"What, you don't want to check out my posters?"

"Shut up." Kieran's lips were against the back of her ear, he was leaning forward to scrape scruff along her neck. It raised goose-bumps all along her hairline, and Avra grinned.

"Not even the Fall Out Boy one?"

"I said, shut *up*," Kieran said, gripping her waist and turning her forcefully around. She spun and caught herself on his shoulders, laughing. "Please," he amended, before kissing her again. She wanted him annoyed. She wasn't sure why. It seemed easier, maybe, to fuck a version of him she already knew—angry, domineering, off-kilter.

"You know, I think Will likes Fall Out Boy."

"Could we *please* not talk about him right now?" Kieran was working the clasp of her skirt with his large hands, and Avra reached toward Kieran's front buttons, letting her knuckles drag slowly against the seam of his jeans.

"Does College Guy like Fall Out Boy?"

"Give it a rest," Kieran commanded, pinching her hip. She smacked his hand away, dragged his zipper down, and the thrill of a flesh-and-blood cock right in front of her, of something hard and aching and not made of silicone sparked a vulgar curiosity.

Avra had always enjoyed dildos, always cooed and writhed prettily when her partners had strapped, but she craved the mutual sensation of this more than expected. The potential reactivity. She stared openly at Kieran's cotton briefs. Avra wanted to memorize the outline of his trapped erection, curved toward the left, the damp spot next to the seam of his underwear, the way Kieran gasped urgently when she drew her palm along the mark. When she pulled her hand away, his hips followed automatically.

"Think this will qualify as hate sex?" she asked cheekily.

"In that I really fucking hate you right now, sure." Kieran tugged Avra's hand back toward him, but she pushed him onto her bed, climbing forward to straddle his thighs, her hands bracing on his shoulders. Her skirt was coming loose, the fabric teasing gently along the tops of her thighs as she stretched them wide. If she shifted her hips a few inches forward, she could slide her failed, soaking panties along the bulge of Kieran's hardness. They were each trapped by infuriating layers of fabric. Avra rocked experimentally, and the way Kieran's head dropped back rewarded her efforts.

"Take this off," he demanded, tugging the hem of her shirt. She did so immediately, wanting Kieran's hands on more of her skin. She was unselfconscious—had learned how to be over years of affectionate sex with women who provided easy praise, comfort, and affirmation. She had been seen naked dozens of times, been called beautiful in equal measure. When she'd expressed some anxiety about the half-cup-size difference between her breasts, a one-night stand had insisted somberly, "They're supposed to be sisters, not twins." She'd ceased caring after that. Now, Kieran's eyes locked on to her chest in such a stereotypically male way that Avra grinned.

"You've seen tits before," Avra chided falsely, before tugging

Kieran up for a kiss. She fucked his mouth slowly with her tongue, ground down to gauge his response, and his fingers scrabbled for purchase across her back. They broke apart panting, breath mingling in a heady fog.

"I've never done *this* before, though."

"What?" She was speaking directly into his mouth, still rocking, more confidently now, gasping intermittently as the friction between their bodies curled pleasurably along her nerves.

"Fucked you."

Avra was exultant.

"I've never fucked a guy at all," she said, matter-of-fact, and Kieran groaned with something like satisfaction, burying his hands in her hair to tug her mouth back toward him. He turned her chin roughly, licked a hot line up the side of her face, and Avra whined. "Knew you'd like hearing that," she said, breathless. Kieran's spit was cooling on her face. "Do it again," she said quietly, almost embarrassed by the request. Kieran didn't have to ask what she meant. He turned her face in the other direction, eyes open and staring into hers as their noses brushed softly, before licking a wet stripe from her chin to her temple. It was outrageous. "Damn it."

"What is it?"

"I don't understand why I like that."

"No?" Kieran, taking his cues, flipped Avra off of his lap and onto the bed. She landed clumsily on her side, one leg still draped over his thighs. When she tried to pull her leg away, however, Kieran grabbed it roughly. "Wait." He raised her bare foot toward his face and pressed an open-mouthed kiss against the stubbled skin just above her ankle, where she had missed shaving. She had actually *shaved* for this. De Beauvoir and Steinem would be so disappointed. Avra pushed the thought of her submission to antifeminist beauty standards out of her head. They had no place in a bedroom with her and Kieran. Or, maybe they did, but she didn't know quite how to square them, and she was far too distracted to try.

Curiously, Kieran licked again, a hot path up the line of her calf toward her knee. Avra knew she was spread open obscenely, her skirt half off, underwear visibly wet. Her cheeks were flushed, breath catching as Kieran nipped at the skin above her knee with practiced precision, his palm now cradling the bottom of her foot.

"I think you like it when I degrade you a little bit." Kieran's other hand was sliding up the inside of her thigh, and Avra opened her legs automatically. "That's why you want me to lick your face. The ownership." He paused and looked directly at her. "The power."

"What makes you say that?" Avra could feel her defenses climbing, even as she recognized the IV drip of shame at his correctness.

"Because I'm here. Because I treated you like shit in high school—knocked things out of your hands, called you names, made fun of you—and you still kissed me last night and today. You still invited me to your house. Into your room."

Avra's laugh came out dark and furious. "Are you saying I'm coping with your history of being a vicious bully via a humiliation kink?" In response, Kieran planted Avra's foot on the mattress so that both her knees were bent, her heels braced, her thighs wide open. He was looking up her skirt, which had finally come undone. Kieran reached forward, eyes focused, and ran one finger lightly over the warm, damp cotton of Avra's panties. Her clit ached and pulsed ferociously, nerves chasing the friction. Patiently, painstakingly, Kieran did it again, his fingertip barely grazing the fabric stretched across her clit.

"Not so much a *humiliation* kink, no," he said, thoughtful and slow, as he rubbed one finger back and forth, over and over while the sensation built. Avra let her head tilt back, closed her eyes. "More that you want me to do whatever I want to you, I think, just so you can figure out what it is. I think you want to see what I'll do. And you don't really care if it hurts you, or insults you, because it's not really *about* what I'm doing. It's about observing what I *choose* to do, and being able to take it. Deciding to take it. It's what you were like back then."

Avra considered this—or, tried to consider it—as the sweet, infuriating friction of Kieran's fingers made her clit throb responsively, desperately. Sparks swam over the backs of her eyelids.

"I think . . . I think that's right. I do want to know what you want to do to me. And I'm interested in seeing how far you'll push, and if you'll want to hurt me, or to humiliate me, because that's valuable information. Just like it was then." Her voice was quivering as she spoke, her cheeks burning. "I want to see what you want from me. But I have some hard limits."

"Name them."

"No hitting my face," she said, and Kieran's fingertips stilled for a second. She whined, and he resumed that repetitive, teasing contact.

"Done."

"And no calling me a bitch. I don't have a problem with name-calling, really, I just don't find that one particularly sexy."

"I can call you a whore, then?"

"Shut up." She didn't really mean it.

"No, I'm serious, I want to know." He was pulling her underwear to the side now, sliding a fingertip up and down against the folds of her labia to check if she was wet. He made a small, savage sound when his skin met the dripping, slick openness, the warm glisten of her. His hands were shaking. Avra could feel the tremble even as he dipped a finger inside of her body, and a soft, eager *hmm* pulled itself from her throat. "While I'm fucking you, would you let me call you a whore?"

"Yes," she said. She hated her own breathlessness. He pushed his finger forward, up to the first knuckle, and Avra opened her eyes. Kieran was staring at the glossy folds between her legs, watching his finger slowly disappear inside of her body, his mouth slack and open as if he couldn't quite believe this was happening.

"Could I spank you?"

"Yes." A bit further, another knuckle. Avra was holding back a desperate urge to beg.

"What about leaving bruises? Marking you up? Pulling your hair? Spitting on you?" He paused, as if considering what else he might want from her. "Coming on you?" He punctuated every question with a short, controlled thrust of his finger, just barely curling, in and out, maybe half an inch. Avra didn't know when she'd fisted her hands in the blankets, but her palms were sweaty against the comforter, her thumbs white.

"Not on my face, but anywhere else, yes." Her voice was strangled. She tried to breathe.

"Can I choke you?"

"Yes."

"Fuck your face?"

Her mouth watered. "*Yes*."

"Jesus, you'd really let me do all that to you?"

Avra was beside herself.

"Kieran."

His head snapped up and when their eyes met, Kieran's expression wasn't sadistic, but disbelieving, wrecked. His eyes were wide, cheeks flushed, jaw tense, the *responsibility* of this sinking in like bare feet in mud, down, down. Avra—understanding tumbling over her—shifted her hips forward slowly, and Kieran's finger slid further into her body. Gaze still locked on Avra's face, measuring, observing, Kieran pulled his finger out, lined up a second, and pushed them both forward until they were buried in Avra's cunt. She let her eyes flutter closed again and her tongue swipe hotly along her bottom lip, before leaning up onto her elbows. Kieran met her for a wet, panting kiss, the positioning awkward, both of them reaching, his fingers moving inside her soft and yielding body, and Avra whimpered against his mouth as the erotic force of this moment crashed into her.

"Just be gentle with my face," she whispered against Kieran's mouth, drawing a line under the boundary, "and you can do whatever you want to me."

"I want to fuck you."

"Fuck me, then."

They each endeavored toward an impossible calm. Kieran drew his long, beautiful fingers slowly out of Avra again and she sighed at the loss before lifting her hips to roll her underwear down her shuddering thighs. Kieran stood to remove his pants, which he kicked into the corner of the room. He had to drag the waistband of his briefs away from his body to free his cock. The head was purpled and shiny, glistening against his belly. Avra stared until Kieran, not quite self-conscious, cleared his throat. There was something holy and weighty about the casting away of their clothing. Socks set in pairs, as if it mattered. Skirt puddled in an oval on the floor. T-shirt hooked on a dresser pull. Earrings on the bookstand, each removed item a confirmation that this was happening. When they were both naked, Avra shifted to the center of the little twin bed, and Kieran—achingly hard—crawled between her thighs. He had a condom wrapper in his hand.

"You came prepared," Avra said, praise coloring her tone.

"Does that surprise you?"

Avra didn't answer. The condoms she had purchased just a few days before sat slyly in the top left drawer of her dresser. She had thought of Kieran when she bought them. Kieran, who was kneeling between her legs, ripping the wrapper open with his teeth, rolling the latex down his cock with one broad palm. Avra was watching him, watching him.

"Why do you think they call it missionary?" she said, interrupting his careful preparation.

"I'm sure you have a theory." Kieran's voice was unsteady. Avra grinned.

"Just seems like a Christian way to fuck."

"You really want to bring up religion right now?"

"I'm Jewish."

"I suppose that means we'll have to try other positions."

Avra's grin widened. "You mean this is going to happen again?"

"How else would I possibly learn the *Jewish* way to fuck?"

Avra's heart was drumming in her chest and Kieran's breath was on her face. "Well, there must be a Joel or Elijah *somewhere* on your campus."

Kieran put his hand over her mouth once more, but he was smiling. Avra licked it. As if succumbing to the suggestion, Kieran ran his thumb slowly over her bottom lip. Their eyes were locked, and Avra's warm tongue was on the pad of Kieran's thumb, and Kieran's hardness was pressed right against her wetness, sliding a little as his hips rolled unconsciously.

"Ready?"

Avra nodded.

The glide forward was slow and perfect and Avra was opening, opening, opening. It felt like being pulled apart, like the universe shattering. She had been fucked before, straps and dildos, warming lube and toys that buzzed. And it had all been excellent, pleasurable, fun, scorchingly hot, sometimes awkward and silly, deeply human. But she'd never been fucked after years of waiting. A half-decade tease. The long game. She felt a moment of wild kinship for all of the girls who had ever wanted to fuck their bullies. It was something like losing and winning, but unlike a tie. Confusion swam her brain and she let it. Kieran felt hot inside her, and Avra was still adjusting to the fullness, the depth, the little strain of holding her thighs open, when he pulled out a few inches and pressed into her again. She moaned contentedly, eyes on Kieran's face. He put a large palm on the back of her thigh, pressed one leg up toward her belly, and began to fuck her.

There were parts of this that Avra would rehearse internally over the course of things, forever. The pressure of Kieran's fingertips on her thighs, the filthy dripping friction of his cock inside her body, the way his face broke in awe as she brought her own fingers to her clit and mimicked the little circles he had drawn, sliding small, wet Os in time with Kieran's rolling hips, while he panted and groaned. The first time he slowed his thrusts, Avra whined a high-pitched "Please" and Kieran actually said "Oh God" aloud before driving forward again, as deep as he could, as much as Avra could stand.

It wasn't hate sex, but it was rough. The next day, Avra's cheeks would warm at the thought of Kieran's palm, firm but careful, against her throat; of her own hands clawing a line across his back; of his mouth right next to her ear, his voice wretched and fractured while he said "fuck fuck fuck," against her neck and her orgasm built like a mighty, hectic, cresting force. The first time Kieran came, he bit her hard enough that she would bruise: a pretty, purple half-moon over her right shoulder. It took her slowly sucking his tongue, mewling a little in his ear, squirming with her fingers on her clit, asking him to please keep fucking her, wrapping her hand around his cock and pulling in a teasing, coaxing rhythm before he was hard enough to go again.

"Condoms in the top left drawer," Avra breathed against his cheek, greedy, wanting more.

Kieran was clumsy walking across the room, pleasure leaving him dazedly bowlegged. He dropped the first, spent condom in the little wicker wastebasket beside Avra's mirror, and returned to the bed with an expression of such soldiering determination that Avra giggled.

The second round was cruder, messy, and Kieran held a fistful of her hair and pressed her cheek down against the mattress. Dug his fingertips into the flesh of her ass, punishingly hard.

"I've always wanted to do this to you."

Something inside Avra cracked like a bell. "Don't stop."

Kieran panted heavily and Avra keened and he was urgent and anchored and she was generous and encouraging, squirming at the delight of being impaled, babbling in her desperation, her fingers working a slippery rhythm against her clit. She couldn't mark the passage of time, couldn't tell if it had been two minutes, or twelve, or twenty. The world seemed to slow. Kieran was fucking her. Kieran was holding her waist, then her ass, then her thigh, then turning her toward her side for another angle, for depth, to fuck her, and she was taking it, acquiescent and pliable underneath him, moaning and begging even as her own voice sounded far away. When her orgasm finally crested, Avra made noises so loud and bright that Kieran kissed her to swallow them, as if he could taste the sounds of her pleasure. Avra knew he could feel her lips forming the chant "I'm coming I'm coming I'm coming" against his own mouth, her tongue on his teeth, her spit mixing with his spit. Avra's cunt squeezed mercilessly, pulsing around Kieran's cock, and his hips snapped and stuttered a dozen more times before his orgasm hit him, and he gasped and groaned against her cheek, her throat, and Avra wanted to memorize the sounds, but her ears were still ringing from the aftershocks of her own pleasure.

When Kieran collapsed onto Avra's chest, both of them covered in a sheen of sweat, the entire room smelling of sex, the echoes of their desperate noises still seeming to reverberate from the walls, his smile was stricken, goofy. He told Avra, shock in his voice, that his vision was spotted, and she licked his nose proudly.

The next day, Avra would be sent foolish and off-kilter at the memory of their shared laughter, at the incredulity. They laughed so hard they wheezed, so hard Avra said she might pee, laughed until it was as loud as the sex, until they could taste the salt. When they settled, Avra draped an arm across Kieran's chest and he covered her small fingers with one large hand; their joined hands rose and fell over his heart, which Avra noted, rosebud romantic as she could be. Kieran smoothed his thumb over her knuckles. They breathed in a melodic synchrony, in-out, opposite one another, so Avra inhaled Kieran's exhale, their lungs collaborating.

It was unreal: a dreamy impossibility, marshmallow fluff, sugar-spun, decadent.

After a few minutes, Kieran asked, "Where did you learn to talk like that?"

Avra explained, "I started reading erotica when I was like fourteen. After a few hundred stories, you pretty much know the lines." She didn't mean for it to be insulting.

"Were those just lines, then?" He sounded nervous in a way that charmed her, and Avra kissed the underside of his chin.

"Meant everything I said."

Eventually, once the mood sobered and their sweat cooled uncomfortably, they rose in a trance to shower together in the empty house. Avra, face as peaceful as a dandelion, washed his hair. Her shampoo smelled of vanilla and coconut. They would match. They would smell like each other, even clean, even after. When she asked

Kieran whether he remembered that massage in the senior lounge, the first time she had ever really touched him, Kieran admitted he had jerked off to the thought of it at home, later that same day, years ago.

"You did *not*."

Kieran kissed her, bit her tongue, licked up the side of her face again, crowded her possessively against the cool tile wall, and Avra shivered.

"Yes, I did."

She was quiet when they got out of the shower, thoughtful as she handed him a towel. Kieran, with uncharacteristic sweetness, wrapped Avra in it before retrieving another from the linen cabinet. When Avra spoke again, a few moments later, her voice was different.

"I know you only want me because I'm the closest thing you've ever had to queerness. And that's okay. I just thought I should name it." She was being *adult*. This wasn't her being a glutton for punishment. No. She was being responsible. Cautious. *Realistic.*

"Shut up, I want you for other reasons." Kieran's tone was gentle, but he didn't actually name those reasons, and Avra didn't ask, and it was impossible for either of them to deny—to each other, to their insides—that one of them was certainly proximity to queerness. When they returned to Avra's room, she sat on the bed in her towel while Kieran gathered his clothes. She threatened to keep his underwear ("proof of my conquest"). She petted his soft, slowly drying hair when he sat beside her. Kissed him once more, licking the tip of his tongue, shifting on the mattress to assess her soreness. He almost got hard, but Avra's body was twinging warningly, and Kieran was exhausted, and they both knew they'd see each other again. He helped her into a pair of warm, worn sweatpants instead, along with a moth-eaten chenille sweater. Kieran stuck his fingers puckishly through the holes in the elbows. He ran his fingers through the damp ends of her hair while Avra pulled on a pair of fuzzy socks, wrestled on her boots, and tutted reluctantly about the drive.

Avra, wanting to do pretty much anything else, returned Kieran to his parked and patient car. On the way, she glanced intermittently at his hand settled on her thigh, maintaining their thread of connection, fragile as it was. She stole looks as well at his profile, the line of marks along his neck, as he squinted against the shock of the intrusive afternoon sun.

They maintained a smooth, comfortable, stunned silence: the silence of two people who had just revised the world of the other, edited their very comprehension of what existed, of what was possible. When the car stopped, Kieran made a pained face before reaching for the handle of the door. Subdued, and after several attempts at final kisses, Avra watched Kieran step out. She watched him walk over to his own car, open the driver's-side door, buckle his seat belt, check the rearview, and start the engine. She stared determinedly at her own hickeys in the side mirror rather than watching him drive away.

CHAPTER 12

APRIL 2012

Ellie and Nico were kind enough to listen to Avra regale them with tales of the party, kissing Kieran, the bookshop bar, kissing Kieran, the ride home, finally sleeping with Kieran, the shower, which she shared with Kieran, and her close analysis of Kieran's behavior over break. She even favored them with a dramatic recitation of the one and only text she'd received from him in the week after she'd straddled him on her childhood bed.

"He said, *good to see you.*"

"A poet," Ellie replied, with a frozen smile.

"But it's nice that he's reaching out, right?"

"How many days since you hooked up?" Nico was always prepared to provide what he called "a dude's perspective."

"Five."

"And is this the first you've heard from him?"

"Yeah, but it's not like we texted a lot before."

"You texted almost every day before break," Ellie reminded gently, pulling her hair back into a high ponytail—she repeated this ritual when she was nervous. Avra counted approximately a dozen

ponytail experiments during especially suspenseful episodes of
HBO series.

"Do you think this is bad?" Avra directed the question toward
Nico, who shot a look at Ellie before responding, slowly: ". . .
I think it's respectful to text someone you've just hooked up with
within forty-eight hours *max*. Just to check in with them. You know,
asking them how they're feeling or about their day. But then, I'm an
old-fashioned guy."

Ellie took her ponytail down, walked over to Nico, and kissed
his cheek. Obnoxious.

"I've never done this before," Avra said plaintively, staring down
at the phone in her hand. She noted the subtle tide of abandonment anxiety coming in—rising disappointment, rising distress.
The obsession with Kieran was back, furious and untameable. Her
old therapist would have probably called this "anxious attachment."
Her old therapist would have been correct.

Over the following weeks, Avra leaned into the art of fantasy,
blurring fact and fiction by imagining a whole future sans input
from Kieran. She wanted to plan what was next for them, or—
more accurately—next for *him*. She imagined selecting his clothing,
something with leather and mesh. Sitting across his lap and brushing on blush, smudging eyeliner. She imagined tugging him out of
a closet and determinedly ignoring his kicking and screaming. Any
protestations, she would insist to soothe the scandalized onlookers,
were just for show. In her head, Avra considered that this display
may be cruel, unethical, the opposite of consent-conscious. In her
head, Avra made him crawl.

She fantasized about outing Kieran at some lavish event—
during a wedding toast, while he froze across the room in his
tuxedo, a lost penguin. On the town green, with a megaphone,
while he stood beside her somberly, head bowed. At a high

school reunion, in a speech to their classmates, while he huddled behind her in a fit of anxious pique. She fantasized about walking him around on a leash, holding his shaking hand while he got a "faggot" tattoo, licking the shell of his ear while a stranger with a cropped haircut and rippling pectorals sucked Kieran off and he cried his relief like a psalm. In her fantasies, Kieran was always at least a little afraid.

Several weeks later, only two days after her return from a cozy home visit for Passover, Avra woke at 1:37 a.m. to the blue light cast from her phone.

free next weekend?

Yes, why? She watched the ellipsis bubble appear and disappear several times, before

coming to visit

As in, you would like to come visit me? Or you would like me to visit you? Or someone is already coming to visit you and you want to discuss it?

ill come 2 u

Avra didn't tell her sister, or her dad, or Karly, or Tati, but she did tell Ellie and Nico, mostly to arrange a free room during the weekend. Ellie put up the barest struggle.

"This means I have to spend a whole weekend in a house of men. Gross."

Nico, ever present and comforting, attempted to soothe her. "I'll tell the boys to be on their best behavior."

"*The boys.*" Ellie made a dramatic gagging sound. "What is this, a Bruins game?"

"No, but there is a playoff matchup this weekend. So at least we know *the boys* will be occupied."

"Stop calling your friends 'the boys' immediately, at once, now, please." Ellie batted her eyelashes warningly at her boyfriend.

Nico grinned before rounding on Avra. "So, you gonna let us meet him?"

Avra balked at the question. "Why?"

"Because I'd like to assess the dude who has intermittently made your life a messy hell, texted you incessantly, kissed you against a car, taken your penis virginity, made himself scarce, and then messaged you at like two a.m. basically inviting himself to your campus."

Ellie raised her eyebrows at Nico following his fastidious summary. He blushed under her scrutiny. "What? I pay attention."

"You know virginity is a social construct, right?" Avra said, avoid-y.

"Hence my specificity, and don't dodge the question."

"You can meet him. Probably. I just kind of . . ." She trailed off, and Ellie cleared her throat once to prompt an explanation. Avra finished her thought: "I just kind of want him to myself."

When Kieran arrived, Avra met him at the entrance to the parking garage. It was a spring day, the sky a repulsive shade of forget-me-not blue, the kind of warming weekend that inspired allergy-prone students to stockpile loratadine. Avra was going to suggest a walk.

Kieran's black duffel had a Nike swoop on the side, and she thought fondly of his backpack on the couch beside her in the senior lounge that day he'd pressed his shoulder blade against her shins. He greeted her with a hug, one-armed, like he hadn't watched his fingers move in and out of her body the last time they had seen each other. Like he hadn't come, cursing, while she cooed in his ear. It was a hug for insecure men who couldn't abide genuine affection. For a wild, annoyed moment, Avra pictured him being hit by a car. Kieran refused the walk. A truck, then.

"What about food? There are a few neat hole-in-the-wall places
. . . ?"

"Can we wait a few hours? I'm not really hungry."

Avra interpreted this as a request for privacy. *Intimacy* of the
kind he couldn't manage around people. She led him back to her
dorm room. They made predictable conversation: about Kieran's
classes, Avra's classes, the drive, the weather. The *weather,* Avra
thought witheringly. The discussion happened in fits and starts.
Each time they saw each other, the intervening weeks or months
had roughed them back to an earlier square.

The energy was timid and clumsy and wrong. Kieran wouldn't
make eye contact, didn't laugh at her jokes, couldn't banter. When
they got back to Avra's dorm room and sat on the bed, Avra reached
for his hand, attempting comfort. He squeezed her fingers passively, placed her hand back in her own lap, and grabbed his phone.
The air was burdened with his angst, and Avra's frustration at her
own failure to alleviate it. She had expected something else this
weekend. She had expected sex that she would blush to recall. She
had expected an anxious thrum of barely bridled passion, the kind
they'd shared in her bedroom. It didn't come. She half hoped Ellie
and Nico would interrupt them so they'd at least have something
to talk about.

"I'm glad you came," she said. Kieran looked over at her, and
Avra noticed his eyes were glassy. "Did you drive here high?"

"I haven't done anything since last night."

"Ooookay. Is it possible you're *still* high?"

"I don't do anything that hard."

"Look." She kicked her heels on the bed, mature as a three-
year-old, and Kieran blinked. "What's wrong?"

Kieran blew out a breath and looked down at his phone. He
could have been praying. "I wanted to come see you."

"But you've hardly said a thing since you got here," Avra complained.

"It's only been like twenty minutes."

"Still, you don't seem—"

He cut her off, as if he had found courage for a moment and couldn't give it the opportunity to abandon him. "I just think I'm really unhappy."

Avra didn't speak. His admission seeped into her lungs, insidious and toxic. She wanted to fix it. She didn't want to deal with it. She felt responsible for dealing with it. She resented the feeling of responsibility, and his unhappiness.

"I'm . . . I'm sorry you're hurting."

"You seemed like someone I could call, maybe. If I was unhappy." Kieran moved one shoulder up, then down.

"And you're unhappy."

"Yes."

"Very unhappy?"

He nodded, "Yes."

"What happened?"

"I don't want to talk about it."

"Then why are you here?"

He leaned over and kissed her, as if meaning to start something, but broke it after a few seconds. Avra watched his face and sensed, with no small amount of horror, that he was going to cry.

"I thought you'd make me feel better."

"Like, with my pussy?" Avra knew this was brash, and tried to soften the allegation with a smile.

Kieran laughed. A little snot bubble popped out of his left nostril. Avra leaned over to her desk and grabbed a box of tissues. She tossed it at him, and he caught it adeptly, as she knew he would. *Athletes.*

"Not necessarily. But maybe, yeah." He blew his nose.

"Did something happen with College Guy?"

Kieran didn't flinch this time. "I said I don't—"

"Course not."

Kieran looked at her, hard, and Avra yielded, "Okay, I'm sorry. I'm sorry. We don't have to." She knew she'd bring it up again later. When he was tired, or maybe drunk.

"Can we just watch a movie?" He sounded tired.

"Sure. Have one in mind?"

"Wouldn't hate a Lord of the Rings marathon."

"*Excuse* me?" Avra, taking the opportunity, leaned enthusiastically into her theater expertise. She repositioned herself on her knees, both hands on Kieran's shoulders, and looked seriously into his face. "I'm sorry. Wait. Pardon me, sir? What the *fuck* did you just say to me?"

He laughed again, the box of tissues hopping in his lap. "I said Lord of the Rings."

"I *know* what the fuck you said!" Avra cawed, feigning fury. "How *dare* you? How *dare* you wait until I have known you for years and years and been a target of your ridiculous big-boy bullying and intermittently hated your stupid popular handsome jock-bro guts to admit that you are a *fucking nerd?!*"

"A closet nerd," he countered, and then hesitated, as if the entendre had struck him a second too late.

"You're goddamn right," Avra said, and kissed Kieran's cheek before pulling away and swatting the side of his head. Any excuse to touch him, she supposed.

"I admit it. You caught me. I'm helpless to the directorial whims of Peter Jackson."

"Who's your favorite character?" Avra asked, expecting Aragorn.

"Samwise the Brave."

"WHAT?!"

The mood lightened considerably after that. They walked to a charming Vietnamese place for dinner, between the first and second films. They split summer rolls with peanut sauce, and Kieran ordered fried rice, and they drank two full pots of tea. Kieran didn't like spicy food. Avra mocked him for this, despite her own Ashkenazic limitations. On the walk back to the dorm, Kieran jostled Avra's shoulder with his own, and Avra felt it in her throat, in her heels.

About halfway through the Battle of Helm's Deep, Kieran fell asleep with his head in Avra's lap. Lit by the blue glow, his face looked vampiric and morbid, but his forehead lines had released, and he made little snuffling sounds when Avra repositioned her legs. Her feet were beginning to go numb. In the background, the Ents marched on Isengard, but Avra wasn't watching. Kieran's hair flopped magnificently into his eyes. He was resting. He was in her room, in her lap, passive, vulnerable. Drool gathered gradually at the corner of Kieran's mouth. Heart distorted and overly large in her chest, Avra swiped her thumb gently through the spit, smoothed a sticky line down to Kieran's chin, and sucked whatever saliva remained carefully off her thumb.

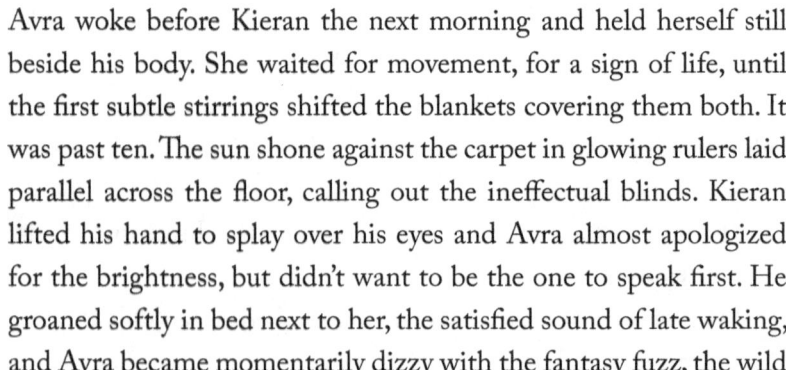

Avra woke before Kieran the next morning and held herself still beside his body. She waited for movement, for a sign of life, until the first subtle stirrings shifted the blankets covering them both. It was past ten. The sun shone against the carpet in glowing rulers laid parallel across the floor, calling out the ineffectual blinds. Kieran lifted his hand to splay over his eyes and Avra almost apologized for the brightness, but didn't want to be the one to speak first. He groaned softly in bed next to her, the satisfied sound of late waking, and Avra became momentarily dizzy with the fantasy fuzz, the wild improbability of his presence, of their proximity.

Sometime near the end of the movie, Avra had gotten up to brush her teeth. When she returned, Kieran was already under her blankets, fully in his day clothes—she'd scold him for that later. Pajama-clad, Avra had joined him, but not before spraying her hair and collar with a sweet vanilla perfume. If he woke in the night, she wanted him to think she smelled nice. She wanted him to want her to stay. She could have crawled into Ellie's bed. She chose not to.

Avra slept with her nose tucked under his chin, breathing softly against his throat. His intermittent murmuring moved the tiny hairs at the top of her head. Now, as morning curled around them, Kieran spoke into her eyebrows. One of Avra's arms was slung over his chest. It was immaculate. Unbelievable.

"Sorry for falling asleep."

"You must have really needed it," she soothed.

"I think I really did." Kieran stretched and Avra's arm rose with his rib cage. She tried to remove it casually, to erase her own presumptiveness, but he grabbed her wrist and brought her hand back down to where it had been before he stretched. Avra's fingers skated along his back. His shirt had come up. She could feel his skin, warm from sleep, and she opened and closed her hand experimentally. Kieran made a low, satisfied hum. She did it again.

"I should brush my teeth," Avra said.

"Me too."

"I don't want to get up."

"Me neither."

"You could kiss me, you know," Avra suggested.

"I'm going to," Kieran declared.

"You are?"

"In a minute."

"You're not going to brush your teeth first?" She was joking.

Kieran tugged her earlobe in lazy reprisal.

"No, I'm not."

Avra shifted closer, and felt his morning hardness against the front of her thigh. Neither of them mentioned it, but his pelvis moved forward infinitesimally, and Avra slung her right leg over the top of his left so her thigh was pressing him in place.

"Good morning," she said.

"Good morning."

When he kissed her, his breath was sour and his mouth a little dry. Avra thought she should have offered him water, or gotten some herself, but then Kieran palmed her ass, lifted her toward him so their chests were pressed together from hip to shoulder, and Avra's brain short-circuited. His other hand came up to cradle her jaw with uncharacteristic gentleness, his fingertips fitting in the notch below her ear so precisely that Avra sighed. Her mouth watered responsively at the sensation of his tongue against her lower lip, waiting. Kieran breathed so that she could taste the air from his own lungs, breathed like he knew it was just a matter of time, and he was right. Avra returned his kiss slowly at first, and then with force. The kiss devolved into messy sparring, punctuated by frantic sounds, wet enough for both of them, gaining momentum, a snow-ball weeping glittering fractals as it rolled downhill. Avra's sighs hitched chaotically when Kieran turned her face to the side and licked a stripe up her neck, over her jaw, along her cheek, the way that had rattled her back in her bedroom. She had run that moment over in her head like a film reel.

"It feels territorial, when you do that." Her voice was stupid, breathy again, and she couldn't care, couldn't be embarrassed, she just couldn't.

"It is." Kieran was harder now, his erection pressed demand-ingly against the soft insides of Avra's legs.

"I like it."

"I know you do."

Avra didn't have to ask him to do it again. He licked a line from her temple over her eyebrow, over the opposite eyelid, down her cheek, back to her mouth, and she imagined she could taste her own skin on his tongue. He was painting her with his spit. She would wear it to breakfast.

"I think you should fuck me." She made the suggestion against his mouth as her hips rocked involuntarily, her heel hooking invitingly around the back of Kieran's thigh. There was a growing damp ellipse at the front of Avra's underwear and pajamas from how wet she was already. *Already.* All he had done was kiss and lick her, touch her waist and throat, and she was weak. It rendered her useless, submissive, needy.

"I'm going to."

"You are?" She nipped Kieran's bottom lip, as was characteristic of their play, carded her fingers through his hair, and pulled his head back so that he had to work to reach her mouth, had to pull away from the resistance of her hand. It might have been hurting him. She didn't care.

"In a minute."

Undressing was as clumsy as the last time, as fraught with finality. They climbed down from Avra's lofted twin bed to pull off clothing, as if the vulnerability of asking for help was beneath them, despite everything. Avra reached toward levity.

"You slept in your street clothes last night. Your grimy pedestrian pants touched my sheets." She was smiling.

Kieran whipped his shirt toward her dresser, understanding that she was being playful. "Too tired to get undressed."

"But you're not too tired now."

He stared openly at her, naked in the middle of the room, and

Avra froze, knowing herself to be on the target side of a scope.

"No, not too tired now." It took two steps for him to crowd into her space, tuck his thumbs into her collarbone, slide his palms down over her breasts, across her peaked and sensitive nipples, down to her waist, and dig his fingernails into the soft flesh on either side of her hips. "Get on the bed."

"I have condoms," she prompted.

"I brought some with me."

"Yes, but I thought about you when I bought mine."

Kieran's face flamed, flexed into a series of hard lines, and Avra felt herself glow with the pride of having rattled him. "Where?"

"Desk drawer."

When he opened it, her vibrator was next to the box, charging. Kieran retrieved it, holding the thick wand in his hand and testing the weight as if it were a baseball bat, or a weapon. Avra pictured Aragorn unsheathing Andúril, mentally corrected the image to Samwise and Sting in the battle against Shelob, per Kieran's stated preference, and had to resist the laugh bubbling up from her toes.

"I've never used one of these."

Avra was dazed, smitten with the moment. "I'll show you how."

He handed Avra the wand and she tucked it next to her pillow before settling back onto the bed, her legs spread in clear invitation.

Kieran took his time fucking her, tucking one of Avra's legs over his shoulder so that she was split apart, and then lifting the other. He rolled her onto her side and spooned up behind her, biting a hot line across the back of her neck, licking the skin beneath her ear again and again until she was whimpering into the corner of the pillowcase and grinding the heel of her hand over her clit.

"No." He grabbed her wrist, held her hand away, and fucked into her slowly, infuriatingly slowly. "You said you'd show me."

"You want to see what I do when I'm alone?"

"I want to do it to you," he corrected, possessively.

"Hand me the vibrator, then."

"Yeah." Kieran's breath hit her throat on the *h* and Avra's shoulders erupted in goosebumps. "You told me in that bookshop that you never enter a bedroom without one of these," he remembered.

"I don't."

"*We* didn't use one the first time."

"Yet another way you've been an exception to my rules." Avra could practically feel the smugness on Kieran's face.

"You like it better with, though, right?"

"Yes," Avra said as Kieran fucked her languidly, and she pressed her thumb into the power button. The vibrator rumbled as it switched on, the sound low and insistent. "I think you'll like it better, too."

"Which position is best?" He was speaking into her ear, and Avra tried to inscribe the sensation, commit it to memory.

"It works with any, really, but I like it best on my stomach."

Kieran flipped her without difficulty, and Avra folded her left leg so she could fit the vibrator underneath her body. "It's easier if I hold it this way, but I'll show you how to use it on me later, if you want."

Kieran was already lining up his cock, sliding into her again, and Avra made a purring, satisfied noise before pressing the head of the vibrator against her clit. The sensation was sweet and immediate. Pleasure swam enticingly along her limbs. Her pelvic floor tightened as the vibrations hummed across her vulva, and Kieran swore behind her. He was sweating. She could feel the slickness of his chest against her back, his knees on either side of her thighs. One of his hands was flat against her spine, pressing her down. The other was in her hair. He turned her head to the side, worshipful and deliberate, so he could watch her face.

"I can feel it." His voice was tight, surprised.

"Good, right?" she said, gloating. Kieran responded with a rough thrust, and another, and another, driving her into the mattress. Her bed frame was starting to creak threateningly. Avra was certain the people who shared her wall could hear them.

"I want to watch you come like this."

"Where the fuck did you get such a mouth?" she asked, wanting to encourage him, wanting to play.

"Like I could even compete with you."

"You feel so good like that. I love feeling you inside me, pushing into me over and over. Every time you press me down against the vibrator—" As Avra spoke, Kieran punctuated her words with deep, intentional thrusts, and leaned down so his mouth was against the back of her ear again. Avra writhed. "It's amazing."

"It's intense. I didn't know—" Kieran sounded drunk, eradicated.

Avra grinned. "Do you like it?"

"Fuck, yeah. *Yes.* I can't believe I've never done this before."

"Welcome to the wonderful world of vibrator-accompanied fucking," Avra trilled. Kieran grabbed the back of her neck at her subtle display of sexual snobbery, but she could tell he was smiling.

"Will you be able to come like this?" Kieran's question lapped against her cheek, and Avra wanted him to talk to her like this for hours, just fuck her slowly and ask whether she would be able to come. Tell her not to, maybe. Tell her to wait for him. Make her hover on the edge like that, before tumbling over.

"If you keep going, yes. Yes. Just take your time."

"I'm not sure how long I'll last."

"That's okay," Avra said. She reached up with the hand not holding the vibrator and braced herself against the wall so she could press back into each of Kieran's thrusts. "I'm not sure how long I'll last either." Avra's pleasure was building, low in her belly and up her thighs, her clit pulsing, shock waves pulling her toward her orgasm, sensation sparking along the base of her spine. Her body was tightening, squeezing Kieran's cock as if trying to keep him inside, and Kieran was moaning low in his throat, breath hot and ragged against Avra's ear.

"I'm not going to come until you do."

"Good boy."

"And then I want you to show me how to use the vibrator on you."

"I promise." Blessed, like so many women, with the briefest of refractory periods, Avra knew she'd be ready for more within minutes.

"Fuck, you're hot like this."

Avra's eyes were closed while Kieran watched her. She could feel the warmth high on her cheeks, her lips were parted, mouth watering, and Kieran released her hair to run his fingers over her chin, the corner of her lips, her teeth. She licked them, tonguing the pads of his fingertips, wrapping the slick silk of her mouth around his index finger and sucking lightly. Kieran groaned. He pressed another finger into Avra's open mouth, another, sliding them against her tongue, the insides of her cheeks, while Avra whimpered and stayed open. He was fucking her pussy and her mouth. Filling her. Making her take it. There was spit sliding down her chin. She could feel his slippery thumb smearing a warm line along her jaw. When he finally pulled his hand away, Kieran licked his own fingers next to Avra's cheek. She was beside herself.

"I can't wait to do that," Avra said, and Kieran didn't need to ask her to clarify.

"Really?"

"I've wanted to suck you off for a long time."

Kieran shook his head in amazement more than disbelief. "God, you're serious, aren't you?"

"Yes. My mouth gets so wet every time I think about it. Like,

I actually start drooling. I want you to fuck my face, like you said, while you kneel over me."

The noise that came from Kieran wasn't human. "You can't talk like that when I'm trying to wait for you."

Avra laughed again, joy breaking like sunshine over the bed. They were bantering while Kieran fucked her, his fingers covered in spit from both of their mouths, his cock deep inside her body, and she was going to come like this, with his voice petting her ear and his sweat dripping onto her shoulder. She was going to come with him trying to hold himself back, feeling the hum of her vibrator around his cock with every frantic thrust.

"I'm getting so close," Avra warned.

"I want you to come, but—"

"I'm getting *really* close."

"Wait a second. Just a second." Kieran sped up his movements, the hand that was on her back now grabbing roughly at her hip, his weight braced against his elbow and pinning her down.

"Kieran, I can't—"

"Wait for me," he murmured, earnest and soft, encouraging, right against her skin. Like he had read her mind, like they understood this power exchange and agreed to hang in the balance together, giving, taking.

"Okay. Okay." Avra was gulping in breaths, trying to hold off, grasping the edge of something wild and bright as a lightning bolt.

"Now, say please."

She might have dreamed it, made it real, fantasy unfurling itself across their paired, tormented bodies.

"What?" She wanted to hear it again.

Kieran moaned urgently into her ear, and Avra didn't think she could get any wetter, spread her legs any wider, didn't think she could feel this good.

"Say please."

"I— Oh god . . ."

"I want you to be begging when you come." His voice was all gravel, all silver.

"Jesus Christ."

"I mean it." Kieran insisted, wretched and ominous. Avra obeyed without further thought.

"God, *please*." It spilled from her mouth like wine. "Fuck, please. I want to come on your cock. Kieran. Kieran. I want to come while you're fucking me."

"How badly?" This was impossible. Unreal.

"I need to. I'm so close. I need to." Avra was almost crying. "I want—I need—fuck."

"Say it again."

"Please."

"Again."

"Please. *Please*. Let me come on your cock. Let me come while you're inside me. Fuck me through it, please. Kieran, I'm begging— I need—I need—fuck. *Fuck*. I don't know if I can stop. I don't know if I can wait." Avra knew she was babbling. Knew she was carnage, disaster. She sounded strung out and pleading, voice raising in pitch, tenor off and trembling. If she took one more deep breath, if she lost focus for even a moment, she would come.

"Now, then," Kieran murmured, conceding. "Now. I want to feel you." His voice was cracking and low, frantic, and Avra knew he was shattering into orgasm, too. Knew he had made her wait so they could come at the same time, symmetries of pleasure blooming between them, synchronicity of delight, reward sugar-sharp and victorious. Avra's orgasm rolled over her. Blood rushed in her ears and her heart pounded so ferociously, she could feel her pulse in her clit, in her thighs, across her lower back. As Kieran moaned, sound dragged along by his own orgasm, Avra swore she could feel his cock spasm inside her, feel it jump, warmth spilling into the condom, which he gripped from the base even as he was rocked by the tempest they had summoned, the gale they had made.

Kieran's snapping hips slowed and stuttered as he gasped and made soothing sounds against Avra's temple. When he rolled gently off of Avra, his sticky chest separated audibly from her back and shoulders.

One minute passed. Another. Another.

"Goddamn," Kieran said, like, *We did it again.* Like, *It wasn't a fluke.*

"Yes," Avra confirmed, and waited for full sensation to revisit her tingling, heavy limbs. After several deep breaths, she turned to look at Kieran, who was still watching her face, his eyes wide open, expression stricken, once more, by whatever magic made this possible. They were each grinning, sharing in the absurdity, the fucking joke.

"You made me feel better," Kieran declared, a clever recall.

"With my pussy," Avra quipped back, and Kieran snorted, recognized the parallel humor, the mutual understanding, the building of something heady and persistent. The honesty came from his chest—for once, Avra thought.

"I have never wanted to fuck a woman the way I want to fuck you."

"I know," Avra said, both flattered and noting his specificity. The minutes passed slowly, and then gathered speed. As her sweat began to cool, Avra shimmied across the bed to kiss Kieran. She wanted something soft, something warm and permanent. Wanted to steal the heat from his skin and wear it as her coronation mantle. At the now-familiar taste, she hummed, dizzy and satisfied. Kieran smiled widely enough that Avra thought several times she might have been kissing only teeth. Eventually, they separated.

"Okay," he said, "all right. Now show me what you like when you use the vibrator."

"Say please."

"Pretty please," Kieran replied, deadpan.

"I'm going to," Avra said, stretching both arms over her head and rolling onto her back.

"You are?"

"I am. In a minute."

CHAPTER 13

MAY 2012

Later that day, Avra broached the topic she had been waiting to broach since walking Kieran to her dorm. She waited until he was well-fed, a strategy for man-management she had learned in high school.

"We should go to a club tonight. If you want."

"A club?" He sounded sated and lenient.

"A gay club."

Kieran's mouth wobbled. "A *gay* club."

"There's one downtown," Avra began, quickly explaining. "Nobody will know you. And it's dark, and there are pretty boys who dance on bar tops, and I could do you up all fancy."

Kieran had his head in Avra's lap again, and she was twisting a lock of his hair into one perfect honeyed ringlet. "What do you mean, 'fancy'?"

"I mean I think you'd look just beautiful in some glitter."

". . . Yeah," Kieran said, after a moment of consideration.

"Yeah?"

"Yeah." Right, then.

"Did you bring anything remotely acceptable for a club?"

"Honestly? I really wouldn't know."

"The jeans you wore yesterday could do, but I think you need a sluttier shirt."

Kieran grabbed a pillow off of Avra's bed and hit her in the face with it, lightly. She could have blocked it. Instead, she welcomed his goofy faux resistance. It was part of their game.

"Guess I'll just borrow something of yours, then," he said. *Cheeky.*

A few hours later, Kieran was in a pair of dark-wash jeans, white sneakers, and a tank-top of Nico's that Avra had liberated from Ellie's closet. Avra had to admit, watching Kieran's shoulders shift as he checked the ensemble in the mirror, that it really wouldn't matter what he wore. He looked like a closeted jock, nervous and twitchy and gorgeous and built like a D1 athlete, about to step into a queer space for the first time: the wet dream of aggressive men seeking a challenge. His naivete was written into each stiffer-than-usual fillet of his body. He might as well have had "fresh meat" stamped across his aquiline cheekbones.

"Good?" Kieran prompted anxiously.

"I'm going to be an insufficient bodyguard tonight, you must know."

"I don't need a bodyguard."

"Sure thing, Sparky." She didn't say, *You really might, looking like that.*

"You ready to head, or . . . ?"

"One more thing." Avra grabbed her makeup bag from the closet and shooed Kieran into her desk chair. She straddled his legs with the traditional confidence of a queer girl and her gay bestie, though this had never been their dynamic and it didn't quite suit them. She was too aware of his thighs under hers, too aware of the heat from his throat. "I'm going to doll you up a little."

"I'm all set, actually."

"Just a little." It was not a negotiation. Kieran sat still and obedient as Avra rooted through her bag, pulling out palettes and pens. He allowed her to settle into his lap, brush highlighter over the swell of his cheeks and his brow line, glide a flavored Chapstick over his lips. Strawberry. On impulse, she leaned forward and licked. Kieran caught her mouth, and they kissed slowly for a moment before she pulled away.

"Don't distract me," Avra scolded mildly.

"You started it!"

She applied another layer of the Chapstick, and resisted the urge to tug Kieran's shirt off, to crawl back onto the bed, and to keep him to herself for another night, another few hours. When she pulled the slim black eyeliner tube out of the bag, Kieran shook his head, but Avra—used to ignoring his protestations, willing to push further than he would typically license—gripped his chin in her left hand, digging her thumb and fingertip into the cut line of his jaw. "Hold still and behave yourself or you'll ruin all of my nice work and you won't look sexy, you'll just look a mess."

Kieran didn't speak, and when the kohl black had smudged across his lash line, he appeared cabaret-stage-ready. His eyes were enormous. They watered as he endeavored to hold them open.

"You are a pretty, pretty man," Avra cooed.

"I feel fucking ridiculous, Av."

"Call me Av again."

Kieran kissed her wrist, rolled his eyes toward the ceiling, and settled one palm against the front of her ribs. Avra licked his nose.

"Av."

"So we've arrived at pet names, then?"

He stood, and Avra stumbled backwards, one step, two steps.

"This is probably a bad idea," Kieran said, suddenly just like a grade-school kid staring down a pack of cigarettes. Under his shimmer and ink hovered something green.

"Kieran. Have you ever been to a queer community space?"

"No."

"Have you ever spent time around a group of gay men?"

"A group?" He thought for a second. "No."

"Have you ever let your guard down, even one time, in your exhaustingly limited life?"

"Why do you talk about my life like that? Why do you assume I've never done anything?"

"Because you haven't," Avra said, certain. Kieran looked toward the window, over the bedspread, toward the door. This was starting to feel the crummy kind of familiar. "Let's just go." Avra tugged her skirt up over her stomach, gave herself a quick review in the mirror, and continued to determinedly disregard the discomfort on Kieran's face, the hesitancy. She wouldn't enable his cowardice. She wouldn't conspire toward his oppression. She wouldn't submit to his insidious self-loathing. He did that all well enough on his own.

"Okay."

When they arrived at the club and entered the flashing, pounding, gyrating haven, it was just past eleven. Avra ordered cocktails with tequila, and Kieran hovered behind her like a Doberman, glowering and long-limbed and doing his best imitation of intimidation. It was wholly unconvincing. The bartender said something about "new blood," and Kieran stared at the floor.

"Go easy," Avra said, smiling, "he's *shy*," and the bartender—cute, in a common, scruffy way—winked. Kieran twitched.

By Avra's third tequila cocktail, the night was sliding by her like the view out a car window, everything hazy and streaked around the edges. She could see the club lights even when she closed her eyes, which she tried not to do, because watching Kieran lit a slow-burning satisfaction in her middle. He was outpacing her nearly three drinks to one, chasing bravery but not his shots. There was a spot of sweat on the lower back of his tank, the warping lights were painting him green then yellow then orange then red, and his hands were up, light glancing off his palms—a pair of fluttering suncatchers. It had only taken about two hours of drinks and coaxing and modeling confidence before Kieran had succumbed to Avra's influence. He was—magnificently, gloriously—wasted. Messy, but so pretty with it, and loosely holding something like joy in his body. She thought if she kissed him, he'd taste like triumph, but this was not the place.

Avra didn't touch Kieran while he danced, just moved her body in undulating waves and tossed her arms into the air and let all the nearby women drag their hands across her shoulders and waist and felt the *pump pump* of heavy bass up through the soles of her stompy boots.

They dragged each other on and off the dance floor, and back to the bar, and back to the floor, then back to the bar. Men approached Kieran over and over again, and he held eye contact while shaking his head, twisted away from their hands if they reached out. Avra thought a few of them might have a shot, but Kieran seemed to quell under the weight of actual possibility, or imagined expectations, and each boy eventually shimmied away. Avra stepped in exasperatedly when a puppyish guy with an Eiffel Tower tattoo on his left biceps tried for a second and then a third time. The thrice-rebuffed boy rolled his eyes before returning to a pack of shrugging friends who had watched his failed attempts from across the dance floor. Kieran gave Avra a look that said, quite plainly, *Thank God.*

"I'm going to tell you something." Avra had to yell over the music.

"What?"

"I used to fantasize about this."

Kieran's smile bloomed slowly, on a several-second lag. "About what?"

"About bringing you to a club, setting you up with some good-looking dude in a dark corner, and watching you finally kiss boys."

Kieran didn't answer, just guffawed toward the ceiling, took a step toward Avra, and rested his elbows on her shoulders. His dancing didn't quite meet the tempo of the bass, and matching his inconsistent sway felt to Avra like trying to share a trampoline, the mesh rising up in the wrong time to meet her feet, her knees wobbling out of rhythm.

"What did the boys look like, when you imagined it?" Kieran shouted back. The heat from their bodies hovered thickly around them. Sweat was curling the little hairs on the back of Avra's neck, her Jewish ancestry looping it into softly frizzing ringlets.

"They were a bit smaller than you, I guess. Shorter, stockier, longer hair, bigger arms. Nice eyelashes. I don't know why! They always had these thick, long eyelashes."

Kieran brought his head close to her face so she could detail the image into the pink shell of his ear.

"And what happened?"

"Mostly you'd make out, and I'd stand guard." She didn't say *I'd keep you safe*, but that's what she meant.

"Seems unlike you to just stand and watch."

"Well, no. Sometimes I'd tell you what to do."

"Like what?"

"Like, kiss him harder, or back him up against the wall, or I'd tell the guys they should suck you off." She felt Kieran's grin against the side of her cheek. Someone walked by and sloshed their drink.

Droplets hit Avra's forearm, the strip of skin showing below Kieran's tank. The fabric was tacky from heat. Avra could feel it riding up along his back. And then there was another voice.

"Want to dance?" Nasally, loud, heavy breath smelling of Jägermeister in both their faces. The new man tugged Avra back from Kieran, whose lack of sobriety was generously accompanied by a matching lack of coordination. Kieran lurched forward as Avra was pulled away, and his hand caught the shoulder of the speaker: tall, bronzed, muscular, with a buzz cut. He'd have looked military if not for the stark glint of a nipple ring through his mesh top and the neon strip of his briefs—an advertisement, a welcome sign—above his low-slung jeans. Designer, Avra was sure. He was handsome, glitter-club royalty, masculine enough to make the twinks fluttery, big enough but too clean-cut to meet the definition of a bear. Avra could smell the stereotype-defying entitlement rolling off of him as he gave Kieran the up-down, before cupping the back of Kieran's neck and pulling him forward, fitting one of his thighs between Kieran's legs. It was such a familiar move, expertly executed in seconds, that Kieran was still adjusting his balance when the stranger started his slow grind.

"My ffffriend," Kieran slurred, gesturing toward Avra.

"I'm okay, dance if you want to," she tried to reassure him. Club King was undeterred.

"No shortage of pussy in here tonight, she'll be okay."

Avra hated that, the way gay men could be just as sexist, the reduction of queer women to "pussy"; the dismissal, as if Kieran couldn't possibly prefer someone else's company. She decided, emphatically, that she did not like Club King, who didn't seem to notice or care that Kieran's drunkenness was melting his limbs, that his eyes were seeking out Avra. She felt the thrill of threat, the proactive urge to sober up, as Kieran was marionetted. His joints looked loose and pliable as the bigger man looped an arm around his back and mashed him forward, chest to chest. His mouth was on Kieran's neck in a second, and he was whispering things that Avra couldn't hear while Kieran's nostrils flared like a horse mid-race. Avra watched the panic melt to a laugh, and then jump up again as the stranger spoke.

Kieran's head was rolling sickly, his pupils contracting, one of his hands reaching up between his own chest and the stranger's, and the room was turning slowly, and Avra was being jostled by warm bodies, damp clothing. The floor was sticky. Someone else's hair whipped close by and hit her in the mouth. She spat. She felt a little diamond of anger crystallize between her eyebrows as Club King grabbed Kieran's wrist and tried to bring it around his own back.

"Take it easy, guy!" she shouted toward his shoulder, over the pulse, the inattentive beat. When he didn't respond, Avra reached up to jostle the hock of beef that was his shoulder. Rather than respond, Club King slunk around Kieran with all the predation of a jaguar, so they were both facing Avra, Kieran's face wild and over-whelmed, Club King's dark eyes narrowed to you're-bothering-me slits. Avra was too tipsy to select her words with care. "Go slow, is all. He's *ne-ew*." She hiccuped halfway through, and thought it rather softened her point.

"I can go slow," King replied, one arm around Kieran's chest, the other hand dragging from his opposite shoulder down along his front, palm along Kieran's belly, over his hip, lower, and then Kieran was bucking forward and back, away from the hands, and grabbing for Avra like she was a lifeline.

His momentum took her through the throng of sinuous bodies, across the floor tacky with trodden cocktails, past the blacktop bar and the scruffy winking bartender, and out into the cold spring night. The fresh air hit Avra's face—a tonic, the relief of an open fridge door in a midsummer swamp—and her ears rang with tinnitus as the sounds of the club were muffled behind them.

"Very stealthy escape—" she began, gulping in the evening, a sweatless chill coming off the concrete, but Kieran was already bent over a streetside trash bin, vomiting spectacularly, shoulders shaking with what could have been fear, or relief, or something else.

When they dragged themselves back into Avra's dorm (she dropped her key card twice on the attempted entry, swore, apologized, tried again, and considered just sitting on the front steps for a moment while Kieran settled a protective arm around his stomach, as if he could hold his sick), Ellie was there. She yelped and sat up abruptly when Avra flipped on the lights, and Kieran jumped wretchedly himself before making a hasty exit to the bathroom. He didn't even say hello.

"I'm sorry," Ellie hissed, shielding her eyes with both hands as she flopped back down. "I'm sorry, I know you wanted the room. But I had this *stupid* fight with Nico, and—"

"It's all right," Avra whispered, flipping the light off and walking across the room to reach the desk lamp instead.

"I'm really sorry."

"I know, it's okay. Go back to sleep."

Ellie turned onto her side and pulled her hands from her eyes. She glanced toward the door, which was cracked open. Avra thought she could hear the wet, gagging sounds of Kieran throwing up again from the bathroom down the hall. "Obviously there's nothing sexy going on tonight anyway."

"So, that's him, huh?" Ellie asked. It sounded like "This is what all the fuss is about?" to Avra, who was tired and on the descending branch of her intoxication and moderately nauseous herself, with a threatening headache.

"Yes," Avra replied. Firm, one syllable.

"Is he okay?" They were listening to him puke.

"He drank too much," Avra said, pulling her sweaty hair into a bun and settling a clip over it. The prongs bit the knot into place. Ellie shrugged as if to say *What can you do?* before turning onto her back again and closing her eyes. Avra looked toward the clock on Ellie's dresser—2:23 a.m.—and heard the toilet across the hall flush. At 2:26, she grabbed a set of towels from the closet and a small green bottle of shampoo, rifled through Kieran's duffel for his toiletries, and carried her bundle to the bathroom door. She knocked twice before trying the handle. Locked.

"It's me," Avra stage-whispered.

"Unffff," came Kieran's pitiful reply. The heavy sounds of someone dragging themselves off the floor muddled through the thick wood.

"Open up." Avra knocked again, and heard the metallic slide of the deadbolt.

"'S open." Kieran took a few steps back as Avra came in. He leaned over the sink and turned on the cold tap. "Too much tequila," he announced, trying to bend far enough forward to fit his mouth beneath the faucet. He steadied himself with a flat palm against the counter and seemed to reconsider his strategy, instead cupping his other hand beneath the water. Kieran sipped, swished, and spit. "I feel like garbage. It is too early for me to feel like this much garbage."

"I brought towels," Avra said, as if this could fix things, before piling her bundle onto the counter and beginning to roll her skirt down over her thighs.

"Why are you getting undressed?" Kieran sounded so confused that Avra couldn't help but laugh. She was sobering up much more quickly than he was.

"I'm not trying to seduce you, I swear."

Kieran looked suspiciously over at her but waited.

"Every time I feel like shit," Avra said, pulling off her top, "I sit on the floor of the shower, and I turn up the hot water, and I try to drink a little of it at a time."

"That is so weird."

"You need to hydrate," Avra insisted, "and cold water can be a shock to your belly. I don't know why, but sitting on the floor of a hot shower always works for me."

Kieran was trying to open the top button of his jeans, but his fingers had all the dexterity of kielbasa, and Avra moved forward to help him. He put his hands on her shoulders while she dragged the denim down his thighs and he stepped heavily out of each hollow leg.

"I'm going to help you rinse off," Avra said, "and I'll wash your hair." She pointed toward the green bottle of tea-tree shampoo on the counter. "The smell will help with the nausea."

"Always so prepared," Kieran said, lifting his foot clumsily again so Avra could help pull off a sock. It was like taking care of a small boy. His forlorn pout said, "I drank too much and threw up," the way the crumpled face of a six-year-old might say, "I ate too many cookies and threw up." It was pitiful, and darling.

"I've got you." Avra worked the tank up over his armpits and past Kieran's mussed and sweat-salty hair.

As promised, Avra turned the water as hot as she thought Kieran could stand and crowded him under the spray. When he sat, she kneeled behind him and worked the minty shampoo into a lather, told him to take deep breaths, and combed the suds through his hair with the tips of her fingers. She moved as predictably as she could so as not to provoke the nausea. The water beat around them, a steaming maelstrom. Once his locks were fully rinsed, Avra instructed Kieran to open his mouth like he would to catch snowflakes and take small sips. She coached a dripping Kieran, still seated on the shower floor, into brushing his teeth, and could tell afterward how proud he was that he hadn't thrown up again, because he said so. Twice.

A little past three a.m., Avra toweled him off and herded him back toward the room. Kieran was too tired to speak, except to mutter a spent and earnest "Thank you" when Avra pulled her own bathrobe out of the closet and fitted each of his arms tenderly into a sleeve. She rubbed a makeup remover wipe across his closed eyes to smudge away the leftover kohl, and Kieran sighed gratefully. She dabbed peppermint oil gently beneath Kieran's nose with a cotton swab, and warned him that it might burn his skin a bit but that the smell would help settle his stomach. She said all this in soothing, parental whispers, half hoping that Ellie was awake to catch this moment of affection. Avra curled up against Kieran's side in a set of soft pajamas and spoke soothingly until he began to snore. He tilted unconsciously toward her, his own body outrageously swaddled in Avra's too-short bathrobe. The two shared a single pillow. When Avra followed Kieran into sleep, her breath slowed to match his. Their slumber party pinkies linked reassuringly in front of their near-kissing mouths. Their wet hair tangled together like lovers, woven locks soaking merrily through Avra's pillowcase.

Kieran wasn't talkative the next day.

Embarrassed, Avra texted Ellie when Kieran barely mustered a greeting. Ellie raised an eyebrow at Avra across the room, but didn't press. It was awkward, Avra trying to facilitate a conversation with Kieran—hungover, intermittently rubbing his palms against his temples—and Ellie, whose face was puffy from interrupted sleep, her mood slanted from her argument with Nico. As Kieran maintained his terse quiet, Avra's stomach coiled with the whiplash from the prior night. How could she go from shampooing his hair, wrapping him in a bathrobe, whispering him to sleep, to attempting engagement with a wall? She was short with him, and trying not to be. Kieran must have sensed her disappointment; it raised his hackles the way it always did.

Kieran packed his bag mid-morning and walked out of the room without so much as a "Nice to meet you" in Ellie's direction. Avra's indignation coiled softly at the back of her wrists, tense from starting her day with closed fists. She pressed two fingers into her palm and watched her tendons shift.

They walked to his car in an agitated silence, not having discussed plans to see each other again. But if one of them was going to be brave, it would have to be Avra.

"Think you'll make it back for another visit?" She tried to lighten her tone. It bounced the landing, false and frenetic.

"Yeah, because this one was such a success." Sarcasm and bile. He didn't even look at her as he opened the passenger door and threw his duffel onto the seat.

Preferring a fight to a hasty goodbye, Avra tossed out a retort: "Whose fault is that?"

Kieran was shitty at saving face, went all toxic masculinity and hegemonic power trip, couldn't stand the vulnerability of feeling unwanted.

"Look," he began, hotly, "I just came here because I was sad, and I thought you might make me fucking feel better."

"You mean you thought *fucking me* would make you feel better."

He laughed, manic. "So what if I did?"

"Might have worked better if you weren't too wasted to get your dick out half the weekend." It was mean, she knew that. But Avra liked being mean sometimes.

"Dude, your roommate was right there. Great surprise company, by the way, and it's not like you made a move, either." Defensive, clamorous, casting around for someone or something to blame. They nursed their mutual sense of rejection, the mounting threat of isolation; watched their tenuous connection fray in the incursive light of a hungover morning.

"Maybe you should've gone home with that guy from the club then. *He* made a move." Avra knew she had stepped over the line. Kieran wasn't ready to be touched like that. If the target had been Karly and not Kieran, Avra might have called that jerk's behavior assaultive. She might have recognized his persistence as a violation. Instead, she weaponized it, callous and brutish, wanting Kieran to hurt.

He retaliated with force, seeking out an even plane of power, his expression angry and heartbroken and lost and a little reckless. It must have burned, Avra thought, that last night was his first time in a queer community space and it had been so overwhelming, invasive, volatile. It must have hurt him the way he always wanted to hurt Avra. Because he was kissing her again, more teeth than tongue, rough and unpredictable. His canines sank into her bottom lip, not a game, not a play, but a punishment, and Avra's hands rose automatically—an echo of Kieran's own body last night, across from Club King—to create some distance.

Kieran pushed her up against the wall of the parking garage, a block of cement in the middle of her back, and this wasn't fun. It was resentful, and bitter. Kieran could break bones. The gravel was cutting, cold against her skin. Avra tried to say as much.

"Kieran, hold on." He put a palm over her mouth; rattled her once, then twice, his other hand finding her shoulder, her waist. She bit the skin she could find, and he smeared his fingers along her jaw before kissing her again, pressing her even harder. He was bigger than she was.

"Kieran, stop."

"Shut up."

"You're hurting me."

He laughed again. The sound was a reckless little bark that Avra didn't recognize. There was a clink of warning ice in her throat.

"I thought you liked it when I hurt you," Kieran rejoined. Acknowledgment slit a sharp thrill into Avra's belly.

"I think I'm bleeding, stop." Rock scraped the waistband of her jeans. There was no space to move, her lip stung from the bite, her palms tried to find purchase against Kieran, who was strong, stronger than she thought. It was noon on a Sunday. The parking garage was empty.

"Say it again—tell me to stop, and I'll stop." He kissed her, bit her. "Tell me to stop, and I'll stop. Tell me to stop, Avra. Tell me to . . ." He was saying it against her mouth, repeating it like a mantra, like a prayer, gripping one wrist fiercely in his hand, fingers pressed into her pulse point, teeth dragging down along her throat. Her skin would be red. She flexed the hand still held in the cuff of his fingers. Brought her other hand to the back of his neck and grasped his hair in her small fist.

"STOP it, Kieran." She pulled fiercely, unexpectedly, and he staggered backwards, following her hand.

Several strands of hair fell between them like blades of grass when she opened her palm.

Kieran was panting, a smear of blood from her own mouth, Avra guessed, stark against his chin. "God, what the fuck is wrong with you?" Avra knew she sounded harsh, knew her voice was raised, and didn't care. Kieran reached around the back of his head, ran his palm over the stinging spot, and stared at Avra as if he couldn't see her at all.

He reached for her after a moment of pale contemplation.

"Let me," Kieran said. The note of pleading in his voice was pitiful. Another day, Avra might have softened, might have thought him sweet and helpless. But her mouth tasted like copper, and she could feel a trespassing bruise rising against the skin of her left lower back.

Kieran moved slowly toward Avra. His arms, starkly gentled compared to the minute before, twisted into meandering vines, hands easy, like he could make them safe, make them threatless. When Avra remained still, Kieran held her face, kissed her eyelids, the tops of her cheeks, each kiss landing like daisies, like the apologies that he didn't know how to give. It was deplorable. Avra stood for a moment, allowing Kieran to try, willing him to soothe her, but the anger rose like a snake when her lip and back continued to hurt. Palms open and flat against Kieran's chest, she shoved him away again.

"Enough."

Kieran's hands shook as they ran through his hair, as he struggled to gain advantage, as he neglected to muster an apology. Avra watched the flush on his cheeks waver between humiliation and regret. He couldn't look her in the eye. "I don't even know why I came here." He interrogated their connection, minimized it, while Avra tried and failed to feel bad for him, while her mouth and body ached.

"Let's make this your last visit then," she spat.

"That's fine."

"Do you even fucking care, Kieran? Can't you even fucking look at me?"

"I don't know what you want me to say! This was stupid. I don't know what I'm doing." It sounded true, and miserable. "I'm s—"

Avra raised a hand to silence him, and his apology was

amputated before she could investigate its genuineness.

"I'll go," Kieran promised, defeated.

"Go, then."

He did.

Avra walked out of the parking garage into the gray afternoon, the sunlessness matching her suddenly stormy mood. She brushed dirt, dead skin, and dust off her lower back, which smarted. She sucked her bleeding lip until the penny flavor faded. She kicked the ground, scoffed, and refused to let the shame of failed communication reach her. The undesired shadow of her course reading on the romantic lives of bisexual women swam to the forefront. The phrase *bidirectional violence* flipped itself over like a trick dolphin. She blanched. She blinked it away.

CHAPTER 14

MAY 2012

Ellie probably had every intention of being magnanimous about Kieran's poor impression, but when Avra returned to their room forlorn, moving gingerly, face shuttered and distant, her roommate's nostrils flared.

"Are you okay?"

"I'm fine," Avra lied. "Sore from the club."

"The club?"

"Drop it, El."

"Did he hurt you?"

"Of course not." So easy. It shouldn't be so easy.

"Don't you want to know what I think about him?"

"I already know that you're going to tell me," Avra sighed, expecting the worst.

"He didn't even *introduce* himself."

"He was drunk! ... And then hungover."

"He doesn't seem all that consistent with his effort."

"He drove to see me, didn't he?" Avra's defenses were scaffolding, reinforcing, insisting upon maintenance. Ellie took a deep breath like she was ramping up to say the thing she had been waiting to say, then said it.

"He seems . . . kind of broken, Av."

Avra barked a laugh, ignoring the twinge in her lower back. "Isn't everyone?"

"No," Ellie responded with force. "No, actually. *You're* not— you're smart, and so funny. Political, engaged, creative, queer, confident, and ambitious. You're going to go places, and you're going to *do thing*s, and he's a partially reformed bully from your hometown who only sometimes texts you and shows up to fuck and then throws up in your bathroom."

"Gee, thank you ever so much for the subtle, gentle, tender way you did that just now."

"Avra, *you don't even like men.*"

"You don't know anything." Avra rarely snapped at Ellie, and Ellie rarely handled it well.

"I will never understand why the gay-ass queen who helped me hang a Pride flag out of our window is letting herself get fucked around by this . . . this hetero hoop-bro."

"You don't know anything," Avra said again, finality and dismissal laced in her tone. Ellie gathered her bag in a huff and left for the library.

Avra sank into her obsession, a full week passing in a dissociative blizzard. May caressed the campus with rainbow fingers, trailing blossoms across the walkways, painting the grass an adolescent kelly green. Avra didn't smell anything. Her universe was monochromatic. Her bruise faded, and she missed it. She could roll over in bed without thinking about him. She thought about him anyway. She missed three classes just before her finals, and handed in assignments she'd have been embarrassed to submit one single month prior. She took edibles at five p.m. and let the evening subdue her, fog heavying her limbs, stomach full of dollar-store candy, her own lack of productivity bolstering the press of anxiety. She didn't hear from Kieran.

Ellie and Nico made up. They cuddled in that infuriating, self-aggrandizing way that only long-term couples could cuddle. Eight days into Avra's flattened, charcoal depression, the pair interrupted her blankness with matching worried expressions to ask if she'd want to find a summer apartment, because Nico's parents were overbearing, and Ellie couldn't stand to be without him for three whole months, and they could use an extra person to split rent. Avra weighed the balance of a lonely summer in the relative rurality of Ridgefield versus the shock of independence: graduating to a full-sized mattress (even if she kept it on the floor), making minimum wage at a local library or interning for some research professors.

Ellie hugged her when she said yes. She and Nico sent Avra silly memes and went on apartment tours and sat next to her as she swiped through the pictures.

"We liked the kitchen in that one," Nico said.

"And that little balcony was cute," Ellie agreed.

Avra thought about creatures that mate for life: swans, wolves, beavers, coyotes, foxes, field mice, marmosets. Even the vulture. Even the albatross.

After ten days of misery, her phone lit with promise.

hey

Despite Nico and Ellie's curious urging to see what Kieran wanted, and against every screaming impulse of her blood and throat and reward system, Avra ignored it. She would not swivel to attend to his every beck and call. She would not chase a ghost. Whatever this was, she could win. Instead of responding, she called

Naya, spoke in hushed and urgent tones into the mouthpiece, apologized for her impolite tendency to dredge up the past, and opened the door when Naya knocked. Ellie left the room without a word.

They fucked and it was decent. Avra came twice. She cried out gently while Naya curled two fingers inside her and swiped a hot, wet mouth over her clit. She kissed Naya gratefully, guided a silicone dildo into her own body, and did not picture Kieran's form above her, did not think about the sweat of his chest against her back, did not feel his tea-tree hair under her fingers.

Avra maintained a stony, determined silence through the last week and a half of the semester and into early summer. Her Intro Psych professor would call it "withdrawing access," and she imagined a set of parents refusing their darling child a predictable allowance. Her friends called it "manipulative," but never to her face. Avra thought of her behavior, privately, as abusive, but made her peace: She ruminated on his years of cruelty, on the splash of latte over the floors of Ridgefield High, on "dyke." He had earned this. Meanwhile, Avra passed her classes, despite retaining next to nothing. She left Kieran squirming on a hook, retribution for torment, and confusion, and her unacceptable distraction from women. Naya was between her thighs. She had to focus.

Avra was aware, somewhere, in the recesses of her ethical code, that she was justifying her own lack of availability—withholding the one queer safe haven this devastatingly beautiful, lost, sad, lonely, occasionally mean, and deeply closeted boy knew—in service of resistance to the kind of violence he could hardly perpetrate anymore. But the power was sweet, and seductive, and she couldn't quite give it up. She did crave vengeance; vengeance for making her want to fuck men. Vengeance for corrupting her queerness, which felt pure and true before him (Naya was beside her in bed—she had to focus).

Avra spent six glorious weeks lording her silence while Kieran texted her, and double texted (*hi* and *u awake?* and *im sorry* and *please say something*), and liked her Facebook posts at midnight, one a.m., four a.m. Satisfaction licked up her spine. She swiped through his new photos and did nothing. The first week of July, Avra put together an actual bedframe, began an eight-week internship at the advocacy center, and filled her living room with resilient plants. Ellie and Nico slept one room over. Her phone rang, an actual call.

His voice scraped, slurred, lacerated his words, and Avra knew he was very drunk, maybe too drunk to remember this tomorrow. He sounded as if someone had rolled an eighteen-wheeler over his resolve, over any sense of grace. He sounded, as Ellie had suggested, broken. Her chest cracked, fragile springtime ice at the foot of a glacier, no longer able to support the sinuous choreography, please, not one more pair of skates.

"Av? Avvvvra? Are you there?"

"Hi," into the phone, quiet and concerned, compassion flooding through a gap, a stupid vulnerability, a slit in the armor. The same pity, that hapless hound, which always got the best of her.

"I've missed yo-ou"—he coughed, burped—"I didn't know, I didn't—where'd you go?"

"I'm right here." Fuck.

"You are?" *Who's in control now?*

"I am, I'm here."

"Good." Kieran's laugh was a brook over pebbles, a force of nature, inevitable, relieved, gurgling and bursting. "Good. That's so good, Av. Av, will you come? Come and see me?"

What witch, what devil, could resist such a plea?

"Sure."

CHAPTER 15

JULY 2012

A few weeks later, Avra loaded a canvas Trader Joe's bag with her clothes, dodged Ellie and Nico on her way out of the apartment, and typed Kieran's summer address into her phone's map app. The drive to Kieran's place lasted an hour and forty-seven podcast-accompanied minutes. She checked the ETA every several seconds, and time passed with the callous nonchalance of a construct unable to empathize with the ache of missing someone who so recently bruised you against the concrete wall of a parking garage. Avra forgot how to take deep breaths. She missed an exit and had to double back. She did it again. She tried *three times* to talk herself out of the trip, while her big toe applied rebellious pressure to the accelerator and several farms passed in between a peppering of identical beige strip malls. The beauty of Western Massachusetts. She arrived at his apartment a bundle of rattlesnake nerves. She parallel parked and panted as if she'd dashed on foot over town lines, through zip codes. She examined the windows of a handsome three-story building, trying to guess which curtains were his.

Her finger on the doorbell might have snapped in half, might have sunk through the brick like a spade through sand, might have jabbed Kieran directly in the eye. He came to the door in a pair of sweatpants and a plain white T-shirt with several animal hairs stuck close to the collar. His face was shadowed, unshaven, his hair still damp from a shower. He smelled like pine, soapy and crisp. Avra opened her mouth to greet him but was met with the soft armpit of his shirt, his chin sharp against her forehead.

He was hugging her. She didn't register the sound of her bag hitting the floor. She barely registered the pain in her foot as the hard edge of her computer landed clumsily atop both of their toes.

"You came." His voice, a bird reformed after months as a bat.

His roommate, Braden, had a cat. Braden wore soft cardigans with leather pads on the elbows and color-matched leather loafers. He had three earrings and a messy bun pulled against the anchor of his neck. Avra liked him immediately. The cat was Xena. She was almost completely blind, with a breathy, bullet-train meow that seemed to zoom right past. Braden regaled Avra with a big-eyed recitation of the day Xena had wandered under the front steps of their first-year dormitory, "so pregnant. Like, very, very pregnant. And I just couldn't leave her out there! I was friends with the RA, anyway, Mason, and Mason has two cats at home, so he really *got it*, you know? And about a week later she had this whole big litter of kittens in a dog bed I set up under my dresser. Kieran was so cool about it, and he didn't have to, but he helped me clean up after them." Braden remembered the name of every one of the litter—Stacy, Orange, Tuukka, Khudo, Myers, and Mouse. They had been christened the Dorm Cats. He doled them out at the end of the semester in a kitten adoption ceremony, with each bundle traded (for, it seemed, weed and high-fives and promises of lifelong cat photos) to the "trustworthy" boys on the floor. Mason hadn't said a word. "But I knew he wouldn't—because of Mew and Two"

(Mason's cats, Avra gathered). As the conversation scurried, Avra warmed.

In no time at all, Braden herded Avra into a blotchy velvet chair in the living room—"We picked it up on the side of the road, but I doused it in *so much bleach*, I'm sure it's safe. Might still smell, though"—and tossed her a throw pillow, which she settled into her lap. She leaned forward on her elbows, tugged toward the gravity of Braden's startling earnestness. Kieran brought Avra's duffel bag into his room while Braden explained how Kieran and he had been paired in the freshman roommate lottery having both noted a preference for, "someone quiet. Which is unsurprising," Braden said conspiratorially, already behaving as though Avra was a fellow authority on Kieran, "with all those siblings." It was clear that only Braden had gotten what was promised in the deal. "And then the summer was coming, and I knew I could either send him home to share a bathroom with like a zillion people or keep him here to hang out with *meeee* and I'm so glad he said yes because otherwise I'd have to find *another* roommate to bless with my shower singing, which shouldn't be hard—I'm not terrible—but who has the time?" Avra shrugged indulgently and cast around the room for Kieran, who was hovering in the doorway of his bedroom as if unsure he should join them. His cheeks were pink. Braden, settled into a squishy, scratched-up leather couch, patted the space next to him, and Kieran trod obediently forward. Xena batted his shins with her small gray head, and leapt lightly onto his lap as soon as he sat down. "So how do you two know each other, then?" Braden was tucking his toes comfortably under Kieran's thigh. Kieran shifted automatically so his feet would have more room. Avra turned to butter.

"Ah, you mean he hasn't shared?" Avra asked archly. Kieran picked at the corner of a couch cushion and muttered something that sounded like "privacy" while Xena purred aggressively on his lap. Braden buried his toes further and rolled his eyes.

"He gives me no information, except moping for months and months until about, oh, three weeks ago. Say, *gee,* that's when you planned your trip to see us, isn't it?"

Kieran flicked his ankle. Braden grinned at Avra, who grinned back, disarmed.

"We met in high school, sort of," Avra explained, haltingly. "I mean, we grew up in the same hometown, but we didn't actually, like, *talk* until high school."

"But I thought Kieran was a piece of shit in high school."

Avra laughed loudly, and Kieran sank deeper into the cushions. Xena dug her claws into his sweatpants, a clear admonition: *Stay put.*

"He *was.* He absolutely was."

"So how did you two end up friends?" Braden was bopping along to an imaginary tune as he inquired.

"We didn't, really."

"We're friends," Kieran insisted, sotto voce.

"We are *now,*" Avra countered, as if it were that simple, "but in school we were more like . . . orbiting planets."

Braden nodded solemnly, as if he understood her from top to bottom, and then knocked sharply on the side of Kieran's head with his knuckles. "Tough nut to crack, eh?" He was ludicrous, and so charming. Avra thought she quite loved him already.

"Man, I should have known this was going to happen," Kieran was covering his face with two large hands over the top of Xena's fluffy back. The cat nuzzled against his elbows. Even through his disinclined display, Avra could tell Kieran was pleased.

"What, that we would get along?"

"Yeah, my two biggest bullies."

Avra wished she'd had water in her mouth, if only to spit it at him. "Pot, meet kettle."

"I *knew* it! I knew he was mean!"

"He was the worst." Avra appraised Kieran from across the coffee table, and he seemed poised on a precipice, waiting for the rest of her assessment. "But, he's getting better."

"Under your wise tutelage?"

"And, apparently, yours."

Braden's eyes sparkled proudly. It was just too much.

"Well, this is very cool, thanks to you both for the character development." Kieran said with a sarcastic salute. The evening skated easily with the three of them. Braden retrieved a trio of beers from the fridge and glasses of water ("Stay hydrated," he urged, as he placed them down on coasters in the shape of Illinois, Braden's home state). He guided them through the requisite conversations about majors, and summer jobs, and somehow around to his stepmother's subpar cooking, his well-above-par girlfriend, Victoria—Avra looked at Kieran as he said this—and his beloved improv troupe, which made sense.

"It was that or a capella," Braden admitted.

"I've known you for less than an hour and neither option surprises me."

"I'm taking that as a compliment."

"Oh, you should." Avra sipped the beer, mid-evening light glowing against the mouth of the bottle. Hops and lemon. Kieran had his long feet up on the coffee table.

"I'm bored out of my mind without them all summer."

"Hey." Kieran feigned reproach.

"Or, I mean, I would be, but I have such *excellent* roomie company, truly *wondrous* and just so darn *verbose*, *what* boredom, boredom *where*?" Braden leaned forward and planted a wet smack on Kieran's cheek. Kieran pushed him away, so absent ire that Xena barely shifted.

"You spend most of your time at Vic's anyway."

"Correct!" Braden confirmed, gingerly removing his feet from under Kieran and wiggling them back to full sensation. "Taking advantage of the NRE."

"New relationship energy," Kieran explained, as Braden stood. At the commotion, Xena exited Kieran's lap. She found a slat of sunlight on the hardwood and showed her belly to Braden as he crossed the room. He immediately dropped to pet her again; spineless or generous, Avra didn't care. "I'm heading there in a few, actually. Figured I'd leave you two to do whatever it is you do."

"Very subtle," Avra replied.

"Subtlety is not my forte," Braden insisted gravely, and Kieran scoffed on the couch. There was space beside him now. Avra could move closer. The couch looked almost too large. The two of them could fit shoulder to shoulder, laid flat.

"When will you be back?"

"I'll do my best not to interrupt anything." When Kieran just stared at him, Braden pivoted hastily toward real data: "I'm staying the night there, but I was thinking—group brunch tomorrow?" Avra's stomach tangled at the remarkable ease of this meeting, of the meeting Kieran should have had with Ellie and Nico, all together at her favorite corner diner: tater tots and omelets and hot coffee and repartee. "We'll call it a double date."

"Wow, you weren't kidding. Subtlety? Not your game." Avra kept her tone breezy, so Braden didn't feel chastised.

He pulled a brown messenger bag off the coat rack by the door and slung it over one shoulder before saying, with an exaggerated hip pop, "Honey, you should see the way I lose at poker."

"*Spectacularly,* I'm sure."

Braden winked, "See you cuties tomorrow." And then he was gone, the lock clicking behind him with finality. The air seemed to settle in his absence, the spiral dust aftermath of a whirling dervish.

"He is just—"

"A lot, I know," Kieran said, but Avra finished her thought with sugar beneath her tongue.

". . . darling. Absolutely darling. I like him."

"I like him, too."

"He's flamboyant. In a great way, I mean," Avra said quickly, because Kieran's eyebrow had twitched defensively. She wondered if he'd been put in the position to defend Braden before.

The momentary sobriety disappeared, and Kieran cleared his throat before saying, with forced insouciance, "He's bi."

"Oh?" Avra wanted Kieran to steer.

"He dated one of my teammates last year."

"Oh."

"They had to keep it on the down-low, because I don't think a bunch of the guys would have liked it, but you've met him now. How good do you think he is at down-low?"

"Really, truly not very."

"Isaac was pretty obvious, too, to be fair. Both of them were *wrecked* when it ended. Braden lost like fifteen pounds and Isaac was benched for over a week. Kept picking fights with the coach. Stupid stuff, you know. The kind of stuff you do when you're really fucked up about someone. Reckless, hurtful stuff." Kieran was rounding the corner of their conversation, heading down a new hallway, and Avra wanted to reassure him that it wasn't necessary.

"I know what you mean."

"I was a dick," he said heavily. "When I came to see you, I really wasn't—"

"It's okay." It was not okay.

"No, I really feel like I owe you some—"

"You don't owe me anything," Avra promised, although he did.

"Damn it, Avra."

She stared at his face, at the tight line of his mouth, the downcast of his eyes. He looked up and his spine was a kite string, taut, tethering him to the couch. "I'm trying to tell you something."

"All right."

"Braden doesn't know."

"Okay."

"They broke up, and Isaac came on to me." His face flamed magnificently.

"Shit."

"He was a mess, and the coach was all over him at practice. And Braden wasn't talking, or eating. And he came on to me after practice one day, and I just—" Kieran lifted his feet off the coffee table, tucking them under his body like he wanted to shrink. Avra moved toward him on autopilot, rising from the chair, stepping over a still-outstretched Xena, dropping into the spot next to Kieran on the couch.

"And you let him."

"No, not really." Kieran sniffed, rubbed his wrist across his nose. "I told him to fuck off, actually. Braden's my friend, you know." He shot a hard look at her, like she should expect better, and Avra tried to appear contrite. "I told him to fuck off," he said again. "I was kind of nasty about it, I think. I almost hit him. I was angry. I was out of— I was just so angry."

"But . . . but you *wanted* to let him?"

Kieran didn't answer.

"How many opportunities have you had, really, to be with men?" Avra asked. Kieran said nothing, but he shifted back into the couch cushions, and Avra went on. "You never really got to explore anything at all. I mean, I don't know how many men you've been with, if any, but I can't imagine it's *lots*, or that you were able to feel all that *safe* kissing guys, or holding hands with them. Certainly not where people could see. I remember how the boys would talk about you and Will, just barely touching each other. And, God, Ridgefield?" Avra whistled, the sound of an incoming missile. "Ridgefield is an absolute garbage fire for queer kids. You know that. And then you come to college, and you're supposed to have more freedom, more space, and the *first guy* who comes onto you is your best friend's ex?"

"Not quite the first," Kieran corrected.

"College Guy?"

"If that's what you want to call him."

"And that was bad?"

Kieran flinched. "That was bad too."

Avra was drawing conclusions. Cogs were clicking and firing and whirring and landing. "The Isaac thing—that was just before you came to visit, wasn't it?" She kept her tone pacifying, tranquil. Kieran nodded stiffly. "So your best friend's ex comes on to you, and you have to turn him down, and it's alarming and disappointing, so you come to see me, right?" Kieran stared at Avra. Avra stared back. "You come to see me, and I take you to a club— your *first real gay club*—and the guy who comes on to you winds up being a pushy fucking creep." Kieran was holding something fragile with his insides, doing his very best not to crack apart, to leak all over the couch. Avra scooted toward him and laid her head against his shoulder, the soft white of his T-shirt wrinkling beneath her ear. "I'm sorry," she said. "I'm sorry this hasn't been easier for you. I'm sorry that so many quintessential queer experiences have been—been denied, or stolen, or corrupted. That the foundation of your queerness has been so unsteady. It isn't fair."

When Kieran shrugged, Avra's head rose and fell. "You deserve better."

"I'm not sure what I deserve. I'm not even sure what I am, Av. I don't know if I—"

"You deserve better. We all do."

Kieran's arm wrapped around Avra, his palm pressed flat against her lower back. He pulled her into another bone-crushing hug, half on his lap. Avra coiled around him, armor, but also doorway, his bridge between worlds. When he pulled away, his grateful eyes were honeyed, bottomless pools. When they kissed, it was just the same.

CHAPTER 16

JULY 2012

They didn't make it to dinner. Kieran offered takeout sometime after eight thirty, halfway into an early episode of *Buffy* (when he agreed to watch the series pilot, Avra squeezed his cheeks in a frenzy of affection-aggression and kissed him full on the mouth). They were splayed across the couch, half-empty food containers strewn over the coffee table. Xena sniffed the air curiously, stalking around the foot of the table as if considering the consequences of theft. Avra's head was resting on Kieran's thigh, his sweatpants bunching beneath her right ear. On screen, the pretty blonde was killing evil things.

"Okay, but I have a question," Kieran said.

"You promised not to talk during the show," Avra scolded, but Kieran was twirling his fingers around the ringlets at the nape of her neck, and she was too comfortable to do more than gesture at the screen.

"It's *about* the show!"

"Well, that's fine, then." Placated, pleased.

"This is supposed to be canonically queer, right?" He sounded skeptical.

"Right."

"Who are the gay characters?"

Avra shook her head hard enough that her hair escaped Kieran's fingertips. "Nuh-uh, no, abso*lutely* not. No spoilers. You will patiently wait for season four like the rest of us."

"Don't tell me what to do," Kieran said. Avra smiled.

"Wait for season four," Avra insisted. Kieran huffed.

"What if we're not still hanging out four seasons from now."

"Then you'll watch on your own," Avra replied, calmly.

"No, I'm serious." A rotation in timbre, reproach.

"Don't be absurd."

"I didn't hear from you for months."

Avra reached for the remote, looked pointedly up at Kieran, and pressed pause. "I'm sorry about that."

"No, that's not what I—" Kieran let out a breath. "You were right, probably. I mean, not to talk to me, if you didn't want."

"Of course I wanted to. It *sucked* not talking to you."

"But you ignored all of my messages." His tone was bald, confrontational. Avra stared toward the screen, discomfited.

"Yes."

"Until I called you." Kieran's fingers had stilled in her hair. She pressed back against his hand in nonverbal encouragement.

"I was *playing it cool*."

"You were punishing me."

"That, too."

Kieran gripped her hair from the base of the neck, slowly curling his fingers into a fist. Gradual, subtle, painless pressure. Avra froze.

"You were punishing me for doing something like this."

"You were hurting me, then."

Kieran tightened his grip, and Avra could feel his hips shift, his thigh flexing beneath her head. The air was humming, suddenly, a crackle forming somewhere around Avra's earlobes, an awareness low in her belly.

"Am I hurting you now?"

"Not yet." A firmer grip, Avra's head pulled back so her throat was bared. Kieran trailed two fingers beneath her jaw, stroking the softer skin. Avra's mouth was open, her breath coming shorter, her head spun. Her scalp was starting to ache, in that way that promised tomorrow soreness.

"Now?"

"Harder," Avra suggested. When Kieran slackened his grip instead, Avra opened her eyes. She tried to mask her disappointment a second too late, but Kieran caught her expression. He smiled a wry, baffled smile.

"It's confusing," he said, earnestly, "that sometimes you like it when I hurt you, and sometimes you don't. I got confused last time, and I'm sorry."

"How about, in the future, you wait for me to tell you that you can hurt me."

Kieran shifted guiltily, disappointment on his own face now. He looked across the room, self-conscious. "Doesn't that kind of defeat the purpose?"

"Of what?"

"What we talked about, at your house. About us seeing what you can take." He flattened his palm over her throat, pressure on either side of her neck, and looked back down to gauge her reaction. Another hypothesis to test. Avra stopped breathing—not because her breath was actually *constricted*, not because she *couldn't* breathe if she wanted to, but because Kieran was asking her not to breathe. Checking if she would obey, encouraging her toward dizziness. *This* was submission, the acceptance of him wielding power, enough to alter her access to pleasure, to pain, to oxygen. Avra felt the blood in her face, the pulse beginning near her temples, before Kieran released the suggestive pressure. She took a deep breath. Kieran went on: "I like seeing what you'll let me do to you."

Avra was squirming. *This* was what she wanted from partners, always—a willingness to push, to measure and then calmly disregard her discomfort. A willingness to hurt her, a little or a lot. She didn't want to examine that too closely, preferred not to parse the origins of her masochism. Face flushed, chest visibly rising and falling, Avra took in deep, intentional breaths. "I like that, too."

Kieran gripped her hair again, tilted her head back, twisted her neck to the side so that she was forced to look up at him. She could feel the fabric of his sweatpants stretch beneath her head. He was hard.

"So, how do we keep getting to—to experiment with this?" He tightened his fist, pressed a palm over her throat, and Avra gasped at the constriction, the sting, deeper before, uncomfortable now, but good. Still so good. She kept herself pliant. She held his gaze. He went on: "Without me hurting you, like last time?"

"Safeword," Avra said simply, and it suddenly struck her that *failing* to establish a safeword earlier in this dynamic was probably a reckless oversight. Irresponsible. Negligent.

"Explain."

"We have an agreed-upon word that means 'stop.' That way I can still resist, if you want. If you like that," Avra offered. Kieran's jaw was hard, his lips slightly parted, and Avra knew what he liked, what he'd always liked: hurting her, surprising her. "I can tell you that it hurts, that it's too much. I can tell you that I don't think I can take it. I can even tell you to stop, or beg you to stop, and as long as I haven't used the safeword, you can force me around. You can ignore me. You can hurt me, or punish me."

Kieran's throat moved as he swallowed, nostrils flared as he nodded. "What's the word?"

"Well, I like the stoplight system, personally. You can check in with me when you need to, and if I'm fine, I'll say green. And vice versa, because sometimes I'll want to check in with you, to make sure you're okay. If this keeps going, we'll probably try some new things."

Kieran made a noise of agreement.

"And if I need you to slow down," Avra continued, shrugging unconcernedly, as if this were unlikely, "or to give me a little break, I'll say yellow. That's the cue that I'm approaching my limit, or that we should pause." She looked at him. "But if I say red, you stop. No question, no testing. I don't mean you slow down. I don't mean you switch it up. You just stop, immediately. Okay?"

Kieran hesitated for a moment, and Avra understood with a dark little thrill that he didn't love this option, didn't love that she could say "red" and he wouldn't be able to use his own confusion as a rationale for hurting her. Avra knew it because she didn't love this option either. It meant she might never see what Kieran would do to her, or know how far he wanted to push. She would be the impediment to that insight: her own discomfort, her own boundaries. She'd be responsible for her own pain, her own limits. It felt . . . cheap, somehow. But it was also smart. Smart, and safe, and necessary, even if it added a layer of disingenuity to whatever this was.

"Okay," Kieran confirmed.

"You know I might want to push you sometimes, too," Avra noted. "I wouldn't consider myself toppy, really. I'm not a domme. But I like you vulnerable."

Kieran's fist was sadistic in Avra's hair, reactionary, dissenting. He displayed her throat again while he scraped two fingernails over the pale skin of her collarbone. Her nerves sang. It hurt. *Green*, Avra thought. *Green, green, green.* She laughed. "I like to see what you can take too. In your own way."

"But it's my turn right now," Kieran stated, an observation, not an argument.

"It is, for now," Avra replied. Kieran's eyes were elsewhere, roving unpredictably, his mind clearly racing with all the things he could do to her. Avra could sense his cool beginning to splinter, his patience and composure fraying.

"I've wanted you in my room since you got here," Kieran said, eyes settling on his own fingernails scraping along Avra's pinkening skin. He watched them dig in harder, press deeper.

"Tell me to go to your room then." Something was fracturing, heaving itself apart.

"Look at me." Kieran's voice was laced with silver, the kind of glamorous arsenic you know to open your throat around. Avra looked, did as he said, and Kieran released her hair, cupped one hand behind her neck, and pulled her face toward him. She rose in a trance.

Kieran stared at her for a moment, held her up with one hand, and Avra reveled in the feeling of being small, of gratefully relinquishing her own control. Power exchange with Kieran was always brutal and blade-sharp and stunning. The retirement of Sisyphus. "Stay still," he instructed again. Kieran didn't kiss her, didn't lick into Avra's mouth the way she wanted, but pressed his lips against her jaw, her cheek, her forehead, his mouth open, inhaling like he wanted to taste her, steal her air, invade her space and raise a flag. "Okay," he said, shaking his own head, as if attempting some impossible earth landing. "Okay," he said again, and pressed Avra up to a seated position. "Avra." Her spine tingled, something lewd and ardent sweeping through her stomach. Kieran stood, and Avra swayed impatiently, waiting for what she knew would come. "Go to my room."

They helped each other undress this time.

Kieran had dark blue sheets, satin-striped, classier than Avra had expected, and she complimented them. "Not fratty at all."

"I'm full of surprises."

"Not really," Avra said, testing. Kieran tugged her shirt up over her head in a fluid motion. Avra's arms rose to follow, but Kieran wrapped the fabric around her wrists before her arms were free, clutching them in one large hand. A reprisal.

"You take that back." His grip was unyielding, pitiless.

"So proud of yourself," Avra retorted, aiming for bratty but landing somewhere in the realm of breathless.

"If I told you to keep your wrists together like that, would you do it?"

"Yes."

"If I told you to take off your underwear"—all that was left—"and get on the bed, would you do it?"

"Yes."

"What if I told you to crawl there?"

"Do you want me to crawl there?" Avra could feel the warmth in her own cheeks.

"I want to see you on your knees." He pulled her shirt off of her wrists. Avra held her arms aloft, wrists touching. Kieran's mouth twitched in approval. Not a smile. "You can lower your arms." She did. "I want you to kneel."

Avra was already sinking, anticipating the cool hardness of the wood floors against her shins.

The tiny internal war—obey, rebel—was tilting toward submission. Kieran hadn't done this with her before, and she wanted to listen, wanted him to know what it could be like when she listened. "Help me get these off," he decreed. Avra began working the drawstring of Kieran's sweatpants before he was done speaking.

"And look at me." Eager, always, for the opportunity to perform, she raised her chin, widened her eyes, and paused with her hands over Kieran's hip bones, her thumbs tucked into his waistband. She let her mouth slacken, licked her lips slowly so they were spit-shiny.

Kieran held his hands at his sides, carefully not touching her. He scrutinized her face, the wanton expression, shameless, inebriated. "What are you waiting for?"

Avra leaned forward, dragged her open mouth against the front of his sweatpants, like she had dreamed. She licked over the bulge, her demanding tongue leaving a dark, damp spot. Kieran made an inhuman noise, coarse and chaotic, before tugging his sweatpants and boxer briefs down.

He looked even better from this angle. He was hard, cock curved toward his belly, downy hair along the base, skin flushed pink along the shaft, and a needy kind of red at the tip.

Avra breathed against his skin, warm and ghosting contact, an intentional tease, while Kieran waited, impatience beginning to whirr and crunch. Avra stared at the glossy tip and felt the wetness of her own mouth like a demand, a craving.

"You told me before that you've wanted to suck me off," Kieran said, light mockery in his voice, a dare, while he watched Avra's eyes, hungry and roving.

"Yeah . . ." Her breath coasted along his sensitive skin. Avra's face was burning, her weight shifting in a soothing sway as she labored to hold herself back. Kieran tilted her face up again with a palm against her cheek. Her articulation, her envious vocabulary, was gone.

"I want your mouth." His thumb was pressed against her lower lip, smearing her spit the way he liked, already making her messy, and Avra nodded, feeling punch-drunk and whorish. She'd beg if he wanted her to. She half-hoped he'd make her.

"You can have it."

Kieran's head dropped back, his gaze trained toward the ceiling while his fingers found Avra's jaw. He squeezed her chin, rough, reactively, and Avra purred. "Say that again."

"You can fuck my mouth, if you want to."

"Ask me." He looked at her again, and Avra's mouth was so wet, her knees spreading against the hardwood, blood thrumming through her body in a ketamine rush.

"Fuck my mouth. Please," she added, for good measure, and Kieran tangled his hand in her hair. Avra opened her mouth wide, reception red, luxurious, and Kieran lined himself up, his eyes locked on her face.

Desire and shame twined helplessly along Avra's throat. She had wanted this, in spite of herself, for years. Wanted to know what he tasted like—what combination of salt, earth, grain, and heat. Her mouth was puddle-slick, viciously warm, and Kieran pushed forward, hanging on to his control with steely resolve. The head of his cock slid wetly along the roof of her mouth, against the back of her throat, and Avra was tilting her head to take it, staring up at him as if to say *See what I can do?* Settling back onto her heels, opening and opening, breathing through her nose, ignoring her gag reflex. He pulled out, pushed in again, stared down at her with a fierce and rapturous incredulity, and Avra wrapped one hand around the base of his cock while her eyes watered.

"Jesus Christ," Kieran said, breath rushed and awed the way he couldn't help but be when Avra did what he wanted when he wanted it. She bobbed forward, took him as deep as she could, spread her spit over the base and shaft of his cock with her dainty hand—the size comparison flattering, stunning—and licked over the tip with a lazy, dripping tongue. Kieran's head rolled back again. Avra squirmed, satisfied and eager, open and waiting. He fucked her face like that for several long minutes, slow and intentional, thumb rubbing over the corner of her mouth, along the place her spit met the shaft. Avra felt his fingerprints along their meeting place, again and again as he moved, like he wanted to feel where she started, to touch the way she took him.

He didn't buck his hips, didn't press beyond what she could manage, and Avra kept her throat open, her head tilted submissively, small sounds coming unbidden from her chest, tiny whines when he took his time, encouraging moans when he moved a bit faster, until Kieran's hips were snapping in eager bursts, and Avra could taste the sea-wave salt of pre-come against her tongue while his broad fist squeezed recklessly, haphazardly in her hair. She was coaxing him, letting him fuck through the soft C of her palm into the slick whirlpool of her mouth, and it was perfect, rhythm consistent, glide lascivious and hypnotizing.

Avra sank into the pattern, the heady pressure, the meditative force and slide, over and over while she stayed wanton, stayed willing. Kieran was in a trance. Avra closed her eyes and could feel the damp shock of endurance tears against her mascaraed lashes. Her face would be messy, stained, after this. Her lips were tingling, sensitive and just this side of sore. She knew they'd look cinnamon-oil pink and filler puffy when he was finished, knew her throat would feel raw and empty, knew she'd think about the way he tasted for months, years.

"Wait, wait, fuck," Kieran finally interceded, voice demolished. When he pulled Avra's head away by her hair, her lips separated from him with a small pop. The sound stirred them both, satisfactorily. A string of spit connected Avra's mouth to the head of Kieran's cock, and he stared at it in obscene fascination before it trailed and broke.

Avra licked her lips, wet smeared across her chin. She missed

the taste of him already, missed the consistent pressure and gra-
tuitous carnality. Wanted her mouth on him again. Would have
pleaded, if he made her. She wanted him to make her.

Kieran's eyes looked black-magic barbaric. Avra could see the
beading sweat across his forehead, and his palm was trembling
against the back of her head. "I want to come while I'm fucking you."

Avra grinned from her place on the floor. Kieran grinned back,
automatically. *Green*, Avra thought again. *Green, so fucking green.*

"Will you fuck me, then?"

"Ask nicely," he urged, half satire, half scolding.

"Please?" Avra was blushing, embarrassed at him forcing her to
ask, basking in the heady rush of shame, enjoying it.

"Again."

She took a deep breath, paused, lifted her chin, held between
his fingers, and knew her mascara must be prettily smudged around
her wide eyes.

"*Please*, I want it."

"Again."

Humiliation laved along her spine and Avra's mouth was
impossibly wet and she wanted to spend entire weeks ruining
Kieran beyond recognition, beyond sense. Wanted to do what he
said, wanted to resist *just* enough, make him punish her, make him
force her, test and try and see if he really would.

"Please, Kieran, will you fuck me now?"

"Crawl," he said, taking a step back, his cock gleaming bruise-
dark against his abdomen. "Crawl to the bed."

Her knees pressed unforgivingly against the hardwood, aching
and terrible and exactly what Avra wanted, to *prove* something:
*Look, I'll be in pain for you. Look, I'll debase myself, if that's what you
want.* Kieran walked behind her, watching her crawl with a quiet,
steady encouragement. He reached forward once to trail his palm

along her back, down her spine, a single finger over the curve of her ass, and Avra whimpered through the goosebumps, the degradation.

Kieran was practically thrumming with energy, shifting from foot to foot, impatience scrabbling along his limbs. When Avra was finally settled on the bed, her lower back pressed flush against Kieran's duvet, weight against her elbows, Kieran summoned a condom from his dresser drawer with near-superhuman speed. Avra rolled her own underwear down her thighs. They separated from her wetness in a slick valediction.

"I missed you," Kieran said, kneeling between her thighs. Avra was spread open, unselfconscious.

"I missed you," Avra returned, hooking one heel around the back of Kieran's leg, encouraging him forward.

"Do you want me to fuck you now?"

"I always want you to fuck me," Avra said, honest and comforting, "but especially now."

Kieran steadied himself over Avra's small, soft body, his palms flat on either side of her shoulders, his chest hair soft and perfect in front of her nose. He bent to kiss her once, twice, Avra's mouth open and pliant and responsive beneath him, and she wondered if he could taste himself on her tongue.

And then, shocking like it always was between them, Kieran was sliding into Avra, deep, deep, as far as he could, while her toes curled and her back arched and her body reminded her, *Yes, this is what it's like, yes, this is even possible.* When he reached around her head, Avra expected him to cradle her. Instead, he retrieved a wand vibrator, previously hidden under his pillow—it was blue, like his sheets, and Avra's favorite brand. She glowed.

"You remembered!" The praise was interrupted by a sharp gasp, because Kieran was sliding forward again, pressing the power button, forcing the gift into one of Avra's hands.

"I want you to use this while I'm inside you."

"I can do that." Avra was already guiding the rumbling toy to her mound while Kieran pulled out slowly, slid in again, and steadied himself with a forearm across her chest, pressing her down into the mattress. The weight of him was soothing, threatening.

"I want to see how many times I can make you come while I'm fucking you." Kieran sounded authoritative, resolute, and Avra's nerves were frayed, pleasure rolling generously along her spine and down her thighs and over her clit. She didn't know what to say, was still formulating a response (something like a "Yes, please" or a "Dear God" or "Are you even real?") when Kieran finished his thought, "I always want you to feel good, you know. Even when I'm hurting you."

Fairy dust ricocheted through her, fast and glorious, as she nodded, knowing, agreeing.

Kieran leaned down, dug his teeth into her neck, and Avra's reactive yelp turned to a sigh as he soothed the bite with the heat of his tongue. One hand closed roughly around Avra's free wrist, and she twisted her palm reflexively. Kieran's grip tightened, a clear expectation that she stay fucking still for him carved into his hold.

"You do feel good," Avra extolled, beginning to tremble.

Kieran was panting along her jaw, roving his tongue over her neck, her ear, and Avra was making small noises, little broken pleas, grinding down into the force of his cock, turning up the vibration settings so that they both swore.

"I want you all the time," Kieran said.

"I want you, too." Avra's orgasm was teasing, assembling itself along Kieran's impossible patience and affirming words and the pressure of each long, filthy thrust.

"I don't understand why I want to hurt you," Kieran said, biting again, hard enough to mark, "why I always want to do this." He emphasized *this* with another slow push, all the way into her body, and Avra practically giggled, her laugh turning to champagne and frosting as Kieran slid into her over, and over, just right, pace dragging and glossed and victorious.

"I've never understood this." Avra's nails were in his shoulders, in his back, and she wanted his sliced, discarded skin beneath her fingernails in a grotesque and morbid way. Kieran was still fucking her, unhurried, correct, and Avra was close to coming, could probably come if he told her to.

"What if I'm not . . . what you think I am?" He didn't really mean it as a question.

"Into guys?" Avra tried to concentrate, but Kieran was gripping her wrist, laving his tongue along her neck, kissing her until she couldn't take a full breath without tasting him, and the force of him inside her body was storybook-perfect, and the rumbling vibrations over her clit blurred her intellect.

"What if I'm straight and I've been letting you live in this extravagant fantasy of me just so I could do this?" He rocked his hips deeper into Avra, and the lusciousness was enough to make her whine. "What if I'm just a—a normal guy"—*Normal*, she wanted to scoff, to protest—"and you made this all up?"

"I didn't."

"What if I'm just using you?" He pulled back to look at her face, to watch her react to this additional degradation, and Avra's cheeks burned. It might have been more convincing if he didn't sound so satisfied, if they hadn't spent all evening dancing around his experience with Isaac, his guilt about Braden. He pulled out, achingly slow, and pushed in again. They groaned in unison.

"You're not."

"How do you know? How do you know this isn't just about getting to fuck you? How do you know this isn't . . ."—he cast around for a word, pulling out almost entirely before sliding in deep—"manipulation?"

It was like he was licking a sticky line over her nightmares. Avra couldn't help but feel a little tingle of shame—the kind that makes you want to purr—at the suggestion. He knew which of her buttons to push, the same way she had always known his, and this was the beauty of the thing. Avra tried to summon the energy to argue, but found with a small startle that she didn't mind, really, if Kieran fucked around with her, if he played this ridiculous game, as long as he kept moving like that. She strung her response together with effort.

"Because of the things you do and say." It was obvious. "Because of the way you act."

"What if it's just that? Acting?" He circled her clit with his finger in a small, liquid swipe on the next thrust, competing for space with the vibrator, and Avra could feel the rumbles through the pad of his thumb. His fingers were slick from Avra's wetness. His free hand moved to clamp, vise-like, on her thigh. He bent one of her knees up so that it pressed against his chest, so he could bear down while he fucked her. Avra was momentarily grateful for her own flexibility, her malleability, that she could do what he wanted, whatever he ever fucking wanted.

"It isn't."

"I could have just figured out what to say, you know. I wanted to have you like this. You're always"—he smiled, waiting to catch her eye before finishing the thought—"such a bitch." He thrust, and Avra let her eyes roll back. "I wanted you to think we had something in common. Make it easier to do this to you." He circled his thumb around her clit again while pushing forward, and Avra grabbed at his shoulder with one hand, the other hanging on to the vibrator with a desperate clutch, soft noises coming unbidden from her chest as he continued his play. "What if I just googled it?"

Avra laughed, delighted and horrified and entirely unconvinced. "You can't borrow the existential dread of queer coming of age from something you read on the internet," she insisted. Kieran shrugged, and it was such a contrast to his tirade of threats that Avra ran her fingers affectionately along his neck and shoulder, a mimicry of camaraderie. "And you couldn't perform it convincingly enough even if you did. Don't forget—I've seen you act." Kieran reached up from her thigh and pinched her nipple softly in admonition. She sighed and arched her back, which drove his hardness into her body again with a satisfying yielding. "I'm getting close."

Kieran licked along her neck, her jaw. "Come, then, and I'll keep fucking you, and then you'll come again."

Avra's orgasm was the slow and tumbling kind, like car tires over gravel when you're sneaking out of the house. It was a heist, an escape; she was getting away with something.

Her breath came back to her in shivering gasps, and the vibrations were almost too much on top of the aftershocks. Kieran held a hand against her wrist, kept the vibrator still, almost overstimulating, as if he knew.

Avra kissed him once, twice, made a grateful noise against his mouth, and writhed encouragingly. "You can't just *fake* gay." Back where they had left off. She tensed her muscles experimentally, punishingly, and Kieran's breath caught. "Admit it—" She panted as she spoke. Sweat was gathered in the hollow of her collarbone and across the small of her back. She was twisting her hips so she could feel the friction of him, the slick pull against her insides, so they could keep moving together. The impulse to turn tables was shuddering through her bones, and Avra knew how. "You'd love to have a man underneath you right now."

He must have been expecting it—was probably goading her

toward exactly this—but Kieran's jaw dropped anyway. Avra, with her insolent mouth and her arousal eliminating any kind of filter, knew what to say next. Emboldened by her orgasm, immodest, flagrant, Avra began narrating: "Squirming and hard. You wish you could wrap your fist around a thick cock while you fucked some guy—maybe one from class. Maybe one from your basketball team. Slow, like this." She arched her back, moving her hips down onto his cock languorously. Avra was still dripping and open. "You could touch him the way you touch yourself." She reached between them to feel the obscene slide of Kieran into her body as she spoke, stroking the base affectionately while he moved into her, a pantomime of his thumb against her mouth less than an hour before, when he pushed past her lips, slid across her tongue. His shaft was slick from her. "You could fuck his ass until he was too sore to even get out of bed."

"What are you doing?" Kieran asked, voice ragged with the torn tension of wanting and resisting. His hips were rolling automatically, filling Avra again and again as she spoke. "Why are you doing this?" It was a rapid power exchange—theft, really—and Kieran was rattled, off-kilter, even from above, and Avra was smiling, soaking, superior.

Avra continued: "Imagine getting to feel him under you, opening up around your cock. Imagine listening to the noises he'd make for you."

Kieran growled, low and frantic, and began to thrust in earnest, hips snapping, one unyielding hand around Avra's thigh. The other found its way to her throat. He didn't squeeze, but the promise of force was a second away. He leaned over her, and the pressure on her throat ratcheted up as his lips brushed hers. "Shut the fuck up," he said, breathing chaotically against her mouth.

Avra kissed him fast and hard, licking his tongue, his teeth.

Swallowing his spit while he fucked her. She imagined she could taste the copper of adrenaline, the panic at his own wanting. "I can feel how hard you are, you know, just listening to me talk about it." She bit. He growled. "This gets you hot, thinking about fucking men while you're inside me, knowing you have my permission, that I want you to imagine it"—she ran the fingernails of her free hand over the front of his throat—"in full sensory detail."

Kieran was panting, mouth against her cheek, tongue along her temple, listening to Avra's filth. "You can't even deny it," she cooed, knowing the shame was weaving him into knots, building like a flood. She thought briefly that she could probably humiliate him like this, make him beg to fuck her while she detailed all the things he'd never permit himself to want, make him say thank you. "What if there was another guy here, watching us? You could make him sit in the corner and jerk off while you fucked me."

"I said shut *up*." He put a hand over her mouth, but Avra licked between his fingers and Kieran groaned again, desperate.

"You could tell him how to touch himself." She was talking between his fingers now, and he splayed them over her chin. "What if he came over to join and I watched him go down on you? What if you got to come with your cock in his mouth and his fingers inside you?"

"God damn it, Avra." Kieran's eyes were squeezed closed, as if eye contact might prove her right, as if she would read an admission of guilt in the ink of his pupils. Avra could feel him, impossibly hard, his rhythm a wild staccato as she spoke.

"What if you flipped him over and ate his ass? You could make him spread his legs and beg while you used your mouth, licked him open."

"Jesus." Kieran was fucking her hard, moaning on every long, deep thrust, and Avra could see his orgasm threatening to overtake him, like a confirmation, a benediction.

"Or maybe . . ." Avra ran a hot tongue over Kieran's fingertips and pulled him flush against her so she could do the same to his neck. The vibrations were ruthless. ". . . you want the reverse. What do you think? Maybe you'd want him to have all the power. He could boss you around. I bet you'd be obedient, for the right guy. Think you'd get on your knees for him?"

"I don't—I don't know—oh, fuck." He was babbling a little, eyebrows drawn in concentration. Trying not to come, Avra knew. Trying to hold off his orgasm, to stay in control. Avra didn't like that—she wanted him strung out, vulnerable, honest.

"Green?" she prompted.

Kieran's eyes snapped open, and Avra grinned—*gotcha*. He let out a near sob, the requirement of confirmation clarifying the utter bullshit of any denial. "Green," he whispered, face blooming, blood molten to his core, breath steaming against Avra's lips, across his own fingers.

"You're going to come thinking about some guy," Avra insisted. Kieran's hand twitched over her mouth. He nearly looked away. "Whichever guy just came to your head"—she gripped his chin and forced Kieran's face toward hers—"*that's* the guy." Kieran nodded wordlessly. "You know this is proof of how badly you want men, right? You're thinking about a cock in your hand or your mouth or your ass even while you fuck me." It was true.

Kieran laughed, unrestrained, a little hysterical, as his repudiation was shredded, brutalized.

"Come on." Avra said it low and encouraging, smiling devilishly as surrender loamed across Kieran's face, seafoam covering a shoreline. "I want you to come imagining him fucking you." She was whispering now, a stream of consciousness right by Kieran's ear, and his pulse was leaping. "Some big, strong guy licking into you and fingering you open. Making you ask him to fuck you." Kieran's forearms were corded, his head bowed as if in prayer. "Think about rubbing against him until you're sticky with his pre-come. Imagine him coming in your ass, all hot and tight. Imagine him using you the way you think you're using me." She laughed again and the sound huffed against Kieran's neck.

He looked entirely gone, heroin-beguiled. His jaw was slack, his eyes closed, and Avra wanted so badly to get him off like this, to just talk him through all the things he'd never allowed himself to have. "Imagine him telling you what a good job you're doing, just taking it. Maybe he'd make you say please." She moved intentionally into every thrust, tightening her body around Kieran in a searing rhythm. His legs were trembling. The vibrator was on high. Kieran was making rough, frustrated noises on every exhale. "Do it," Avra whispered, commanding and urgent, watching Kieran's face in erotic wonder. "Do it. Beg him to fuck you." She waited. It barely took Kieran a second.

"Oh fuck, please . . ." His voice was wrecked.

"Please what?"

"Fuck me. Please. Please fuck me."

"You want to be fucked by a hard cock?" Her tone was light, contemptuous. Avra licked the shell of his ear. "Want some guy to pin you down and mess with you? Fuck your ass open until you can't sit down without thinking of him? Want to come begging with a dick inside you?"

"Ple-ease, I want— Fuck, I—"

"Want him to fuck you through it, leave you filthy and panting. Wish he could see you like this right now, see the way you're needy for it. Come on, baby." Avra gripped his hair in one hand, pulled, knew she was hurting him, knew they both liked it. "Come while he fucks you."

"Oh god oh god oh god oh god oh god"—a consecration, a mantra. Avra could feel Kieran's cock pulsing hotly inside the condom, inside her, as the orgasm hit him, swift and overwhelming. Her own orgasm took her quite by surprise, and Kieran's face broke open as his pleasure rocked them both, his expression painting crepuscular rays of relief. He was loud. The window was still closed, for the neighbors, but they could probably hear him on the street. "Fuck, *god*, this feels so good."

Avra crooned encouragement against his cheek. "Good boy. So hot like this. Think about how hard he could fuck you. How deep."

Kieran was unraveling on top of Avra like a broken thing, gasping out moans, shuddering through aftershocks. It took him a few long moments to stutter and then still his hips. He whined a little as he held the base of the condom and pulled out, holding himself above Avra on trembling limbs. He opened his eyes and looked quickly at her face, registering her gleeful expression.

"That," Kieran said, voice a sonata of gratitude, a submissive concerto, "was fucking hot." He looked stunned, dismantled, and close to actual tears.

"You're goddamn right," Avra sighed, just this side of sore, the twinge as delicious as a cotton-candy lake. She switched off the vibrator. Kieran's shoulders were shaking, covered in a salted sheen. Avra caught one of his hands—he collapsed clumsily onto her belly—pressed a kiss to two of his fingertips, considered for a moment, and then licked his palm.

"You don't get that from Google," Avra asserted, petting Kieran's hair as he came back to the room, to himself. She ran her fingertips through the gathered sweat of his hairline. His chin rested on her navel. "I promise. That's not the internet. It's not some play-pretend, make-believe bullshit. It's you." She skimmed her fingertips down the back of his neck, and felt goosebumps rise to meet the whorled prints as he scooted closer. "It's what you want."

"How do you know?" Kieran lowered his face, and his voice was muffled against Avra's breast, his hair damp and curling under Avra's chin. She turned to press a kiss to his forehead.

"I've always known."

She had always known.

"Green?" Avra prompted, wanting to reassure, to check in.

"Green."

Green.

Kieran stopped any pretense of resistance. Almost sweetly, appreciatively, he lifted himself onto his elbows again, shuffled all the way up her body, and kissed her cheek. This was all the admission Avra would get, she thought. She'd take it anyway.

"It's your turn." He still sounded absolutely destroyed.

"I came when you came." She snickered at his look of surprise, so caught up had he been in his own experience.

"I want you to *tell me* when you do that." He sounded almost put out, and she resumed petting his neck and back to soothe him.

"We can play more in a bit," Avra assured him. "First, aftercare." She drummed her fingers. "Then, maybe a nap." Kieran's jaw cracked on a yawn. Avra continued: "Then we can talk more about the things you want to do, to have done to you . . ." Kieran was already shifting his hips again. His cock was still half hard against her thigh, the condom clinging to him determinedly, Avra's wetness coating the outside like stained glass. "How do you like to be taken care of after sex?"

"I've never really thought about it."

"Well, think about it." She kissed the softened lines of his face, tasted his cheek, nuzzled the warm skin beneath his ear, and smiled wide. "Think about it, and let me know."

CHAPTER 17

JULY 2012

They fucked twice more that night; keening, barely-vanilla sex that made Avra want to drip like blood down the walls and stain the ancient baseboard molding. When she commented that Kieran's room was starting to smell like the two of them, he opened the window. She closed it again, because of the noise, "for the neighbors." The shirt Kieran loaned her for sleep hit around mid-thigh and stayed on for approximately half an hour. They fell asleep past two in the morning, slick condoms discarded like Legos, scattered stepping hazards, throughout the room.

Braden careened back into the apartment at nine a.m., clickety-clacking his fingernails against Kieran's door to encourage them toward waking. When Avra opened the door—Kieran's shirt retrieved and donned for the occasion—Braden did a puckish little golf clap.

"Did I earn applause?" Her mouth tasted like dead things.

"I can't speak to your performance, but certainly the hair does, darling." A nest, a disaster. Avra patted it twice before taking a single deep breath. She smelled the vulgar umami of dried ejaculate,

shared salt, and she conceded the necessity of a shower. Kieran was
still snoring.

"I'd tell you to wake him, but I'm not sure he's decent," she said.

Braden scoffed as Avra scooted past, "He never is."

Avra hurried off to rinse while Braden, ever brazen, bounded
inside to jump on the bed. Kieran stirred behind her, groaning at
the rude awakening. Avra thought she heard Braden say "Ouch!" as
she closed the bathroom door.

Brunch was indulgent and delicious, a necessary injection of cal-
ories after hours and hours of cardio. Avra enjoyed Vic, who had
enough unflappable bartender energy to offset Braden's mania, as
well as the social grace to ask open-ended questions. She ordered
for the pair of them, one savory dish, one sweet, to split, and Avra
got the impression of an experienced nanny wrangling a frenetic
toddler. Braden habitually seized the conversational thread like
a football and ran it down pitch. Vic would smile, pet his collar,
hum agreeably, and return them to topical center field. Braden
would scold her for the change of subject. She would note his
whimsicality. They would meet in the middle, bravely peppering
Avra with personal questions and nudging Kieran to do more than
quietly caffeinate. Avra experienced a brief rush of pride, self-effi-
cacy, at her own social graces, vastly improved since high school.
She nodded excitedly at Vic across the table, laughed with her
mouth open, and did a small internal tap dance at the comfortable rapidity of a new-buddy bond. By the end of brunch, Avra
and Vic were following each other on social media, grasping
hands across the syrup-sticky table, and promising sincerely to "do
this again."

Braden pledged Kieran an empty apartment for one more night

("But just the one, I know how you miss me"), winked at Avra ("I prefer your morning hair"), and left with Vic. Again, Avra basked in the slowing social inertia, the Saturday-suited plod of Braden's absence. She enjoyed his presence, in the spent and long-suffering way she was sure most would, but marveled at Kieran's ability to live with him. Kieran maintained that he had sufficient practice—a brother plus four sisters versus one Braden? It might actually be a balanced scale.

When they returned to the apartment, Kieran collapsed across the couch. Xena settled herself above his head, plopping her belly down onto the arm before taking up a motorcycle purr, and Avra allowed herself a moment of admiration for the kind of man whose presence soothed a cat. Kieran pet her soft fur absentmindedly. Avra slid off her shoes.

"C'mere." He was gesturing, arm outstretched, beckoning Avra toward the coffee table with a twisting wrist.

"You seem tired."

"I am tired." His eyes were closed.

"You just mainlined coffee."

"You wore me out then, I guess."

Avra grinned at this, settled onto the couch while Kieran made room.

"I like your friends," she said affectionately.

"I like them too."

"I bet you'd like my friends, if you spent any time with them."

Kieran cracked an eye. "I'll do better next time."

"A bit presumptuous, eh?" She was half kidding, settling back into the space Kieran had left for her.

"Figured you would give me a second chance on that one."

"*I* will. Ellie might not."

Kieran opened his eyes fully, twisted his head to look at Avra.

His brows were pulled together in concern. "Did I fuck it up that badly?"

Avra watched her feet, in a pair of Kieran's too-large socks, the bump of the heel protruding diseasedly from the back of her ankle. "Do I even have to answer that?"

Kieran reached an arm around her middle, flattened his palm along her rib cage, and pressed his nose into the side of her breast, almost childish. "I'll fix it."

Avra thought for a moment of the soreness in her body when she returned to her shared room, Ellie's flared nostrils, the bruise that took a week to fade, the sound of Kieran vomiting from down the hall, and tried to let the pressure of his palm sugarcoat the sour.

Unable, as usual, to fully tame her reactivity, she presented a challenge. "You don't have to, you know. You don't have to ever meet my friends, if you don't want. It's not as if we're dating." This was the incorrect time for a pop quiz. The weekend was going so well. Avra cleared her throat, coasted a finger along the back of his hand, and watched a water stain in the corner of the popcorn ceiling. "I mean, I'm not your girlfriend or anything." Kieran's mouth quirked at the corner, and Avra's sudden annoyance shimmered like the thick air above midsummer pavement.

"No, you're not." His tone was easy. Avra guessed he was still comfortably buzzed from several last-night orgasms and the convenience of noncommitment. She knew from college-girl stories about this: Men became Magellans of avoidance when prompted with romantic labels.

"I'd never expect you to settle down with a woman, anyway, before experiencing more." Avra said, like it didn't matter, even as her gut fizzed anxiously, even as it very much did.

Kieran turned his face, his cheek resting against her back, nose hidden between Avra and the couch. His voice was muffled. "My family would be psyched, though. If you were my girlfriend." Avra hadn't thought of that before.

"Because it would mean you aren't queer?" Kieran lifted one shoulder in response. Avra pressed on. "Does your family even know who I am?"

"My mom always liked you, actually. She said you were good in the play."

Avra's belly oscillated with craving. She didn't garner benevolence from mothers—not her own, not her girlfriends'. "Does anyone in your family know that you're not straight?"

"I spent literally all last night fucking you—*I'm* not even sure that I'm not straight," Kieran said. Avra made a *don't be ridiculous* sound and waited. "I think Brigid suspects something, but she's never asked. She *has* pointed out hot guys in front of me before, though, and then, like, *stared at my face,* which is pretty classic for her. Mom might be in denial. I've never brought someone home, but she makes all these jokes like I'm just playing the field. Dad . . ." He hesitated. Avra shifted onto her side so she could see his face. "Dad knows something. He walked in on me and Will once."

"Walked in on you and Will doing *what,* exactly?"

"Not really the point, Av."

"We've got time—answer both." Her eyes were glinting, curious and possessive. She was finally, finally getting some details.

"We were just kind of fooling around. Roughhousing, I guess." Kieran flushed. "I was touching him. We weren't kissing or anything."

"God forbid," Avra retorted.

"Actually, yeah," Kieran confirmed.

"And your dad came in?"

"I think he'd been suspicious for a while, you know. Asked Will lots of questions about girls. He'd walk in kind of randomly if we were ever in a room with the door closed, and we were usually pretty careful."

"Usually?"

Kieran shot her a *please don't interrupt* look and Avra returned a *do go on* frown.

"So he came in and obviously we pretty much ran to opposite sides of the room but I knew he could tell. And I thought he was going to beat the shit out of me or something. Yell, or break something, or kick Will out. But he just left the room. Didn't even look at me." Kieran's face was boarded up and ramshackle, a faraway haunted house.

"And that was it?"

Kieran laughed, the least funny sound Avra had ever heard. "No. That was not it. I thought it was done, right? It had been a few days, and my dad hadn't said anything to me. I was too nervous to have Will over, so I was spending all this time at his house, or at Garrett's. And one night I came back for dinner, and my dad asked if we could go to my room. And my dad isn't, like, a *conversations* guy. He'll talk *at* you, but he's not really—" Kieran made a sound like the air sputtering from a balloon and shook his head. "It's not as if he wants to know what you have to say. And I didn't think we were actually going to talk. I figured he'd say he was disappointed, or that I was going to hell. Eternal damnation and a lost soul and all that. But instead, he showed me this thing." Another laugh, bitter and mustard-yellow. "He put a lock on my door. Like, the outside of my door, not the inside. He locked me in that night. I couldn't eat, and I couldn't leave."

"Like Harry Potter," Avra said, unthinking.

"Yeah, just like Harry fucking Potter, Av." Kieran shook his head, disbelieving, and Avra apologized.

"I don't mean— Obviously it was horrible. That's— God,

Kieran, that's really fucked up."

"Unexpected is what it was. He's just unpredictable, my dad. Like, you think everything is fine, and he's joking around, or seems like he's in this good mood, and your guard is down *just* enough, and then he'll—"

"Lock you in your bedroom?"

"For example. I had to pee out the window in the middle of the night. I didn't want to try the door, in case he heard me. It was unlocked in the morning. But he did that a few nights that week. Not every night, just a few, and never consecutively. Keeping me on my toes. Always right before dinner. I started stashing snacks under my bed just in case. I'd hide the wrappers and throw them away in the kitchen trash when he wasn't home so he wouldn't suspect anything."

"So he wouldn't suspect that you were *eating?*"

"Yeah, self-sacrifice is a big thing for my dad."

"How long did he do all this?"

"Eh, not long." He said it like *no big deal* and Avra wanted to burn his father's house down. "Like a week, maybe two. Brigid asked what was up, one time. She asked why I wasn't eating dinner with them. And he just said, 'Kieran knows why.' And I did, so I guess there wasn't anything else to say about it." He shrugged. "He can be passive-aggressive."

"This sounds just plain aggressive to me, but continue."

"He left a Bible on my bed one of the times he locked me in, and these little booklets on the sins of homosexuality and mastur-bation. I don't even know where he got them. I mean, how do you find stuff like that?" Avra shook her head. Kieran's hand was sweaty on her side. He was watching Xena's tail flick back and forth, sym-pathetically frustrated. "And a few days that week, Mom sent me to school without lunch, and that was just shit, you know, because

I didn't think she'd ever—" He stopped talking, and Avra watched him blink, felt his fingers shift along her waist. "I bought hot lunch when I remembered money. And I stole a lot of french fries."

"Your dad is the fucking worst, dude."

"He's . . . he's not great. Brigid was, though. She figured it out, I think—always been the observant one of the lot of us. She started bringing these extra huge lunches to school and sneaking over from the middle school wing to hide her leftovers in my locker." Kieran laughed again, warmer, truer, like the sun hitting when the wind slows. "I don't even know how she learned my locker combination. Pretty sure she was giving Dad a hard time about it, too, because he didn't talk to her much that week."

Avra felt her affection for Brigid surge, a grateful instinct grappling roughly with her ambient rage toward Kieran's parents. Avra was rooted half to the heat of Kieran's hand on her waist, half to the certainty that her own father wouldn't *dream* of this, would rather drag himself exhausted through a kitchen, heave out his largest cutting board, and accidentally chop into a knuckle than let one of his daughters sleep hungry, queer or not. "I'm glad Brigid took care of you," Avra began, softly. "But you have to know—you didn't deserve that. From either of them."

"I mean, I never fooled around with Will again, so, mission accomplished, I guess."

"No," Avra said, and folded herself into Kieran like an origami chest plate. "Mission definitely not accomplished. You can't starve and isolate kids out of *being gay*."

"You can try . . ." Falsely light, unconvincing.

"I'm sorry they did that to you. Jesus, even your mom?" Avra jerked her head in refusal, as if she could shake off the possibility, and Xena made a low, unhappy sound. "You can share my dad, if you want."

"Yeah, like your dad would ever let me near you after the way I acted in school."

"My dad is fairly forgiving. Soft-hearted. I mean, don't get me wrong, you'd have some work to do, but it's not an impossible task." She nosed Kieran's chin, then his cheek.

"Not that it matters, and I know it isn't an excuse, but that week—the time I called you . . ." Kieran looked at her, looked away. "I don't want to say it."

"Right now, you can say it."

"When I called you a dyke," he began, extra quiet, and Avra smiled at his stage whisper, at the reticence, at the worlds-apart comparison between right now and their sophomore year of high school. "That week, you know, I was just really, really hungry."

Avra held his face softly between her two small palms and kissed him.

CHAPTER 18

AUGUST 2012

Four weeks later, Avra made the trip for the third time, letting herself in with the key that Braden left for her under the front flower box (all the blooms were dead, neither boy attentive enough to regularly water them). On the second day of her visit, she and Kieran spent the afternoon in a syrupy liminal space between cuddling and snoozing. Avra's body ached in that well-ravaged, satisfying way she had come to expect from Kieran's company. Kieran was a furnace, and the potent combination of summer sun oozing beneath the blinds and body proximity elevated the afternoon's stickiness factor. Avra woke beside him on the couch to feel her worn T-shirt moss-damp against her lower back. When she grumbled discontentedly, Kieran murmured against her forehead.

"What is it?"

"I just showered this morning and I'm already all gross."

Kieran licked her eyebrow. "There, better."

"I'm sorry, what?"

He didn't open his eyes. "It's how Xena cleans me."

"Right, and those two things are totally the same."

Kieran was post-nap playful, bizarre and invasive, tucking his toes beneath Avra's feet and winding his fingers into the hem of her shirt. "You're just going to get dirty again anyway."

"Oh, *am* I?"

Kieran licked over her temple, swiped his fingers through the sweat of her lower back, and poked the sole of her foot with his toenail. "Probably."

They rolled and fumbled for a few minutes, kissing unhurriedly, before Avra slid a thigh between Kieran's legs, expecting the promising suggestion of arousal. When it wasn't there, she pressed open-mouthed kisses along his neck, his ear, dragged her palm over the front seam of his jeans, and wiggled enticingly. Still nothing.

"I can see that my novelty is failing." Avra bungled the bon mot. "I mean, there was only so far your infatuation with my gayness was going to take us."

"Yellow," Kieran interceded, warningly, and Avra paused.

"I'm sorry."

"Just—guys don't really love it when you rough them up about stuff like this."

"Yeah, I know. I was trying to be self-deprecating. I didn't mean—was being stupid."

"It's okay." He kissed her again. "Just give me a minute."

"Would it help if I made you mad?" When Kieran raised an eyebrow, Avra bit his collarbone; not hard, but not lightly. "You like to fuck me when you're mad. You get pushy and sadistic in a way I find kind of dreamy."

"You find my moments of sadism *dreamy?*"

"Well, yeah."

"How does that even happen?" His tone was light.

"Abandonment trauma? Mommy issues? Self-consciousness regarding my own delight in being *used* as a sexual object despite never actually wanting to be *perceived* as a sexual object?"

"I appreciate the clarification."

"Lots of people cope via kink." She said it like *lots of people like lemonade.*

"Oddly, I am not in the mood to hurt you right now."

"Bummer for me."

Kieran's laugh cracked open like a geode between them. "Yeah, huge bummer for you. My apologies."

"As long as you promise to be mean again later," Avra chirped.

"You can pretty much count on it." The guarantee landed like a weighted woolen blanket over their floaty flirtation. They both knew it was true.

"Well, as long as we're not playing, maybe now would be a good time to do something sensible. Like, we could maybe take a quiz?" Avra posed an invitation.

"What kind of quiz?" A hedge.

"A kink quiz."

Kieran raised an eyebrow. "Go on."

"Well, apparently it's *sexually responsible*"—Avra rolled her eyes over the phrase—"to talk about wants and hard limits in a nonsexual context."

"Says who?"

"My professors."

"Your major is so weird."

Avra ignored this. "I can find one of those comparison quizzes to take. They go over what you really want to do, what you'd be down to do for a partner, and what you don't want or won't try. And the other person answers the same questions, and it creates a kind of matched list."

"I thought I already knew what you dislike," Kieran said over a yawn. "No hitting your face, right?"

"Sure, and we have safewords, and all of that is smart and good, but I want to know what else you want. As in, what else we could play with together." Avra kissed his neck, licked, hummed against the sweat-sticky skin, and shook herself back to the moment. "Like, I want to know how much of the rest of the . . . sexual repertoire we could try." She drew a little circle on his chest with her fingernail, over and over, until it began to darken. "Or whatever else I could *help* you do, or watch you do, with someone else."

"I don't want to take a quiz." It was abrupt, defensive.

Avra pulled back, laid her hand flat over his chest, and sat herself up. She used the spot over his lungs for leverage. "Why?"

"It's kind of like what we talked about before. I want to experiment, to gauge how you react to things."

"And if we take the quiz, you don't get to use the try-it-and-see method?" she asked.

"What's that?"

"Self-explanatory." Avra was exasperated at her suggestion being rejected, frustrated with Kieran for being calm and flaccid, annoyed at this obstacle to further insight, grumpy at hearing no, in whatever form, from this man.

"What is wrong with you?"

"You make a suggestion, then, if mine are crap." She knew she was being outrageous.

"No, I mean—" Kieran's arm swept behind her like a whip, a shock. He dragged Avra back down onto the couch by her waist. In a second, Kieran was above her, pressing into her with his full weight, his bare chest still marked with a pink O from her fingernail, one long leg between her open thighs. He licked into her mouth, covered her throat with both hands, thumbs notched beneath her jaw, and Avra yielded, deliquescent. ". . . this." Kieran pulled away, watched Avra's face with a morbid fascination. When he applied

pressure, squeezing thoughtfully, gauging her responses, Avra's eyelids fluttered. "I mean"—he licked her cheek—"what the fuck"—he
shifted his thigh upward, parting her legs—"is *wrong* with you?" He
squeezed a bit harder, and Avra whined. She could feel him, half
hard now, against her thigh, and was ecstatic at the shared want for
this, precisely this. At the symmetry, the barbarous synchronicity.
"How do you get off on all this shit? Why do you always want me
to hurt you?"

"Just one of the broken people, I guess."

Kieran removed his hands. "No, you're not."

"No," Avra confirmed, her throat suddenly too bare, "I'm
really not. This isn't damage, or trauma. This is"—she selected her
words—"radical acceptance."

"Explain."

"Power play is *hot*. Submission, especially. Submission is hot.
It just is. It's liberating. It's the best fucking game. And I certainly
will explain." Avra took a deep breath. Kieran settled his elbows on
either side of her, preparing for a tirade. "I have to be so *on* in my
life—I'm this gifted student"—they both knew it, no reason to be
humble—"and an activist, and an educator at work, and an ally to
my friends, and to all of these other hurt and oppressed people. I'm
juggling roles that require me to be in charge, in a thousand different ways, and to stay in charge, to stay in the fight. All the fights,
actually. The fight against patriarchy, the fight against homophobia,
one after another. And while I'm over here, doing my very best to
be the *right* kind of empowered person, the world is still telling
me that I'm a whore." Her voice was rising in pitch, the stalag-
mite quality shooting sharp and jagged. "A slut! A harlot!" Kieran
grinned at her theatrics. "Just for being a woman, or for being bi.
Or! Or, that I'm part of some evil global bank–based mafia because
I'm Jewish. Or that I'm one of the lost, hopeless girls for really,

really enjoying sex, or whatever. The world tells me that I'm this fallen woman, a cursed woman, and guys just stare at me all the time, and girls either think I'm a little too gay unless I'm sating their curiosity, or they tell me I'm not gay enough, because of how badly I've always wanted to fuck you, and it's too much." Avra was gathering speed, transmuting from pretty femme into steam train the way she could when she had a lesson to impart. "It's just too much, and I'm in all of these stupid, unwinnable social wars, scrapping for my humanity, and defending myself, and keeping up the walls, and joining the fourth-wave feminist guard, and on and on and on, and do you know what I love? What I really, *really* love?" Avra could feel the flush of cheeks, the softness of her body beneath Kieran while she ranted and he stared at her. At her face. Her eyes. Her jubilant, open mouth. "I love just *giving it up.*"

The eager profundity shimmered in the air between them. Avra meant it. She went on.

"All those fights? I love laying them down. I love it. I love *resting*. I love just saying, Okay, world, you want me to be a slut? Then yes. *Yes*, I'm a slut. You say I'm here to be used and discarded? Use me. You say I'm good for fucking and not much else? I'll be the best goddamn lay in the galaxy." Avra wound her arms around Kieran's shoulders, buried both hands in his hair, and pulled him down for a kiss, hard, then teasing, patient, velvety and mellow. "For all of the cognitive dissonance"—she spoke directly against his mouth—"of fighting oppression. For all of the cognitive dissonance of resisting systems of power so much goddamn bigger than I am. For all of the cognitive *fucking* dissonance of demanding that I am not a Fleshlight in a world that insists that I'm pretty much a set of holes, there is cognitive assonance—beautiful, peaceful, blissful, *easy* simplicity—in just getting to *submit*. There is a stupid, inebriating, glorious relief in Just. Not. Fighting it anymore. *That's* why I'm like this. *That's* what the fuck is wrong with me." Avra licked over Kieran's mouth, punctuating her finale.

She knew he didn't understand, that he couldn't really, but hoped he found her galloping perspective illuminating regardless, hoped he found her dagger-sharp and genius. She wanted him to learn, to be impressed by her. She wanted this to stick.

Kieran waited a moment to be sure that she was finished. When she merely gazed at him, inoffensively expectant, Kieran responded in a halting affirmation, ". . . I hear that. And I don't doubt it. But— and don't think this means I'm all finished hurting you—but what if I just want to be nice to you sometimes?"

"Like how?" Amazing, Avra thought, registering her own reticence, that she could be suspicious of this but not of his hands around her throat.

"Like, taking care of you. Or—you let me fuck your face again last night, and it was so hot. I mean, it was really . . ."—Kieran blew out a breath and squirmed as his cock leapt with interest—"it was obviously really fucking good. But I have no idea how to go down on you." At this confession, Avra's eyebrows flew into her hair. Kieran flushed. "I mean it, I really don't. And you could teach me how to do that."

"Do you have any interest at all in vulvas?" She paused, thought, continued, "Vulvae?"

"I think I've made it clear that I have a lot of interest in yours."

"Okay." Avra was shifting beneath him, kissing the corner of his mouth. "Okay, then." She pulled away. "It'll take some getting used to. For me, I mean. I've never coached a guy through doing this before."

"It'll take some getting used to for me, too."

Avra laughed, the reactive sound of hurricaning wind chimes. "We'll add it to the list, then."

"Where do we start?"

"I'll draw you a diagram."

Avra did, indeed, draw him a diagram. Mostly as a joke. A canoe shape, with a lamp at the head. Kieran pointed. "Does it glow in the dark?"

"Shut up."

"Just tell me what you like."

Sitting next to Kieran on the couch, Avra fidgeted under this kind of scrutiny. The revelation of her own tastes constituted an intimacy, a *vulnerability*, that made her want to hide somewhere six-walled and small. She cleared her throat and blushed. She stared at the lined lavender paper, which had been ripped out of her own journal.

"I like consistency."

"Be more specific."

"Okay, like, if you find a pattern, and I tell you that it feels good, just keep doing that *exact* thing. Don't switch it up. Not even if I'm starting to react, or to move. That just means it's working."

"No problem."

"Sometimes people think noises or reactions mean to be more intense, or to go harder or something, and I'm just saying that's not what I—"

Kieran nudged Avra's knee. When she looked at him, he was nodding solemnly, all wide-eyed and earnest, the ideal performance of a captivated pupil. His eyes glittered as he clocked Avra's uncharacteristic self-consciousness. "I can do that. What kind of pattern?"

"Usually small circles. And it helps to keep your tongue flat, because you're less likely to miss."

"Vote of confidence, there." His ears went magenta, but he smiled.

"No—" Avra puffed another laugh, grateful to Kieran for

keeping the mood light, as she herself tried to force away the tor-
nado of fear threatening to uproot her. "I think there's so much
porn out there where people are eating women out and they lick
kind of like a cat, you know. Quick and intense and messy. And it's
supposed to be sexy. Or, really, it's supposed to *look* sexy. But that
doesn't actually work! At least, it doesn't for me. I can't speak for
everyone else." She kept bringing in other people, and porn, and
generalizations, to diffuse the targeted focus. It felt easier to pivot.
We, not I. *They*, not me.

"I hear you. So, tongue flat, little circles, don't switch it up.
What else should I know?"

"It might take a little while." The most significant concern.
What if he lost interest?

"I'm not worried about the time commitment."

"Like, twenty to thirty minutes." Avra was acutely aware of
Kieran's proximity, of his mischievous grin, of the fingers he was
grazing along the outside of her thigh.

"I'll plan to take my time."

Something inside of Avra was curling in on itself, the charred
edges of a fire starter. This was excessive. The instructional—not
a lecture, a provision of insight into *her*—felt like spilling trade
secrets, collaborating with enemy forces, spying on behalf of an
antagonist. And she would have to be vulnerable in front of Kieran
somehow. And she couldn't perform, couldn't play some coquette
role. She would have to be real, and open. She would have to *relax*.
It seemed an impossible task, unreasonable. Easy with women,
Rubixian with men.

"Want to move to my bed?" Kieran suggested. "We can spread
out, have a bit more space?" Avra felt her blood protest, felt her
anxiety twine and barb around itself. She should have named her
nerves, probably. She should have said "Yellow" so Kieran could

further inquire. She should have said, "This is scaring me, this is intimidating, and I'm afraid you won't like it, and I'm not sure why."

Instead, she said, "Okay."

It was, predictably, a disaster. Or, it wasn't a success. Kieran followed Avra's instructions to the letter, while Avra's realm of existence narrowed to a small, self-conscious black box in the back of her head. She registered little physical sensation, despite the wetness of Kieran's (perfect, plush, gorgeous, damn him) mouth, and the calmly insistent ring pattern of his tongue. She made the requisite sighs and noises of approval. She willed herself back toward the bedroom, but never arrived, never returned to their company. At one point, she found herself bobbing along the ceiling beside the fan. Avra threaded her fingers encouragingly through Kieran's hair. She thought about how she wasn't clean shaven, and didn't men prefer the false, perverse veneer of pre-pubescent pussy? She wondered whether she smelled, and if so, whether Kieran hated it. She perseverated on the dehumanizing taco comparison and cursed patriarchy. She wondered if Kieran was loathing this, every second, if he was bored, if he was disgusted, if this was a job, or a chore, or some burden of expectation that he took on with regret and reproach. She thought about that asinine rumor that good cunnilinguists spell the alphabet with their tongues, and promptly found the ABCs stuck in her head. Five minutes passed, then ten, with Avra splayed open like a cornucopia, and all the food was plastic, and she was residing in that little black box, and she couldn't feel a thing.

Avra let out a forced, obviously fake moan before interrupting. "Do you want me to wear a strap?"

"What?"

"Like, we could try that instead, maybe." The air hummed with the static pall of mutual insecurity, and Avra interrupted herself.

"You're doing great, I just—"

"Is this not good?"

"No, it's not that."

Kieran was looking up from between her legs, weight on his elbows, one broad hand across her rib cage. His hair was mussed, his lips shiny, a look of impending dismay on his genuinely stupidly beautiful face, and Avra felt a ridiculous urge to laugh. She didn't. "You're doing everything that I asked, I swear."

"Then what is it?"

"I just . . . can't convince myself that you actually want to be doing this." She hurried on, "I brought a strap with me, so we could—"

"You *what?*"

"No, like, just in case this wasn't actually what you wanted." Avra's voice had a bent of needle, a shot of whine, stabbing straight through the middle. Defensive, like maybe there was something wrong with her, and making this about Kieran would be so, so easy. Making things about Kieran was always so easy.

"You mean, just in case *you* weren't actually what I wanted."

Avra didn't answer.

"Why do you always do this?"

"Your hyperbole is unhelpful," Avra deflected, shifting backwards along the navy blue sheets and gingerly closing her legs. She reached for her shirt on the side of the bed, while Kieran rubbed the back of his wrist over his mouth. She internally cataloged this as proof of his revulsion and fought the urge to point and yell "Aha!"

"Av." The tone of voice (soothing a mule, bathing a cat) made Avra want to kick and leap and run. "Sometimes I really do want it to be just the two of us."

"What do you mean?"

"I mean there doesn't have to be an imaginary man in the room every time we fuck." He said it with the long-suffering grace of someone managing a persistent poltergeist. As if the specter of men was haunting him, plaguing him, and Avra was the conjurer. Avra led the séance. Avra navigated the Ouija board. Avra invoked queer men fucking in her stuttering, ardent Latin.

"You love it when there are imaginary men in the room."

Kieran blushed but didn't argue. "I also . . ."—he cursed quietly to himself, as if steeling for something preposterous—"I also love being alone with you."

All the air left Avra's belly. Her esophagus turned to aluminum. Heat crawled up her skin like botulinum, or poison ivy. Pleasure and fear, panic in the gut, toxic disbelief singing in a spiked ring around her throat—*not possible not possible not possible*—even as she recognized the proof. Kieran, following her into kitchenettes and practice rooms, out of graduation ceremonies and through dimly lit bookshops, into dorm rooms and gay bars. Kieran's desperate texts and purloined photos saved saved in a folder on her computer, then obsessively downloaded onto her phone, several anxious voice messages preserved where they could never be lost. Kieran, inviting her to subsequent visits within hours of her departures, every time something a little sweet and desperate, like "When will I see you again?" Kieran, chasing her down over and over, for years now, her own apparition, a phantom of something adjacent to care.

"Red," Avra said.

"Yeah, I kind of got that," Kieran replied, then paused, then backpedaled. "Wait, red to the sex? Or red to this conversation?" She ignored the question, which effectively obliterated the whole point of the stoplight system.

"I love being alone with you, too." Avra realized with a start that the view of the grain pattern of Kieran's wood floors was swimming in front of her vision. Tears were such a useless intrusion.

This was unforgivable, and if she could hide under the floorboards she would do it, and if she could wish herself into the walls, she would make a stunningly patterned paper. She wanted to blink the salt away, but she held her eyes open stubbornly. "I just don't know how to be alone with you like this." Avra looked at him, at the W between his brows, the downturned corner of his mouth, and willed herself away from crying, didn't understand the acid on her tongue, couldn't abide it.

"Okay."

"It always felt easier with—with women." It wasn't exactly what she meant to say. Kieran's jaw tensed in that familiar jealous L, and Avra's eyes found floorboards again.

"Okay."

From the little black box in the back of her skull, Avra imagined fucking women again like crawling out of a grave, like escaping her own funereal dirt, and saw for a moment Kieran wielding a shovel, and couldn't tell murderer from liberator, and didn't care to investigate the difference.

She left for home a few hours later, feeling utterly cannibalized. She practically smashed an eyeshadow palette in the pace of her nervous packing, and on her disassembled drive ignored the rankly rotting caterpillars in her lungs, the dead and dusty butterflies, the possessed and vile vampire bats.

CHAPTER 19

SEPTEMBER 2012

Avra spent the last two weeks of summer in a creepy Victorian manse on the coast of Maine with her extended family. Her father and uncles cooked wood-fired pizzas in a massive brick oven on the patio while her aunts shared workplace woes and gossiped happily about the younger generation. Avra and Emerson chopped pizza toppings and dropped eaves and exchanged significant looks and laughed giddily when it all became too charmingly Jewish.

Sometime during their languid vacation, Mom reached out via Facebook with another "it will be *totally* different this time, I miss you, baby" invitation to reconnect. Avra showed Emerson the phone screen. Emerson commiserated with several similar notifications, and they both ignored them all. The solidarity of refusal, the dedication to estrangement, was a shared sibling dialect; if it hurt either one of them to stretch the silence, neither ever said so.

Kieran texted with thoughtful regularity, an obvious departure from his adolescent inconsistency, very *see, I can change*, while splitting his time between his older sister's Atlanta apartment and Braden's family boat (of *course* Braden's family had a boat). He recounted dreams to Avra of her spread open on a snowbank, or in the back seat of a car. He confessed—a bit frantically, as Avra's responses went tersely self-conscious—that he was measuring the passage of time via their contact. Despite his seemingly ballooning affection, the weekends before fall semester were efficiently eaten by Avra's end-of-summer plans and Kieran's preseason basketball. Avra was relieved. She sent him pictures of burnt pizza crusts and some rabbits in the yard, and ignored any mention of the cunnilingual catastrophe, or Kieran's corrective fantasies.

Although Avra performed the appropriate level of sadness at being unable to see him before the semester began, something had been arsenic-injected. She ignored the creeping unease, the haunting of her selfish, entitled mother. She tasted the familiar urge to dash away from intimacy on her tongue, felt the heaviness of avoidance in her palms. Avra was nervous to trust Kieran, who might one day realize that men were to him what coke was to Mom: inevitable. Even though she missed him, she waited for him to say it first. Testing, always. Looking for proof. The message came after the stretching days of Avra's experimental silence.

miss u

She responded, after about thirty-six hours: *thinking about you*

A few hours later, Kieran sent a YouTube link: *think youd like this song*

Before bed, Avra replied: *Have sweet dreams*

The next day, Kieran sent a request: *tell me a story*

Midafternoon, after a brief tale of woe, Avra presented a challenge: *Send me a picture*

A few moments later, a picture of Kieran burst onto the screen of her phone: bare chest, just out of the shower, steam on the mirror, hand in his hair and nose scrunched up like, *This what you had in mind?* Avra saved it to her Kieran album with a smile she had to bite down on like a bullet. She considered setting the picture as her phone background, considered having it printed at a Staples just so she could tuck it into her wallet like some possessive 1950s husband. When they weren't texting, Avra ruminated agitatedly about their last attempt at sex; at the numb, empty space between her thighs, at her own consciousness hovering passively, unreachably, beside the ceiling fan.

Being with Kieran, she decided, was simple when she was *giving*. Providing pleasure to a man felt instinctive, hereditary submission to a spoon-fed gender paradigm. Getting Kieran off was like retrieving mail from a mailbox, or clearing the table, or brushing her teeth, albeit more enjoyable. It was what young women were *raised to do*. Avra thought she must have absorbed this socialization via osmosis, in spite of her many years of exclusively fucking women. She admitted to herself that some of the unidirectionality might have been internalized during high school—from the way she accepted Kieran's abuse as typical, predictable: just another fated burden borne by the hated gay Jew.

In the weeks absent Kieran's company, stewing in her own self-conscious rehearsal of the unsuccessful head, Avra's pornographication parted at the seams. She spent hours trying to imagine herself beneath Kieran's mouth. The thought spilt a bucket of shame over her skull—Carrie at the prom, drenched and baffled. She texted Ellie incessantly, but never about this. She took Emerson to farmers markets and helped her dad plan a small renovation of the downstairs bathroom of her childhood home. She added Isabella on Facebook, and liked a photo, then another. When she pictured Isabella between her thighs, the shame never emerged, and how *backwards*, she thought. But *homophobia*, she thought.

Back in her fall semester apartment, unpacking her summer suitcases, Avra finally brought it up with Ellie. Better in person, she assumed. And besides, considering Ellie's easy affection with Nico, her own bisexuality, their matching rainbow flags, her friend could probably share relevant expertise.

"I have a question for you."

Ellie was sitting on the edge of Avra's bed, swinging her feet in a harmlessly bored way, prepared to absorb inquiry. "What's up?"

"Kieran went down on me a few weeks ago."

Ellie waited. Avra didn't elaborate. "That's not actually a question, babe."

Avra held a T-shirt over her face, made a tiny sound of frustration, and peeked over the fabric. "It was horrible."

"Damn, really? I figured the only thing that was keeping y'all in this thing must have been the sex."

"Okay, first of all—ouch? Second, no, the sex is usually so great, and I swear he was really . . . attentive?"

"Ew," Ellie said.

"He was! I gave him all of these instructions and he listened and he did exactly what I wanted him to do, but I just couldn't *be there*. Like, I didn't feel present at all. At one point, I swear to god, I almost started singing the ABCs."

Ellie's answering laugh was not unkind. "Couldn't get out of your head?"

"Not even a little." Avra's fists were balled in the T-shirt, her eyes mournful.

"And your question is . . . ?"

"How did you get used to it? With Nico? How did you figure out how to even stay in the room?"

Ellie sighed, stilled her swinging legs, and patted the comforter beside her. Avra sat, the blankets making a *thwump* sound in perfect symmetry with her mood. "You know what I love about you?"

"What?"

"You always ask such easy questions." Ellie's sarcasm, like the laugh, was good-natured.

"I'm not saying you're some kind of pleasure-reception virtuoso," Avra whined. "I just really don't know how people do this with guys."

"Okay. Well. I'm not going to lie, it took a while for me to . . . adjust. And a *lot* of positive feedback. I kept asking him if he was having fun, and it helped to hear him always say yes. And then he'd tell me other things." Ellie blushed and looked at her hands, and Avra respected that her friend respected Nico's privacy, and tried to look appreciative of this insight without looking too interested in the details, which she was not. "He'd say that he liked the way I tasted, or he loved making me feel good, or the best part for him was knowing that I was enjoying myself, and the more I heard it—"

"The more you believed it?"

"Yeah, pretty much."

"So I'm not the only one who finds this just impossible?"

"Girl," Ellie said, with a tone suggesting absurdity, "absolutely not."

"I never had to feel this way about women!" Avra burst out. "I never had to worry they wouldn't like my body, I mean. Or worry they'd think of my pleasure as a waste of time."

"That must have been amazing."

"It *was!*" Avra wanted to stomp her feet, to jump into a chlorinated pool and emerge full-body decontaminated, to slap patriarchy across its stupid evil face. "But even teaching Kieran how to hold a vibrator felt so bizarre. I did it!" she announced, proudly, "and he listened! But I was embarrassed, and I'm almost *never* embarrassed." Ellie nodded, knowing this to be true of her friend. "He's the first guy I've ever—" Avra stopped, restarted. "He's the only guy I—" Another pause, briefer. "I just don't feel like I have to hold the vibrator when I'm with women," she intoned, defeated. "And I always assumed it was because the ones I've slept with all had similar bodies to me, and I trusted that they would know what to do, but I told Kieran exactly, *exactly*, what I like, and it just felt like I was asking too much."

"I promise," Ellie said soberly, "it gets easier."

"Such a stupid fucking adjustment."

"It isn't stupid!"

"Like, god forbid I ask someone else for their time, or labor, or energy, or effort. I feel ridiculous for even worrying about it. I feel like a . . ."—Avra cast around—"a shitty feminist, I think. But I did what I was *supposed to do*. I pushed through the self-conscious bullshit and told him what I prefer, and still nothing! I physically couldn't feel anything. Nothing at all, really."

"Sometimes it helps me to feel the pressure of my own hands," Ellie said, shrugging. "I'll press my palm against my upper thighs or my stomach, or touch my fingertips together, and it's a reminder that I'm in the room, and to focus on some sensations that feel safe, or soothing. Any sensations that I don't associate with shame, I guess."

"And that works?"

"Yeah, actually. I did a lot of somatic grounding stuff with my last therapist, for my social anxiety, you know." Avra didn't know. "And it translates pretty well to the bedroom."

"Okay. Like what else?"

"I know this might sound too easy, or too woo-woo or something, but literally just deep breathing helps. Although, then there's the self-consciousness about how your stomach looks."

"Fuck," Avra said.

"Fuck," Ellie confirmed.

"I hate this shit."

"Me too." The air was displaced with their sighed commisera-
tion, their companionate efforts to reach for pleasure deservingness,
for pleasure assertiveness, and to actually find them.

"I don't want to have to *adjust* to receiving orgasms from someone!" Avra spat the word like a curse. "I want to just . . . just know
how to do it." Her voice was bladed and lemony.

"You're not even twenty, dude. How would you possibly be a
sex expert?"

"Fanfiction?"

"No." Ellie was laughing again.

"Coursework?"

"Insufficient!"

"God damn it." Avra flopped back onto the bed. Ellie took the
T-shirt from her hands, folded it, and laid it beside her thigh.

"I know, babe."

"Well, thanks for listening." Avra tried to feel relief, but her
stomach was still turning, a familiar worry buzzing beneath her fingernails. Ellie patted her knee and stood.

"Anytime. I'm gonna make some lunch. You want?"

"In a minute," Avra replied, still huffily horizontal. When Ellie
left, Avra turned the conversation over and over, examining its
myriad sides: How the receipt of kindness from men, the receipt
of sexual generosity, felt simply *unnatural*. How women were so
socialized into the brutality of gender, so burdened with expectations of abuse and dehumanization, they apologized shamefacedly
for their own sexual enjoyment. How they learned to police their
bodies, to hide their bellies, to hold their breath. How they were
all—consciously or unconsciously—laying across the tracks and
waiting breathlessly for a slaughter, bracing for the train of harm to
finally bisect them.

After lunch, Avra sat full and agitated on the couch, her feet curled beneath a soft purple cushion, a pilling throw blanket across her lap. Ellie was flipping through streaming options, suggesting movies while Avra grunted noncommittally and sipped from a large sweating glass of iced peppermint tea. A text came in from Kieran, asking about her return to campus. She ignored it. She felt a brutish urge to block his number and ignored that, too. Better to be less available. Better to leave him wanting . . . something, she supposed, even if she had such trouble believing that something would ever actually be her.

A few weeks later, she told Ellie about the get-in-touch attempts from her mom, and Ellie smoothed one of her eyebrows without speaking. Half an hour later, Ellie was baking Avra a sugar-crusted chocolate-chip banana bread with small ravines of buttery cinnamon shot through the loaf, while Nico listened thoughtfully to Avra's disclosures from his designated seat at their kitchen counter.

"Makes sense why you might be a little more nervous about staying in touch with Kieran," Nico mused benignly. "I mean, you keep getting all these reminders of a Very Important Person"— Avra heard the "TM" that Nico didn't say—"who left you. I'd feel insecure, I think, if it was me."

"You know, you really should consider switching your major," Avra repeated for about the sixteenth time. She had spent the last year encouraging Nico toward psychology with ever more ardor. Ellie placed a steaming slice of bread onto one of her grandmother's china plates, decorated with dainty baby-blue flowers. She followed the bread with an enormous pat of Irish butter from the yellow tub that lived in the door of their refrigerator. Melted fat and chocolate smeared together across the knife's edge as Ellie pushed it in Avra's direction. Avra's mouth watered at the promise of something delicious; her eyes watered at her emotionally generous friendships and Nico's measured insights, at her own feelings of unworthiness, the little left-behind girl still living in her body and wondering what was so repulsive about her that her mother could fail to choose her daughter. The tide inside Avra pulled seductively toward self-sabotage, as it always did when things felt comfortable, when people were kind, when her friendships were good. She took a large bite of the banana bread and swallowed the urge to say something nasty, just because.

——————✿——————

Avra texted Kieran incrementally less as the inertia of fall semester hit a rumbling stride. She tried to measure her retreat—one text to each of his three, four days apart and then five—so that he had to chase her, to prove his affection.

I'm just really swamped with work, she said, and then

Sorry, I know it's been a few days, and then, almost a week later:

How's Braden?

She reflected not on the afternoons wrapped around Kieran in warm sunlight, or spread across his chest on the couch, but on their high school years. Her mom reached out again despite Avra's consistent nonresponse, and Avra spent one venomous afternoon writing moody poetry about Kieran's violence and cruelty, his staggering unreliability, the dangerous discrepancy of both affectation and affection. The projection was so obvious, Avra considered setting up a therapy appointment with the campus counseling center, but didn't.

Meanwhile, Kieran woke to panic attacks in the middle of the night. She knew this from Brigid, who sent her a series of loosely related texts under the patent pretense of needing help on essays for an AP English class.

Kieran gave me ur # and id super appreciate your help

Then

You were always so smart in school, it drove him nuts but he talked about it a bunch, and I have no idea how to write this paper. I rly want to get good grades so I can get into a super killer college and I can't ask mom and K isn't really in the place to help me rn

And

hes in kind of a rough shape. Not sure if u kno abt the panic attacks. *frowny face*—might help if you reached out to him. Braden (roomie) says hes in bed a lot more now & B seems nice and I know hes trying to be a good friend but he spends all this time at his gfs house n I dont want K all alone.

And

No pressure tho, I honestly rly just need yr help w the essay

Then

<3

Then

Thx so much

Avra thought this quite the flimsy excuse for a concerned sister reach-out, an intermediary encouraging her toward communication reciprocity, particularly because Brigid had been a straight-A student her entire life, per Kieran's proud reporting, and also she never asked for Avra's email. Avra responded with effusive warmth, trying to communicate to Brigid, *I am forever obsessed with your brother but a small troll living beneath a bridge in my brain is constantly telling me he thinks I'm human garbage.* She didn't word in quite like that. She wasn't certain she got the point across at all. But she was nice, and apologetic, and nice, and agreeable, and nice.

Avra's imagination filled in the blanks of Kieran's supposed suffering. Maybe Braden—worried, annoyed with Avra, dishing to Val on the weekends—tried coaxing Kieran out of bed, with a poor success rate. Maybe Kieran refused to preseason train with the team and would be benched. Maybe he missed calls from his mom, worried texts from his teammates, and assignment deadlines. Maybe his whole life was falling apart without her.

Despite the accumulating heaps of evidence, aggregating into a chronic guilt that lived behind Avra's left lung, she refused to acknowledge, mostly, that he missed *her*. That the craving was a shard of glass deep in his spine. That it might hurt Kieran to breathe, hurt to move, until she reached out again.

They visited one another in dreams, their subconscious link fueled by alienation and mutual obsession, fear and resentment and insecurity and codependence. Avra woke at three a.m. to the wild urge to call him just so they could breathe back and forth over the phone. Once, she nearly packed a bag and drove to his apartment, but she worried about facing Braden, who would undoubtedly be bodyguard-furious and unimpressed. The nights she didn't dream of Kieran, Avra revisited a recurring dream from her childhood: She was breaking her mother out of a dragon's lair. Together, they hopped a river of magma via large, flat, gray stones and Avra's mother stumbled, as she always did. The dragon loomed, and Avra—body between the beast and her grinning, seemingly unaffected mom—stood in full knightly finery, wrapped in bright steel armor and wielding a sword. When the dragon insisted her mother remain behind, Avra refused, brandishing what appeared, in comparison to the dragon's immensity, a metal toothpick. When the dragon enveloped her in its bored, flaming breath, Avra woke knowing she was dead.

On her twentieth birthday, it had been nine days since their last text. She half expected Kieran to show up as a surprise. He didn't, and Avra practically spat out the candles on her birthday cake. She hadn't invited him to the party. She wasn't even sure if she wanted him there.

Somewhere in the back of her mind, Avra knew that she was approaching the self-conscious crux of queer adulthood where the rebellious fervor of being *out* and *proud* and *certain* of one's mission and *eager* to break barriers is overtaken somewhat by an insidious, impressible curiosity: What if all those other people are right? Avra mulled it over, staring at a large orange number 2 helium balloon hovering by the kitchen window. What if she actually *was* bad, broken, cursed, and wicked? What if she was a shitty queer, but she was failing, entirely, at her one chance to be straight? What if bisexuality was a naive little myth, a self-centered performance of those silly people too narcissistic to *just decide already?* What if her mother could sense this absurdity, sense Avra's incurable evil, and coke was just her way of coping with the sin of the daughter? What if people left because rebels are, actually, quite difficult to love? What if Kieran had burned out, permanently, on his chase? What if he decided she wasn't worth it? After all, he wasn't here, and her birthday cake tasted like dust, and she tried not to shriek thinking about that afternoon two years ago—their first, heady kiss in that white-walled practice room, which may as well have never happened, because it obviously didn't mean what she wanted it to mean. Clearly it meant nothing at all.

Besides, Avra reminded herself as October closed, no degree of effort could transform her into an appropriate proxy for men. She couldn't open jars, couldn't hock a loogie, couldn't throw a football. And people were horrible at self-denial, truly. Mom was the metaphor and it was so obvious, so pathological, Avra wished she could kick herself in the shins. Fundamentally, Avra thought one day while she was peeing and holding her phone in both hands and looking through that ridiculous Kieran album once more, the world was rocking her gently toward self-loathing. She had always been just on the cusp of it, tipping back and forth between performative egoism and a hatred so pure, it could have cauterized the festering wound of her self-esteem. Her own willingness to participate in this scalding embrace reinscribed her self-diagnosis as terribly, terribly unlovable and horribly unhappy.

In the first week of November, when she didn't hear from Kieran even once, Avra decided—bitterly cursing at herself in mirrors for no reason, ignoring affectionately concerned voicemails from her father—that all these unwinnable wars may actually be the kinds you aren't able to win. You may actually lose, she thought, twisting dramatically under a woman she would never call again. Because what kind of person could love a girl who fucks everyone? And what kind of girl who fucks everyone could even know how to love?

CHAPTER 20

NOVEMBER 2012

Avra's fall semester was characterized by ping-ponging competition: approach versus avoidance. She tracked each incoming text from Kieran, whom she forced to swallow his pride (like molten metal) again and again.

happy belated bday, saw the pictures.

Nothing. Then,

Im sorry I missed it
did ellie make the cake?

Nothing.

On the days Avra didn't receive texts from him, she stared disappointedly at the message thread despite the disproportionate debris piled along her end of the reciprocity highway. She missed him, resented it, missed him, tried desperately to turn the volume down, missed him, and wished ardently to perseverate on anything or anyone else. On one occasion, she opened their text thread to find a promising set of floating dots. All at once, she imagined a marathon of Kieran's patience, minutes or hours of halting attempts to say what needed to be said. The dots disappeared moments later, however, and Avra wondered tempestuously how often she had overlooked this infuriating phenomenon. He plagued her imagination during classes, movie nights, conversations with Ellie. Avra thought of his fingers inside her body, his mouth sealed along the line of her throat, his teeth, his arms, his back. Anytime someone walked by wearing his cologne, Avra craned her neck, breathed a pranayama breath and held, like she could lock the smell of him in her respiratory system, hold his ghost hostage in the oxygenation of her blood. When Avra's attention drifted thusly, Ellie snapped her fingers in front of Avra's face before gently pressing her finger against the tip of Avra's nose, and Avra apologized distractedly for the sixth, seventh, eighth time.

The second week of November, Avra's phone buzzed. She expected Kieran, hoped for yet another humble appeal prior to their holiday break, immediately considered ignoring this one too, but it was an unknown number.

Hi honey! its mom. I messaged you on Facebook a while ago and I didn't hear anything so I thought I'd try your phone. I hope it's okay, I asked Emerson for your number.

Avra reminded herself to call Emerson and pick a fight. She filed away a few lines for her "I thought we were silent co-conspirators" confrontation.

I hear your doing so well in college and that youve been auditioning for shows. You get that from me, you kno!

Avra rolled her eyes. Her dad was an *excellent* singer, a *fine* dancer. Any performer's charisma she had was certainly a contribution of his genetics. Besides, she hadn't auditioned for a show in over a year. After her last audition, when she didn't get the part, Avra decided without consultation that all roles must have gone to the performing arts majors. She comforted herself by insisting she hadn't actually had the time.

I'd love to catch up whenever your ready. This is my new number—text or call me when you get the chance. luv you.

Her new number. Avra understood what that meant—her old number had been turned off, or she had peddled the phone for booze money, or one of her many unsavory associates had stolen it, or, in a state of intoxicated euphoria, she had simply given it away.

Unthinking, Avra closed the text and opened her messages with Kieran.

Hi, she said, reaching her palms through the muck of their bond, through the silt and the sand, all the way up to her wrist. *I'm sorry I've been so unavailable. I think I'm just having a stupid little crisis about this whole thing.* It hardly seemed enough, "this whole thing," but she figured he'd know what she meant. *I hope we get the chance to reconnect.* She didn't say *falling in love scares me to death because my mom left when I was a kid and once your mom leaves you, you pretty much assume that everybody else will, too, so you turn into a bit of a sadist and kick the people who matter over and over to see if they'll keep coming back and I truly hate to say it but I've been really enjoying kicking you.* Instead, she hit send. She stared at the message afterward, at its startling insufficiency. It was a half-truth, the "stupid little crisis." It was a test, too—she wanted to see how quickly he'd respond. Avra hadn't heard from her mom in two years before that Facebook message. There had been a two-week gap in between Mom's last message and this text. In the space of two minutes, before the screen had even darkened, her phone buzzed again.

I think we should talk. I could come see you? Fuck. Punctuation. Kieran was using actual punctuation. And capital letters? Acid pooled in Avra's stomach.

I'm home for Thanksgiving in like a week and a half. Want to meet up then? She replied.

okay—hope ur doing alright. Avra read the pity into this one, the concern, the empathy, and suddenly wished to take it all back. No, she was fine. No, she didn't want to talk.

You too. She said, also using punctuation, also practicing a manipulative brevity. It seemed only fair.

Thanksgiving hobbled toward Avra with a halting clumsiness and then, as if coming into its identity, arrived declaratively: I am here. She sampled sixteen kinds of dessert and let her cousin French braid her hair and watched her dad and uncles make the turkey bones into stock and didn't do any homework at all, not one single assignment.

She didn't confront Emerson about the Mom problem. It wasn't worth it.

She and Kieran arranged to meet up the night after Thanksgiving at that same bookstore bar, like a full-circle moment, like a regeneration. She drove over in the dark, her headlights staring down the road, and petted the wheel as though soothing a horse. Probably she was the horse, because the car was inanimate and didn't need her. Avra's panic rose and fell, her desire rose and fell, and Kieran wasn't real, wasn't quite a human to her, until she recognized his green family Subaru parked out front. If his car was real, then certainly he had to be real, and then so was this. See? She could do logic.

When she walked into the shop, he was actually reading, and this was the worst. She experienced a moment of greasy annoyance at him doing something she found so instinctively attractive. He never struck her as "a reader." His hair was blocking his face, but his body stilled when she entered, and Avra knew he was stopping himself from looking up, trying to appear unconcerned, trying to play chill. He barely pulled it off.

"Any good?" Avra asked upon approaching. When he looked up at her face, her whole body thawed, and the absurdity of her several-month semi-silence hit her with the emotional blunt force of a truck. Stupid. So stupid.

"Really good, actually." Kieran's eyes didn't move from her face. They were locked, relieved, and it really was good to see him, actually, really good to see each other finally. She thought she could stay in the room, perhaps, if his mouth was between her legs right now. She thought nothing could tear her out of the room at all this time. Not even fear, not even God.

Avra looked at the book jacket. Kieran's thumb was covering the author's name. *This Is How You Lose Her,* by Junot something. Díaz, Avra thought, filling in the blank. She knew that name. Her belly swooped again, at Kieran reading Junot Díaz while he waited for her in a bookshop.

"I like him," she said.

"My TA recommended it a few weeks ago. Found it on the shelf when I got here," Kieran explained, though he didn't have to.

"Your TA has good taste."

Kieran blushed at this, and Avra filed the response away.

"Yeah, Jordan is pretty cool." For a second, Avra had an intrusive fantasy of Jordan bleeding on the side of a road somewhere. *Mine, mine, mine* curled around her tongue, hummed prettily against the soft insides of her cheeks, and she smiled carnivorously.

"Want to order?"

Kieran's guard hovered around waist-height as he selected a cocktail—no old fashioned for him this time, and Avra made a joke, and Kieran self-consciously praised his own maturation, and they commiserated over a shared dislike of snooty cocktails. Avra's GI tract had been tart with worry all day. She ordered a spearmint tea, and added an overcorrective proportion of honey, and tried to be honey-sweet herself, making up for her prolonged absence. Kieran was defrosting, grinning more easily as they quipped, and

when his knee pressed against hers for the first time, Avra ran a fingertip along the back of his hand, just because.

"Been a while," she said.

"Hated it," he replied.

"I'm really sorry." She meant it, and it jolted through her just
how much.

"Want to tell me what the fuck happened?"

Avra sighed predictably, held her warm mug in both palms, and
twisted her mouth as she tried to figure out an answer. "How much
time do you have?"

"I have all night," Kieran said. "Do you need to be somewhere?"

"I told Dad I'd be back by like eleven," she lied, providing herself
an out, and Kieran masked his disappointment with some difficulty.
"But I can maybe stretch it." Avra liked allowing herself an escape
route, liked giving herself some latitude.

"All right then. Tell me what happened," he prompted, and
then, "please."

"A few things, I think," she said. "I freaked out a little. I really
. . ." She took a sip as she decided to be honest. "I've never had to
navigate patriarchy in my relationships before." She could start with
the nonspecifics, with the bird's-eye view. "I've never had to con-
tend with the needs and desires of men. I haven't had to consider
a man's feelings, I haven't had to think of myself in relation to men.
And I haven't had to think about men thinking about me in relation
to them, you know? Like, I don't have to imagine the way women
imagine me. Basically, I just haven't ever had to figure out what it
means to be perceived by men, or to deal with them. Masculinity,
sure, but not *guys*. It's one of the best parts of being with women,
really. I feel more worthy, and it's all so much simpler. I mean, you've
known me since we were kids. Being queer is *who I am*, and this
thing with you always felt like . . . like betraying it, somehow. Like

failing the community, or turning my back on women, and I find it hard to stomach myself when I think about it that way. I get all this twisted, persistent self-loathing. And I really never wanted this! I never wanted to have this idiotic fucking crush on you. I don't want to think about you all the time." Kieran grinned, the relief so obvious it was charming, and Avra shoved his knee in a *kindly shut up* sort of way before continuing. "And with you, patriarchy takes up space. You've said it yourself: You treated me like shit in high school, and I managed to get this *emotionally invested* in you anyway. *And* you're a dude, and you have all this power, and sometimes I don't know how to let you be nice to me. It's an adjustment, and I think the last time we saw each other, it hit me how huge, how ridiculously massive, the adjustment is."

She took another sip, and Kieran's eyes were on her nose, her cheek, her throat. She could tell he was listening, but he was devouring the sight of her as well, wolfing the sounds of her confessional, a starving beast. The heat between her thighs unfurled like a kite. She wanted to climb him. She wanted to talk. "And I'm not sure I know how to be nice to *you*, either. Sometimes I don't actually think of you as a person, and I know this is so fucked up." Kieran's head tilted over his right shoulder, his eyes narrowed, but he didn't interrupt, and she respected that about him. "But when you text me, or try to get in touch, I don't always think of you as Kieran-who-wants-to-go-down-on-me." He blushed. There were three stools between them and the next person at the bar. The lights were low, Norah Jones played softly in the background, but Avra's voice carried, and the bartender grinned as she shook a cocktail. "I think of you as Kieran-who-pushed-me-around-a-lot. And I don't feel like I owe you anything when I'm remembering you that way. Not my time. Not my responses. It's selfish and shitty. And on top of that"—and she hoped he got it, she really did—"my mom keeps trying to reach me, and it makes me feel like a worthless little garbage person every time I hear from her, and I can't imagine a universe in which the people I love don't leave me." She said the word "love" by accident, but now it was out there and she couldn't capture it, couldn't hide it like a grasshopper in her cupped hands. It halted her in her tracks, all the momentum stolen from her lungs, and Kieran took the space while Avra stewed in her sour confusion.

"Okay," Kieran said. Then, "okay," again, as he took a long drink of his not-an-old-fashioned. "I have a few things to say, if you don't mind."

"Say them."

"First of all, thank you for what you said, because I think I get where you're coming from a bit more now. But things aren't all better just because you told me this stuff, you know?" His voice was carefully strung, violin-taut, and Avra knew he was swallowing hurt, anger, the way he knew how. "You don't get to just say 'I don't really see you as a person' and keep failing to see me as a person. Like, doing a fucked-up thing doesn't become *not* fucked up by you recognizing you're doing it. I *am* a person, and I've been really mad at you. And sad, too. And embarrassed, because I *am* . . . Kieran-who-wants-to-go-down-on-you." He had forced out the words, and Avra blushed magnificently and the bartender was eavesdropping and this was so brave, Avra knew, so brave of him, and she wanted to house this moment in ice, to live in its igloo forever. "And I don't know how to change or make up for the fact that I'm also Kieran-who-was-a-piece-of-shit-to-you. I want to do that, and I think I'm afraid that I'm never going to, and you're going to decide I'm just *that guy,* or that I'm still *that guy.* And part of me worries, too, that honestly, maybe I *am* that guy, because you walked in . . ." He lowered his voice, and Avra tilted forward subconsciously. "You walked in, and my first thought was how maybe if I get to fuck you hard enough, I won't be so mad at you anymore. Like, maybe if I get to hurt you, to mess you around a little, I won't feel so angry." Avra's body responded with such keen interest that she almost rolled her eyes at her own underwear. "I don't know what that is." His voice was rough and chaotic, the self-disgust palpable. "I don't know what's wrong with me."

Avra wanted to touch him, so she did. She coasted a palm along his forearm, lingered over each of his fingers, dropped a hand to his knee, and his legs shifted open, almost imperceptibly, the pattern of his body meeting the pattern of hers. "And there's stuff I've wanted to talk to you about, too. Because Braden's the best, he really is, but he's never met a conversation that he can't make about himself, and I really thought that we were going to be that, for each other. Like, I want to hear about your mom, when you're hurting about it. I want to talk about how patriarchy shows up in our"—he hesitated—"I never know whether to call it a relationship. In our whatever, I guess. And also I want to take you apart, sometimes."

"I daydream about making you crawl," Avra said, interrupting, conversational.

"I daydream about fucking you until you cry," Kieran responded, even-toned. "What's that all about?" They both laughed in a haha-we're-probably-terrible kind of way.

"Okay, well, we're in public right now, so in lieu of all that, talk to me about what Braden doesn't handle well," Avra invited, and Kieran did.

He talked about preseason training, and the guys, and navigating around Isaac, and how he finally told Braden about Isaac's come-on, and how Braden cried but wasn't angry. He talked about his major—business, *gross*—and how much he hated it, and how he thought maybe something else, but didn't know what. He talked about how his dad was an asshole, judgmental and controlling, and how he should start therapy, maybe, because he kept hiding snacks around his bedroom, and it started as a weird little trauma joke just with himself, only now they had mice, and he couldn't stop hiding the food. Time scrambled along the anecdotes and Avra was pressed thigh-to-thigh against him, laughing until she leaked tears and smudged eyeliner, leaning against Kieran's shoulder, trusting her guts enough to order a cocktail, and then Kieran cleared his throat and Avra knew this was something he'd been waiting to say.

"I wanted to talk to you about Jordan."

"What about him?"

"He hits on me, and he's nice, and he's smart." A few months ago, Avra probably would have felt pride, would have soothed her possessiveness with the assertion that boys should *always* kiss boys, would have encouraged this with an enthusiasm well past the line of fetishism. But that was a few months ago.

"So, are you interested, or . . . ?"

Kieran could read her shift in tone, and made an attempt at comfort, which was interrupted by a toothpick of resentment. "I wasn't! I wasn't into him at all. I mean, I noticed that he's good-looking, because I have eyes, but I didn't think anything—only then, you know, you went all unresponsive and I kind of just assumed you were done with me."

"So, what, he was next on the list?"

"I didn't say that."

Avra thought it had been close enough. "Kind of a fucked-up power dynamic, don't you think?"

Kieran actually laughed. "Right, fuck you, like it's any different from this one."

It didn't sting so much because he was clearly correct, but Avra's mind flashed again to a dead imaginary Jordan on the side of a darkened road and it soothed her covetous grumble.

"I had a crush on a TA once," Avra said, changing the subject. Kieran allowed it.

"What did you like about her?" His accurate pronoun made Avra want to waltz along an entire ballroom floor of being seen and understood.

"Her handwriting," she clarified instead. "She graded in actual red pen, and her *a*'s had this little curl at the bottom, and she'd write all the praise stuff like *good job* in cursive, and I just found it kind of winsome. That attention to detail. I assumed she'd be a thoughtful lover." Avra wondered if a competitive jealousy was roiling in Kieran's belly as well. But he had never risked invalidating Avra's love of women, never clarified their boundaries when it came to possessiveness and control, and seemed to shrug it off. Sort of.

"You weren't worried about the power dynamic?"

"Well, I didn't fuck her, did I?" Avra countered.

"Didn't you?"

"No." An obvious relief, to both of them.

"I haven't even texted Jordan, if it makes you feel any better."

"I wasn't worried," Avra lied again.

"There's something else I wanted to talk to you about," Kieran said, and his cheeks were red from a second cocktail, and his chin was sitting in his hand.

"What's that?"

"The ghosting."

Avra gulped, worried her lip, flexed her palm.

"All right."

"It was fucked up," he proclaimed. Avra didn't speak. "I think it was mean. You pretty much disappeared immediately after the *one* time sex wasn't, like, perfect. You make all this noise about how sex is messy and complicated and clumsy and that sexual communication is super important, right? And I believe you, and I listen, and I try really hard to communicate and ask for direction. And then I mess up, literally once, and you don't let me fix it." Kieran didn't like talking about sex in public. Or, maybe he just didn't like revisiting the spectacular pain of Avra's vanishing act. His voice was metered, self-conscious, his posture defensive and rigid. Avra didn't think now would be an ideal time to remind him of his own communication style, years ago—how she had learned this avoidance, in part, from him.

"I already told you, you didn't fuck it up," Avra began, her tone a shade of orange, but Kieran interrupted her, which he rarely did.

"I really wanted to learn. Like, I *still* want to learn. I tried texting, like, to prove it. I wanted to show you. But you were all shady and detached. I didn't even get the chance to get any better." Something about Kieran's sincerity always made Avra's chest cleave open, her eyes swim, the guilt from her own lack of communication coating her skin in a film of shame. A week ago, she had been enjoying the possibility of hurting him. She wasn't enjoying it now.

"I hate that I did that," Avra said, and Kieran breathed out hard through his nose. "I hate that I kind of disappeared right after we tried to focus on me. And I'm down to try it again. I want to, actually. I just dissociated."

"What does that even *mean?*"

"I got so nervous that maybe you weren't actually enjoying yourself, or you weren't into it, or you'd rather be with somebody else—a guy, you know—or maybe you found my pussy just horrifying," Kieran's eyes went wide and disbelieving, and Avra was certain her face was scarlet, that her freckles themselves were darkening in the shade of her openness. "I didn't know how to let you take care of me. I didn't know how to stay. I wound up floating around the ceiling fan and totally abandoning my body, and it was harder to give direction, and then I thought, well, it doesn't really matter if I give direction anyway, because no matter what he does, I'm not going to be able to feel it. And so I got too anxious to ask, or to say something. Being vulnerable with you like that scared me." Kieran was touching her again, curving his arm around the back of her chair, settling a broad palm against the back of her neck and rubbing his thumb along her hairline, feather-light and slow, the way he liked, the way he knew she liked.

"I've been scared of you for years."

Avra scoffed. "Yeah, whatever."

"It's true. Especially when we were kids and I knew that you knew. About me, I mean. I've been scared to death of you. That day you were handing out the GSA fliers, and I'd seen you watching me and Will, I just—I knew you could fuck up my life. And if I'm being *honest and introspective*, yeah, that's why I was such shit to you."

"I know that," Avra said.

"Of course you do," Kieran replied. "Just, you were so intense and weird and you looked right through me and I didn't enjoy it, back then. I knew, like, if anyone could out me in a sentence, in a word, you could do it. So I was mean about it, and then I'd ruminate about what might happen if I pushed you too far, and part of me wanted to find out. And at the same time, I think I also knew, fuck, if anyone is brave enough to make me feel brave enough to do this, it's her. And I hated your guts for that. I hated that you could fuck up my life if you wanted. And I hated wanting to know what would happen if you tried, and hoping a little that you *would* fuck up my life just so I didn't have to do it myself. And I keep thinking I'm going to get over that thing, right? That thing of putting you on a pedestal because you're out and loud and ballsy as hell and so much smarter than I am. Of resenting you for it and wanting to shove you around and clearly

I'm still kind of lost." He said it with a shrug, like it didn't matter, but Avra knew this was the performance, the minimization of fear like he wasn't losing acres of sleep. "Basically, I think I'm an idiot for seeing you as some kind of authority because you're also pretty obviously fucked up. And nobody can live on a pedestal. And you still scare me to death. Like, I'm afraid of what I want to learn from you." He shook his head, as if to clear some image, some scandal, and dug his thumb into the meeting place of her neck and shoulder, pressure point contact and katana control, before saying, "I'm nervous about what you could make me do, if you wanted to. And I'm definitely scared of the things I want to do to you."

Avra was smiling, and probably she should not have been. She didn't know when it had started. The pressure of Kieran's thumb was grounding, soothing, and if he pushed any harder, she would shift her head just so.

"I think we need to figure out how to not terrify each other," Avra said, matter of fact, and Kieran dragged his thumb smoothly along the few fine hairs that had escaped the base of her ponytail. Goosebumps followed.

"Deal."

The bartender was turning off lights, collecting cash, reminding people in a kind but insistent tone that it was eleven, the end of last call, Avra's dishonest witching hour. Kieran swore, surprised. Avra hummed a few lines of "Closing Time."

"That was so fast," Kieran said.

"Time flies, et cetera," Avra replied.

"But we didn't even get to talk about all of your stuff. I feel like I've missed so much. I mean, your mom—"

"No, that's okay." Avra found, categorically, that she didn't want to discuss her mother. "We'll talk about it another time. Let's get out of their way."

Kieran pushed back from his stool and stood, large and gorgeous, his silhouette framed by bookshelves and hazy lighting. He paid for the Junot Díaz novel, and their drinks, and Avra thanked him sincerely, and it was so obvious that he loved her, so obvious that she felt like hurling her cynicism into a canyon, dancing on its grave, relieving the odious burden. They were the last two to leave.

"Lucky nobody we know decided tonight was a bookshop night," Kieran said as they stepped out into the crisp November evening. Avra was grateful for her lined layers.

"Because . . . ?"

"Because I'm twenty and still using my brother's ID. You know, they didn't even ask, when I came in?"

"Me neither. But I'm looking all mature college-girl, with the tights and the turtleneck, and you sat at the bar reading Junot freaking Díaz. Maybe we just seem convincingly *adult*."

Kieran slid the small paperback into his jacket pocket and laughed, as if the possibility of being perceived as an adult was really all that absurd. Avra provided a counterpoint: "Or maybe they're just trying to make some cash off of those naughty underaged boozehounds."

"Either way," Kieran said, "risky."

"Oh, for *sure*," Avra affirmed, somewhat tongue-in-cheek. "Dangerous."

Kieran's hands hung at his sides, thumbs tapping a staccato rhythm against the pocket of his jeans. He kicked the ground and hesitated in his characteristic, awkwardly stalling way, and Avra grinned again. They had wandered a step or two away from the bookshop door. The bartender exited, shot them a *this is kinda cute* look, locked the door, tested it, half smiled at Avra, and walked toward her car. They watched her go, and Avra wondered how many couples had hesitated under this same broad awning, biding their time. A pair of headlights curved across the parking lot, illuminating the two of them, the mouth of the little plaza alleyway, and Avra's Prius before highlighting the road. Avra and Kieran maintained a stretched-taffy silence. He took several steps toward the wall before turning to watch Avra and leaning thoughtfully against the cold brick. She stared at his impassive face.

"This feels weird," he said.

"What part?"

"The part where I'm not kissing you."

"Oh, *that* part." She took a step toward him. "I could fix it, if you want," she said, and the breath between them was mist, curling as it rose. The pair of them steamed together on the covered walk.

"That would be good," Kieran said, losing some articulation now that Avra was in his space. She wondered whether he could smell her same spiced-vanilla perfume. She wondered if he realized, as she did, that he hadn't held her in months.

Avra stood on tiptoe to reach him, and his arms came up around her back automatically, practically lifting her forward, like she was light as air, like he'd been waiting an age. She could feel the tense tremble of his forearms, his broad hands against her shoulder blades. The kiss was all gasping gratitude and apologies, *thank fuck* and *please, harder* and *why would anyone ever run from something so good?* Kieran tasted like grapefruit and desperation and Avra was curling her hands around his jacket his shoulders his skull his ears his back his hips, pulling and grabbing like she really could find some purchase and climb, and he was retaliating urgently, burying his fingers into the flesh of her lower back, flattening a palm up over her spine, tugging her turtleneck out from the waist of her skirt. Her breath hitched at the temperature of his fingers.

"Sorry," Kieran said, but he didn't remove his hands.

"Better not be," Avra insisted, and her mouth was open and wet, and god, this was just as good as she remembered, toe-curling the way she remembered, and Kieran was making small noises of relief as they pawed at each other, and headlights rolled by once every fifteen minutes, and no one could see them from the road. What passed could have been an hour, or several, or some infinite stretch of pleasure. Kieran maneuvered them into switched positions, Avra's back against the stone, Kieran's thumbs in a favorite place under her jaw, and he was looming over her as they kissed, using his body to box her in, and she was so tiny, completely hidden. He licked over her bottom lip and pulled away, and her mouth chased, and he did it again, and she whined a little, annoyed and delighted. In a petty rebuke, Avra thrust her own cold hands inside Kieran's coat, lifted the soft weave of his thick red sweater, and touched her frigid fingertips to the sensitive skin of his belly. He hissed at the cold and reached for her wrists, capturing them in one hand.

"Not sorry," Avra said, moving as if to touch him again, but Kieran held fast.

"Are you ever not a brat?" His lips hovered just above her ear, his thigh parting her legs slowly, the way he knew made her insides turn to glitter and molasses, and the cold was immaterial, and it was a genuinely good question.

"Pretty much only when I'm tamed," she replied, barely resistant, and she *was* a brat, sure, but a bad one.

"Such an obvious challenge," Kieran admonished, and dipped his head to kiss the side of her throat, right below her jaw, in front of her ear, the fragile skin helpless to bruising and bites. Barely there pressure, then another, open-mouthed, then another, slow, and Avra's skin was singing the way it always did when Kieran fucked around with her. Her clit ached, and her resolve to withhold from grinding against his leg frayed with each brush, over and over, the repetition itself a leash, a warning. His breath coasted along her collarbone, and she wanted him with a brutality close to mania. She tried to twist her wrists and his grip tightened infinitesimally, an obvious *no. not yet. stay still.* It was well past her witching hour, and Kieran must have known the witching hour was bullshit by now, but he didn't call her on it. He never called her on things when he was smack in the middle of getting what he wanted and wasn't that just like a guy?

He kissed her neck again and her hips rolled forward desperately. She must have looked vulgar, balancing over his thigh, head tilted back, panting, while Kieran licked a molten line across her neck and followed it with another soft, open-mouthed kiss, so indulgent, so unhurried, she might actually die.

"Are you ever not a tease?" Avra managed, meaning it, her voice strained and wobbly, and that must have been the straw, because then Kieran was pulling her along the brick wall, her tights catching once against the rough stone. Kieran was pulling her toward that little decorated alley, iron tables set up for outdoor reading and deadened twinkle lights looped around mounted hooks, and Avra knew before they even rounded the corner that Kieran was going to fuck her here. He was going to fuck her in an alley in their hometown just after midnight, maybe laid across one of the frigid patterned tables, maybe pressed up against the unforgiving brick. She saw the image before it happened—her tights rolled down around her thighs, underwear pulled to one side, skirt bunched around her waist—and it was so pornographic, so idyllic, she was tempted to describe it aloud.

Kieran crowded back into her space, released her wrists so he could tangle his hands in her hair, and kissed Avra hard against the red wall. It was all tongue and panting, wet and slick, and Avra made an inhuman sound, eager and tormented. Her jacket absorbed the cold and she felt the chill seep through to her skin, hold fast, and she was minutes from shivering. The dim light from the awning lamps caught their breath so that Avra and Kieran appeared enveloped in a cloud of their own making, each panting, the air around them a heavy, refracting silver. Kieran paused to look at Avra's face, to kiss her temple, her cheekbone, then returned to her mouth, taking time in a *be patient* way that made Avra want to fight. She bit back, rough and rushed, the *fuck me* entreaty between her teeth. They didn't have to say a thing. Kieran spoke anyway.

"Knock it off." He didn't mean it, not really. She bit him again. He placed his palms flat on either side of her neck, held her chin between his thumbs, and ran his tongue along her bottom lip. *Wait a second, just a second more.* Avra knew she wouldn't listen, knew she wanted to ignore any invitation, any demand, because they were alone in an alley and he could do whatever, anything at all, and so could she. When he spoke again, his words were welcomed by Avra's open, expectant mouth. "Knock it the fuck off. I'm trying not to hurt you." He said it even as his fingers dug deeper, as Avra's nails slid up his back, along either side of his spine.

She bit him again, harder, wanting the blood.

He retaliated by fisting a hand in her hair, sharp, merciless, and tilting her head up.

"I *said* I don't want to hurt you right now." It was absolute garbage and they both knew it. Avra smirked and raised a dark eyebrow and let out a condescending tinkle of a laugh.

"Fuck you, yes you do"—his own curses flew back in his face. Kieran crushed her with the next kiss, bit along her bottom lip and jaw, clawed a set of fingernails down the side of her throat, and Avra knew the trails would glow red-hot and she loved it, she loved it. It was always so good like this, the two of them rough and furious. And he was fucking her mouth with his tongue, and she was reaching beneath her own skirt, rolling her fleece-lined tights down with

one hand, clumsy and desperate and a little obscene. Kieran helped
her when he noticed, tugging the waistband down with a disbelieving, grateful, wretched sound before reaching back toward her face,
covering her mouth with his fingers, and licking between them, so
their tongues met between his knuckles. The air was cold around
Avra's bare thighs and something in her blood was screaming, her
cunt was dripping, and she wanted Kieran to choke her until she
passed out, to split her lip until she bled down the front of her shirt.
She made a distraught sound against his fingers, and he turned her
around so quickly her head whipped. She almost smacked her forehead on the wall, but Kieran's hand was back in her hair, tugging
her painfully toward safety.

Kieran swore when he saw the pale strip of thigh between the
lowered nylon of Avra's tights and the hem of her skirt. "You look
fucking good," he said, breath bursting hotly against the back of her
neck. Avra mewled, spread her legs, and Kieran dropped the hand
that was tangled in her hair to grip her hip, fingers punishing and
vicious, and Avra flashed back to cut lime and tequila, to her prayer
for proof. When she arched—an invitation, a demand—her cheek
scraped gloriously along the stone wall. She raised her forearms
to steady herself, dropped her head between them, and her wrists
were bare and frozen, her fingers going numb, and she could hear
Kieran's zipper behind her, hear him fumble to get his pants down
with one hand. He practically shoved her underwear to the side,
gathering it in a fist.

"Thought you said you weren't trying to hurt me," Avra mocked,
coy and infuriating, as she felt the fabric pop a stitch.

"Shut the fuck up."

"Oh, *please*," she retaliated, squirming. "Tell me you don't get
off on this."

Kieran reached up around her face, grabbed her jaw in one

broad hand, and suddenly his palm was the protective barrier between Avra's cheek and the wall, and it should have been a relief, but it wasn't.

"I told you to shut up."

"You also told me you fantasize about fucking me until I cry."

"Goddamn it, Av."

"Hey," she said evenly, licking along the pads of his fingers, holding herself together by a single, spidery thread. "Your words."

"I don't have a condom," Kieran warned, an afterthought, and Avra briefly considered the fact that her period had ended two days ago, and that the chance of her ovulating was low, and also that she didn't give a single fuck right now, not one, she really didn't.

"Don't come inside me then. You can make me a mess, if you want." She paused, shifted her hips back, and promised, "I'll wear you home."

And then Kieran was pushing into her, all the way in, slow at first, one long, savage glide, then out, then another, and then fast, all of a sudden, as if waiting was actually impossible, and the hypocrisy was palpable, him warning her slower, warning her patient, when his own resolve was stripped bare and he was hurtling forward, needy. The open zipper of his pants pressed hard against the flesh of Avra's ass on every thrust, and it was brutal and immaculate and thorough. He was making noises like a broken thing, half moaning into Avra's neck, using her hip bone as leverage while his palm curved around her warm, freckled cheek, and Avra was spreading her thighs open, further, more, and dropping one trembling hand to work quick circles over her clit, feeling the way Kieran slid into her with the tips of her fingers and swallowing the urge to tell him he could do whatever the fuck he wanted to her, maim her if he wanted, brand her, hurt her, forever and ever, in perpetuity.

"I missed this so much, Jesus Christ," Kieran said, laughing recklessly as he fucked her.

Avra said, "Moses, actually, but whatever," and Kieran bit the back of her neck through another laugh, and tiny stars dotted Avra's vision. She wanted to sob, wanted to curse him, wanted to never stop, wanted to stay like this for weeks, spread open and impaled and dripping onto his cock in the back alley of some bookshop while he worked her over, bruised her, confessed to missing her, pushed into her again and again.

Kieran mustered a lion tamer's control, short bursts of energy followed by languid, intentional movement, and Avra considered begging but knew it would be over the moment she said please and wasn't ready, wasn't ready, had missed this. Minutes passed like flames along a sword, like a tongue holding ice, burning and melting all at once, and Kieran varied his pace, and Avra whined, pleaded, adjusted as best she could. Her hair had fallen out of her ponytail, locks tumbling around her shoulders, and her hairband found its way to Kieran's wrist and she didn't know when it had happened. Kieran moved her hair with his free hand, releasing her hip for a just a moment so he could nip at the sensitive skin under her ear, kiss the side of her throat, and he was moving inside her with absurd patience, and Avra couldn't remember ever feeling this fucking good.

His orgasm took them both by surprise.

"Shit," he said, panic coloring his voice as he teetered along the edge, and made to pull out, and Avra's knees almost buckled.

"No, don't stop." She wanted to feel him, wanted to know what it was like, wanted to sleep with him inside her body, to absorb anything he left inside her, to mix him into her own blood and tissue, macabre and wanton. "Just keep—stay. Staypleasepleasestay." She said it quickly, packed together, one word, and Kieran listened like he'd been waiting for this, like he knew.

"Fuck. *Fu-uck.*" His voice cracked on the *u*, and Avra sighed acquiescently. She could feel him spill, feel warmth paint along the inside her body, feel him twitch, and she cataloged her senses: the press of her chin into his palm; his forefinger against the corner of her mouth; his bottom lip along the back of her ear; his other hand broad along her hip, over the curve of her ass; the ravaged, annihilated noises; the smell of winter air like maybe snow was coming; the raw sting of her lungs from sipping in the cold. She committed it all to crushed-velvet memory.

When he pulled out of her—so slowly she felt tugged from the inside out—a rivulet of something warm and wet snaked down her inner thigh. Avra hummed contentedly.

"Good?" he asked, satisfaction laced through his tone.

"Very, very good."

"I'm going to go down on you now." It wasn't a question.

"That would probably be easier in a bed, you know." She wasn't really protesting, and Kieran haphazardly yanked up his briefs, half-zipped his pants, didn't bother buttoning them.

"I don't care. I'm going to go down on you right now."

"Sir, yes, sir." It was cheeky. Kieran's come was dripping down the inside of her thighs, and this was debauchery. Filth was happening here, pure and simple, and she had missed him in a brutal and murderous way, and she thought she'd be able to stay.

"Will you show me? Talk me through what you want?"

"I will," she promised. Then, "It's cold."

"Good," Kieran turned her around slowly, fit his thumbs below her chin again, and rubbed his nose over hers, twice, three times. Sparking, live-wire affection pulled through Avra like an oath, a vow. Kieran ran one thumb down the front of her throat, kissed her chin, her left eyelid, her right, and Avra's chest ached and she thought she would break her body over rocks, leap off of a bridge if he asked it of her. "Cold is good. It'll keep you here with me." He kissed her mouth, almost chaste, and Avra opened her eyes. He was staring, waiting for her to look at him, and this was what she needed, what she always needed from him. The watchfulness, thoughtfulness, checking in, making sure. "Be cold," Kieran said, murmuring against her mouth, his eyes boring into hers, so wide. "Be cold and stay here with me."

Avra nodded, jerky, body beginning to shudder from the press of chill, and then Kieran was leading her over to a steel table, lifting her onto it, encouraging her onto her back, rolling her tights and underwear from mid-thigh down around her ankles so she could widen her knees. Her feet were bound, and Avra didn't need to look hard to find the appeal of that. Another way to be held, to be trapped.

Kieran spread her skirt below her ass and thighs so she wasn't directly against the metal, a bizarre attempt at gentlemanly consideration. The positioning was awkward, a little, and Avra almost shifted, almost spoke, but then Kieran was leaning over her, blanketing her thighs with either side of his jacket, flattening a palm over her mound and pressing toward her bellybutton so that her dripping labia parted in front of his face. He dipped a thumb into his own mouth before sliding it through her wetness, rubbing slow circles up, up, finding her clit in the dark, and Avra keened softly.

His mouth was a warm, wet relief, and noises crawled out of Avra's throat over and over again, reckless pleasure rising, escaping the depth of a well, the swelling cavern of her. Kieran stayed, licking slowly, so slowly, circles wide and flat, mouth soothing and open, hot breath over her cunt, and Avra's vision was blurring, in and out, her fists opening and closing in his hair, in her own, grasping for some kind of grounding. And the cold kept her there. Her hands on her belly and against Kieran's forehead kept her there. Her deep breaths kept her there. Kieran's mouth, hot and urgent and still so patient and willing and coaxing and perfect, kept her there. And Avra knew he was eating her out in a public alley, in the middle of the night, dirt and dust and stone around them, after pulling her hair and fucking her against a wall and roughing her up the way she liked. She knew she wouldn't normally come like this, hadn't expected to be able to come like this, but it felt correct, and time stretched like a housecat, and Avra didn't mind the passing minutes, didn't mind that she was shivering. Cold, but not numb. Near frozen, but certainly not numb. Avra could feel everything, everything, everything.

Kieran was glorious, scalding, sloppy, gliding his tongue over her clit in wet, indecent swipes and Avra was guiding his head, directing his mouth with one hand soft in his hair, positioning and precise. She leaned up on her elbow, watched her own breath curl, haunted, leaving her body, and the sight of Kieran was holy, blessed. Her orgasm crawled promisingly up her limbs, spiraling and tensing, approaching like a wild thing, skittish but determined. It hit her in stinging shock waves, tearing her apart from the inside, shattering again and again, and Avra was arching, wailing, weeping into the echoing alley. She could feel hot, grateful tears on the side of her face, and she could feel Kieran's wolfish smile against her as she shook through her orgasm, his tongue barely moving, prolonging her pleasure as it shimmered incandescently through her clit, her navel, her thighs, her nipples, her red and wild mouth.

Avra was still cursing and panting as Kieran pulled her forward by her cold hands, helped her sit up, and kissed both of her wrists, her palms, before kissing her lips, her nose, all over her face. Short, peppering kisses that made her sigh, and then snort with contagious, unselfconscious laughter. Kieran was beaming. When he pulled away, Avra sagged against his shoulder, exhausted, while he rolled her tights back up with shaking hands, over her knees, her thighs, stopping right below the hem of her skirt.

"You're hard," Avra observed, noting the bulge against Kieran's half-done zipper, against the inside of her thigh, and it sent another little flutter of sparks through her low belly, filled her veins like lava and licorice. Avra shifted, sensitive, already feeling the promise of that well-fucked soreness, her thighs and hamstrings loud from tensing, holding. She thought for a moment that Kieran could maybe fuck her again before sending her home. She was still wet. It would be so easy. She reached for him in wordless invitation, pulled his jeans and briefs down over his hip bone, and cupped a palm over his erection through the stretching, damp fabric. Kieran huffed a breath against her cheek, her throat. "Want to go again?" Avra invited.

"I'm already close," Kieran admitted, and Avra grinned against his jaw, pressed two kisses against his temple, licked along the lobe of his ear. "Give me your hand?" he asked, shyly, and the request was almost romantic. Kieran dragged the briefs down to free his erection, and Avra smiled dazedly. The tip of his cock was slick from pre-come. He settled her hand along the shaft, shifted forward once, twice, and Avra imagined she could feel him aching. It must have turned him on to get her off, because he swore loudly the moment she touched him, kept up a trail of quiet curses as they moved. Avra and Kieran kissed wetly, the crackling hearth of them warming the space between, and Kieran wrapped his own hand around Avra's smaller one before thrusting gently into their entwined fingers. Avra panted against his neck, watched his eyes flutter closed, watched his cock move against their paired palms, and thought she'd replay this scene before bed each night, every night, until she died.

Kieran fucked into the soft C of their fingers, and Avra slid her thumb beneath the ridge of the slick head the way she'd seen in gay porn, just barely pressing, and began to talk, stream-of-consciousness filth, and Kieran's breath was right at the top of his chest, his jaw tensed hard enough to break. His eyebrows pulled together while she spoke, like maybe he actually couldn't take it, like this was impossible, a devastation for which no one could prepare.

Avra praised his mouth, his perfect tongue, the look of their hands, the way he kissed her, how she could already tell she'd be sore tomorrow, slow-moving, and she'd think about him when she sat down. "I missed the way you hurt me," she said, and Kieran groaned. "I missed you messing with me," Avra urged, and the hand that wasn't wrapped around Avra's reached for her waist. Kieran dug his nails in, all frantic force, and Avra said, "yes," said, "please," said, "You look fucking hot," said, "Bruise me. I want to know you were here. Want to look at my skin tomorrow and see the proof of you. I love it when you fuck me up like this." Kieran was trembling, breath ragged, mouth open against the side of her face, and Avra licked his throat, his cheek. "Kieran"—he shivered at the sound of his own name—"I missed this. I missed you. I *missed* you. I really—" She lifted the hem of her skirt, moved their hands closer to the milky white of her thighs, and Kieran came with a rough, aching sound. He dripped over her leg, across her knee, obscene and mussed, and Avra made a show of dragging her fingertips through it during the comedown, while she kissed his cheek, his ear, his eyebrow, his mouth.

Elsewhere on earth, people battled worry and boredom and sexual frustration, and Avra pitied them from the comfort of her own satisfaction.

"Gonna wear me home?" Kieran asked eventually, sounding like he just smoked a pack and a half. Avra slid gingerly off the table, tugged her tights and underwear up over her thighs and the curve of her ass in confirmation, and then Kieran was reaching for her again, kissing her again, worshipful and gratified, desirous, utterly pleased. Kissing her until she couldn't taste any air that wasn't his. Kissing her until her tongue was sensitive, her breath hitching in little hiccups as the cold got the better of them both. Kissing her until Avra had to fight back the frantic, endorphin-fueled urge to confess, to swear it all, to crack open, to declare, *Jesus, fuck, I am so fucking in love with you I love you so much I love you goddamn it I love you and think it could actually kill me I love you so much that I want it to kill me* against his mouth. She didn't say it. She didn't say anything. But after they dressed—Kieran touching her as much as possible, straightening her turtleneck, fixing her jacket, twirling a lock of her hair—and laughed and checked the time and acknowledged that it was past one a.m., Avra promised to text him, to stay in touch, and Kieran kissed her in thanks, kissed her and kissed her, and Avra said it again.

"I'll text you soon. I'll talk to you soon. I swear I will."

Kieran nodded, grinned dazedly, wrapped in the glow of another catalytic reunion, and Avra wanted to mean it; she hoped he believed her.

CHAPTER 21

DECEMBER 2012

Avra kept her promise. She texted him almost every day—silly jokes and gossip about Ellie and updates on her classes and a countdown to winter break, when they would both be home and she could see him again. Kieran texted back: sneaky desk selfies from the middle of a lecture hall, a blurred video of the first campus snow, a favorite paragraph from that Junot Díaz book, and once *i cant stop thinking about u. its annoying.* Avra took a screenshot and saved it and resisted the urge to set the photo as her profile picture on every single one of her accounts. She was in such a spectacular mood that she hummed while getting ready for bed, giggled abruptly while tying her shoelaces, and bounced around while Ellie baked yet another steaming, seductive sweet bread. Nico laughed openly from his perch.

"You should always be texting Kieran."

"Do not encourage her, dear god," Ellie admonished, mitts-deep in the belly of the oven.

"What? She's happy!" Nico replied, grinning, gesturing toward Avra, who was wiggling her butt along to Ellie's Spotify selection.

"Yeah, El. I'm *happy*," Avra agreed with an exaggerated shimmy.

"I'm resisting the urge to be a dick about this," Ellie said gravely, but she smiled when Avra did a little bunny-hop over to the stove, and reluctantly agreed that the snowfall video was charming, and the book paragraph well-chosen, and the clandestine classroom selfies handsome. Avra showed off each with the obnoxious pride of a parent introducing disinterested neighbors to their child's trophy shelf. Nico peeked over her shoulder.

"Damn, Kieran is kind of slutty."

"What do you mean?" Avra said, prepared to leap to the defensive.

"Well, the smolder alone . . ."

Avra stared at the photo—his dark eyebrows, the tiny I-could-talk-my-way-out-of-a-shoplifting-charge quirk at the corner of his mouth, the barely parted lips, the mussed hair that had probably been intentionally ruffled just prior to the photo—and nodded.

"If he knew how to be a slut, he would indeed be a very, very good one."

A text from Emerson dropped from the top of the screen, and Nico and Ellie withdrew in part to allow for Avra's privacy, and in part to snack.

Mom in rehab, South Carolina.

Then

:(

Then

Classic

Avra texted back:

Could have called that one. You okay?

Even as something adjacent to shame, to disappointment, curled octopidly around her spinal cord.

Fine. You?

Entirely unsurprised.
Word.

And that was that. She tried her best to pivot back to flutter, to contentment, to her suite of jokes with Nico and Ellie, but the bottom had dropped out of her joy, a chink in the dam, and the wet of her hurt was coming through, ready to flood the pastures and rot the grain.

Another interesting non-Kieran text (these felt fewer and farther between to Avra as the positive feedback loop of consistently texting Kieran overloaded her dopamine receptors) came in several days later. It was Karly.

Hey bb, throwing a certified RAGERRR over winter break. Garrett's turning 22 & im leaving for study abroad in a few weeks (eek!) & Tati needs her glorious homecoming bash. Thinking Sat after Xmas. U down?

Then

Say yes plz i miss u

Then

Kieran is coming—as if she knew to throw this line, this hook, half warning, half promise, left over from years of observing her two warring, wanton friends.

Avra replied immediately.

Of course I'll be there. Love you miss you can't wait.

Then

Garrett's gonna be insufferable, isn't he?

To which Karly replied, with a little laugh emoji:

>:D Count on it.

Kieran texted Avra a few hours later.

going to karlys thing?

That's the plan!

go together?

Sure—give em something to talk about. Avra allowed herself a little flush of pride, a glow of success. She did it. She had him. And they would know. And it would be good, she was quite convinced, it would be excellent. Vindication and validation folded neatly into one.

they talk abt us already, Kieran insisted.

???

karly asks me abt u

Then

garrett too

Oh, Avra responded, noting the mutual marionetting, the string-pulling, directed toward them each in turn, like even footing, like no footing at all.

nosy, Kieran asserted.

That's Ridgefield! Avra confirmed.

Time blurred spectacularly, revving like a motor. It was December ninth and her finals were pressing in on her, December nineteenth and her finals were over, and she was certain she had done well, and Kieran texted her appropriate praise, and she responded with a selfie of her giving him a thumbs-up, the pad of her thumb covering a quarter of the screen. And then it was December twenty-ninth and she was standing in the foyer of her father's house wearing that same pair of fleece-lined tights (laundered, to her chagrin), and her skirt was A-line and high-waisted, and her lipstick was a cheery cherry red, and her belly was flipping, fluttering, at the thought of seeing Kieran again. At arriving together, as a pair, on purpose, in public, like a daydream.

His car pulled into the driveway. That green car, and Avra felt glitter at the base of her spine, in the bowl of her pelvis. Tonight was a wheelbarrow carting her toward the fresh dirt, the potential to thrive—Kieran as her chauffeur, his grip around the handles, tipping her into fertile ground.

He came to the door like a gentleman.

Avra opened it before he pressed the doorbell.

"Hi," he was smiling, front teeth a little crooked, maybe promising future orthodontics, and Avra wanted to kiss each of his canines in turn, and held herself back on her toes (which hurt, because her heels were many inches high).

"This is bizarre."

"Because I'm not kissing you?" Kieran asked, his recall phenomenal.

"Because you're at my door like a Jane Austen–style Regency man about to whisk me off to a party."

"I've never read any Jane Austen."

"Yes, you have—we had to read her senior year."

"Correction: *You* had to read her senior year. I read SparkNotes." He was still grinning, and Avra took a presumptive step forward, her feet crossing the threshold, her toes aching, her body warm from the closeness of Kieran's body.

"Such a slacker," she scolded, her hands reaching up to clasp the open collar of his jacket.

"Such an overachiever," he retaliated, his own hands fitting neatly along her waist as their paired hips held open the swinging door.

They kissed in the December frost, two days before a new year, and he tasted like peppermint gum, like he had planned his own freshness, and Avra's vanilla enveloped him, clung to the soft weave of his sweater—another wholesome woven sweater—and their faces were lit from the string lights spiraling around the Christmas tree in the sitting room.

"You're Jewish," Kieran noted when they pulled away, a string of spit connecting his mouth to Avra's like a garland.

"Dad loves Christmas," Avra explained, her nose against Kieran's nose, and she felt him smile, felt his bottom lip against her bottom lip as he kissed her again, slow.

"Where is your dad?"

"In the office."

"Can I say hello?"

Avra's chest squeezed, and her hands buried themselves in Kieran's hair, and she grinned so hard he might've actually heard the jubilant muscles tensing across her wide-open face.

"If you'd like."

Kieran pulled away from her, a recalcitrant boat abandoning port. He wiped his suddenly sweaty hands against the front of his jeans and cleared his throat once, twice.

"Okay," he said.

"Okay," Avra repeated.

"I'm nervous."

"My dad doesn't hold grudges," Avra reminded him, like she hadn't pep-talked her dad into kindness just three hours ago, like she hadn't shown him Kieran's adorably sneaky class selfies and the Díaz paragraph, like she hadn't worked to soothe the rough edges of parental protectiveness in anticipation of this meeting, which had to go well, because it mattered, because it must.

Kieran reached for her hand, held her fingers gently, turned to kiss her forehead, and squeezed her forefinger, her thumb, her palm. Avra blushed down to her bellybutton, smiled into Kieran's shoulder, and squeezed back.

"Fuck," Kieran said, blowing a warm breath against the fine, light hairs curling Hebraically around the crown of Avra's head, before stepping into the house. The front door closed softly behind him, not quite latching.

"You'll be fine."

Avra's father must have heard this reassurance, because he was suddenly framed between the French doors bisecting the sitting room and office. An impressively self-possessed expression was on his would-be defensive face.

"Mister Kieran Monahan," he said, name in full, the way he did when Avra was misbehaving, when Emerson was exercising her sass.

"Mister Bergmann," Kieran replied, chin down, posture appropriately deferential. The men reached toward each other, fatherly grip firm against suitorly sweat.

"I'd say something about having her home by eleven, but my daughter is a grown-up, apparently." He was smiling in a wry, regretful sort of way.

"Yes, sir." Kieran nodded, somberly.

"I can't believe you're in my house." It was a joke, a jab, and clearly true.

"Me either, sir. But I'm glad, obviously." Kieran's cheeks were purpling, his eyes locked on Avra's father, and Avra wanted to smack both of their heads together, but didn't.

"Your mother is a kind woman. I've always liked her, you know," David Bergmann assured him, and Avra knew this was meant to be comforting, but *gods* her dad was awkward.

"She likes you too, actually," Kieran said, and he could do this, church-boy charm settling in like it had waited until college to finally fruit. "She told me once that she was impressed by you being a single dad." Kieran coughed a little, self-conscious in his candidness. "Excuse me. I mean, she thought Avra was talented, in the play and everything, and Emerson was always nice. I think she's glad I had the chance to meet your daughters. Like, that they were good for me."

Avra's insides were molten, liquid, melting into the carpet in the foyer, and her father was much the same, a gleam of approval in his wide brown eyes. Flattery was smart.

"Yes, well, tell her thank you."

"I will, sir."

"And take care of Av tonight."

"I'll do my best, sir."

It was all so preposterous, Avra snorted. *"Sir, yes, sir,"* she mocked, so they both could hear, and her dad reached forward to muss her hair. She dodged him, grinned impishly, and licked her teeth. "Men are so weird."

"Now you're ruining a perfectly nice moment."

"Learned from the best," Avra rebutted, before reaching for Kieran's coat sleeve. "Too bizarre. Can't cope. Leaving now. Loveyoubye." She dragged Kieran toward the front door while her dad belly-laughed in the living room, the tree lights painting his beard a Santa-esque silver.

"Ho ho ho," Kieran murmured when they closed the front door behind them.

"You're not wrong," Avra said, and then she was walking around the passenger-side door, opening it, and sliding into Kieran's car, like a girlfriend, like his partner, for the very first time.

CHAPTER 22

DECEMBER 2012

The ride to Karly's house was tensely expectant. Kieran's car fastened the road behind them like a zip closure, binding reluctant halves. Avra's leg jittered with the intensity of a toddler-bearing pogo stick, until Kieran reached out and ran his palm soothingly along the top of her knee. She stilled, with some effort.

"It'll be fun," Kieran said, as much to himself as Avra.

"Our coming-out party," Avra joked back, and Kieran's thumb—previously rubbing a small rainbow along Avra's kneecap—paused. "I didn't mean."

"No, I get it," Kieran said, and there was an unexpected smile tugging at the corner of his mouth. "It *is* something like that."

Karly's enormous house loomed out of the winter dark. Tea lights in each window gave the impression of many tiny creatures peering curiously onto the sprawling, inky lawn. The house glowed from its dozen golden eyes. Avra noted the cars lined along the drive: Tati's SUV, Garrett's Jeep, Matt's Lexus, Will's Audi, and a handful of shiny additions—a bulky silver Acura, a cherry red Mazda Miata, a blue Toyota with a few scratches on the bumper

(*Solidarity,* Avra thought, subconsciously seeking someone more on the "middle" side of "upper-middle class").

"You ready?" Kieran asked, and Avra noticed that he was watching her watch the house, a vague concern tugging at his eyebrows. She paused to see if he would look toward Will's car. He didn't.

Avra blew out a humid Tic-Tac breath and gently removed his hand from her knee—practicing a performative distance, for his sake, for his reputation, in a way that didn't match their mutual arrival.

"Let's go." She shot him a still-eyed smile. Kieran didn't reach for the door.

"Everything all right?"

"You sure you want to do this? Like, with me?" Avra was staring at the house like it bore her some ill will, despite the years of friendship linking her to the clique inside.

Kieran unbuckled his seat belt. "Give 'em something to talk about," he muttered as he leaned toward her, echoing her own weeks-old text against her ear. She turned to face him, and his mouth pressed generously against hers. It smeared clumsily over her bright lip stain, and Avra's belly flipped at the possessive, warming thought of Kieran walking through the door of a Ridgefield party sporting her particular shade. They pulled apart, several inches of distance between their noses, and Avra sighed.

"It's okay. Okay. All right. I'm okay."

"Was it Shakespeare who had that line about protesting too much?" Kieran kissed her face several times as he posed the question. Soft kisses against the corners of her mouth, the groove above her chin, her nose.

"Did you just ask me to clarify something about Shakespeare? On purpose?" Avra kissed back, finding his cheekbones in the dark, the dent beneath his lip, the fronts of his teeth.

"I've heard it helps to remind people of their areas of expertise when they're nervous."

"What makes you think I'm nervous?"

"You were staring at the house like it's haunted."

"You never know," Avra said, kissing him once more. "Could be a murder house."

"House owes me money," Kieran said, grinning enough that Avra could feel it.

"House beats its wife," Avra replied, feeling her own eyelashes catch Kieran's eyebrow.

"House is a little racist."

"House is a little gay."

Kieran laughed aloud, seeing the joke in the dark. "All right, time to go." He kissed her hard, licked her bottom lip once, pulled away, and reached for the car door.

"Fuck. All right. Okay." Avra stepped out onto the lawn.

The front door was cracked open, ambient sounds of "party" drifting up from the finished basement. Kieran led their way down the stairs, Avra several feet behind.

Karly was waiting at the landing, smiling maniacally as she took in the mutual arrival.

"Oh, *hell* yeah," she purred.

"Called it," Tati chirped, carrying two candy-colored shot glasses over in her pretty manicured hands.

"Matt owes me twenty bucks," Garrett added jubilantly from the pong table. Kieran laughed.

"Goddamn," said Avra, "y'all need *hobbies*."

"Or, like, Jesus," Kieran added, draping his jacket over the banister.

"Whatever," Karly rebutted. Then, "If we get you drunk enough, will you tell us everything?" Avra directed an urgent look toward

Kieran, and he interceded.

"Not for all the shots in Connecticut."

"We're gonna make a dent in those," Matt promised, ruffling his own blond hair and passing Kieran a shot glass, already full of something. Kieran downed it without looking, handed the glass back, and clapped Matt on the arm as if to say *Good man.* Avra rolled her eyes. *Boys.*

She mentally corrected herself, watching Matt and Garrett and Kieran together, a trio she had known since childhood. *Men.* And that was weird, the adultification of their collective. Karly was graceful in glittering platform stilettos, wafting around as people arrived, less performative than her high school self, more assured. Tati was preening, glowing, reunited in a high school town with a group of also-in-college friends, enjoying her own I've-joined-you-at-the-top-of-the-food-chain moment. Garrett stared at her with a longing close to pain. Clearly, she was continuing to spurn his advances. Clearly, Avra thought—as Tati dazzled in Garrett's direction before flitting to Karly's side, whispering something low-throated, laughing—this was a short-term resistance.

The party swung forward with the assistance of lubrication and a loud bass, which thumped from enormous matte black speakers in the living room. Six people trickled in that Avra didn't know, then eight, then twelve, friends of friends and siblings who were cool enough to hang and popular kids from several towns over. The basement filled with muddy inches of strangers, unfamiliar voices, and the high-pitched buzz of flirtatious energy. Avra felt her hackles raise the way they always did in her hometown. Will ambled in with a tall, exquisitely beautiful young woman whom Avra was certain Karly would hate if only for the limelight theft. Avra watched from across the room as Will made a forced little show of introducing the girl to Kieran, who nodded a hello and gave Will an awkward one-armed hug, searching for Avra over his shoulder. She held his gaze for a long moment. *Yes, I'm here. I've got you.*

As the party catapulted itself into the frenzy of post-introduction, pre-rager imbibement, Avra hung on to Tati and Karly. She avoided the newcomers. She avoided small talk. It felt as if she could curl herself against the risk of social harm by sticking close to the devils she knew, who were nice to her now, she reminded herself impatiently, tipsily. Nice devils. Good, friendly devils. And she could be cool. She could totally just be fucking cool.

Avra took two peppery shots with Tati, Karly, Sarah, and a new girl named Amanda who had a pierced eyebrow and a Dali-esque tattoo of a spiraling, half-melted grandfather clock on her forearm and seemed to be Matt's younger cousin. The alcohol burned phenomenally on the way down. Avra stared at Amanda's ink.

"Jalapeño gin," Karly said, jostling Avra's shoulder, "it'll make your kisses spicy."

"Not that you need any help, I bet," Tati joked. Avra blushed self-consciously.

The girls huddled in the kitchenette while the guys cornered Kieran out on the patio. Divide and conquer, quite the strategy.

"I'm not trying to make fun or anything," Karly began, offering another round of shots, this set with a sprinkle of pink sugar around the rim of each glass, "but it took you all the fuck long enough."

"I have no idea what you mean," Avra said. Tati blew a raspberry and Karly pushed the glamorously feminine shot into her waiting hands.

"Oh, bullshit bullshit bullshit. One hundred percent crap. You owe us *details*, Avs. You owe us a *blow-by-blow* description."

"Maybe literally," the new girl Amanda said dryly, grinning unapologetically when Avra caught her eye. "Believe it or not, I was filled in before you even got here."

"No," Avra said, covering her face with one hand.

"Yup," Amanda confirmed, knocking back her own shot. Avra followed suit, and Amanda reached forward immediately to take the glass out of her hand. Their fingers brushed softly before Amanda set the sticky glass down on the counter, and Avra thought automatically that Amanda would have been her type, pre-Kieran. Wry and charming. Brazen, comfortable around new people, confident enough to rib a casual acquaintance. Avra cleared her throat, glanced down and then up to find Amanda still looking at her. Good, then. Okay. Instincts still intact. A familiar itch stirred in her lower back, whispered along her throat and over the roof of her mouth, buzzing with the jalapeño booze. *Women,* it taunted. *Women. Women.*

"Spill, babe." Karly reminded, interrupting the simmer between Avra and Amanda with a rapidity suggesting their conspicuity.

"There's not much to tell. We've been texting for a while, pretty much since last summer. He came to visit me at school. I've been to visit him a few times. It's all very casual." She said the last part with a dishonest wobble.

"Casual my *entire ass,*" Karly was shaking her head. "Y'all have been ridiculous about each other for years."

"Garrett's banking on a wedding announcement any second now," Tati ribbed. "And just think—your freckles and eye color? His hair and that jawline? Imagine the *babies.*"

"The *what* now, excuse me?" Avra choked. Amanda patted her twice on the back, a gesture of long-suffering solidarity.

"You'd make pretty kids, is all I'm saying."

"Okay, please calm down. How did we get to *kids?* We're not even, like, officially *seeing* each other."

"Absurd," Karly said. "Stupid of both of you."

"Not really," Avra responded, noticing the booze making her flush, noticing her own defensive reactivity clawing to deny a heteronormative trap while Amanda smirked and observed. "I mean, who's to say I'm ready to give up girls?"

"What girls?" Karly challenged. "You haven't dated a girl since that one your roommates didn't like, right? The one who made you read all that stuff? And wasn't she like a year ago?"

"I've still been fucking girls!" It was too loud.

"Recently?" Karly challenged, archly. Avra thought back before shrugging as if to say *Recently enough,* and Amanda shifted her weight with some judgment, and the kitchenette was small. Avra remembered Kieran's intimidating seduction years ago, her back against the sink, his breath on her cheek, fingers unforgiving around her wrist. She remembered Karly, then, interrupting with concern. The way their classmates used to watch her and Kieran orbit and scrap. She thought thornily of how their friends *still* watched them, still lived vicariously through Avra, her bravery, her sexuality, even now.

One of Avra's hips rested against that same sink, and how had she gone from the neighborhood queer to marriage and babies? The familiar impulse to kick out with both feet and dash away danced along her insteps.

Matt, Will, and Garrett walked in, perfectly timed for a distraction, and Avra experienced a moment of relief before Kieran followed, looking stung, like he'd heard her last declaration. Like he didn't know.

And he didn't know, Avra realized, the alcohol slowing her cognitive-processing speed just enough so that she didn't school her face toward contrition before Kieran looked away. Amanda offered Avra another shot. She took it in wordless thanks. That was four.

The room hazed clumsily while Avra watched Kieran. He glanced from the floor to the sink back to Avra—looking at her, hard—and she knew he was remembering, too. His thumb pressing a bruise into the thin flesh over her hip bone. His tongue chasing her spit across a sliver of lime. Salt on his hands. The charged air, and all the rage of adolescence, and the way they wanted to hurt each other, and how that part hadn't changed a lick. Avra felt the tentative, infantile thread of interest between herself and Amanda snap, sever, sliced clean through, burned to a crisp.

Nothing had ever felt like him.

Avra crossed toward Kieran in several strides, her heeled boots pulling the thrumming bass up through her thighs, and Kieran rested a large, possessive palm against her lower back when she reached his side.

"Having fun?" he prompted, while their friends tuned in, as usual.

"Should have expected the inquisition," she quipped, wondering if he would get the joke. His mouth twitched in response.

"Pretty sure not a single person in this town is Spanish."

"My nana is Cuban!" Tati interceded.

"And thus, the point is proven," Avra muttered. Kieran's twitching mouth opened into a grin. Avra took another automatic step into his space, his hand guiding her gently forward.

"Fuck you guys." It was Garrett. "This is that fairy-tale shit."

"Look at them, *joking* together," Karly cooed, proud and condescending.

"It's almost like high school never happened," Tati said, with a dreamy smile, like this was what all of them would have wanted. The group nodded amicably, as if they weren't the exact same people who had eagerly swallowed the *best years of your life* dogma twenty-four months prior.

"All grown up and in love," Matt affirmed.

Will was silent.

Avra tried to ignore the bead of anger grating along the center of her palms, the shiver of resentment at the performance of shared persecution, the way they had let Kieran get away with years of adolescent torture, the insufferable *straightness* of it all, the erasure of Avra's entire history, their patterns of queerphobia and tokenization. She thought of Karly leaving a hickey on her neck, the commodification of queer femme sexuality distributed to bored small-town kids as a party favor, *thank you so much for coming*. Kieran must have seen something in Avra's expression, because he elbowed Matt in the stomach, many seconds too late.

"What?"

"It's enough, dude."

"We're just messing around," Garrett said loosely, lumbering to Matt's defense.

"Make a different mess then."

"Besides," new girl Amanda piped up after a casually masc swig of beer, "who's to say Avra"—she gestured with her bottle and the looseness of her wrist suggested intoxication—"is all done with girls?" The defense could have been better timed, Avra thought with some confusion, as Kieran's forefinger tapped reactively against her lower back, his thumb pressing warningly forward.

"Pshhht, call it a phase," Garrett said in response, tipping his own drink toward Avra without looking at her, and Avra nearly spat, nearly clawed like a cat, leapt in fury. If looks could kill, this kitchenette would be a sudden bloodbath, Avra knew, her eyes narrowed to slits, her mouth opening with the courage of four shots and bisexual rage. Kieran beat her to the fray.

"Shut the fuck up, dude."

Garrett was confrontationally drunk, leering toward Avra now as Tati looked on with kinetic anxiety. He spoke to Avra in a mocking baritone: "If you found a way to pray away the gay, you know you could market that shit." Avra could feel the urge to transform,

knives and elbows, edges and teeth, fingernails and a bulletproof
vest; wanted to remind people of her queerness like someone fighting for their fucking life, because, honestly, that's what it was.

"Women," she said coldly, stepping away from Kieran's touch,
"are my calling."

"Hear, hear!" Amanda said, shoving away from the counter.
"Three cheers to rural queers!" And then she stomped out, as if any
of this was being directed toward her, as if homophobia in a town
like this was the mushroom that flavored every interaction, because
it could, because it did. When she left, Avra's eyes went with her,
and so did her guilt. Karly was scowling at Garrett, at Avra. Tati
was flitting nervously by the doorway. And Kieran was sentry-still,
mountain-still, ceasefire-still by Avra's side, no longer touching her,
hand vaguely outstretched like it wasn't sure where to land.

"Will, what about the girl you came in with?" Avra began,
shifting back toward the circle, seeking a change in the subject, an
alternate target. She sharpened her claws against the silence and went
for the moment's soft underbelly. "Didn't figure her for your type, if
I'm honest." She smirked meaningfully, the alcohol making her reckless, and Will gawped. Kieran moved beside her as if considering an
interruption, knowing that Avra was lashing, a wild thing caught in
a bear trap, prepared to gnaw off her own foot, but Matt spoke first.

"Hold up. Wait. If women are your *calling,* what's this, then?"
He gestured clumsily between them, protective of Kieran, leaping
in to defend one of his dudes, and this was dreidling out of control,
Avra knew, and she didn't care.

"Dalliance," she lied, the distance between her and Kieran growing into blocked marble, and the back of her head shrieked, *Please
know I don't mean this I don't mean it I'm just fighting I just have to*
in Kieran's direction. Avra followed up, condescension pointed, all
those teenage reasons the group had so disliked her coming out to

play: "Do you need me to define 'dalliance' for you, or ..."

"I think they get it," Kieran interrupted, and his voice was pinched with reproach.

"I'm getting another drink," Avra spat, sandpaper-irritated by Kieran's split loyalties. She marched out of the kitchen, toward the back patio, where she knew the coolers lived.

Karly, the reluctant peacekeeper, followed her out.

The winter chill belied the need for ice. A line of bottles—beer and wine, ciders and harder options, a dusty few that must have belonged to Karly's parents—lay cuddling along a baby-pink towel. Avra reached to grab the closest one, and her fingers protested the sudden cold. A wind tunnel breeze lifted the baby hairs along the back of Avra's neck, and Karly closed the slider behind them, wrapping her arms around herself for warmth. The noise from inside now muffled, the two of them quite alone, she stared shrewdly at Avra before she spoke.

"That was shitty." Ever the audacious.

"Yeah, okay," Avra said, and twisted off the bottle top.

"He really cares about you, you know."

Avra laughed dismissively, taking a swig of something dark and thick, even as the lawn tilted forward and back, a frothing sea. Karly tried again.

"I've never seen him like this about someone."

"Did you all just *forget* how he treated me in school?"

"Did you?" Karly shot back.

"No, which is why this is all so fucking weird. One of the zillion reasons. At least women are *nice* to me. Like, at least I can trust that girls are going to be kind."

"That's not always true and you know it," Karly reminded her, impatiently.

"*This* wasn't always true, either!" Avra knew her voice was getting louder as she gestured back into the house. "He fucked my shit up, for years. *Years!* And yeah, he's stupid hot, and we have bonkers chemistry, and I can't help wanting to . . . to ride him like a carousel, but that's *got* to be all it is, because I just can't—I can't really . . ." Avra didn't know where she was going. She cast around for words, for any clarity, her own disorganized attachment turning language into a labyrinth. "He was cruel," she said, voice small and pleading, before taking another drink, slow and deep. Karly waited. "He was violent. And he scared me. And he called me names, and he followed me around."

"Yes, and that was shitty of him," Karly affirmed, "but has he done any of that since graduation? Anything like that since you've been seeing each other?"

Avra thought back to the parking garage, his hesitancy about safewords, how he'd looked her in the face and said he daydreamed about fucking her to tears. "Not exactly."

"Then maybe he's grown. Maybe you just have to—and I'm sorry to be blunt but I think I'm right about this—get over it."

Avra scoffed, ignoring the needling sense of Karly's correctness. "Yeah, because that's something I can totally just *get over.*"

"Then what are you doing here with him?"

"I don't know! We're both home, and he lives like two miles away, and the sexual spark is definitely there. It's fun, sometimes. He knows what he's doing. It's not like I'm in love, or anything. He's just there when I need him. He's just really . . . convenient." As soon as she said it, she knew it sounded horrible.

Karly's face twisted into disbelief, rejecting the premise. "Catching feelings for a guy you insist you can't forgive is *convenient?*"

Avra was halfway through this bottle, and had to focus on Karly's face to stop it from blurring. "'Convenient' is a bad word, maybe."

"Ya think?"

"I don't know what I'm doing."

"That," Karly said, opening the slider and turning back into the warmth of the house, "is obvious." She left Avra in the chill.

Avra walked back into the party a few minutes later to find Kieran hesitating inside the doorway, his face a shallow pond of frustration. Will was kissing the probable model in the corner, her slim fingers in his hair, their tongues moving pink and thick between their faces. Avra wondered if this had contributed in any way to the sourness of Kieran's mood, or if she was solely responsible. She resentfully expected the former, but hoped narcissistically for the latter.

"What is it?" she prompted Kieran, unceremoniously.

"I'm taking you to bed." Toneless. Not a happy, sizzly promise.

"Why?"

"You're drunk."

"So?" Avra snapped, unreasonable.

"You're being a dick."

"Well, it does seem to be my fucking turn, doesn't it?"

Kieran reached toward her, wrapping his fingers around her wrist *that* way, slow pressure and threat, some visceral urge toward punishment, and Avra couldn't help it, it was all so absurd: The party pumped grotesquely around them, all these beautiful popular people talking and drinking and dancing, and she looked at Kieran's serious face, and laughed. It was fucking stupid. How was *she* the inappropriate one while his thumb found her pulse point and his grip tightened, ominous, as if nothing had changed, not really, and nobody noticed, nobody interrupted, and she could read his urge to hurt her in every shift of his body?

"Upstairs," he said.

Avra flushed, embarrassed, turned on in spite of it all, angry at everyone and everything, including herself, including him. "Okay."

They went.

Karly's guest room was one floor up. The music muted beneath the plush carpet. Avra kicked her boots into the corner before flopping dramatically onto the bed. Kieran toed off his own shoes beside Avra's and closed the door gently, the curved golden handle falling and then rising with the hushed rub of brushed metal.

"All right. What even happened down there?" Kieran said, and Avra considered withholding, considered making him guess and cajole and fuck her around until she finally broke and babbled her fury, but she couldn't hamper her tongue.

"None of these people fucking know me, and they were absolute shit in high school about me liking girls. No, they were," she sped forward when Kieran opened his mouth, her words playing bumper cars. He closed it again at her cue, and nodded. "They were shit to me. And then once I got *hot* enough, and *desirable* enough, it was *so cute* that I was gay, but pretty much only when I was gay for their entertainment. When I was introducing them to queer erotica, or teaching them how to go down on girls, or letting Karly suck on my neck as a fucking party trick, *that* was the kind of queer I was allowed to be here. The slutty kind, or the fuckable kind, and now I show up with *you*"—she spat the word like an accusation, automatic, accidental, and Kieran's look hardened—"and all of a sudden they're talking about marriage. *Marriage?* And *babies?* Seriously, what the *fuck?* Like, you can't be okay with that either."

Kieran shrugged. "What if I was?"

Avra leaned back on her elbows and swung her feet out from the foot of the bed as if she could kick the invasively vanilla normativity out into the hall. "I'm not going to be your little picket-fence wife, dude." She spoke as if it was absurd, like it would be terrible, and wondered if Kieran could feel his own blade coming out, the urge to throw her out a window, the rejection so swift, so thought-less. "I'm not doing it."

"I didn't ask you to be my *little picket-fence wife*, Avra. Goddamn it."

"Well, don't bother."

"We're not even twenty-one."

"I don't mean *actually*. I just mean—being with you, whatever we're doing, that doesn't make me straight. You know that, right?"

Kieran rolled his eyes. "Have I ever, even for a moment, suggested that you're straight?"

"*They* do." She pointed through the floor with her toe.

"Well, I'm not *them*."

"You know, I've always had trouble with that, given that you were pretty much their shining-beacon popular basketball boy." Kieran didn't speak, and Avra felt the swift, heady want to shove, so she did. "And I don't care how much they want us to get *married* and have *babies* so that your *special dick* can have fixed the sick little broken gay girl—I'm not fucking doing it."

"Avra." Kieran's voice was lethal—gravel, oil, and matchstick. "I daydream about bruising you. About causing you actual, literal pain." He swallowed, self-conscious, and went on. "You're here, and then you're not. You chase me, and then you run. You let me fuck you, and hold you, and stay at your place, and then you disappear. I don't know what this is. I don't know why you keep me around, or what the fuck we're doing. You seriously think I'm going to try to tell you what to do? Out in the real world, I mean," he said quickly, because Avra was quirking an eyebrow. "Not when we're—in real life. Do you seriously think I'd *propose?*"

"Even you're too smart for that," Avra quipped, cruelly.

Kieran growled, convulsed; seventeen separate murder methods seemed to be crawling along his imagination, that sick and ugly box at the bottom of his skull where he stored the urge to do violence to Avra, where we all store fantasies of hurting the people we love most.

Avra went on. "And, like, hypothetically, you don't even know what you could be missing. Will is right downstairs. Jordan has been coming on to you." Dead, roadside Jordan. "I'm doing this weird little dance with you and always wondering if it's women, ultimately, for me."

"Well, first of all, go fuck yourself," Kieran said, matter-of-factly. "Second of all, do you think you could let me be happy with what I have, maybe?"

"You aren't happy, though." Avra sat up again, pushed off the bed, and she was standing in front of him, feet planted wide, grounding herself in what she understood as truth. Her hands were on her hips, power pose, as if she could trick herself into a bravery she didn't feel. "I make you miserable. And you don't *have* me." It was utter bullshit, and both of them knew.

"You don't make me miserable," Kieran argued, and Avra shook her head.

"Yes, I do. I know I fucking do, because sometimes I'm doing it *on purpose,* just to see if I can."

Kieran's expression was softening, like he knew this and found it soothing, like the confirmation was a comfort, not an admission of sadistic guilt. "You make me happy sometimes," Kieran said, reaching for her face.

Avra wanted to stomp on both of his feet, and the room was wrapping around them in that hazy, seasick-making way, a warning of impending mess. She wanted him euphoric at the thought of her, wanted him aching, wanted something enormous, to make up for the rest of it, to keep her from ever feeling lonely.

"*Sometimes*," Avra rebutted, scathing, before Kieran's palm reached her cheek, before he smoothed his long fingers over her brow, one nail catching along her eyelashes, clumsy, like the booze was rattling him, too. He pushed his fingertips into her cheekbone with unnecessary force, molding his prints into the warm clay of Avra's skin.

"Yes, *sometimes*. That could be enough, I think."

"Enough for *what*, dude?"

"I love you." He was watching her face when he said it, gauging a reaction, and Avra tried not to shrink, wanting to laugh, wanting to hurl herself down the stairs and out onto the lawn.

"Whatever."

He was advancing on her, and his palm was warm under her chin, fingers splayed across her face, thumb beside her mouth, and Avra examined a freckle next to his ear, avoiding his eyes.

"I love you," he said again.

"Now is a really shitty time for you to say that." Her laugh sounded panicked, discombobulated.

Kieran grinned a little chaotically, his teeth in two skeletal, jack-o'-lantern rows, and pressed forward until the backs of Avra's knees hit the edge of the mattress. "Fuck it," he said, caution to whatever wind could possibly exist in the stale, still room. "Fuck it, I don't care. There hasn't been a *good* time for me to say it, right? I love you."

"Could you not, though?" Avra's eyelids were fluttering in spite of herself, and Kieran nosed her nose, and she could feel the anger seeping out of her, air from a balloon. She would have begged it to stay.

"I'm going to kiss you now." He did, sighing into her mouth, relieved at his own confessional, and Avra's tongue was slick and acquiescent, and her lungs were empty from panting. The kiss accomplished what it always had—summoned that fierce firework pop, hummed along her skin like a bass note. But the raw wouldn't leave, the sting of someone squeezing lemon juice over heart tissue, hydrochloric acid self-loathing eating through the possibility of being loved. He said it again, pleading and bunny-soft against Avra's mouth, and the walls closed in, enveloping her in a tomb of velvet, and Avra might have been able to let it happen if she wasn't so fucked up. Because people left, really, when you stopped being what they want. Avra had never known how to remain the kind of person that someone might actually choose to keep.

"Stop it," she said, fluted, forceless.

"You really have to deal with this abandonment shit you have going on."

"Shut the fuck up."

"I get that your mom screwed you up but—"

"No worse than your dad," Avra retaliated, trying to be cruel.

"It's not the same."

"It fucking is." And finally, unable to open, to peel herself away from the wallflower terror of being left, avoidant even in her affection, Avra kissed back. She traded her anxiety for aggression, and bit hard, pressed forward, tried to fit slivers of Kieran's skin beneath her fingernails.

He squirmed, kissed her temple, held her waist, stilled. "I'm not going anywhere."

Avra flinched against his face, flinched into the bald insight, comfort she would never have requested. "We'll see," she said, and shrugged, and thought she might be touching blood, under his shirt, and the room lurched in the resultant wave of guilt. Or it lurched because her balance was off, casting her sideways, bucking her toward the wall. Kieran steadied her.

"You all right?"

"Drunk," Avra said, noting the word—guttural, harsh, accurate. "Want to lie down?" Always a gentleman.

"Shower first." She pulled herself from Kieran's arms, reached toward the wall for a reliable hold. Something inanimate, dependable. Kieran sat heavily as she left, fight drained, relief at his declaration leeching slowly into the floor.

Avra faced out in the hallway, away from his exhaustion.

When she returned to the room later, hair dripping, Kieran was asleep.

The next day, Avra wouldn't remember whether she threw up, or how many times, or her reunion with Karly's shower floor, or crawling into bed next to Kieran. The black-and-blue impression of reaching for his phone, tapping in the passcode he had entrusted to her once upon a time, opening the App Store—missing, she would swear, to herself and to Ellie, guiltily. A gritty TV-static crackled over her vague recollections. That flame emoji. The small square boxes with handsome and less-so faces inside. The pictures from her own saved album, a typo-laden bio, an easy selection of preference—men. Men only. She set a radius of ten miles, which looped like cattle fencing around several neighboring boroughs. It would return to her in flashes, fleeting, clarifying, another uncrossable line in a Lincoln Log pile of uncrossable lines, each now full meters behind. The final test of her thesis: *Everyone leaves, regardless of how desperately they want to stay.* The for-his-own-good cord-cutting, freedom for them both, liquor hazing over a human menu as she tried not to vomit, and swiped right, and right, and right.

When she awoke, teeth practically moldy from open-mouthed hangover sleep, head pounding and pounding with the cruelty of a pernicious percussionist, Pepto pink comforter reminding her conveniently of her own urge to be sick, Kieran was gone.

CHAPTER 23

DECEMBER 2012

Once Avra awoke, she cajoled Karly—already sober and well-hydrated and pink-cheeked from morning yoga—into a ride home, during which Avra stared out the window and Karly turned down the radio volume and neither woman spoke.

She dressed chaotically, forgot to brush her teeth, swished with mouthwash in the car and spat out the window on her acute hangover drive. Avra pulled hesitantly onto the tree-lined street of Kieran's childhood home, where she had never been. Not invited. Not wanted. Kieran wouldn't know how she had the address, only of course she did, of course she knew exactly where to go.

Avra's eyes were bloodshot, shirt wrinkled, hair pulled messily into two frayed braids. She smelled like Listerine and the deodorant she kept in the center console of her car. She took a single panicked inhale when she pressed the doorbell. She waited like she could erase the unwanted intrusions of the prior night; the reminders that she had fucked up, really fucked up, stupidly fucked up.

She had expected Kieran beside her when she woke.

Brigid answered the door, began to smile, looked Avra up and

down, halted the smile skillfully on her face, and called for Kieran.
She shot Avra an apologetic half-shrug and wrinkled her nose for
good measure before leaving her standing out on the stoop. Avra
waited, patience impossible, pulse sludge-thick, imagination con-
juring the desolating visual accompaniment of a Kieran who didn't
have reason to be furious with her, a Kieran who might have taken
the steps two at a time.

What felt like several head-pounding weeks later, Kieran came
to the door. He stared into Avra's face through the storm screen,
assessed the handbags beneath her eyes and the expression of rip-
ening anxiety on her face. Appearing to find what he was looking
for, Kieran stepped outside and closed the door decidedly behind
him. He did not invite Avra in.

"What are you doing here?" No mood for games or avoidance.
No squalling submission.

"You were gone this morning." Her voice was cactus, crinoline.

"Like you're going to be in about five minutes."

"I thought you'd want to hang out today, maybe." It was a long
shot.

"I don't." He was direct, at least.

"Look, I'm not sure what happened last night, but—"

"Fuck, Avra. Just—" He sighed, scraped a hand across his face,
and Avra noticed the puff of red beneath his eyes, lids raw above his
lashes, like he'd been crying. Her stomach flooded with something
oxidizing and corrosive. She breathed through her nose. "Don't you
dare," Kieran said, his voice tangerine-bright and awful.

A different route, then. A needling voice. "Can we talk?" Avra
wasn't above begging, if it came to that.

"You're literally talking right now. Just say what you have to
say." He said it like *This is your last chance*, and Avra knew it was,
and she pivoted toward the lie as automatically as breathing.

"I don't even remember what I did."

Broken camel, its spine in two. Kieran's laugh, dry and humorless, was straw scattered on the stone slab beneath their feet.

"Bullshit yourself, if you want, but I'm done. I'm done. You don't get to bullshit me anymore."

"Kieran, look, I'm sorry—I'm sorry, I don't know what happened. I swear. I didn't mean it—to do what I did. Whatever I did." She remembered. She was a terrible liar. Or maybe Kieran had finally learned to see through her, to look past the wanting and hypnosis, the fascinating bluntness, toward that ugly part just underneath. Her streak of manipulative obsession. That punishing urge to test. Avra watched the muscle jumping in his cheek as she fumbled for a convincing dishonesty, a performance clumsily rehearsed in the car. "I just want you to be happy."

"Happy?" Like a fistfight. "Don't give me *happy*. You don't actually want me to be happy, you want me to be yours. Your little fag mentee. But I don't have to be gay the way you want me to be gay, and I'm not your fucking puppet. Not anymore."

"I know that. I know you're not. I didn't mean—"

He cut her off again. "You couldn't even be subtle about it, could you? Couldn't even leave us an out?" Kieran stared at her like he couldn't possibly understand. Like this was the betrayal, the negligence, beyond the action itself. "I was awake, you know," he went on, "when you finally tucked the phone back under my pillow. I was *awake*, and keeping my eyes shut, and I couldn't believe it, but then I could, because of course you would do this. Of *course* you would. And those pictures?" He croaked in reproach, in rejection of Avra's inexplicable clumsiness. "I hadn't seen some of those before. That one of us on the couch? Did Karly send that to you?"

Avra stood frozen, stunned by her own carelessness. Kieran didn't have to dig to know it had been her. Barely had to think at all. A final test. Permanent and cruel. He didn't even have to ask. And this was the unholy mess, the shortsightedness, the peak and pillage of mutual sabotage. She had left no deniability, no escape route, no halfway-fucked foundation for future bliss.

She had outed him.

She had left a blinding, iridescent trail while doing so.

The bio had full punctuation.

"You even swiped on a few people!" Kieran said, voice a half-shout. "Some of them were good-looking, too. You have great taste." He said it like *You have excellent marksmanship,* and Avra felt it like a bullet, wanted momentarily to die on his front stoop. "You know we went to high school with two of those guys?"

"No," Avra said, before she could stop herself.

"Yes," Kieran assured her, venom beneath his tongue. "One of them was at the party last night, you fucking bitch." He half laughed, half sobbed. Raked a trembling hand across his face again, and Avra knew with a sudden clarity, hangover dissolving into the acid of this interaction, that no "sorry" could be sufficient, no grief appropriately convincing. "I cannot believe you. I just—Avra. I cannot fucking believe you."

"I'm so sorry—"

"Shut up," Kieran demanded. Avra felt her teeth clack together from the force with which she closed her mouth. "Shut the fuck up. I listened to you. I trusted you. Believed that you cared about me. Believed you knew what you were doing, like you were some authority on all this, and wow, I was just completely fucking wrong." Kieran laughed again, primitive and terrible. "That's such shit. It's garbage. Despite everything you might think about how genius and enlightened and informed you are about literally all of the things, you're not any better at *this* than I am." Avra squirmed and Kieran watched her for a brutal second before plunging on. "For real, what makes you think that your experience could be anything like mine? That it could even compare? *You* can just hit on the first tatted girl you see, the first tipsy chick in a rainbow bracelet, and it's fine. You can find an Amanda at any goddamn party you want. *But I didn't want people to know.* I didn't want—I don't want people to know. It's *different* for me. And you swore you'd never make me say it, you promised that, and I never should have believed you, because you'll say whatever you can to get whatever you want, and I've known that about you for years. And still, I thought you really had something to say, I thought I could *learn* from you"—he scoffed, the sound like chalk—"when you have no idea. No idea. Men and women are just different."

Avra opened her mouth—to claim some sameness or to insist she already knew that, or whatever Kieran needed, but he held up a broad hand. "It's fucking different. You don't have to worry about your parents tossing you out of the house, or telling your siblings they can't talk to you anymore. You don't have to worry about your dad telling you you're a piece of shit, or broken, or disgusting. And that's before the sex! Before even dating!" His voice was pitched high and reedy. "You don't have to worry about some *girl* punching you in the face, or kicking you in the nuts, or telling all your friends that you're a fucking freak. You don't have to worry about disappointing your teammates or scaring your friends."

"I already did all of that," Avra insisted, attempting wildly to prove some commonality. "I already did the freak thing."

Kieran went on. "You don't have to worry about some *girl* who isn't going to take no for an answer." But this was another bridge too far, and Avra never could stay quiet for long.

"Um, yes. Yes, I do. You think girls can't be pushy and coercive? You think queer women are *safe* from this shit?" She laughed back, horrified and despairing, and it was the hollow sound of a belly scraped clean of all its sugar, all its salt.

"*YOU'RE* MY PERSON WHO DOESN'T TAKE NO FOR AN ANSWER!" Kieran was trembling, hands clenching and unclenching, weight shifting haphazardly from foot to foot. "You're my person who pushes, and pushes, even when I'm not ready. I'm not ready." He was crying, eyes bulging a little, the funeral march for his own agency tracking a wet line down his face. "Just—fuck you, Avra. *Fuck you.* I wasn't fucking ready."

"If I listened every time you said no, you would never experience a single thing but me." She said it small, a corner-pissing-kitten defense against a righteous buffalo stampede.

"Maybe I wouldn't! And maybe then we could actually be fucking happy! Imagine it, just imagine," he said, his tone yearning, pining for what already laid in a grave. "You could be happy! If you listened to my no, maybe you'd just let me be in love with you!"

"But I'm not what you want."

"YES, YOU ARE! Yes, you were. Sure, I think about men. Yes, I've wanted men. And yeah, all right, I'm curious." Kieran was defiant, face blazing but determined, voice low enough to crawl along the pavement between them. "I'm *interested,* okay? But I could have had everything I wanted with you."

Contrite was not where Avra lived. Deference was not a home. Avra found them both uninhabitable, cumbersome. When she reached for her regret, it left a film of dust on her fingertips. In search of something sturdy, Avra turned, as she always did, toward snark. "A perfect little Tudor house with babies and two-point-five golden retrievers and a submissive little wife who would let you fuck guys?"

"I have literally never asked you for that!"

"But it's what you want."

"You. Don't. Always. Know. What. I. Want. We are *both* fucking adults. We're goddamn adults now. We're not in high school anymore, and how is it that I stand in a room with you and feel like I'm back in those same hallways with those same assholes?"

"On your knees in the locker room?" Avra quipped.

"God, can't you stop being a smartass for five seconds?" Kieran looked like he wanted to strangle her.

"Sorry."

"You're not. Just—I was *never* on my knees in the locker room, and you know that. I've never experienced anything but you. I've never done anything but you. And I think I've been in love with you for a long time, and I *hate* you for it. For fucking me around. For outing me. Shut up. No. You outed me. And there is no excuse. Not even you, with all your pretty words, all those well-phrased rationalizations you always seem to find, not even you can come up with an adequate excuse for this." He fiddled with his phone for a moment before thrusting it into Avra's hands, bio screen open, and Avra received it passively. Her eyes remained on Kieran's face, which was contorted in a way Avra had never seen. "I hate you for constantly making choices like I don't get to be in charge of the way I do this." He pointed at the phone, finger jabbing Avra's knuckle accidentally. "Not even *this*. For lecturing me, and for pushing me. For getting scared, and for being so fucking selfish. For constantly forgetting that I'm even a person. And for running away like you're any different from your mom, really." It hurt. It hurt. He wasn't wrong. "For running every. Single. Goddamn. Time things get good for us." He was gasping, nose dripping, fat tears clinging to the bottom of his chin. His breath fogged the air. "And I hate that everything I know about queerness I learned from you, like you're some kind of *expert*." Spit landed on her cheek. "Some shining example, and you're not. You've been an *absolute nightmare*. A fucking *terror*. Disappearing and reappearing whenever you feel like. You've been an *asshole*. And I hate that I still fell the fuck in love with you, like an idiot. And that I even told you, like an idiot. And I hate that I can't do this by myself."

Kieran's shoulders collapsed, like his bones were too exhausted to hold up the rest of his sorry carcass, his wretched frame. Crumbling, crashing, a hollowed-out mine, pilfered and raw, littered with dead canaries. He moved them further from the door, both hands pushing Avra backwards, out onto the lawn, away from his family, from his home, where she had never been, where she could never go. "I hate that I don't know how to do this by myself."

Avra's voice was lonely and final and sad. Kieran's hands were warm. She wished she hadn't noticed. "Nobody knows how to do this by themselves."

The sound of an approaching car cut the quiet. Kieran's mother had finished her grocery trip. From their place on the lawn, Avra imagined the expression of puzzlement as she assessed the scene. Her blotchy son, trembling and rageful. His nervous friend, twitchy, head bowed.

This was not how Avra would have chosen to meet anyone's mother.

Kieran balled his sweatshirt sleeve in a fist and passed the fabric over his face, attempting to erase the wetness, smearing it toward his temple. His mother approached, grocery bags in her willowy arms. Kieran's voice barely made a sound. He stared hard at Avra.

"I don't know how to forgive you for this."

"Then don't."

"My dad is going to kill me."

"No, he won't. No locks on the doors." *Please,* she thought, *see how I remember? I love you. I'm sorry. I love you.*

"Hi, Mom," Kieran said, his tone flipped like a switch, crude oil ease.

"Trunk is open!" she hooted back, smiling joylessly at Avra's pained expression before raising a protective brow at her son. The curtain of this opportunity was closing, end of scene. Avra hoped that Kieran's mother, at least, would look back. She wanted to fit the fullness of apology onto her face, wanted some familial absolution, but she was already walking inside, letting the storm door slap shut behind her.

Kieran took a harsh breath, swore softly, took his phone back from Avra's hand, and turned to walk toward the car. Avra, body on gray autopilot, followed. She split from him in the driveway, her head hung with the gravity of a mistake you can't take back.

When she opened her car door, Kieran addressed her spine. He was several paces away. She couldn't reach him. Couldn't smell him anymore.

"This—what you did, Avra—this wasn't a favor. This wasn't for me."

Avra directed her heavy agreement to the Prius, which would drive her away, which Kieran wouldn't sit in, not ever again. "No, it wasn't."

CHAPTER 24

SEPTEMBER 2013

Avra left for France the following fall, abandoning another New England autumn, escaping the monotony of a campus without the anticipatory buzz of Kieran, and his hands, and his mouth. She wanted to meet French girls, she told herself. *Women.* She wanted to meet French women with severe haircuts who would say her name with that beautiful glottal reverence. She wanted to outrun the haunting love, the phantom of Kieran, who had not spoken to her, not returned even one of her approximately forty-seven (exactly forty-seven) texts, approximately fifteen (precisely fifteen) calls. She thought about dying, about the muffle of loneliness, how it casts a pall over the entire world. She considered methods—bathtub wrists, painkiller cocktails, an oncoming car—but her father's face invaded, benign smile and thick beard, and the acceptability of death waned. It would be humiliating to die over a boy. Embarrassing. She couldn't face her fellow feminists in the wherever-after. She'd have no way to explain herself.

France would distract her, console her, hold her with the identity erasure only a new time zone could offer. She was Carmen

Sandiego. She was determined to fall out of love. She was hapless, hopeless, failing, just like her mother, who called her once a month to leave sad messages. She wondered how long it would take her to buy a burner phone, set up a fake number, and call Kieran once a month to leave sad messages.

Kieran had removed Avra from his Facebook, had blocked Avra's number after call six, text thirty-four. It had been a gut-punch, a shot through the lungs. Three whole months later, Avra cried at two in the afternoon across an ocean, and nobody noticed.

ACKNOWLEDGMENTS

Oh, my heart. Oh, the enormity of my gratitude. Writing this is utterly surreal.

Thank you from the very depths to so many wonderful people. To my father, Peter, for understanding that shame is not an effective parenting tool, for believing that his daughter has always had something important to say, and for absolutely everything else. Thank you for being my company across every bridge, when so many fathers assume they are meant to be their daughters' muzzle. To my sisters, Julie and Emily, for being sounding boards over a lifetime of my fascination with the erotic and the boundary-defiant. Thank you for never telling me, "ew." Thank you for always listening. To Little Moo and Cal-Pal, for a type of joy I didn't encounter before each of you were born. To Emily F., my sister-turned-soulmate, for every moment of compassion you have offered since I was the same kind of reckless, anxious, frightened, insecure, and rageful girl as Avra: you have always been such a soft place to land. To the Bogen aunts, Leslie, Karen, and Debra, for teaching me to be intellectually curious, to give unwavering voice to my ideas, to write, to edit, and to approach challenging conversations no matter how unnerving or destabilizing. I could not possibly be prouder to be your niece. To my uncle Karl, for shepherding everyone in his life away from bullshit and toward a lively truth, without self-consciousness. To the Bogen and Leshko and Beresford and Moskovitz cousins—Shana and Talia and Sarah and Geoff and Teddy—for understanding that I'm a freak who cares. I adore every one of you brilliant and fantastic darlings. To Olivia and Gus, for over a decade of gentle and generous friendship, for being my first phone call, for the constant kindness and non-judgment, for so much good in the span of so little time. Every beautiful bit of friendship in these books I learned from you. To Jay, for sushi dates and hot sake and solidarity and the courage to combat injustice and the wisdom to sit with pain— I am so blessed to know you and to be your friend. To my PhD mentors, Drs. David DiLillo and Tierney Lorenz, for acknowledging that working on this creative project was necessary for my wellbeing in the context of a rigorous program, and for never asking me to turn away from my books. Your support over the last five years of my life has been instrumental in the development of my craft as a writer, my curiosity as a researcher, my empathy as a provider, and my ethical growth as a human being. To Barney Karpfinger, for reading the first draft of this book and saying, with enthusiasm, *yes*. Your email is framed and hanging on my wall. I get I-love-my-agency butterflies every time your name comes up in my inbox. I am so grateful to the universe for placing you at my father's Bar Mitzvah, over 50 years ago, and so grateful to you for knowing when the universe has spoken. To Sam Chidley, for reading every single draft, being on every frantic call, fielding every question, and continuing to champion my work over *thirty six entire rejections*. I could not have done this without your warmth, sense of humor, patience, and gracious encouragement. You are the dream agent. I will never stop singing your praises. I hope all of your predictions come true, but even if they don't, having a reader and friend as earnest as you has made this process worthwhile. To Andrea, Amanda, Saimah, Lydia, and the team at The Future Of, for making sure this book marched its determined way into the literary world and the hands of readers. To Nicola, for a cover design so spectacular I see it in my sleep, and for the pleasure and privilege of your friendship. To Douglas Mahoney, a soldier of accountability, who made it possible for me to fund the publication of this book—15-year-old Katie is forever grateful to you for your advocacy and support. To my beta readers, for your time and care. Your early feedback on this work gave me the bravery to continue when I asked myself whether I had indeed ever written a single worthwhile line. To Umnia, my precious, my sweet, who gave me my first review, and sat with me on a hotel bed in Paris while I read aloud for stretched, indulgent, giggly hours—finding our connection through this process has added meaning to my life, and to this experience, in a way I will forever struggle to put into words. To Joy Castro, of the UNL English Department, who gave me sound advice during my first ever writing retreat: "say all the ugly stuff." I think of your wisdom often. To Will Thomas, who organized this retreat and provided space for me to grow in a community of writers and thinkers: you will never know the impact you have had not only on me, but on the broader collective of UNL graduate students. Culture is the people who shape it. I feel so lucky to have been in your orbit, however briefly: much love to you and your family. To Karen Shoemaker and all of my Larksong comrades (Brad, Cathy, Monty, Christine, Pam, and so many others), my world will not be the same without you. I can only hope to bottle some of the camaraderie and sweetness I experienced at Larksong and to share it with other creatives. To anyone I've ever loved, and who has ever loved me: you taught me the worlds of romance, sensuality, desire, heartache, and (God help me) obsession. I hope you see the echoes of us in these pages. I hope you feel something.